THE ENCHANTRESSES BOOK ONE

PAULLETT GOLDEN

Print ISBN-13: 978-1-7328342-0-0
eBook ISBN-13: 978-1-7328342-1-7

Print ISBN-13: 978-1-7328342-0-0
eBook ISBN-13: 978-1-7328342-1-7

Author Photo by LaNae Ridgewell
Cover and book design by Fiona Jayde Media
Interior Design by The Deliberate Page

This book contains an excerpt from the forthcoming novel *The Duke and The Enchantress* by Paullett Golden. This excerpt has been set for this edition only and may not reflect final content of the forthcoming edition.

Also by Paullett Golden

The Enchantresses Series
The Earl and The Enchantress
The Duke and The Enchantress
The Baron and The Enchantress
The Colonel and The Enchantress
The Gentleman and The Enchantress
The Heir and The Enchantress

The Sirens Series
A Counterfeit Wife
A Proposed Hoax
The Faux Marriage

All listed titles coming soon

This book is dedicated to my mother for her endless support and motivation, as well as her willingness to read outside of her preferred genre to offer critiques.

A special thanks to Ishtar who made this book possible.

Chapter 1

May 1790
London

Lizbeth's chest tightened as she searched the room for a means of escape. Over her pounding heart, she could hear the swish of silk and muslin, the click of dancing heels, and the tune of the gavotte. The ballroom oppressed her, full of sweaty bodies, fake smiles, and shrill laughs.

Safety beckoned from the far corner of the room, a red paneled door. Eyeing the route, she strategized shadowing behind three columns.

A beast did not pursue her through the glitz of the London ballroom, rather the well-meaning intentions of her family. They were bent on arranging each set with a sympathetic bachelor, namely the aging and infirm who wouldn't mind dancing with a spinster or wallflower. This set would soon end, and she loathed to see on her aunt's arm another partner with eyes of pity making his way to her. Escape was the only option.

She side-skipped to the first column. Coast clear. Two columns remained. As she slipped behind the second column, she could smell freedom over the musty air.

One step towards the third column and she stopped short. Her sister blocked her path, teeth bared.

"Don't you dare, Lizzie." Miss Charlotte Trethow hissed.

"Don't I dare take advantage of a better view of the dance?" Lizbeth flashed her sister a smile of nonchalant innocence then turned her attention to the room, undaunted by the delay and as determined as ever to leave.

Groups of young girls stood along the sidelines gossiping behind gilded fans while the social matrons studied every dance step for a hint of favoritism towards their charges. Liz curiously noticed none of the women looked at each other while talking. Rather than eye the object of their conversation, their hawkish eyes roamed the room for signs of scandal and for eligible bachelors of wealth and title.

"Don't think I don't know what you're doing." Charlotte glowered. "You're heading for that door. Auntie will suffer a fit of vapors if she finds you hiding in a parlor."

Shaking her head, Lizbeth argued, "Aunt Hazel knows I'm a lost cause. Her only concern now is you. You're enjoying yourself, so don't let me rain on your sunshine."

The dancers slowed to a stop. Liz cast a pleading glance.

Sighing, Charlotte said, "Very well. Escape before Auntie sees you, but don't say I didn't warn you of her wrath."

Lizbeth's sister turned with a huff to follow the perimeter of the room, her embroidered train swishing behind her, a sea of peach pastel and lace. The young hopeful was a sight to behold this evening, her golden-brown ringlets flirting with onlookers and her milky white skin accentuating her dark eyes, a prize for any man in search of a bride. Lizbeth glanced down at her own humble appearance and shrugged.

Unlike her sister, she wasn't the least interested in becoming someone's property, a dependent upon some aloof man who controlled her life but ignored her person, fulfilling his jollies elsewhere.

Returning her concentration to the red door, she resumed her mission, desperate to flee the smothering room. If she heard one more giggle from a vapid woman or one more wine-infused guffaw, she would scream. The dancers emptied the floor to circulate, and Liz knew she had only moments to spare before her aunt sought her for another arranged set.

Moving surreptitiously, she sidestepped her way to the door, pressing her back against the cool wood to ease it open, then slipping through the gap towards freedom. The noise muffled as she closed the door behind her. After a moment's repose, she breathed in deeply the fresh air of her solitude.

Solitude was far superior to a room full of snots.

Not a single person in that ballroom would be able to carry on a conversation that suited her palate. She doubted any of them read more than the gossip column. This was the age of enlightenment, after all, and she would wager her dowry that not one of them was enlightened. Not that a lady made wagers, but, then, no one had ever accused her of being a lady.

Lizbeth surveyed the hallway. Several doors invited inquiry. One of the doors led to a drawing room, she recalled, but the drawing room would be crowded with septuagenarians and their nodding plumes. That wouldn't do.

A faint memory niggled at the edges of her mind. Hadn't she seen a library the last time she was here? Oh, a library would be divine!

Determined to find it, she closed her eyes and inhaled a belly breath to let the fantastical scent of freshly printed books guide her to—yes! She was sure she remembered which door. Heading for the second door on the left at the far end of the hall, she walked with purpose to repress any helpful footman's desire to reroute her to the ballroom.

The door sighed open at the lightest suggestion of her hand, as if the room had awaited her arrival. A fire flamed in the hearth, the glow lighting the room. Before relaxing, she glanced around the room for signs of life. It appeared vacant.

Alone at last.

Leather bindings decorating the walls aromatically romanced her nostrils, and the shelves of bound and color-coded books tantalized her. What would it be like to spend the day with myriad reading choices at her disposal? One goal in her life remained steady—to have her own home library. She wouldn't stoop so low to sacrifice her independence by marrying a man for his large library, but she couldn't deny she would be sorely tempted.

Although a matching chaise posed under a damask draped window, temptingly comfortable, the lighting would be better by the fire, and she was eager to absorb herself into a tale. Two grommet chairs faced the fire, one with its chair-back to her, the other inviting her to nestle into the cracked-leather seat.

Lizbeth removed one of her gloves to feel the bindings of the books as she browsed the shelves. Her fingertips caressed the gold-tooled spines, trailing along a set of histories with black leather and gold leaf, and atlases of light tan with a flower pattern.

Two bookshelves over, she found plays and dramas, nine volumes of Stern, five volumes Murphey, nothing that cried out to be read. Wrinkling her nose at Cowper another shelf down, she continued searching until, aha, something she could never read enough of, *The Faerie Queen*. She freed Spenser from his shelf, inhaled the scent of leather, and touched the wove paper.

This topped any romance she would ever find in a ballroom. Reading to herself the first lines of the opening canto, she immersed herself quickly and thoroughly.

Her satin shoes instinctively found their way to one of the chairs in front of the hearth as she read while walking, entranced.

As she sank into the cool seat of the chair, a deep voice growled.

"Shouldn't you be in the ballroom hunting your prey?"

Chapter 2

Liz's head jerked up, eyes wide. A man sat in the opposite chair, one leg crossed over the other, a book held with long fingers in his lap, the gleam in his eyes predatory.

"I beg your pardon?" Lizbeth questioned, affronted.

"Has no one told you begging is demeaning?" he replied, his unwavering stare that of a lion eyeing his quarry.

"How dare you, sir." She lifted her chin defensively, looking at him down the length of her nose. "Why did you not announce yourself when I entered?"

The nerve of this man not to say something when he most assuredly heard the door. A respectful gentleman would have left promptly at seeing her, for they'd not yet been introduced and shouldn't be alone together even if they had.

"Not to belabor the point," he challenged, "but you disrupted *my* privacy, and thus you should have been the one to ascertain if the room were vacant, and if not, take your leave."

She bristled, narrowing her eyes. What a horribly rude man!

The stranger didn't wait for a response, rather eyed the book in her hands and sneered. "Sentimental drivel, I presume?"

Refusing to be intimidated, Lizbeth glared, raising her chin a fraction of an inch higher. "Edmund Spenser, actually," she snapped.

That should shut him up and give her a chance to flee. The likelihood of him knowing Spenser was slim to none, just as all the other fops and dandies in the ballroom, too busy socializing to read.

One corner of the stranger's mouth lifted in a sly smile as he said,

"And thou most dreaded impe of highest Jove, Faire Venus sonne, that with thy cruell dart At that good knight so cunningly didst rove, That glorious fire it kindled in his hart,"

Her world turned topsy-turvy in that moment. She gaped at him as he recited from memory *The Faerie Queen*. Any plans of departure abandoned from the sheer shock of meeting a potentially intellectual person at a human meat market, Lizbeth studied him, stunned, fascinated, even a touch smitten despite his rudeness.

He certainly didn't look like a fop with his bronzed skin and crinkles around his eyes as though he spent too much time squinting into the sun. There was something almost feral about him. Conservative clothing framing a powerful build and a tamed mane unpowdered and confined by a large brown ribbon conjured a vision of a caged animal.

While she couldn't put her finger on it, there was decidedly something familiar about him, something that invited her to stay despite his obvious attempts to dissuade her from lingering. She had never met him, of that she was sure, but she recognized his wistful tone when he recited Spenser.

Unfamiliar to her was his Roman nose, almost too large for such a slender face, his sardonic grin, his quizzical eyebrows as he waited for her to respond. Unfamiliar, too, was the color of his eyes, so dark a brown they nearly matched his raven hair.

Yet as she studied him, those eyes brightening from impenetrable black to an unclouded, intelligent brown, she realized what about him she recognized. His were the eyes of a dreamer, of a thinker, of someone who had stood on the edge of a cliff and wondered what it would be like to fly.

She knew, then, the reason behind the sense of familiarity, for she knew his eyes as well as she knew her own reflection in the mirror. His initial intimidation waned with this realization. He wasn't a rude or abrasive man, rather someone like her, someone who preferred solitude over company, someone who enjoyed reading over socializing.

Or she could be misreading him.

Relaxing her guard, albeit cautiously, she smirked, changing her tactic, desirous to test her theory.

"Well recited." Lizbeth set her book in her lap and awarded him a slow clap, mocking his cleverness with an arched brow. "But you can't fool me. Cupid has not struck you with an arrow today."

"Can you be so sure?" He remarked, his smile broadening, teasing. "It's not every day that a woman sequesters herself in a room with me...alone."

Lizbeth snorted inelegantly, her gaze dropping to the book in his hands. "And how's *your* sentimental novel progressing?"

He scoffed, closing his book and leaving it to rest on his crossed thigh. "You would hardly be familiar with what I'm reading. John Locke—a far cry from feminine reading preferences. I'm surprised to see you with Spenser and not Samuel Richardson, a favorite of yours, I'm sure."

Refusing to take umbrage at his goading, especially from a man with a faint Scottish burr, the rolling r's hinting at a northern dialect, but eager to prove her literary prowess, she accepted his implied challenge.

Casually, as though she had such conversations daily with strangers in a library, she said, "Personally, I'm not a believer of Locke's philosophies, but not from ignorance of them. And funny you should imply that I'm a reader of Richardson rather than Locke, when Richardson's book embodies the very philosophies of Locke's *tabula rasa*."

Touché! She thought.

Perhaps she felt starved for quality conversation, or perhaps she wanted to best a man. Either way, her tongue sharpened for the duel. She would prove this stranger's assumptions of her intelligence, or lack thereof, wrong.

"I'm intrigued." He prodded, "What similarities do you see between Locke's book on human nature and Richardson's silly romance?"

She took the bait. "Locke asserts we are all born blank slates, molded by experience. Essentially, we are who others make us, nothing more than victims of chance. I would like to think I was born of sterner nerve than to let experience alone influence me."

He uncrossed his legs and leaned forward.

The movement invited her to admire his shapely thighs, thick and pressing against the taut satin breeches. *Don't be distracted.* She schooled herself.

Focus. She had never been in a room alone with a man, much less a man such as this, physically powerful and mentally stimulating. *Focus.*

Focus renewed and determined to champion in the duel, she sat up straighter, eyeing him to ensure he was impressed. "Richardson's *Pamela,*" Liz asserted, "epitomizes a woman born as a blank slate, influenced only by the people around her, a victim of social mores rather than personal values. I do not believe that people are passive creatures to which cruelty and kindness are inflicted, helpless without recourse."

His dark eyes lit with intelligence and intrigue. "You of all people should know the victimization of the sex."

"No one is completely helpless. We can all change our situations, carve our own destinies. Women can control their fates as well as any man." Lizbeth leaned forward in her chair, gripping her book. "Consider this past October. Women marched on Versailles! Women revolted in the streets against the powers that constrained them!"

"Yes, yes, but Pamela, as Richardson writes her, is the only kind of woman I've ever known. Show me a woman who is not false fronted or a victim of circumstance." He waved his hand in the general direction of the ballroom.

Before she could respond, he continued, "I'm surrounded by eyelash-batting frauds. Can you honestly imagine any of those ladies in the ballroom marching? Can you see them dragging cannons, carrying small arms? Preposterous. They have been molded into what they are, simpering sheep. Not a single brain amongst them, all because society dictates silent and ignorant women are more marriageable. Society made them what they are." He leaned back against the chair, smug victory etching his features.

Parrying, she said, "So, you admit you've read *Pamela*."

He snarled.

The silence that followed presented the perfect opportunity to end the conversation, however entertaining, and make her exit, but she couldn't bring herself to do it. She had never enjoyed teasing or even conversing quite so much as with this man.

Gone was the need to prove herself, replaced with the delight to share her opinions without being mocked or ridiculed. This conversation needed never to end as far as she was concerned.

Afraid he, too, might see this as the perfect time to end the moment and leave, she launched into a rebuttal, taking the conversation one step too far.

"I agree most women of my acquaintance wouldn't be amongst the revolutionists, but that's not my point. These women are Pamela made flesh, following the crowd instead of following their own mind. Once we cease fearing society, we can carve our own path. Locke's essays are hogwash! We may be influenced by others, but only we can determine what we do with our lives. No one and nothing controls us or commands who we are."

His face darkened. He withdrew into his chair, retreating. Lizbeth could feel the shared moment pass, as well as see the transformation in his physique—a tightness in his jaw, a deepening furrow of his brow, a subtle shift in his eyes. The depths of those eyes she had just admired shadowed.

Goosebumps rose on her arms from the change in the air around them, companionable to tense. She hit a nerve, however unintentional.

Blast.

Why had she continued to rattle on so vulgarly? She was enjoying the repartee, and beyond that, she was enjoying his company. His combination of intellect, wit, and mystery sent her senses reeling.

Hopefully, she hadn't upset him beyond repair. Hopefully, he would relax again and find a way to resume conversing. Hopefully—.

"You know, you'll never catch a husband sitting with me exchanging literary parley." He tossed his book on the side table next to his chair, then steepled his fingers, elbows resting on the chair arms.

A clear dismissal. Liz laughed self-consciously.

Deflecting, she jested, "Had I realized my plans to avoid the marriage mart were so transparent, I would have disguised my intentions."

He raised one black eyebrow. "Not a follower of society's expectations?"

Holding out her hand, she declared, "Miss Trethow, determined spinster and future lady's companion, at your service."

Only after the words tumbled out did she feel chagrined by the proclamation. Not that she was interested in him romantically, but did she have to stick her foot in her mouth with every conversation?

Nonplussed, he reached for her hand, grazing her knuckles with soft lips.

"At my service? And how shall you serve me?" His lips curved upwards.

Both touch and words sent gooseflesh down her back.

This man was no gentleman. No gentleman behaved this way. No gentleman spoke so brazenly or touched lips to flesh. Was he a rake? He didn't look like a rake, but what exactly did a rake look like? She wasn't altogether sure she'd ever met a rake.

She swallowed, her flushed face belying her affected calmness.

"You haven't told me your name," she squeaked, her voice high and strained.

His voice dropped an octave. "Observant of you."

She waited for him to continue. He didn't.

Feeling notably awkward, she said at last, "Well, it has been a pleasure." She stood unsteadily, the unread book in hand. "Not that I expect anyone to come to the library, but it wouldn't do for us to be found alone and unchaperoned."

Ridiculous words given she'd stayed for half an hour.

Rising from his chair, he chuckled, the sides of his eyes crinkling. "And here I thought you refused to be a victim of society's prejudices."

"What a clever monkey you think you are, Mr. No-Name. It is not for myself that I think, but of my sister. Any sniff of scandal and my sister's reputation would be at stake." Lizbeth returned Spenser to his shelf and her glove to her hand, determined to appear confident despite shaky legs. "I will leave first."

As reluctant as she was to leave, there was truth to her words and impropriety to their situation. She had thrown far too much caution to the wind as it was, enjoying his company more than safeguarding her reputation. She had lied about her sister. It was of herself she thought.

While she didn't so much care about her reputation, she did care that being found alone with a man could force her into marriage. Not even this man with his wit and mystique could tempt her to sacrifice her independence. Of all her talk of controlling destinies, they both knew some situations were outside either of their power. She'd risked too much already. The more fool her.

As her hand met the door handle, he said, "Miss Trethow."

When she turned to face him, he bowed reverently. "Call me Roddam."

"Mr. Roddam. A smart name. It has been a pleasure." With a nod, she departed.

Sebastian relished for a moment his newfound mistaken identity as a Mr. Roddam. He embraced the anonymity it afforded. Mr. Roddam. What would it be like not to shoulder responsibility, not to be a peer of the realm?

He replaced the collection of essays on its respective bookshelf and waited another half hour in the library to avoid being seen leaving after Miss Trethow.

Her words of Locke echoed in his mind as he waited. A well-read woman but sheltered. What did she know of the hardships of life? She made controlling one's destiny sound easy, as though life and other people held no consequence. If she had lived but a year in his shoes, she wouldn't hold to such beliefs. After all he had done to rise from the ashes of his past and build his life into something meaningful, something survivable, it still took every ounce of his willpower to remain sane, all because of what had been done to him, all because of other people.

He should be pleased the conversation had taken such a turn. It served as a reminder that his life overflowed with too much darkness for friendships or romance, not that a woman like her would want to pursue any type of relationship with him once she got to know him. He was no prize.

And yet, he found her enchanting. They had exchanged a more engaging conversation than he'd ever shared with anyone in his life. He admired her boldness to speak her mind regardless of anyone's impression of her, a trait most men would find unappealing.

He was not most men.

For the length and breadth of their exchange, he had pulsed with awareness of Miss Trethow with her sparkling eyes and Cornish quaintness, the latter of which endeared her to him with every dropped h.

Her large brown eyes hinted at a touch of green when reflecting the fire light. Dark hair with touches of red curled across her forehead with long tresses loosely braided atop her head and threaded with a blue ribbon. If he hazarded a guess, he would say she was mid-twenties, hardly on the shelf, but clearly branded unmarriageable either by her brashness and radical views or by her own choice, perhaps both.

While she had styled herself in the newest fashion of the empire waist with a blue sash and bow below the bosom, she hid bare skin with a modest, lace fichu. He had focused on her face, for he was sure if he looked down at the fichu, he would have found himself wanting to unwrap it. Who could blame him the occasional glance, such as to admire the pearl necklace with its gold and amethyst cameo?

No detail had escaped his notice. He had memorized her.

He couldn't even remember the last time he had looked at a woman lustfully. Years. Before his inheritance. But her damned outspokenness had him wanting to undress more than her mind.

It hadn't solely been her words both to incense and entice him. Her eyes had done a fair job on their own. In her eyes he had recognized something he knew all too well. The need for freedom. The desire to jump into a cold sea at midnight and feel the crisp water lap at bare skin. The desire was in her eyes just as in his soul.

To hell with her sheltered beliefs. He wanted to see her again. He needed to see her again. Damn the complications.

Given her declarations of being a determined spinster, she wouldn't see him as a potential mate. There would be no need for excuses or explanations for why he preferred to remain unmarried, no worries she would attempt to trap him or compromise herself. There would be only two equals desiring the same passion.

Chapter 3

At the end of the week, Lizbeth attended another party, one she had no intention of missing by hiding in a library.

She, her sister Charlotte, her Aunt Hazel, and her cousin Walter ascended the steps to Lady Kissinger's townhome on this most auspicious evening. Although the dancing wouldn't start until more guests arrived, music reverberated from the ballroom through the anteroom and out into the foyer. She bit her bottom lip in anticipation.

Preceding them in the queue was a large cucumber, Marie Antoinette, and a mermaid. A faux horse head neighed behind her. Tonight's ball wasn't just any ball; it was Lady Kissinger's fancy-dress ball.

Raising the hooped gown of her Queen Elizabeth costume, Liz followed her troupe into the anteroom, ushered in by the first footman who took their cards. The whalebone of her long-waist corset bit into her rib with each step. Oh, but it was worth it, she thought. Nothing could be more exciting than a fancy-dress ball.

On second thought, seeing Mr. Roddam again would top that excitement.

Her family waited in the receiving line. The hostess, still whinging with the group before them, was dressed as Titania from *Midsummer Night's Dream*, complete with fairy wings.

"The Right Honorable Baron Collingwood, The Right Honorable Baroness Collingwood, Miss Lizbeth Trethow, and Miss Charlotte Trethow." As the footman trumpeted their names, Lady Kissinger, all dangling pearls, glitz, and smiles, stepped forward to greet her guests.

"I keep telling him not to announce names and let me guess who is behind the masks! If he doesn't cease and desist, I'll demote him to fifth footman," Lady Kissinger announced with a laugh.

"Oh, Agnes, darling. You look fabulous," replied Aunt Hazel disguised as a milkmaid with two buckets strapped to her hips.

"So good of you to say, love." The hostess glanced at Walter. "Your son is looking more like his father every day. So handsome!"

Walter, dressed as Hamlet, tucked Yorick's skull behind his back as he took her hand in his.

"And your nieces are living dolls!" she exclaimed. "Queen Elizabeth, and let me guess. No, don't tell me. Little Red Riding Hood?"

"Yes, my lady." Charlotte simpered demurely and curtseyed.

Aunt Hazel kissed Lady Kissinger's cheek before leading the quartet into the ballroom. The faint scent of violets wafted through a room already overflowing with several dozen costumed guests, a few unrecognizable, others merely adorned with a mask and ball attire. Charlotte tucked her hand in the crook of Lizbeth's arm as they walked into the ballroom and worked their way around the perimeter, greeting familiar faces as they walked.

Sconces lit the space. Strung from one to the other and stretching the length of the ballroom waved feathers and colored fabrics. Chandeliers cast a magical glow on the ceiling mural and illuminated the fresh flowers dangling above the dancefloor. Pink chairs and settees lined the walls, each decorated with a mask and short cape.

"Now then." Hazel flicked open an ivory-handled fan. "The mission is to secure dance partners posthaste. Look lively."

"Auntie! Don't be vulgar." Charlotte blushed.

"Fiddlesticks. We're here to see you married, and you can't very well accomplish that without dance partners." Hazel looked knowingly at Lizbeth.

Before Hazel could press the issue, a gaggle of girls approached Charlotte for gossip and costume comparisons.

"Mother, I see some of the fellows," interrupted Walter. "Do you mind if I join them?"

"Go, but don't neglect the ladies. If I see you sitting out a single set, I'll have you walk home to Devon after the Season."

Rolling his eyes, Walter headed in the direction of a chubby Louis XVI, a tall figure in a domino, a knight in rusty armor, and a Paul Revere with a tourney horse.

As per usual, Lizbeth stood alone with her aunt, a wallflower. It was just as well since she had no desire to gossip with the ladies or flirt with the men. All she wanted from the evening was another conversation with Mr. Roddam, but she groaned inwardly to realize she may not recognize him if he wore a full costume with mask, assuming he attended. Unless he approached her or failed to wear a mask, she would be at a loss.

She kept her eyes trained on the double entry doors, watching each newcomer for broad shoulders and tall height. She wasn't even sure why she hoped to see him again. They had met only briefly, and she remembered doing most of the talking, giving him the impression she was the worst sort of bluestocking.

But there was something about him that made her feel he understood her, something that set him apart from other men. She couldn't help but suspect she had stumbled on a hidden gem. If he were to speak to any other woman as he had spoken to her, he would undoubtedly offend their tender sensibilities. Women might also find him less than attractive given his bearing was uncommon to the typically sought-after man.

And yet she found him titillating.

He struck her as a man who wouldn't be afraid to dirty his fingernails, who thirsted for knowledge and loved a challenge, who, above all else, communicated with her.

One of her aversions to marriage was being bound to a man who wouldn't communicate, who would visit her only in the evenings and ignore her otherwise. Such a man would strip her of her identity, leaving in its wake a mindless possession. Her closest childhood friends had succumbed to marriages of so-called convenience, relinquishing their dreams to be supported by the shadow of a man.

After only one meeting, Lizbeth suspected Mr. Roddam to be of a different ilk, to be like her. A communicator, a reader, a passionate lover of knowledge and nature.

Distracted by her thoughts, she almost missed the man standing at the ballroom's double doors, his back to her. The sight of long, dark hair held by a purple ribbon caught her attention. She craned her neck for a better view.

"Has someone caught your fancy?" Aunt Hazel pressed, poking Liz in the arm with her fan. "Which one is he?"

The man turned to face the room. Small nose and beady eyes. Not Mr. Roddam after all.

"No one in particular, Auntie. Just admiring costumes. Have you seen the leprechaun flinging bits of gold paper?" She laughed a tad too heartily.

With narrowed eyes and pursed lips, Hazel said, "I must insist you put this spinster nonsense to rest. Your father tells me you're even considering employment as a lady's companion. Of all the absurdities. It's time you reconsidered a union with Walter. Our plans were interrupted when the baron passed, but it's been three years, Lizbeth. It's time."

"Oh, Aunt Hazel. Not again," Liz replied, exasperated.

"I would feel much better if the two of you came to an agreement before the end of the Season. With your father's property entailed to Walter, it is a sensible match." Lowering her voice, she added, "He needs you. He's been listless ever since his father's death, and I believe it's because he's still grieving. A wife is what he needs. I'll never forget how instrumental you were in helping your father through the death of Elizabeth. You could do the same for Walter. I worry about him—and about you!"

Liz loved Walter as a cousin, but nothing more. Even if she did feel more towards him than friendship, she couldn't be an emotional caregiver, not again, not after the last time. She'd nearly lost herself in the process.

"Walter and I move in different circles. We would never suit. Don't you want him to marry for love?" Liz smiled sweetly against the acrid taste in her mouth.

"Of course, I want him to marry for love, but who wouldn't fall in love with *you* if you gave a man half a chance?"

The dance floor cleared of milling guests, then, distracting her aunt from the conversation. All eyes turned to Robin Hood and Maid Marianne as they stepped out to lead the first dance, a lively cotillion. Other dancers joined the couple. The violins struck the opening notes, and as the dancers clasped hands, those standing about the room clapped in time to cheer the couples.

Liz looked to her aunt in surprise when Hazel huffed and harrumphed rather than joining in the festive atmosphere.

"Why is Charlotte not dancing?" Hazel sniffed. "Who is she with? Who is that man?" Pulling her lorgnette from a bucket, Hazel squinted at a scrawny, costumed Captain Nelson who had replaced the group of girls Charlotte had been with minutes before. "Good heavens. That's Mr. Crawley. A wastrel of a man with no good connections. She'll not find a husband standing about gabbing with the likes of him."

Tutting, Lizbeth said, "Dereliction of duties, Auntie, if you don't see to her rescue."

Returning her lorgnette to the bucket, Hazel pushed past Liz to intercede.

Relieved to be free of the matchmaking schemes, Lizbeth turned towards one of the balconies. From there, she could escape the madness without losing her view of the room. This marked a bright point in the evening, as her aunt's distraction with Charlotte would enable Liz to remain undisturbed by well-intentioned dance partners. Praise be to small favors.

For a full set of dances, she managed to remain out of sight and mind. She was far happier half-hidden behind the curtains, unnoticed and undisturbed.

And then her cousin reappeared.

Cringing, she suspected he would have at his side one of the dreaded dance partners.

"There you are, Lizbeth!" Walter stepped onto the balcony, all smiles and flushed cheeks. "I've been searching everywhere for you. Why the deuce are you hiding out here? Well, no matter. I want to introduce you to someone special." Leaning towards her, he said *sotto voce*, "He's been champing at the bit for an introduction, Lizzie, and let me be the first to say, *well done*. Quite the conquest."

Walter waved over the masked man in the domino. A swirl of black cloak advanced. A tricorn covered the man's hair, and a gold mask disguised his face.

Lizbeth's heart skipped a beat.

Walter said, "May I introduce to you my cousin, Miss Trethow?"

The masked stranger bowed Liz in her Queen Elizabeth costume and said huskily, "Your Majesty."

"Lizbeth, this is the Duke of Annick," Walter enunciated.

Liz curtsied, her heart in her throat. "Your Grace."

The stranger in the library had introduced himself as Roddam, not Annick, and certainly not as a duke. But the resemblance even in costume was unmistakable. Broad shoulders, tall height, deep voice, and northern accent, albeit muffled by the mask. And he had sought out an introduction. Who else could it be aside from her Mr. Mystery?

She felt faint.

How perfectly ridiculous. He was only a man. And a rude man to boot. A man who lied about his name, no less. Roddam could be his surname, she supposed.

Her knees knocked beneath her gown.

"I hope we may become more intimately acquainted over the next hour." The duke took her hand in his and kissed the air above it in an overly dramatized motion. "Call me Annick."

"A pleasure to meet you, Your Gra-er-Annick," Liz stammered.

"Tell me you haven't already promised the next set. Nay, even if you have, you will dance it with me instead."

Inclining her head, she replied, "The dance is yours."

"Shall we step out for fresh air during the first dance of the set and return to dance the remaining two?" Annick asked, his head dipping closer to be heard over the music.

Walter winked at her and walked away, leaving her alone with the duke.

Taking swift advantage of Walter's departure, the masked man did not wait for her consent but instead guided her the remaining steps to the balcony railing, still in sight of the ballroom but cast in shadow.

Was this him? Was this the man from the library? She was sure it was.

"Meet any Pamelas this week?" she jested, wishing she could see beyond his mask, wishing she could see his eyes.

Basked only in moonlight, his face remained a mystery.

He chuckled, "No Pamelas that I'm aware. I was more intent on securing an introduction to you. Why would I desire a Pamela when there is a Miss Trethow of such beauty before me?"

Well, then.

She flushed, not from the flattery but from discomfiture to the overtures.

"Read anything of note lately?" She asked the first insipid question that came to mind, rerouting the direction of discourse.

Resting a hand on the railing behind her, he angled closer. "I didn't request the set to talk books. I'd much rather remark on how attractive I find you."

For half an hour, days before, she met a kindred spirit, a lover of knowledge, someone who wouldn't judge her or patronize her. His words in this moment proved her mistaken. Her anticipation for the reunion faded, replaced with an edgy self-consciousness.

Fidgeting with her Elizabethan ruff, Liz fixed her focus on the parquet floor in the room beyond.

"The moment I saw you, I knew your beauty couldn't be rivaled," he intimated. "I hope you'll give us a chance to become... better acquainted."

With a gauging, anxious laugh, she shied away from him by leaning against the balustrade. "I'm surprised to learn you're not only an aristocrat, but a duke."

"Do you find my title intimidating? Don't. I may have any woman I desire, despite humble origins or age. In fact, I find your maturity advantageous."

He might have flirted with her in the library, but nothing about his words or behaviors had sounded this lascivious, this pompous. Before, his words had seemed defensive rather than genuinely flirtatious, as if he had wanted to shock her or test her mettle.

His tone tonight doused her in cold water.

Shivering, her eyes darted from him to the ballroom. During their first encounter, she hadn't felt awkward, tongue-tied, or agitated. Now, she suffered all three. To top off her discomfort, she was sure that behind the mask, hungry eyes glazed her with honey and pineapple.

"I disagree, Your Grace. You may desire whomever you like, but if the woman in question doesn't return your affection, you will not have her." She punctuated her sentence by crossing her arms over her chest in an unladylike manner.

"Mmm. I like a challenge," he intonated, reaching into his cloak to pull a small box from his pocket.

Her stomach clenched. "Perhaps, I did not make myself clear the first time? I'm a spinster by choice and wish to remain so."

"The first time?" he asked absently, distracted by his struggle with the lid of the gold box. "To what first time are you referring, Miss Trethow?"

Popping the lid at last, he reached in to finger the contents.

"Do you meet so many women in libraries that you can't recall what I said at Lady Starling's ball?" she spat, increasingly vehement to be in this situation, to have thought about him all week, to have looked forward to seeing him, to be misremembered, to be turned into an object rather than an intellectual equal.

More to himself than to her, he muttered, "The devil."

"I beg your pardon?" she demanded more than questioned.

Chuckling, he removed his mask, held his fingers to his nose, and delighted in a pinch of fragrant snuff from his box. Looking up at her, he flashed a devilish smile and smoldering sapphire eyes.

"Miss Trethow, we've not met before tonight. I do believe you've mistaken me for someone else."

Chapter 4

Liz's hand flew to her mouth.

The man before her was not Mr. Roddam. Even unmasked, however, there was a startling and eerie resemblance. Both men shared the same slender face and aristocratic nose, the same dark features, height, and deep voice. All except the eyes. Mr. Roddam had dark, brown eyes with fathomless depths, but this man had deep, blue orbs beneath half-lidded lashes. They could be brothers, and perhaps they were.

Her cheeks heated in mortification.

Removing his tricorn, he unveiled heavily pomaded hair spiraling in stylish disarray, cut short in a Brutus style except the unruly top. "My apologies, Miss Trethow. I will not retract my words, for I spoke in earnest of my attraction to you, but I know a distracted woman when I see one. Your mind is on someone other than me, and that simply will not do."

"The misunderstanding was my own," she admitted, pressing her gloves against her hot face and looking wistfully towards the ballroom.

"Allow me to return you inside. I believe my pursuits have fallen flat this evening, and I can only hope you have a keen sense of humor. Shall we finish the set on the dancefloor to make amends?"

She nodded dazedly as they walked the length of the balcony back to the room. Nothing sounded more dreadful than dancing the remainder of the set with him, but she couldn't very well say no, especially not to a duke.

Oh, how humiliating.

And how like her, adamant about remaining unmarried, yet throwing inhibitions to the wind after a single encounter. So excited about Mr. Roddam, as though she'd discovered a new favorite book, she'd even mistaken this man for him, though it seemed a reasonable mistake given their similarities. But was she so desperate for a friend she'd risk entanglement with a stranger?

When she returned to the ballroom on the duke's arm, she scoured the room for signs of her family or of the real Roddam, but all she saw was the swirl of dancers as they finished what remained of the dance. She didn't have to wait long for the next dance to begin.

"Miss Trethow, our dance?" His Grace directed her to the floor for the allemande.

Discarded on a chair by the balcony doors were his hat and mask. Lizbeth fought the queasiness of what happened on the balcony as she looked up into her partner's face, his blue gems studying her with interest.

And then she saw *him*. Her breath caught.

Out of her peripheral, Liz caught sight of a pair of dark eyes beneath furrowed brows watching her. The voices around her funneled to distant mumbles.

Mr. Roddam stared at her from across the room. Unmistakably Mr. Roddam.

A red ribbon tied back his hair, except for the windswept strays falling around his ears. A knee-length red coat with gold embroidering molded as a second skin across imposing shoulders. His coat opened to a white shirt contrasted by three daggers in a waist pouch, a thick gold chain with a cross, and a sword sheathed at his waist. Gold knee breeches, tied at the side with red ribbons, accentuated muscular thighs.

A pirate.

If she thought him animalistic before, it was nothing to now. He towered above those around him, powerful and primal. How could she have confused the man in front of her for Mr. Roddam? As similar as their features and height, there was a lifetime of difference in their bearing and physique, not to mention their movements. The duke swaggered; Roddam prowled.

Exhaling, she looked to her partner and curtsied as the dance began, at once chagrined to be caught dancing with him. Was she worried her stranger would think her unfaithful? How absurd!

With the first *enchaînement*, she earned a waft of the duke's scented pomade. With the second *passé*, she felt his signet ring dig into her palm. He flashed her a light-glinting grin as they interlaced arms and hands.

She suspected most of the room watched them, not only because a duke chose to dance with a wallflower, but also because he galloped during the promenade. The other dancers followed suit with his figure changes rather than censuring him. Ah, the power of a duke.

Try as she might, she couldn't catch another glimpse of Mr. Roddam. Was he, too, watching? Or had he bowed out to find a hiding place?

The two remaining dances of the set, during which she was trapped in the company of the Duke of Annick, lasted a half hour collectively. A half hour of sheer hell, as far as she was concerned. The man was a pompous windbag.

His title alone would make him the most eligible bachelor in the room. His looks aided in that status. In the eyes of the *beau monde*, he was dashing, far more handsome than Roddam, despite their resemblance.

Roddam had a raw, harsh beauty with his sun-bronzed skin, hard eyes, and muscular build, more in keeping with a laborer than a gentleman. Annick, while sharing similar features, boasted an ivory complexion, a lithe frame beneath the domino costume, and the devil-may-care roguishness that would send most women in the room into a swoon.

Liz found him a nightmare. While he interjected compliments of her *mature* beauty throughout the dance, he mostly bragged about himself. His art collection, the number of his estates, his prowess with a sabre, his personal friendship with the Prince of Wales, and various and sundry other vanities. More than ever, she desired the scholarly reflections of Mr. Roddam.

After making a cake of herself with this buffoon, she would hardly blame Roddam if he avoided being introduced to her. Even without the oafish duke, he may not wish for an introduction, as he could disdain bookish spinsters. Who wouldn't, when it came down to it?

Once the dance ended, he returned her to her family, all of whom were affecting over-dramatized ennui to see her on the duke's arm. The duke, to make matters worse, preened like a peacock.

Walter was the first to speak when they reached the bosom of her family. "Annick, would you allow me to introduce my mother and youngest cousin?"

All devilish smiles, the duke turned to Aunt Hazel and Charlotte.

"Lady Collingwood and Miss Charlotte." Pivoting to the duke, Walter said, "The Duke of Annick."

All focus on Lizbeth abandoned, the duke turned his attention to admire unabashedly a bashful Charlotte who, much to Liz's dismay, greeted him with, "What big blue eyes you have!"

With a throaty chuckle, he reached for her hand. "All the better to see you with, my dear." He bowed over her knuckles before turning to Aunt Hazel with no less an admiring gaze. "This cannot be your mother, Collingwood. This is quite clearly your sister. The pleasure of this meeting is all mine, your ladyship."

Aunt Hazel touched her fan to her chin, simpering as though she weren't thirty years his senior.

After soliciting Charlotte's hand for the next set, Annick took his leave, taking Walter with him. Hazel poked Liz in the arm with her fan, then made her way to the refreshment room with a few fellow matrons. Not but a few moments passed before Charlotte's friends descended on Liz, full of questions and curiosities about her dance with the duke.

She humored them but soon grew tired of the interaction. Their heads were filled with cotton, and she found their company tedious.

One young lady, barely out of the school room and appropriately dressed as a shepherdess, said to Lizbeth, "This is Charlotte's first Season, but she says you aren't married?" Her words lilted innocently, long lashes batting around green eyes.

"Correct," Liz hedged, not sure how this was polite conversation.

"Isn't it terribly embarrassing to have your sister come out before you've married? It's customary for the eldest to marry before the sister is out, you know." She smiled slyly.

The familiar oppression weighed on Lizbeth's chest. The room grew uncomfortably warm. As proud as she was of her decision to remain independent, judgment nevertheless cut deeply.

She'd stayed in the ballroom too long. She'd mingled when she knew better. Anxious to escape further criticism, she glanced to the safety of the double entry doors.

And there he stood, talking with Annick and Walter.

Their eyes met.

Vaguely, distantly, she heard Charlotte's friends moaning about something, but she couldn't tear her eyes from Roddam long enough to return to the conversation.

"My mother told me about him," said one of the girls. "She said he has the manners of a toad. My grandmama says she doesn't care if he's rich as Croesus, for he's a radical and a brute."

The girls tittered.

As the pounding of her heart drowned out their words, the three men walked over. She was instantaneously surrounded by flirtatious squeals and batting eyelashes.

"The big bad wolf has come to collect Little Red Riding Hood for the supper dance." Annick bowed, wiggling his eyebrows at Charlotte.

Roddam cleared his throat, his eyes leveled on Lizbeth.

Annick smirked. "May I introduce Collingwood's cousins? Miss Charlotte Trethow and her sister Miss Trethow." He ignored the other women milling around Charlotte. With a wink to Liz, he said, "And this grumpy pirate is my cousin, the Earl of Roddam."

Lizbeth hoped they hadn't heard her sharp intake of breath. Mr. Roddam wasn't *Mr*. Roddam at all. He was *Lord* Roddam. She should have been far more shocked to learn he was an aristocrat, but after spending a quarter of an hour believing him a duke, an earl didn't seem quite so intimidating.

Still. He was a noble for crying in a chamber pot! She could feel her skin flush with the horror of having called him *Mr*. Roddam to his face.

Without averting her eyes from his, she held her poise and curtsied. Those dark eyes, those dark pools of dreams held her own, unflinching.

"Queen Elizabeth, I presume?" His voice caressed her ears.

"Blackbeard?" she queried.

"What gave it away? My *lack* of a long black beard?" His sarcasm made her laugh, despite her self-consciousness. "Captain Bartholomew Roberts." He bowed.

Lizbeth bounced in her excitement. "Oh, I've read about him!"

"Why am I not surprised?" He arched his eyebrows.

"Yes, in a *General History of the Pyrates*. My mother gave it to me." *Oh no,* she thought. *Here I go again.* She bit her bottom lip to silence herself from not only dominating the conversation once more but from carrying on about books. Again.

"Let me get this straight. When you're taking a break from reading Locke, you read about pirates?" His expression and voice remained unaffected, but his eyes sparkled with mischief.

Faintly, she could hear the voices of her sister, Walter, the girls, and the arrogant dandy. Their presence was easy to forget. Apparently, Lord Roddam thought the same since he hadn't yet acknowledged her sister or the other girls.

"I hope you have yet to reserve the supper dance, my queen," Lord Roddam said.

Sharing the supper dance meant he would also be her partner for the meal after the dance. Dinner and a dance—oh, how divine!

"The dance is to be the scotch reel, I believe," he added.

"I would be honored." Her heart fluttered as she placed her hand on his proffered arm and let him lead her to the dance floor.

Chapter 5

Sebastian led Miss Trethow to the dance floor, anxious to share with her both a dance and dinner. While assuming their positions, he admired her hair's auburn tint, distinguished against the white neck ruff, and the teased style, resembling a crown.

When every other woman in the room favored short hair, her preference for long locks differentiated her. Since meeting her, he had entertained the vision of her hair flowing around her shoulders, imagined unpinning the strands and running his hands through the silk. Long tresses weren't the only enticing feature this evening, for her long-waisted dress emphasized inviting hips, something he hadn't been able to admire in the library.

Having her dancing with him now set his mind somewhat at ease after an hour of unwarranted anxiety. Not only had he spotted her in private and shadowed conversation with Drake, looking flushed, but then he watched her dance with him. For a woman who supposedly preferred the library to a dance floor, she appeared to enjoy his cousin's company.

He had felt murderous when they stepped out from the balcony. He had been disgusted by their flirting. He recognized these feelings for what they were. Jealousy. Ridiculous feelings for a woman he had met only once.

This intelligent and poised woman surely couldn't fall for the rakish charm of his cousin, could she?

But why shouldn't she flirt with Drake? The duke was perfectly eligible. More to the point, Drake was seriously shopping for a duchess, a command given by his mother who threatened to choose his bride herself if he didn't bring home one of his own choosing by the end of the Season. Drake may be a libertine, but he was imminently desirable by marriage minded females.

And Sebastian? Anything but. His title and wealth recommended him, but little else.

Unlike his cousin, he was not in the market for a wife. A friend, perhaps. A mistress, possibly. But not a wife. The dilemma he'd faced throughout the week was how to proposition *this* woman for the role of mistress. She expressed a disinterest in marriage, so that eliminated any concern of being trapped, but one didn't take in innocents as mistresses. Widows, courtesans, actresses, all acceptable. Not innocents. She would be ruined.

He would need to tread carefully, for the only way it could work is if she allowed him to support her, if she undertook the role as a life position, changing her plans from being a lady's companion to being his companion. Ah, but it all sounded so sordid and insulting to a woman of her intelligence.

Having her in his life in any fashion was risky. So many secrets, so many complications, so much trust. But meeting someone like her was an impossible dream come true—suddenly, the impossible seemed possible. He expected at any moment the dream would burst, that he would wake to find her a figment of his imagination or to find she wasn't who she claimed to be.

Trust was in short order in his life. Did he dare trust her? Did he dare chase a bit of light in his dark life?

"Shame on you for not informing me of your title, my lord. You led me to believe you were a *Mr.* Roddam," she scolded, interrupting his reverie.

Standing side-by-side on the dance floor, they waited for the music to strike. Other couples joined their circle.

He couldn't tell if she meant to tease or admonish him about his subtle deception.

Choosing to answer honestly, he turned to her and said, "I would much rather exchange repartee with a Miss Trethow who believes I'm a Mr. Roddam than with a fortune hunter who speaks to me only because I'm titled."

"Be that as it may, I've decided you can't be trusted." She pursed her lips, waited, then dazzled him with a reassuring smile.

The music began. They clasped hands, hers warm in his even through their gloves.

The dance was the liveliest of the evening. They spun, swung, clapped, circled, linked arms and skipped, shuffled feet, raised arms, and laughed without a care in the world. It was unseemly to display such enthusiasm. They didn't care. They made a right spectacle of themselves laughing gaily as they danced.

Sebastian couldn't remember the last time he had danced or who his dance partner had been, but she hadn't possessed the light row of freckles across the bridge of her nose as did this reader of pirate tales. He found himself at a loss for words, entranced by the brightness of her eyes. She looked at him as though she held all the secrets to happiness.

"Have you been enjoying the masquerade?" He could kick himself for such trite conversation.

"Not in the least. Not until now, that is," she admitted as they skipped in a circle.

"Don't all women enjoy parties?"

They snapped their fingers as their feet jigged to the pipe and violins.

"I'm not all women. And you? Are you enjoying yourself?"

He winked. "I have never before enjoyed a dance or partner this much in my life."

They circled the room with arms interlaced, her spontaneous laughter lighting the shadowed spaces in his heart.

"Lord Roddam, are you flirting?" She looked more surprised than coquettish, he thought. He suspected her question was as genuine as her blush.

"If I am, it is because I think we have more in common than anyone I've met. You have my undivided attention, Miss Trethow. Would you consider my friendship?" He hoped his words didn't sound too rehearsed.

His proposal of friendship had been practiced countlessly in the past few days, phrased and re-phrased so he didn't sound too pushy, too flirty, too hopeful, too calculated. He knew what he really wanted. He wanted to taste her lips, redden them with passion. He imagined how it ought to be, the wind whipping her hair about her face as they stood on the beach, her lips parting in invitation for a kiss.

"I accept."

"Wait. What do you accept?" He shook his head from the momentary fantasy of her lips, wondering in trepidation if he had proposed friendship or the far more scandalous position of mistress.

"Your offer of friendship, my lord. I must confess that I've been hoping all evening to see you. I want you to tell me everything there is to know about *Robinson Crusoe*. And when you're finished, tell me your thoughts on Kant, Rousseau, and don't forget Voltaire."

As they linked arms to circle the room again, he inhaled the scent of soap and meadow flowers that permeated her skin. No dousing herself in perfume as did other women.

She smelled like home. Like a spring day after a morning rain. He fixed on the image of her lying in a grassy field shielding the sun with a book. Inhaling meditatively, feeling a warm calm blanket him, he adjusted the image so that in place of the book, his body shielded her from the sun.

"With no small charge you've tasked me, my queen. Wouldn't you rather I told you my thoughts of *Les Liaisons Dangereuses*? I could whisper to you in French while we scandalized all those in the dining room."

"You're a wicked man, and I know you're not serious! Don't you know it's impolite to say such things to a woman?"

"Ah, but as you've pointed out, you're not as other women. And *you're* the one who reads about pirates." He smirked, enjoying being able to share a lighthearted tongue-in-cheek exchange without worrying about offending her tender sensibilities. "Would you prefer me to remain stoic and speak only of the weather or to brag of my riches?"

"Neither! I spent half an hour listening to the riches of your cousin. It is an experience I never wish to repeat." Her eyes smiled up at him.

The dance ended far too soon, and the guests traversed to the dining room.

Guiding her through the traffic of masqueraders towards the long table, Sebastian experienced a startling realization, a sensation he had never felt—this is what it felt to live a normal life. He had lived as a recluse for so long, feeling less than human, an outlier in the world of men, that he didn't know until this moment how good it felt to be alive, really alive.

The past could never be erased or forgotten, and never could it be forgiven, but the future appeared as a chrysalis now, full of promise and transformation. He wasn't entirely sure he trusted it yet. Like an apple for Adam, he suspected the present to be an illusion.

"Tell me your favorite writer of all times," Miss Trethow asked as he steered her to an empty seat.

"Would you judge me harshly if I said it is not a philosopher I favor, but a poet?"

"A poet?" She raised her eyebrows in surprise. "A *sentimental* poet?"

The guests around them cast aside masks and gloves in preparation for dinner. Being the single-minded man that he was, he ignored whoever sat on his other side, regardless that he was supposed to make conversation with that person, as well. He had eyes only for Miss Trethow.

She teased, "After all your derision of sentimental novels, you have a favorite poet. I'm surprised at you."

"Poetry is hardly comparable to a sentimental novel," he rebutted, already enthralled with their banter.

The meal began with white soup, veal, and negus. Sebastian absentmindedly ate, tasting nothing. His mind was too engrossed with her lips meeting the soup spoon. Heaven help him.

"Don't hold me in suspense. Who is this poet?" she asked between bites.

The last thing he wanted to do was talk about himself. He wanted to know everything about her, this well-read, freckled seductress who had sworn off marriage, balls, and all men charming. He couldn't make her out. What did she do with her time? Did she like the ocean?

He had more questions than there were guests at the party, and he was not traditionally loquacious. Her cheeks, he noticed, remained becomingly aglow from the liveliness of the dance.

"Burns," he answered at last.

"Robert Burns?" Miss Trethow laughed. "You're joking. You can never again ill-judge my sex for preferring sentimental novels when you have admitted to liking one of the most sentimental poets alive!"

"Nonsense. He values individualism, freedom, and nature. Three 'sentiments' I happen to think we both value."

He angled towards her and recited with dusky depth the first poem that came to mind.

After a few lines, she interrupted, scoffing affectionately, "Not sentimental, my toe! Burns can call sentimentality 'hair brained' all he wants, but I've never heard more sentimental words. You're a secret lover of that very romance you mocked."

Shame on him for not behaving with better manners, but he couldn't remember the last time he felt this carefree. Sebastian leaned closer still, and as huskily as he could reply without being overheard by those around them, he whispered a few lines from a particularly bawdy Burns poem.

His aim was to shock rather than flirt, to test her resilience. And, devil take it, he certainly enjoyed seeing the blush rising from her neck, creeping with pink tendrils up her soft cheeks.

"Is, um, that the whole poem?" she breathed.

His throaty chuckle accompanied a shake of his head. "The rest is much too dirty for your feminine ears and certainly for our present location."

"Oh. I see." The blush reached her hairline.

The second course arrived in a flurry of footmen. Plates were whisked away and replaced with a delightful dish of hare, scalloped oysters, and sweetbreads.

After they sampled a few forkfuls, Miss Trethow asked, "Are you of Scottish descent by chance, my lord? You have, if I'm not being indelicate by saying, a strong accent."

"Roddam, please." He sampled the wine before answering. "English through and through. I live in Northumberland, naught but 30 miles from the border. I grew up even farther north within an easy walking distance to the border. To be honest, my ancestors were among the northern defenders against the Scots. And you, Miss Trethow, are most assuredly from Devon, Cornwall, or thereabouts."

"How did you—?" Her cutlery paused halfway to her mouth.

Leaning his lips inches from her ear, he whispered surreptitiously, "Your eyes tell me you enjoy cliff diving."

He basked for a moment in her surprise. After chuckling at her wide-eyed incredulity to his brazen statement, he admitted, "Your accent is clearly southern, and I so happen to know your cousin's barony is near Exeter. The clues narrow down my guess, you see. Near Torquay, perhaps? Since you read about pirates, maybe farther south. Penzance?"

Not that he could learn much about her without arousing suspicion, he had managed to learn a few details about her extended family, which proved easier than expected given his cousin and her cousin had attended Oxford together.

Miss Trethow recovered and shook her head. "I live on the northeast coast of Cornwall. In Trevena."

Her words slapped him, crushing his jovial mood.

She couldn't possibly live in Trevena. Not Trevena.

Was this a joke at his expense? Had she and Drake planned this from the beginning or just since tonight? Sebastian had seen them sharing intimate conversation earlier, so it wasn't impossible they planned the joke. Had she known the duke before tonight? Drake very well could have sent her into the library to seek him out, an elaborate ruse. It wouldn't be the first time his cousin had pulled a prank.

The coincidence of Trevena was too extraordinary to be believed. Given how doggedly he guarded his privacy, only Drake would know what Trevena meant to him. Not sure what angered him the most, that she had been so perfect or that Drake would go to this extent for a practical joke, he unceremoniously tossed down his cutlery, his appetite lost.

For a moment, he had felt happiness. A glimpse of a happiness he never thought he would feel, never thought he deserved to feel. With the single word, the happiness crumpled.

"Trevena," he echoed.

"Yes. It's about 60 miles west from Exeter. You may not know this, especially being so far north, but it's believed to be the birth—"

"—birthplace of King Arthur." He cut off her sentence.

Pursing his lips, he erecting walls around himself.

"Yes! So, you do know? How delightful. I haven't met many people acquainted with the histories or the lore. Living in the very parish of his birth, I confess I'm fascinated by the literature about him. Are you versed in King Arthur? How do you know about Trevena?"

"Did my cousin put you up to this before you came to the library or after?" he queried gruffly, unable to tolerate the charade any longer.

He hoped she wouldn't answer. He didn't care. If she were willing to play Drake's game, she didn't matter to him anymore regardless.

But for some reason he didn't understand, the answer did matter. He needed to know if their connection in the library had been real or all part of the joke. But to what end? It was over regardless.

"Pardon? I'm afraid I don't follow." Her brows crinkled in feigned confusion.

His limbs tensed as he shut out further conversation with this trickster. She mocked him. She and Drake both. Remembering the two of them dancing earlier infuriated him, for now he knew they hadn't danced as strangers, but rather as friends plotting against him.

Her hand touched his coat sleeve, startling him. When he glanced over, his stomach flip-flopped to see her brows still knit in confusion, her eyes concerned without a hint of mockery. Either she was the world's best actress, or he had just made a monumental mistake.

No, no, he hadn't made a mistake. Of all the parishes in England, she couldn't possibly live in the parish rumored as the birthplace of King Arthur. While he wanted nothing more than to leave, to escape this bewitching Lady of the Lake, he couldn't cause a scene by leaving mid-meal.

Brusquely shrugging away her hand, he returned to his meal, not caring what she thought of his behavior. She and Drake would not make an arse of him.

A wonder he hadn't realized it until now. This woman was the embodiment of the Lady of the Lake. This woman, this Miss Trethow, had nearly duped him. Fool that he was, even after realizing her to be false, he still wanted more than anything to continue their friendship, to ask more questions, to fall into those happy eyes.

No, he wasn't going to fall for this beguiling enchantress. His secrets were his own, and he would not be trapped by her. According to lore, the Lady of the Lake struck a deal with Merlin to love him if he shared with her all his secrets, taught her all he knew. Merlin did, and the lady trapped him, turning his own magic against him.

From Trevena indeed, he scoffed. He didn't believe her for a minute.

From the moment she walked into the library, he should have known it was too good to be true. He never should have sought her out this evening. Everything had been too similar between them from the start, and now Trevena, the very birthplace of his idol, of the one figure who helped him turn his life around through emulation. This was too much of a coincidence, and Sebastian didn't believe in coincidence.

The room was overly warm.

He was aware his departure into silence left his dinner companion curious, but he didn't care. She shouldn't toy with him.

As dinner ended, he left the table in haste to find his cousin.

Not surprising, Drake had already surrounded himself with women. Crossing his arms over his chest, Sebastian glared menacingly until the ladies exchanged wary glances and left the two men alone.

He could hear the music striking up for a boulanger dance. Drake said not a word, just eyed him curiously as he took a friendly pinch from his snuff box.

"I'm leaving. Are you coming, or shall I send the carriage back for you?" He flinched as the knife hilts in his waistcoat impaled his elbow.

"Be serious, Sebastian. I'm getting on well!" Frustrated, Drake shoved his snuffbox in the pocket of his black cloak.

"Stay if you wish. I'm leaving," he repeated.

"God, man." His cousin ran a hand through his hair. "You can be such a bore. Here I couldn't wait to tell you who I've decided to court, and now you've ruined my good mood."

"I'll not be baited by you. Not now." His stare held Drake's unflinchingly.

Confronting his cousin at the party about the joke he and his accomplice played would be in poor taste, especially when Sebastian wanted nothing more than to plant a facer for Drake's cruelty. He would wait until they were alone.

"As I said. You're a bore. Wait and I'll come with you. I need five minutes to give my regards to Lady Kissinger so she doesn't think we're curs. I've accomplished all I can tonight anyway."

As he took a step towards the hostess, Drake pivoted back to face Sebastian. "On second thought, I'm going to tell you my plan whether you want to know or not. Given your attentions to Miss Trethow this evening, you should know that I will be sending my calling card to Lady Collingwood tomorrow."

His heart skipped a beat. Dear God, they really had duped him.

"This shouldn't come as such a shock, Seb. Is this what it's like to be a hermit? The world keeps moving, and you haven't the faintest clue. I have it on good authority that the Trethow sisters sport lucrative dowries. Come with me tomorrow, if you'd like, and I'll show you how to make a woman fall in love."

That told him all he needed to know. His cousin would be calling on her tomorrow. So, by his cousin's own admission, there was something between Drake and Miss Trethow, proving she had done his bidding by playing a heartless joke. The whole affair left his mouth tasting bitter and his stomach upset.

"Poor choice, Drake. The youngest Trethow is barely out of the schoolroom, and the eldest is a spinster," Sebastian retorted, desperate to end the conversation and leave.

"Nonsense! Miss Trethow could easily be wooed, and her maturity does her credit. She could go toe-to-toe with my mother and force the old bat into the dower house. As for Miss Charlotte, well, she is of age and would make a fine little duchess to mold however I'd like, even if she is a tad prudish."

Drake waited for a reaction, but only received a scowl.

After a few minutes of silence, Sebastian surrendered to anger.

Through clenched teeth, he demanded, "What's your game, Drake? I come here to help you find a bride, and your gratitude is to stab me in the back. Does it go back further than tonight? Did you send her to the library? Or was the ruse only tonight after you discovered we'd met? Tell me now. Tell me truthfully, and I swear to make your throttling brief."

"What library? What the deuce are you on about?"

Sebastian growled. "You know exactly what I'm talking about."

"I haven't the first idea to what you're referring, honestly." With a hand to his heart, Drake said, "I assure you the last thing I would want is to provoke you. I invited you as my guest, you'll recall. While the rest of us are enjoying our lives as gentlemen should, you're holed up in your pile of ruins. I thought a few evenings of merriment would do you some good. I don't know what you're on about, and I don't appreciate being threatened."

Following a long pause, Drake took a deep breath and lightened his tone. "If you get your head out of your arse, perhaps you would be so good as to accompany me to visit Lady Collingwood and her two beautiful and wealthy nieces. If not, that's your prerogative and to my advantage. And I assure you, I do plan to take advantage."

Drake stalked off in the direction of Lady Kissinger, leaving Sebastian to wonder about the odds of coincidences and to reflect on his churlish behavior at dinner.

Chapter 6

The drawing room at Lady Collingwood's London townhome was a neo-classical delight. Stucco walls, wall niches with statues, Chippendale furniture, a rug designed to complement the pastel shades and plasterwork reliefs of the ceiling. A mythology inspired motif repeated throughout the room in the border, the furniture, and even the carved frieze above the fireplace.

"I've always loathed this room," said Aunt Hazel two days after the fancy dress ball.

"Auntie!" Charlotte sat across from her, stroking a cockatoo perched on her forearm. "You chose the design!"

"I know, but I loathe it all the same. I chose it to be fashionable, and I hardly know why. I'd rather this room be pink."

Lizbeth sat at the writing desk finishing a few letters for her father who left most of his correspondences to her way with words.

Charlotte returned Captain Henry to his tree. "Do you think he'll come today?"

"One should hope, my dear." Aunt Hazel reassured Charlotte. "I returned the card yesterday, so he could visit any day. We can assume he has other engagements, but I dare say he won't stay away for long."

The Duke of Annick's calling card arrived the day after the ball. Only this morning had the squeals of delight between Hazel and Charlotte subsided. Liz, on the other hand, was less than thrilled. She wasn't sure his intentions for calling, but she hoped he meant to rekindle his friendship with Walter rather than harass her or Charlotte. She could at least defend herself against the likes of him, unlike Charlotte—too young, too impressionable, and too in love with each beau who paid her a compliment or sent flowers.

Oddly, Liz too had received flowers after the masquerade, but thankfully, no callers. At least five bouquets arrived for her, all from names she barely recognized, no doubt gentlemen who witnessed her dance with a duke and then an earl. Such associations might give the impression she was a catch despite her age, not to mention on the market.

In anticipation of the duke's arrival, Hazel insisted they set up camp in the formal drawing room, at the ready with embroidery and chitchat so they would appear occupied, at ease, and at their best. Although he had yet to appear, they spent the time entertaining a steady stream of callers, mostly friends of Hazel's, a few friends of Charlotte's, and several potential suitors also for Charlotte.

Lizbeth joined the conversation, quill poised above paper. "We certainly shouldn't expect him until after Parliament, should he even call, which is unlikely." She returned the quill to its stand, dusted the freshly inked address, folded and sealed the last letter, and walked over to the duo. "I wouldn't sit around waiting for him if I were you."

"Oh, but Lizbeth. He's a *duke*, and he's so handsome and clever. Did you know that he's friends with Prinny? I'm so taken with him," Charlotte cooed.

Just as Lizbeth rolled her eyes, the butler opened the door, earning the attention of all three ladies. "His Grace the Duke of Annick."

Charlotte rushed to her seat and grabbed her embroidery as the duke entered the room, his multi-caped riding coat swishing behind him. He wore tan buckskin that left little to the imagination and Hessian boots curved just below the knee with a v notch and a gold tassel.

She couldn't help noticing the sheen with which his hair glistened in all its artfully arranged dishevelment. He looked like a frightened owl. The cravat at his neck was truly dandified with a complex knot, lace edging, and sparkling diamonds peeking out of the folds.

So frivolous. Liz tutted.

They stood and curtsied in greeting.

"I've walked into a painting of goddesses!" Annick exclaimed.

"Your Grace, join us. You may sit wherever best suits you. Cecil will return with a tea tray shortly," Aunt Hazel crooned.

Squawk.

All eyes turned to Captain Henry perched on his tree.

Before sitting, the duke walked towards the bird. Captain Henry raised his crest, a fan of yellow and white, and spread his wings, bowing and bobbing to the newcomer.

Squawk ha ha ha ha squawk.

"I've only come to see you, my darling." Annick flirted with the cockatoo who replied with more bowing and squawking, shadowing Annick's movements with aggressive enthusiasm. "Shall we take a ride in the park together, you magnificent bird?"

Charlotte chortled behind her hand as the duke courted the bird.

"If you're this enthusiastic about me," he continued to say to the bird, "why don't we skip courtship and go straight for the wedding? What's your name, beautiful angel?"

Lizbeth intervened, hoping to save the cockatoo from undue stress. "*His* name is Captain Henry, and he's trying to intimidate you to discourage a potential rival."

Charlotte's muffled laughter could be heard throughout the room.

The butler re-entered with a tray of tea, sandwiches, scones, and sweets, far more than any of them could eat in one brief visit.

Aunt Hazel promptly began readying the tea. "Milk, Your Grace?"

"Yes, please, and sugar." He moved away from the upset cockatoo and took his seat with a flourish. "I thought we had dispensed of the formalities. Nothing would delight me more than for you to call me Annick, your ladyship."

His coat still on, teacup in hand, he explained he hadn't come for a lengthy social call, rather to invite them all for a ride in Hyde Park. The door opened, then, and Walter and Papa Cuthbert tumbled into the room, affecting nonchalance and surprise to find the Duke of Annick present. Never had eavesdropping been more obvious.

The clock on the mantel ticked slow seconds as everyone chatted before Walter and Papa whisked away the duke for a cheroot in the study. Would she ever be rid of his company? Courtesy dictated he leave after half an hour, yet three quarters of an hour had passed. And now to think of enduring a ride with him in Hyde Park? Unbearable. Inconceivable. Ludicrous!

Lizbeth's nerves frayed during the wait between the invitation and the ride, especially when Hazel spent the time exclaiming how her machinations were coming to fruition at last, and that one of her nieces would snare a duke. Her aunt even offered unsolicited advice on what to say during the drive, how to behave, and how to accidentally initiate physical contact.

By the time Annick returned to take them for the drive, Lizbeth could stand it no longer. She hadn't enjoyed a single moment's peace since the masquerade, and this was all too much, especially when the duke was an ever-present reminder of Lord Roddam and the dinner debacle.

To the surprise of all in the room, Lizbeth announced when the duke returned, "As tempting as the ride is, Your Grace, I must decline. I am suffering the migraines and must retire. Please accept my apologies."

As soon as they left for the park, she informed the butler to tell visitors she was from home until her aunt and sister returned.

She inelegantly flopped into a chair in the drawing room to relax. The tea tray with now cold tea still boasted more sandwiches and treats than could feed an army. She stuffed a sandwich in her mouth and fell into despair.

Lord Roddam haunted her thoughts.

After a lifetime of feeling out of place, she finally met someone cut from the same cloth. But then it all crumbled. He was exactly the sort of man she wanted to avoid: moody, incommunicative, forbidding.

For a brief time during their dance and dinner, she had entertained the possibility of a future with him, of romance, imagining the two of them sharing their days together talking about anything and everything, two people who understood each other. Not quite ready to cast aside her fears of an unhappy marriage or her plans for employment, she had nonetheless casually entertained possibilities.

Two meetings weren't enough to break her heart, but she felt heartbroken all the same. Not so much over him, rather the idea of him. If she could sketch her perfect man, he would be Lord Roddam—the one man who could change her view of relationships. Before meeting him, she had yet to genuinely enjoy speaking with a man not her relation.

All she wanted was someone with whom she could talk for hours, someone with whom she could share her thoughts. She wanted someone who inspired her and excited her, someone who didn't give a fig about society's expectations and preferred reflection to socialization, someone who would speak honestly and include her in his life.

For the briefest of times, she believed him to be that someone. Having the ideal dashed was more heartbreaking than spending a dinner ignored. While they hadn't entirely lapsed into silence, they might as well have, for the remainder of the meal, he had replied only with curt answers. By the time dessert was served, she had turned her attentions to the person to her other side for a polite discussion about the weather.

What had she done wrong? The conversation repeated through her mind, but no matter how she dissected the dialogue, she couldn't see how she had said something offensive or ruffled his feathers.

This was such a typical male reaction. Instead of being forthright, he ceased communication altogether when all could be resolved through honest conversation. His behavior validated her decision never to marry.

Her father's property may be entailed to Cousin Walter, but that didn't mean she had to resign herself to an unhappy marriage. After all, the money earned from her father's tin mine was his and his alone. Only the estate was entailed. If she desired, she could live without employment, but such an idle life would leave her restless. She need not sacrifice her independence for a marriage because society deemed it a respectable way of life.

For her, marriage would be love or nothing. She couldn't love a man who refused to communicate. She could never love a man who shut her out to live his separate life while she sat at home and knitted by the fire.

She vowed at an early age that she would marry for love or remain a spinster. Love meant communication, mutual understanding, shared views, a shared life. Her parents married for love, as had Aunt Hazel, so she knew what life could be like between two loving people, and that's the life she wanted. That or nothing.

Wedding after wedding, she witnessed her friends married off to caretakers, essentially. She refused to allow that to happen. Her greatest fear was being at the mercy of a man. Despite society's view of women and the laws of entailment, she still felt she had alternatives.

Life as a lady's companion seemed a perfect choice. She would earn her own income, have her own roof over her head, and enjoy the company of an older woman, a widow perhaps, who loved to be read to or go for long walks. At the very least, she could be a governess, a schoolteacher, or any other position that might offer freedom of choice, pay, and leisure time for her personal studies.

She refused to have a man tell her what to read, what to wear, and what to do. Just as she had said to Roddam during their first meeting, she didn't believe in victims. People made their own choices and etched their own futures and were never merely victims of circumstance or happenstance.

No, she would forge her own future. Romance be dashed.

Two meetings with the ideal man shouldn't upset her since they were a subtle reminder that the ideal man didn't exist.

"Am I intruding?"

Lizbeth looked up from her mental diatribe, realizing she had been staring at her hands this whole time, a half-eaten sandwich soggy between her fingers. Walter peered at her from the doorway. "No, of course not. Join me."

"I would say I'm surprised you're not with Mama and Charlotte, but I know you too well to be shocked." He sat across from her and reached for a sandwich.

"Should I ring for fresh tea?"

He shook his head and nibbled at the edges to pull out the cucumbers. "Mama tells me you danced with Annick's cousin, Roddam."

"Yes. And your point?" she snapped.

"No need to be snippy. She said you made a handsome couple. I suspect she heard wedding bells through the whole dance." He grinned playfully.

"I'm most certainly not interested in marrying him. It was only one dance for crying in a tea cup," Lizbeth replied tight-lipped.

Walter stared at his sandwich, lost in thought, before taking another bite.

After swallowing, he admitted, "She's been hounding me, as well. About marriage that is. She means well. She always does. I'm just not ready is all. I want to be married and have a houseful of little ones, but... All the responsibilities of this title are weighing on my shoulders, Lizzie. I'm barely out of Oxford, yet here I am a baron. Sometimes I just want to run away from it all. Move to Wales and live in a cottage on a hill."

Lizbeth nodded, glad to have a candid conversation.

"I do have a confession." She swallowed, her mouth dry. "I enjoyed the dance with Roddam. A great deal more than I wanted to."

Walter met her confession with raised eyebrows.

"Oh? Are you interested in him? He hasn't sent his card, I'm sure, or Mama would have mentioned it."

Walter dusted the crumbs off his shirt before reaching for a sweet.

"I'm not interested in him, Not in the least," huffed Lizbeth. She paused to watch him stuff the entire sweet in his mouth then struggle to chew. "I mean, I might have been interested, at one time, but not anymore."

Walter's eyebrows raised a little higher as he gestured for her to continue, his cheeks full of the sweet.

"We have a good deal in common, he and I. At least I think we do. We seem to. We haven't talked at great length, but the little bit we have talked has been titillating. No, I don't mean that. I mean, oh, I don't know what I mean." She slumped against the chairback.

"Woth th thothem?" He mumbled, mouth full. Pausing, a finger raised, he chewed then swallowed. "What's the problem?"

"Well, we were talking at supper, and he became agitated with me for no discernable reason. I've gone through the conversation a hundred times in my head but can't make sense of what upset him. I shouldn't be overwrought, but I did favor him, if we're being honest." Liz smoothed the ribbon under her bosom with one hand then the other.

"Hmm. I don't know much about Roddam. I know Annick from Oxford, of course, but Roddam didn't arrive until two years later. He wasn't remotely interested in joining our club. All I recall is Annick getting him out of a few scrapes with other lads. I'm sorry to say my memories are a few years old, Liz. He was a trouble maker, is all I remember. No one much liked him. Sorry I can't offer more insight to his character."

Another savored sweet later, Walter amended, "I do know he's considered a hermit by peers. Maybe that's not the right word, but he doesn't venture into society much, never has. He takes his House of Lords duties seriously, one of the more vocal speakers, but otherwise, no one sees him, not even at Whites. Maybe he was feeling out of his element at dinner? It could be nothing you said and all to do with him."

"I wish I knew what he was thinking. I'm sure I said something to anger him." Lizbeth reached for another sandwich.

"Maybe he's just a cur. Ever thought about that? It's also possible, and I'm strictly speaking as a man and not as a representative of the mind of Roddam, that you inadvertently said something you weren't even aware of that brought back a bad memory."

"Well, it doesn't matter. I don't believe we'll speak again, and I'm not sure I would want to if given the opportunity." Lizbeth bit into the sandwich, not the least hungry.

"I think you should give him a taste of his own medicine," Walter concluded. "If I were a cur, I would know I could take advantage of your gullibility if you were sweetness after I had behaved so abominably. But if you bite back, it shows you have a strong backbone and won't tolerate boorishness. On second thought, if you hurt his pride, maybe that advice isn't the best course of action. I know if my feelings had been hurt, I wouldn't want you to rub it in my face." He shrugged.

"That's terrible advice. I couldn't possibly know which way to behave and could make matters worse. You're barred from giving advice."

"How is that bad advice? I rather think I've solved all of your problems." Walter stood up to offer a napping Captain Henry a piece of a scone. When the bird only eyed him from over a wing, Walter left the bite in the food bowl.

"Your advice is terrible because you give me two choices dependent upon the motivation of his actions, which neither of us know. Either I ignore him, or I engage him in conversation, but I shouldn't choose unwisely. That offers no decisive direction," Lizbeth said with exasperation.

Before he could reply, Aunt Hazel and Charlotte bustled into the room, a flurry of noise, excitement, laughter, and chatter, both flushed with broad smiles. Captain Henry squawked and stretched his wings, curious by the ruckus.

"I've decided to host a dinner party!" announced Aunt Hazel. "Next week, we will dine and raise our glasses to the new Duchess of Annick!"

Lizbeth's mouth formed an O of incredulity. "One ride in Hyde Park, and Charlotte's engaged?"

"No, no, of course not. Don't be silly, child. But mark my words, he will propose at the dinner party. I'm too wise not to see to that. Mark my words that in less than a fortnight, Charlotte will be betrothed."

Chapter 7

Fat rain drops slithered down the windowpane in the study of the Duke of Annick's townhouse. Since before dawn, rain had chased people indoors, coating the city in a gray mist of rain and soot. Sebastian leaned against the window frame, looking out onto the park across the street, observing the grass turn to mud.

A week had not been long enough to ease his torment over the masquerade dinner. What a fool he had acted. She must think him a madman.

He laughed wryly to himself—she wouldn't be wrong.

Everything made sense at the time. It had been obvious she played him, that she was part of some joke Drake initiated, or since Drake still professed ignorance, she had asked around, learned of his life's passion and wanted to use it to set her cap at him as a clever fortune huntress' ploy.

Given his life thus far, it all seemed more plausible that she acted out of cruelty than attraction.

However, the more he questioned Drake, and the more he thought about the conversation, the clearer it all became: he was deranged and ruined a chance at the only good thing to happen in his life. This proved he needed to stay as far away from her as possible, even if she were in the right and he in the wrong, for he lived too close to the edge of madness for anything to work out between them, even friendship.

She wouldn't trust him not to snap again. Not even he could make such a promise.

Bah, he was a fool. How could he ever believe she lied about her home when her entire family was in attendance? The truth would be too easy to uncover. How could she have been schooled on philosophy and literature in time for such a ploy? No, hindsight revealed he jumped to the wrong conclusions. If she were in earnest, and he believed she was, his behavior was unforgivable. He didn't know where to begin explaining rationally how unusual it was to find his personal interests echoed.

To exacerbate his melancholy, his cousin had spent every day of the past week visiting Lady Collingwood and her nieces. Drake made sure Sebastian knew of each visit. As part of the provocation, Drake never would admit which sister he courted, knowing the mystery crawled under Sebastian's skin, spreading a rash of jealousy.

It unsettled him to think of Drake courting Miss Trethow. Even if Sebastian couldn't have her, he certainly didn't want to watch Drake parade her around as his new duchess. She may have voiced her dislike of the duke, but he had yet to meet a woman who could resist Drake's advances. No one said no to the Duke of Annick. He felt sick at the thought of them together, of his cousin dampening that raw beauty, shrouding her eager mind.

He pushed his shoulder against the window frame.

To hell with her. Let her have Drake. She deserved what she got if she accepted Drake.

No, no, no. She deserved better than Drake. She deserved better than Sebastian, for that matter. She deserved someone who wasn't haunted by past mistakes, someone who didn't wake nightly from visions of death.

Resting his head against the glass, he let the cool pane chill his forehead. Servants, some with umbrellas, some without, scurried to and fro on the sidewalk below, all battling the rain to deliver messages and complete errands for their masters.

The door of the study opened and closed behind him. Footsteps muffled by the rug creaked their approach when weight met aged wood panels.

"You're going to leave a print on my window pane." Drake settled into a Louis XIV styled chair with tapered mahogany legs. He reached for the cheroot box, lit a cigar, and inhaled the vaporous elixir.

Sebastian shrugged away his solitariness and joined Drake, pulling out his pocket clock. The feel of the etching beneath his fingertips soothed his agitation, the simplicity of the tick-tock mechanism providing order in his tumultuous emotions.

"You're coming to that dinner party if I have to drag you by your hair." Drake puffed the cheroot before blowing smoke towards Sebastian, antagonizing his cousin. "I've arranged a meeting with Mr. Trethow tomorrow. With his permission, I will extend my proposal at the dinner party."

"To whom?" Sebastian gripped his chronometer so tightly the edges bit into his palm.

"What do you care? Either sister. Both sisters. You tell me which I should choose." He didn't wait long enough for a reply before saying, "Miss Trethow would make a perfect duchess, don't you think? She's poised, attractive—freckles aside. She keeps to herself, which will allow me my freedom. I could spend my days with Maggie and only see my wife for the evening visits. Perfection."

Sebastian felt sick to his stomach.

Between clenched teeth, Sebastian hissed. "She's a poor choice. Too opinionated. She would be remiss of the social duties of her station, and her bookishness would embarrass you."

Drake studied him shrewdly as he puffed. "You could be right. Perhaps her poise is pride, and her attractiveness will fade alongside her waning youth."

He ground his teeth.

Drake continued. "A shame you aren't considering her for yourself. There's an appeal to us having a sister each. Miss Charlotte is far prettier, I think. She's as malleable as you would want a wife to be. Eager. Sensual. Her lips drive me to distraction."

"Miss Charlotte is the obvious choice for you, then," he grumbled.

Drake smirked before adding, "Their father is a gentleman, landed, and respected. One hell of an MP. He has some radical ideas, not unlike you, come to think of it, and he doesn't have a drop of blue in his veins, but he is wealthy and well reputed." With a smirk, he added, "Mother would be furious to have him as an in-law, which makes marriage to a Trethow all that more attractive." He dropped the cigar in an ashtray and stood. "Brandy?"

Sebastian shook his head.

"Cuthbert, or Mr. Trethow rather, isn't titled, and he's only parish gentry, not even county gentry, but there's no denying his wealth. I have mentioned he's wealthy, haven't I?" Drake queried.

He poured a drink and carried the glass back to his chair, propping his feet rudely on the mahogany table in front of him. "I've considered other prospects, you know. Lady Patricia is the most eligible, a duke's daughter and well trained, but her breath is downright foul. The Cavanaugh twins are also perfectly eligible, but they're bound to be as plump as their mother one day. Miss Wittles is a wealthy and well-connected contender if she weren't so obstinate. None will do so well as the Trethows." He tasted the brandy before continuing. "I mentioned the possibility of the Trethows to Prinny, and he thinks it's a lark."

"I hardly consider relationship advice from Prince George wise." Sebastian sneered, for everyone knew the prince's reputation.

"If I choose Miss Charlotte, will you be pleased?" Drake asked.

"Indifferent," he answered noncommittally. "I do think your mother would be pleased once she got to know her. Miss Charlotte is exactly the sort my aunt had hoped you would choose."

"That's not what I asked, Seb. I asked if *you* would be pleased." Drake tapped his glass with well-groomed nails.

"I don't see why my opinion matters, Drake. She's your wife, not mine." Sebastian leveled his eyes on the floor, mumbling, "I don't care who you marry."

Drake rewarded Sebastian a sly, lopsided smile. "Liar. I've seen you dance once this entire Season, and that with Miss Trethow. I even caught you *smiling*. Get your head out of your arse and do something about her. Supposing I ask for Miss Charlotte, will you court her sister?"

"I have no intention of it." Sebastian dismissed Drake with a grunt and crossed his arms, his pocket clock tightly gripped in one hand. "I have obligations beyond courting someone who lives on the other side of the country. I have estate business to tend to and little time for such frivolities."

"Estate hogwash be damned. That's why you hire a steward. I say, if she makes you smile, she's perfect. Besides, you'll be the end of your line if you don't marry. Tick-tock, old man."

"And what if I'm the last?" He spat vehemently. "My father's blood shouldn't continue. The line should end with me," Sebastian insisted. "More to the point, you know I value my privacy, something that could never be had in the company of a woman."

"If you wouldn't take pleasure from her company, then she isn't the right woman after all." With a scoff, Drake added, "When did you become so pigheaded?" Draining his glass in one motion, he set it on the table none-too-gently and stood. "Tell your father's ghost to sod off, mate. You're not him and have never been him. But what do I know. I'm just a pompous dandy."

Before admitting which Trethow he would offer for, Drake left the room, the study door clicking closed as he departed.

Sebastian stared at the empty glass, mulling over his cousin's words. His father's ghost wasn't going anywhere any time soon, but he knew one thing for certain. She was the right woman.

Aunt Hazel victoriously divulged to Lizbeth that Annick had come to an understanding with Papa regarding Charlotte, who as of yet remained unaware of her upcoming nuptials. The dinner party was to be that evening, and the shrewd cupid had already devised a plan to ensure the duke and Charlotte would be alone in a room just long enough for a proposal.

In a tizzy, the hostess directed flowers be placed here and flowers be placed there, and no, those flowers simply would not do. Candles were placed in front of mirrors around the room to maximize the light as evening darkened.

The dinner party would be a small affair, only Hazel's closest friends having been invited. She made sure the invitations included those prone to gossip and excluded any young lady who would have dimmed the evening's shining star.

The card games were already set up as entertainment in the drawing room for after dinner. Normally, Hazel would have ushered them outside into the small garden, but mud still saturated the grass from three days straight of rain.

Charlotte was being fluffed and buffed by her lady's maid, the greatest of care being made for her gown and hair this evening. Her aunt wanted the duke to walk in, see his betrothed-to-be, and fall deeply in love. Lizbeth humored herself by thinking the only way that would happen would be if his first sight were of a mirror.

As proud of her success at matchmaking, Hazel admitted to Liz feeling guilty that she hadn't tried harder with Lizbeth, especially after seeing her dancing at the masquerade first with the duke himself and then with an equally eligible earl. Thankfully, Hazel's fretting over Liz's spinsterhood was overshadowed by the glow of a future duchess in their family.

The last thing Lizbeth wanted was her family's interference in matchmaking. Also fortunate was the decreasing appearance of Roddam in Lizbeth's every waking thought. She had been so busy helping her aunt prepare that she had forgotten to worry about him.

Until today.

He had accepted the dinner invitation. She knew it was to support his cousin, not to see her, but her stomach knotted knowing they would be thrown together for the evening.

She hadn't yet decided how to react to him. Part of her didn't want to speak with him ever again after seeing his poor temperament, but the other part of her desperately wanted things resolved. Friends in this world were rare, and she cherished the few she had. Surely their miscommunication could be patched.

Hearing the pit-pat of her sister's leather shoe soles against the wood floor in the hallway, Liz looked at the mantle clock in surprise. Guests should arrive soon.

"Oh, Lizbeth, I'm beyond excited!" Charlotte floated into the room, a cloud of pink and yellow. "A party just for us!" She looked breathtaking in a white frock over pink satin bordered with yellow flowers on tulle. A wreath of fresh flowers haloed her head of curls.

"I do believe the party is for you, not us." Lizbeth cringed, hoping she hadn't given away the surprise.

To her relief, Charlotte was oblivious, smelling each flower vase in turn.

"Will you play piquet with me after dinner?" Her long eyelashes framed her eyes when she looked at Lizbeth, her nose still buried in a bouquet.

"If that's what you want, but I suggest you convince His Grace to partner you in a game of whist."

"Do you really think he'll come? I hope he does, and he did accept the invitation, but do you really think he'll come? Our party is hardly a grand affair worthy of a duke."

"I doubt anything could keep him from your side this evening." Lizbeth smiled reassuringly, hating to think her sister marrying a rakish oaf, but happy Charlotte's dreams would come true.

A flurry of activity occurred, then, of Aunt Hazel rushing in behind a footman with his tray of cocktails, ready to receive guests, Cuthbert and Walter not far behind, taking their places in the receiving line. The evening's plan was a half hour of cocktails in the drawing room followed by dinner, and then a return to the drawing room for games, wine, and cheese.

Lizbeth fiddled with her cameo, worn this evening on a long pearl necklace resting below her bodice. Given no future duchess would want a dowdy sister by her side on this celebratory occasion, Liz's lady's maid had dressed her with care. She wore a topaz blue gown under a white open robe of gossamer. A bandeau of matching blue encircled her loosely knotted topknot, irregular curls strewn over her forehead.

The butler announced the first of the arriving guests. "The Marquess of Quail, The Marchioness of Quail, and The Lady Harriet Quail." Soon after, "The Right Honorable Viscountess of Coombs and Mr. Hock." After which arrived, "The Dowager Lady Leighton, Mr. Covington, and Mrs. James Covington." Before long, "Sir Conrad Stockton, Lady Kissinger, Mrs. Holzingwood, Mrs. Popen, and Lady Sayles."

Poor Cecil's announcements were drowned out by the conversations around the room. The men gathered in one corner, and the women formed smaller sects of friendship circles. The clocked ticked ten minutes, and then twenty, increasing Lizbeth's worry the duke would arrive late to his own betrothal party. Charlotte would shatter if he showed after dinner started. Or not at all!

No sooner had she begun to fret did Cecil announce the final guests. "His Grace the Duke of Annick and The Right Honorable The Earl of Roddam."

Lizbeth gripped her cameo, steeling herself. Lord Roddam had entered the room.

She wanted to hide in the parlor with Captain Henry who would be spending his evening away from the hubbub of the crowd. She stolidly stared at Mrs. Popen a few feet away, hoping she looked wrapped in conversation with a woman who wasn't even talking to her. She restrained her urge to eye the door.

Her spine stiff as a baluster, she shifted her feet to appear more natural, calmer. Did she look too rigid? Would he be able to tell how tense she felt? Blast that man for making her feel embarrassingly uneasy. She still hadn't decided if she should ignore him, speak curtly, or pretend nothing happened.

Did he look wounded after their last encounter, perhaps licking his paw? Heavens, it had been so long since they had last spoken. Maybe he stood proudly at the door, his mane flowing around his shoulders, or—

"You look lovely this evening, Miss Trethow." Roddam stood all of five feet from her, his shoulders pulled back, augmenting his height.

She gaped at him.

He wore a fine white muslin shirt with a simple-knotted cravat, single-breasted waistcoat, and double-breasted tailcoat with knee-high satin breeches and embroidered clocked stockings with leather shoes. His hands clasped behind his back, he was the image of stately elegance and composure. To put it mildly, he took her breath away.

Trying again, he said, "I wish the sky these past few days had matched the color of your dress. Terrible weather, eh?"

She wanted to laugh. After her week of fretting, mulling, and pouting, he greeted her with comments about the weather. Absurd man!

She looked straight into his dark brown eyes and scolded, "I would have expected better from you than talk of the weather."

"Has anyone ever told you your expectations are too high?" He raised his eyebrows.

She had forgotten how attractive she found him. No, she hadn't. She had just pushed it deep down into her belly, weighing his poor behavior heavier than his handsomeness.

She replied, "I suppose you just did, although I hardly consider the desire for deeper conversation than the weather constituting high expectations."

"Clearly, I've been in the wrong company all these years."

They locked eyes, hardly noticing the other guests heading for the dining room. Not until the room emptied did they realize their plight.

Lizbeth reluctantly looked to the dining room doors. "We should proceed, Your Lordship. I believe you're sitting by Lord Quail this evening, near the head of the table."

"I hope to talk after dinner." He held out his arm in invitation. "If that would be amenable to you."

She placed her hand on his forearm, his warmth pervading her glove.

"Yes, I would like that," she confessed despite herself.

They walked into the dining room and took their seats on opposite ends of the long table. Against Hazel's original intention, Liz had begged her aunt not to place him near her. Now she regretted that request. She wasn't even sure what to say to him.

Venison was the meat of the evening, a warm and rare treat that Hazel had insisted on for the occasion. Cold meats, fruits, and wine accompanied.

Liz enjoyed a quiet meal, as the ladies on either side of her were too busy chatting with their neighbors to take any notice of her. As casually as possible, she eyed the opposite end of the table. He too took his meal in silence.

Throughout the meal, she periodically glanced in his direction, and several times, much to her chagrin, she caught him looking her way, unflinching in his admiration of her.

After the meal, the men stayed behind in the dining room to share port and cigars while the women returned to the drawing room to gossip before the mixed-company card games began. Before she had a chance to return with the others or protest involvement in matchmaking plans, Hazel caught her arm.

"Liz, love. Come with me to show Annick the new portraits in the parlor." Hazel winked and nodded towards Charlotte standing beside the duke at the door.

So, this was her aunt's strategy, a portrait tour of the parlor while the guests were distracted. Liz nodded and followed them.

"And this," her aunt explained to Annick when they arrived at the parlor, a curious Captain Henry watching them, "is a portrait of my late husband, God rest his soul. I loved him more than anything in this world, you know. We were a love match from the beginning. And this portrait to the left is of my mother, and next to her my father, or should I say Charlotte's grandparents." She turned glowingly to the trio, then, her eyes widened in dismay, startled by an unvoiced thought.

"What's wrong, Auntie?" Charlotte piped concern from Annick's side.

"Why, I've forgotten to tell Cecil something quite important. Oh, dear me. Lizbeth, come help me find Cecil." She took Liz's hand to lead her out of the room. "We won't be but a moment, but this cannot wait."

Charlotte in her blessed ignorance said, "Here, I will pull the bell-cord."

"No! No, he will be in the drawing room. You continue the tour in my stead, my darling. Annick is a rapt audience."

Spotting the cue, the duke bowed to Aunt Hazel, then distracted Charlotte with questions about the other portraits. Lizbeth slipped out with her aunt.

"Now then. That'll do the trick. She'll emerge an engaged woman, our little duchess. I'm not prone to fainting, but I may need smelling salts on this occasion. A duke, Lizbeth! A duke!"

"You are a remarkable woman, Aunt Hazel." She hugged her aunt and returned to the drawing room, less than enthusiastic about the bridegroom, his title be dashed.

The men were still in the dining room, and she had no real desire to socialize with any of the guests, all friends of her aunt.

She escaped outside to the veranda overlooking the garden. The flowers basked in the setting sun, a hazy glow lighting the flowers and casting long shadows across the veranda. Swift moving clouds blotted the horizon from time-to-time.

Leaning against the railing, she welcomed the crisp air that whipped around the back of the house, pleasant after the previous days of muggy humidity. The grass in the garden was sloshed with mud, but the roses displayed fresh blooms after bountiful showers.

Before long, she became acutely aware of someone standing behind her. Gooseflesh covered her arms, and a distant memory flashed in her mind of Annick in his domino costume flirting with her on a balcony. She shivered.

This time, the intruder wasn't Annick. She could feel discerning eyes gauging her mood, guessing her thoughts. Eyes she knew would appear black in the dusk.

Without turning, and hoping she wasn't mistaken by the identity of her veranda guest, she said, "Tell me what I said to anger you."

Roddam lumbered to the railing to stand beside her. Leaning his hip against the balustrade, his arms folded over his chest, he opened his mouth, then closed it, brows knitted.

When he didn't reply, she launched into an impromptu speech, "Don't play me for the villain. If you want my companionship, be forthright. I only ever ask for honesty, and in return, I offer my own candidness. True friendship is difficult to come by, and I value the few friendships I have. If you want to play games, my lord, play them elsewhere."

Her ears filled with the rush of pumping blood, her heart pounding against her ribcage. This was not at all what she had planned to say.

Turning her body to face him, she held eye contact. Even in the encroaching darkness of night, she thought she saw his eyes alight with hope.

"You're an unusual woman, Miss Trethow. I don't deserve your friendship, but I value whole-heartedly your extension of the proverbial olive branch. I can only hope I won't disappoint you. I—." He paused, looking away, "I am not trusting by nature. My life has been a series of betrayals, which does not lend itself to easy trust. I make no excuse for my behavior. I was a lout. You showed me sweetness of temper, and I showed you hostility. I do not deserve your forgiveness."

Here stood a man she had only met twice, and on one of those occasions he had acted irrationally, yet her heart went out to him. If he spoke truthfully, she had taken his anger personally when it had naught to do with her. Lizbeth moved her hand along the railing towards him, wanting to touch his arm, to reassure him that he did deserve forgiveness.

As if perceiving her intention, he uncrossed his arms and rested his hand on the railing within arm's reach of hers. She gripped the rail, unexpectedly nervous.

From inside the room came cheers and exclamations as, she assumed, Charlotte and Annick made their appearance in the drawing room, an engaged couple.

"It sounds as though my cousin and your sister have come to an understanding." Roddam said, echoing her thoughts. "May I be so bold to ask why you proclaim yourself a spinster?"

Somewhat startled by the question, she said, "You may. I'm not ashamed of my decision." She shifted her weight to lean more heavily on the rail. "I want complete independence. With a husband, unless it were a love match, and I suppose even then, I would be controlled. My money would be his, my time and hobbies his. I want to make my own choices and not have them dictated by an owner."

"I don't see how remaining unmarried accomplishes that goal," Roddam replied. "Women gain independence through marriage. Without a husband, women remain dependent on family. If employed, the employer would control wage, residence, reputation, and reference. How is that independence? Wouldn't it be wiser to make a careful match with someone who would value your independence, affording you the ability to do as you pleased with your own money?"

Liz clarified, "Your own words explain the problem. 'Affording me the ability.' If I were to marry, I would be the property of another person. My husband would need to grant me permission on all things, even having access to my own money. My money would be his by law. My person would be his by law. With a considerate husband, yes, I could do what I willed, I suppose, but it's not just about that."

She drew a breath, garnering strength to resume. "It's an unattractive life, as well. Couples are expected to move in separate circles, never to spend too much time together, even in public. It's convenient for both parties because they live separate lives. I do not wish to live in a shadow. I refuse to live with a man I rarely see or who rarely speaks to me, living his own life separate from me. I would rather live alone than be another piece of furniture, dusted when guests are expected. You may consider me common, but those are my conditions, and as of yet, those conditions have not been met by any suitor."

When he gave no immediate reply, she continued, considering her words carefully.

"I'm not opposed to marriage, Lord Roddam. I'm opposed to any marriage that isn't based on mutual respect and affection. I have seen loving marriages, and if I chose to marry, that is what I would want, but so few examples exist. My parents and Walter's parents were examples of loving marriages rather than convenient unions, even if cut short by death. There are others, I suppose. Never would you find a more loving and chaste couple than King George and Queen Charlotte, for instance."

"And clearly, it's driving him mad," Roddam chided.

They both laughed, lightening the tension. She unwittingly lessened her grip on the railing and inched her fingers closer to his, quite contrary of an action to her censure of marriage.

How could she not be attracted to him, regardless of her concerns and his distrustful nature? She liked the sound of his laugh, a throaty chuckle, and liked how his smile reached his eyes. A compliment, this laugh, a compliment that he could laugh so easily with her, the corners of his eyes crinkling. She suspected he didn't laugh often, not if, as he said, his life had been a series of betrayals, not when he believed he didn't deserve forgiveness.

Everything about him, from his body language to his words, told her he was fiercely territorial, well-guarded, not apt to show any signs of weakness, and to him, emotion would be a sign of weakness. Yet here he was, laughing with her over a distasteful joke. Regardless of misdeeds and misunderstandings, he deserved to laugh more.

Fully aware he had not yet answered her original question of what angered him, she began to understand he would in his own time. He wasn't not communicating, rather finding a way to communicate. Already he had admitted he didn't deserve forgiveness. Was what he had to say so difficult to express?

Liz delved, "And you?"

His words weighed heavy with sadness, his eyes darkening, "Unlike you, I've never seen a happy marriage. I've witnessed manipulation, abuse, and adultery. I believe I could reconsider my own hesitation for matrimony if it were for love, as you say, but I'm not sure what that word means, what that feels like. I've been alone a long time, Miss Trethow, and have demons to exorcise before I could change that. I've…." His voice trailed off, his eyes closing for a moment before continuing. "I've hurt people in my past, people who loved me. I would be afraid to bring anyone new into my life, for she may not like what she sees, and I may not be able to bring her happiness. You asked for forthright words, and that's what I'm speaking. I don't deserve love, and I would only disappoint anyone who offered it."

"Why would you say such a thing?" she gasped. "Everyone deserves love."

Roddam shook his head, his expression pained. "Not everyone. Some people make poor choices, choices that affect others, that destroy lives and cause irreparable damage. Those people do not deserve love."

Silence stretched. Chortling voices reached from within, and outside the wind blew through the leaves of the bushes.

"It's silly in hindsight," he said, reaching for her hand and covering it between both of his. "What angered me, that is." His voice hitched. "The coincidence was too much for me to believe. You see, I inherited my great grandfather's life's work, Dunstanburgh Castle. He spent the family fortune restoring the castle but died before finishing it. It was a brutal undertaking that broke him. When my grandfather inherited, he let the castle fall into dilapidation, focusing instead on replenishing the depleted coffers. My father…well, my father allowed both finances and castle to fall to ruin. When I inherited, I swore I would make it right, restore honor to the family name, and finish the castle."

He laced his fingers with hers using one hand, absently trailing the fingertips of his other hand along her forearm.

"My ancestor believed Dunstanburgh was the Isle of Avalon, where King Arthur found his final resting place, the mystical island of immortality and home of the Lady of the Lake. I've devoted a great deal of my life since my father's death to studying the lore of King Arthur and restoring the castle, a kind of homage to a great man.

"The point being, I stupidly misconstrued our conversation when you said you lived in Trevena. I thought you were playing me. You must admit the odds are marginal that we would each live in a place pivotal to the king's life. I thought, perhaps, Drake had mentioned something to you as a joke or a ploy. I'm not an animal to be hunted, and I thought you had lied as part of your hunt. What other reason could there be for you to live in the king's birthplace when I live in his final resting place?"

"Fate?" Lizbeth said.

He laughed dryly. "I don't believe in fate."

"And yet, here we are," she teased.

"Aye, here we are."

He brought her hand to his lips and pressed the inside of her wrist against his mouth, watching her unblinkingly. "I love the sound of your voice, Miss Trethow. It's musical."

She sniggered a nervous laugh and glanced warily at him. "I thought you said I had a southern accent, like a pirate or a country bumpkin."

"I did say that," Roddam admitted. "But not as an insult. You don't sound like a pirate and certainly not a bumpkin. Your voice could charm the birds from the trees."

She was thankful for the onset of darkness. He wouldn't see the rosy tint of her cheeks. All she could think to say in return was *likewise*, so she remained silent, feeling the warmth of his hands tingle through her limbs, chest, and abdomen. Could he feel her trembling?

Roddam's thumb drew circles on the back of her glove, sending waves of pleasure undulating down her spine. He held her hand to his chest, massaging her hand, his fingers working towards her wrist where his lips had been only moments before. Lowering his head closer to hers, he admired her from beneath long lashes. She had never been more mindful of someone in her life, her senses acutely aware of him. He smelled like soap and leather, an intoxicating smell to Lizbeth.

Her gaze lingered on his lips, wondering what it would be like to kiss him, those moist lips pressing against hers. She imagined away the veranda and envisioned they stood in the moonlight on a cliff, their bare feet in damp grass, the sea air tickling their skin. As his lips reached for hers—

Roddam interrupted her day dream. "Are we friends again, then?"

Exhaling through her nostrils, centering herself in the present moment, she replied with a slight tremor,

"I wish you had been honest from the start. Even if I had known about your castle, which I assure you I did not, I would never have made the connection between Trevena and Dunstanburgh. I thought the Isle of Avalon was in Glastonbury, you see."

"A common belief, and who's to say which is correct? The earlier works regarding King Arthur only describe places, descriptions that match aptly to Dunstanburgh. The king's final battles were even fought in Northumberland, giving credence to the possibility. It wasn't until Malory took liberties to name Glastonbury as the location when the controversy between Dunstanburgh and Glastonbury arose. Malory was a cheeky devil." He half-smiled, making light of the conversation. "I admit I assumed erroneously both your knowledge of the literature and your awareness of me."

Not wanting to spoil their reconciliation, but still determined to make her point, she withdrew her hand from his grasp and insisted, "The point, my lord, is that this whole silly misunderstanding could have been resolved in one conversation if you had chosen to talk to me instead of shutting me out."

He scowled, shifting his weight away from her.

"Our first conversation," she said, "was the most enriching of my life, so I can't understand how someone so willing to treat me as an equal could then ignore me over a simple misunderstanding."

"It wasn't a simple misunderstanding to me." Roddam wrenched out sharp words, arms crossed. "Nothing in my life is simple. Haven't you heard a solitary word I've said? My life is rife with complication, so coincidence doesn't factor in. I only felt confident offering friendship, but it would seem I shouldn't have bothered, not when I can't keep a friend longer than a single evening."

"Stop that this minute," Lizbeth commanded, boldly placing her hand on his taut forearm.

This wouldn't do. She hadn't meant for him to withdraw even further, to erect walls so quickly. Instead of taking his brusqueness to heart this time, she recognized it for what it was—his defense. Had he never let in anyone?

"I forgive you, Roddam. Is that what you need to hear? I forgive you. I'm not scolding you, only asking that you talk to me as a friend. Instead of assuming the worst, talk to me," she pleaded.

His intelligent eyes intense, and his brow-crease smoothing with what she took to be relief, he studied her pensively. Self-conscious under his heated stare, she covered her cheeks with her hands and waited for him to speak.

Uncrossing his arms, he palmed her shoulders and pulled her against him, wrapping muscular arms around her in a loose embrace. Pressed against his chest, she felt nothing else mattered. Did he feel the same? His heart beat against the palm of her hands, splayed open on his chest. Absently, she wondered if she should be reassuring him with her embrace rather than the other way around, for despite his formidable demeanor, he struck her as being vulnerable.

Oh, how easy it would be to fall in love with him, but she couldn't live with him if he didn't open to her, if he set a stone wall between them at every turn, barring her with his defenses. He was his own worst enemy.

"You never cease to amaze me," he said, his words muffled as he moved his lips to graze her forehead.

He rested his cheek against her temple, sending every care in her world flying into the wind. When he brought his lips, soft and moist, down to her cheek, she thought he might kiss her, but instead he leaned his head back, looking down to level his gaze on her. Her skin tingled in the wake of his lips.

"I guard myself against injury, but your words disarm me. I offer friendship when all I want to do is kiss you. What am I going to do with you, Miss Trethow?" he asked rhetorically.

He brought his hand to her cheek, touching the back of his fingers to her heated flesh.

"You're going to be honest with me, that's what you're going to do," she wheezed, trying to sound confident as she trembled in his arms.

With a shake of his head, he said, "That's not at all what I meant." He cupped her cheek in his palm. "God, you're wonderful," he marveled, his stare fixed on her.

Before she could process his words, he released his hold on her and propped himself against the railing.

"I ought not to have acted or spoken with such presumption. Such behavior was inappropriate and reckless," he mumbled, his eyes downcast.

"No, I'm pleased you did. I—I value your candidness, and I want to know you better, to—to be closer to you." Biting her lower lip, she stepped forward and rested her hand on his upper arm, tempted but not brave enough to reenact the embrace by twining her arms around him.

He raised his eyes to hers, half-lidded.

"I'll have you know that my cousin thinks I'm foolish to devote so much time and money to a legend, but in my darkest hour, it anchored me, gave me something to live for, a guiding light, if you will." He shrugged, making light of the words. "And I know it sounds absurd but learning about the king helped me define the kind of man I wanted to be. Do you think me a fool?" He beseeched.

"For what? Believing in legends?" she asked, her tongue heavy and her mouth dry. Her whole body still tingled from his touch.

"No." His eyes reflected the moonlight, feline and carnivorous. "For thinking you a liar."

"I don't think you're a fool, Lord Roddam. And I don't think you ever believed I lied."

He tilted his head. "No?"

"No. You wouldn't be standing here if you believed that. I think you were afraid of someone getting too close, of meeting a kindred spirit. I think you saw someone with whom you could be yourself, and it scared you. Tell me I'm wrong," she challenged.

"You seem to have me figured out." A roguish smile teased the corners of his lips. "So, tell me, what am I thinking now?"

She could feel his body heat through her dress as he took a step closer, widening his stance to straddle either side of her, nestling her legs between his own.

Rubbing a smooth cheek against hers, he purred into her ear. Lizbeth tried to inhale fresh air to calm her nerves, but she smelled only him. Through a haze of desire, she wondered if he flirted because she said the right words or if he flirted to distract her as another defense because her words hit too close to home.

With a breathy laugh, she answered, "You're thinking, my lord, that my words are too brazen, and I'm too outspoken for my own good."

"Sebastian," he replied. "My name is Sebastian. And that wasn't at all what I was thinking."

"Oh." She stuttered. "We're using our given names already? You know, the most respectable members of the ton rarely even refer to their spouses by first names."

"I thought we were kindred spirits." Sebastian stared at her from beneath heavy lids and rubbed his nose against hers.

"You're the devil incarnate, Sebastian. Lizbeth, by the by. You may call me Lizbeth."

"Lizbeth." He rolled the name over his tongue, trying it on, tasting it. "A more beautiful name, I have never heard. Mmm. Lizbeth," he repeated.

She angled her head, not sure what to expect from him. Was he going to kiss her after all? Did she want him to kiss her?

How foolish to want to be kissed by him. She had spent a week fretting about him; he was practically a stranger; and he struggled with verbal intimacy. By his own confession, he could offer her nothing but friendship, so what would a kiss accomplish other than to complicate matters?

Kissing him meant freely giving her lips to a man not affianced to her, plunging herself into an affection that wouldn't be returned. And if he then felt obligated to offer for her after kissing her, she doubted she could live with him, not unless he tore down his defenses, not unless he returned the affection beyond obligation, not unless they came to some agreement that ensured she maintained a level of independence.

To top off the absurdity of the moment, they stood on her aunt's veranda mere feet from the party inside, never mind that the guests were distracted and couldn't see them from the gaming tables at the other end of the room. If so much as one guest wandered over, Liz would be compromised. Was this worth such a risk? He could refuse to offer for her, leaving her ruined, or he could offer for her, trapping her for life with a man she barely knew, a man she didn't want to forgive less than an hour ago.

Oh, it felt worth the risk in this moment. Nothing else mattered but this moment. Nothing was more important than discovering the feel of his lips against hers, the taste of him, consequences be dashed. She wanted to be his, even if only for a moment.

He inclined his head and drew closer, his lips hesitating inches from hers.

His breath tickling her cheeks, he whispered hoarsely, "Have you ever tried Wensleydale cheese?"

Startled, she leaned away and wheezed a laugh. "Not that I'm aware of."

Releasing her from his grasp so unexpectedly that she faltered, he took a full step back. Cool air rushed between them. She shivered and took her own dizzying step away.

"There is Wensleydale cheese in the drawing room that I think you should try. It's a Yorkshire cheese. One of my favorites." He crossed the veranda in quick strides before turning back to face her. "Lizbeth," he said in hushed tones. "I want nothing more than to stay here with you, but tongues could already be wagging at our disappearance. Shall we stealthily make our way to the cheese?"

Steadying herself on the railing and breathing in the fresh air unperfumed by his masculinity, she nodded, trying not to feel disappointed.

With a flourished wave of his hand, he bowed. "After you, my queen."

Resigned to rejoin the party, she sighed and moved towards the door. They returned to the drawing room, no one the wiser of their whispered discussions, a hardy game of cribbage underway in one corner and a game of loo in the other. Several guests circled Charlotte and Annick, animated in conversation. Not a soul turned their direction or paid them any heed. For a heartbeat, she wanted to push him back outside and finish what he started.

When she glanced towards Sebastian to see if the same temptation etched his features, Lizbeth felt a shift in her life. A shift that would change the course of her future.

Chapter 8

The first of the three banns were read in church on Sunday.

In three weeks, Annick and Charlotte would be united in matrimony at St. George's in Hanover Square. Lizbeth offered to accompany Charlotte on her honeymoon, as was customary among the families she knew back home, but Charlotte whined they were to return immediately to his principal seat in Northumberland after the wedding, thus no need for Lizbeth to accompany.

Not that she'd admit to Charlotte, but she was relieved. Without a second thought, she would move heaven and earth for her family, even if it meant following her sister and the duke around the continent for post-nuptial travels. That said, she had already seen the duke more than she ever wanted.

More than that, she would be eager to return home once the Season ended. The London noise, soot, and crowds wore on her nerves. She missed her walks to the seaside, the mornings with the miners, and evenings with Papa. During the busiest days in town, when she most longed for quiet, she swore she could hear the headland calling to her from Cornwall.

The space between now and the return home stretched into eternity, a wide unknown that would determine her future. Now more than ever, she missed her mother. She wished she could confide in her mother the emotional maelstrom raging in her over the man she was falling hopelessly in love with, the man who swore only to offer friendship.

But what if he changed his tune and offered for her? Oh, he was irresistibly almost perfect, but if she were going to throw away all chances for an independent life, he needed to be perfect, or else give some indication that he was willing to drop his guard with her.

Ambling alongside the river in Hyde Park, her lady's maid trailing behind her, Lizbeth relished in the serenity. All of London was abed except for a handful of early risers strolling through the park wishing to be undisturbed, including a few lovers meeting behind trees for secret trysts. Only during her morning walk was she able to find peace in the city. The hustle of business and the bustle of fashion didn't stir for several more hours, leaving sidewalks empty and parks abandoned.

The evening loomed, full of both promise and disquiet. For a week, nearly every evening had been spent in the company of the two cousins. She wouldn't trade the time with Sebastian for the world, but a week of the constant presence of Charlotte and her betrothed was more than enough to last her a lifetime. What made the evenings that much more trying was the growing tension between her and Sebastian as the affianced couple nattered endlessly about their wedding and beyond.

At least from her perspective. She wasn't sure at all what he thought.

This evening, the cousins were to escort the sisters to Vauxhall Gardens for an evening of dining and entertainment. Liz wanted to see the statue of Milton and admire the lush gardens. Charlotte was most looking forward to being seen, a perfect opportunity to be ogled by crowds as she wined and dined with a duke on her arm.

As much as she loved her sister, Liz could hardly wait for more time alone. Since the betrothal, every morning had been devoted to shopping with Charlotte and Aunt Hazel, for their aunt insisted on a new wedding dress for a duchess-to-be. Every afternoon had been sacrificed to the endless stream of visitors eager to take tea with Annick's intended, visitors who hadn't given them the time of day before the engagement. Every evening had been shared with her family and the two cousins.

While Charlotte drew her energy from the excitement of friend and family togetherness, Liz did not. The more time Liz spent in the company of others, the further into herself she withdrew, feeling fatigued with each expenditure of polite smiles and genteel conversation. She couldn't be any more different from Charlotte if she tried, and if Sebastian ever had any inkling the sisters shared similarities, his observations of them this past week should have dashed such suspicions, for better or worse.

Their differences stemmed from birth. Their mother, Mrs. Elizabeth Trethow, had lavished Lizbeth with attention for the seven years before her death during childbirth. Liz grew up romping the fields of Trevena with her mother by her side, bringing pasties to the miners as a mother-daughter duo, and sharing dreams while they guessed cloud shapes in the sky. In the evenings, she curled in her father's lap as he read her stories. Papa Cuthbert was an ardent reader and scholar, Mama Elizabeth a nymph of nature, and Lizbeth their lovechild.

Life changed when Charlotte was born. In place of a mother, Lizbeth had a squirmy, smelly sister who followed her everywhere but would sneeze in the meadows and cry if her feet touched the ocean tide. Even their personalities couldn't be more different, Lizbeth always preferring disorder, spontaneity, the wildness of wilderness, the beauty of a naturally growing meadow, while Charlotte needed order, routine, perfection, the symmetry of a stately knot garden with measured proportions.

As time passed, the gap between them widened, one sister eager to escape the peacefulness of Trevena to be part of the social whirl in the big city, the other desiring a quiet life of nature walks, estate ledgers, and scholarly pursuits.

Lizbeth had dreaded her come-out when the time came, preferring time with her father and the company of local villagers to any promise Society might offer. Charlotte, on the other hand, spent years preparing for her debut. With her aunt's guidance, Charlotte prepared herself for the life she wanted, remaining indoors to maintain her milky complexion, learning the pianoforte, taking dance lessons, studying languages, painting, and mastering all other attributes expected of a young lady.

Everyone loved Charlotte. She had her mother's beauty and an inviting personality, making love to everyone with demure smiles, batting eyelashes, and innocent optimism.

No one loved Lizbeth. Few even knew her.

She withdrew from crowds and was, in this way, rarely seen to be neither liked nor disliked. She knew how to behave when she had to be seen, but in truth, she was still far too blunt, level headed, and critical of thought to be favored in polite conversation. She shared her father's radical political views and her mother's sarcastic humor, neither of which aided her tact in conversation.

This year, Charlotte's dream came true, a dream Liz couldn't understand. She could understand if her sister wanted to marry for love, but she couldn't understand marrying a pompous rake because Society expected a woman of beauty and wealth to do just that. Liz's happiness for the engagement was bittersweet. She only hoped her sister could remain content with the dream she had seen to fruition.

Then, she shouldn't be so quick to judge her sister's circumstances considering her own current straits—falling for a stranger with a veiled past.

But who could blame her when a relationship with a man had never felt so comfortable, so right, despite his idiosyncrasies? She had not lived her life a complete recluse, for she did have her share of former suitors, but they were all of one type or the other, namely widowers or cits.

The widowers saw her as a safe match, a sensible and tender woman who could raise their children. The cits valued her intelligence and sizable dowry, seeing her as a prime catch to live the merchant life and financially back their growing business, not to mention the distant hope of possibly inheriting her father's mine by way of marriage.

Never had a man wooed her. Never had a man physically attracted her. Never had a man earned her respect. Never had a man made love to her with his words, wit, or eyes.

Until now.

The past week only softened her heart more for him. Private conversations were in short order given they had only shared company within the presence of their families and friends, but she didn't need private conversations to enjoy his companionship or the admiring glances he flashed her direction.

During the first evening after the betrothal, Sebastian and Annick visited for dinner and charades. With the family focused on the newly engaged couple, they ignored the shared conversations between Liz and Sebastian. The next evening, the entire Trethow and Collingwood clan ventured to the ducal townhome for a soirée, complete with card games and a performance on the pianoforte by Charlotte with Annick turning the pages.

Two evenings later, they all attended a crowded rout at a *ton* member's home, a squeeze of epic proportions. Eyes had focused on Charlotte and the bridegroom, never regarding the two forgotten figures in the back of the room with heads bowed in conspiratorial conversation.

Sebastian claimed to admire her intellect and value her thoughts. Did he really think her wonderful, despite her manly exploits into philosophy and literature, regardless of her bold outspokenness, even with her advancing age and humble appearance?

He claimed to admire her *because* of those traits. She certainly felt comfortable with him. More than comfortable. She felt at home with him. More than that even. She was physically attracted to him, desperate for his embrace once again, wistful to finish the kiss they almost shared. She shamelessly appreciated his somber elegance at every opportunity.

Throughout the burgeoning friendship, however, their conversation from the betrothal party still echoed in her mind.

Why did he believe he didn't deserve love? Who had he loved and hurt—a former lover, perhaps? She wished she could learn more about his past, but she worried about ruffling his feathers. And that was the very sticking point. If he were her perfect man, she shouldn't have to worry about ruffling feathers.

Perhaps she was deluding herself in believing she understood him more with each passing day. The fact remained, he still held a superior coolness, enshrouding himself in secrecy, never mentioning his past nor his family.

Considering herself a patient listener, she suspected all he needed was time and space to form his thoughts without feeling forced into unveiling his fears. If true, then she could help him exorcise whatever demons he claimed to have. But she didn't yet trust him enough not to push her away if she pressed a sensitive topic. As undeniably attracted to him as she was, she was apprehensive, as well. What if she underestimated his needs and overestimated her ability to help him? She couldn't live in a shadow.

She had declined the suits in the past because they only wanted her as a convenient spouse. What of her desires? She wasn't a convenient spouse to be tucked in a cupboard.

Much of her childhood had been spent in a similar fashion after Mama died. Papa withdrew into himself the years immediately following her death, leaving Lizbeth to run the household, a seven-year-old girl deciding the menu for meals, leading her father to bed when he couldn't move from the fireside so lost in a trance of mourning, caring for an infant who needed a parent, not a sister. Liz learned through the long recovery how and when to communicate with Papa, how to draw him out of his shell.

Choosing to live the rest of her life in a similar situation would be murder to her soul. Spinsterhood was a far more attractive choice than running a household from the shadows or loving an uncommunicative man lost to grief. Was Sebastian any different from her former suitors, any less forbidding than her father in mourning for his beloved?

The physical attraction between her and Sebastian left her breathless. And she couldn't deny the emotional connection between them. But given his brooding moods, his saturnine expressions, his sensitive temper, what would happen over another trifle misunderstanding—would he shut her out completely?

She didn't fancy walking on eggshells the rest of her life. His eyes revealed a good man who had been deeply hurt by something or someone, leaving a possibly irreparable wound. She wanted to believe that with someone to care for him, his defenses would melt. If only he knew tenderness and the loving arms of a woman. But oh, what a risk. She would be putting her happiness on the line, pitting her sympathy against his demons.

She wouldn't doubt him as a potential mate if she hadn't been on the receiving end of his distrust so early in their friendship. When with him, when hearing the timbre of his voice, when seeing his eyes light with amusement, all she wanted was to be with him. Her rational mind clicked into place once apart, though, questioning everything.

This was no easy decision for her. If he were to offer for her, and she accepted, she would never be alone again, which could be both a curse and a gift. If she declined, would he eventually marry someone else? Would she be able to stomach seeing him arrive to Town with another woman on his arms?

Almost laughing aloud at her worries should he propose when he had yet made no indications of wishing to do so, she turned her attention back to the present moment only to realize the park had steadily filled with children and nannies, as well as groups of riders leading their horses to the riverbank. She spotted her maid sitting on a park bench a few feet from her. So lost in thought, Liz hadn't noticed herself stopping by the river or leaning against the tree to watch a family of swans.

After collecting her maid, she headed back to the townhouse. In three weeks, she would return home, and Sebastian would return to Northumberland to his legend-steeped castle, and that was that. She would be happy with the time she had spent getting to know him, and then she would move on with her life, putting him and his hypnotic eyes behind her.

Chapter 9

Upon returning to the townhouse, Cecil took her bonnet and caraco walking-jacket, and directed her to the drawing room where her aunt was entertaining another gaggle of ladies. She could hear muffled voices coming from behind the closed door as she approached.

Just as she reached to open the door, she overheard one of the women say, "He was a dreadful man, and I don't expect his son is any different."

Oh, no! Were the women talking about Annick? She sincerely hoped not. Annick was her least favorite person, but that opinion was hers and hers alone. Surely her sister wasn't betrothed to someone considered dreadful by others. As far as she could tell from the events they had attended post-betrothal, Society was enamored with him, far from considering him dreadful.

She stilled her hand against the door, guiltily leaning to press her ear to the wood.

The haughty voice weaved in and out of audibility. "A tyrant, I tell you. A mystery how his young wife died...speculate her death—well, it would be indelicate to say..."

Her aunt's voice replied loudly and bristly, "He seems perfectly amiable to me. Don't let me think you're being sneaky, Esmeralda, and trying to say naughty things in hopes he will pay attention to Miss Constance instead of my dear Lizzie. He's taken a shine to her, I believe."

Lizbeth's hair stood on end at the mention of her name. Were they talking about Sebastian? If so, whose wife died? She found it difficult to follow the conversation from the wrong side of the door, especially when half the words were muted. Was Sebastian widowed? She could hardly hear the continued chatter over the pounding of her heart.

Huffs and harrumphs filtered through the door. "I wouldn't dare let Constance anywhere near that man. I don't care how many titles he has. Like father like son, I always say."

"I, personally, have no reason to dislike him," Hazel responded.

"Don't say I didn't warn you," said the snippy voice, her words fading into inaudible mumbles again. "Like father like son, I always…black mark on that family...a mystery whatever happened to the little girl."

Hazel's voice piped in again, all in a twitter asking what girl. Wondering the same question, Lizbeth pressed her ear more firmly.

"My memory is as sharp as...," spoke the other woman. Her next words trumpeted, startling Lizbeth before quieting again mid-sentence, half of what she said lost through the wood grain of the door. "He brought them for only one Season, and then we never saw wife or children until…came showing off her daughter…I told Meredith…a *pre*-wedding surprise… they rushed the wedding and didn't invite a soul…

wife died of a 'slight chill'...the girl, I ask you? Did he off her too, bury her in the back garden?"

Her blood ran cold.

Exclamations followed suit with a confusion of voices. All of the ladies talked at once, pandemonium of words and shouts until the same haughty voice said, "All's the better when Constance marries Lord Cornerstone...estate near Brighton, you know."

A third voice piped into the conversation, but all Liz heard were muffled chirps. She squashed her ear as hard against the door as she dared, praying the door didn't swing open in the middle of the conversation. She could imagine Aunt Hazel's expression to find Lizbeth lying prone in the den of ladies. She widened her stance to steady herself better against the door, her imagination reeling over what she had heard.

The bits and pieces of what she heard didn't make enough sense to even form speculations. Had Sebastian been married? Did he have children? She silently mourned how little she knew of the man.

All the same, her ire rose at these busybody biddies dragging his name through the mud, assuming they were indeed talking about Sebastian. So typical of gossip mongers to spread lies and ruin reputations for their own amusement. What malicious whispers were these about offing children and wives? If this was what Society made of him, no wonder he trusted no one and suspected coincidences. She felt defensive on his behalf, protective of his name.

A new voice joined the conversation, an obnoxious, high-pitched shrill.

"He has no less than five earldoms. You do realize he's the wealthiest man in England, do you not?

Poppycock to your tale! Poppycock! I wouldn't care if he were covered in warts. Hazel, dear, do yourself a favor, and marry him yourself. Why, he owns half of Yorkshire and Northumberland. Tell that bookish niece of yours to move out of the way."

The original voice spit another reply, the deeper tones fading through the door, "Ridiculous notion. The north has no society…desolate wasteland...stuck with his company…mannerless brute, not unlike… father."

More dampened words followed, but Liz missed them when her foot fell asleep. She adjusted her stance, wedging her feet against the doorframe. Needles pricked at her toes with the movement.

Her aunt's voice resounded clearly when Liz returned her ear to the door. "I would go myself, except my ankle has been bothering me all day. I think I took a wrong turn this morning."

Squawk.

Lizbeth's head nearly collided with the door as she leapt back, startled by Captain Henry.

"Lizbeth!" Charlotte exclaimed, making her way down the stairs, one hand on the banister and one arm raised to hoist up Captain Henry who looked very much like he wanted to take flight and land on Lizbeth's head. The bird leaned forward on Charlotte's arm, his wings opening wider with each step of her descent. "What are you doing?"

"Oh," Liz stammered. "I, uh, just returned from my walk and discovered Aunt Hazel has guests."

"Splendid! I need advice on my gown this evening." Pausing at the closed door, Charlotte looked Liz from head to toe and said, "You're not walking into the drawing room dressed like that. Change out of your walking dress at least. You look frightfully flushed and bedraggled."

Taking a deep breath to calm her nerves from what she overheard, Liz nodded without arguing. She was too perturbed, too shaken down to her half-boots to be insulted by her baby sister's bossy reproach. Hiking her skirt in undignified indignation over the biddies, she took the stairs two at a time, frantic to widen the distance between her and the gossipers.

How dare they talk about Sebastian with such malice? Even the greedy woman who wanted him for his money rattled Lizbeth's cage. Vexing women! He may be aloof, but she knew him to be kind. How dare they insinuate such vile things? Not that she heard enough to know exactly what it was they were insinuating, but the gist involved murdered wives and children. Bah! Her blood boiled. They weren't half the virtuous person he was. Typical of the beau monde to spread lies about people they didn't bother to understand.

More than ever, she wanted to stand by his side in support, to show him and the world she wouldn't believe Banbury tales of murder and intrigue, that she trusted him to be a noble man worthy of her affection and friendship.

Chapter 10

Her lady's maid, Bettye, fussed over the flower brocading of her scarlet frock and the too hastily curled ringlets dangling from the coil of hair atop her head, attempting last minute touches as Lizbeth made for the door, fighting off Bettye with one hand and reaching for the door handle with the other.

"But Miss Trethow! Your hair still needs a few more pins!" Bettye chased after her, waving hair pins.

Lizbeth dashed for the stairs to dodge her well-intentioned maid and caught herself at the top step to pause, breathe, and descend calmly. She could hear from the drawing room Annick roaring heartily with laughter and her sister tittering.

Standing at the drawing room door, one foot in and one foot out, Sebastian watched her trek with unwavering eyes. Her breath caught seeing his regard.

She smiled, and the corners of his mouth curved upwards. *He doesn't look anything like a killer,* she thought as she reached the bottom of the stairs and moved towards the drawing room, ready for an evening at Vauxhall.

The two pairs took a boat from Whitehall to the garden entrance on the south bank of the Thames in Kennington. More than a few jokes were made by Annick about the stench of the river, much to Liz's dismay given his poor humor fairly ruined the grand entrance to the gardens, not that she could concentrate on much with Sebastian's smoldering stare or her indecision of how to broach the topic of murder and mayhem.

Clearly, the way not to approach it would be to tell him she had overheard a conversation that may or may not have been about him and may or may not have involved gossip about the offing of a wife and child. Determined to substantiate his innocence in a single conversation, she would think of something.

Even her initial observations cleared him of all charges as far as she was concerned. Despite the magical evening being fraught with her anxieties of the gossip mongers, her companions were none the wiser. All along the walk past the supper boxes, orchestra building, and statue of Handel, he and Annick behaved with lighthearted frivolity, jibbing about all and sundry, acting like two children out for a walk in the park.

His mood was gay and his smile broad. *That is not the face of a killer*, she told herself. How dare those women say such things about him? She wanted to embrace him in front of all to see to show he had her unconditional support.

"Dinner isn't for another two hours. Shall we tour about the place, amuse ourselves?" Annick asked, Charlotte on his arm.

"The less time I must spend with the gloating groom, the happier I will be," jested Sebastian, in high spirits.

Annick feigned a friendly punch, and Sebastian overdramatized a dodge, both laughing at their boyish antics.

The mysticism of the gardens took Liz by surprise, momentarily dashing her worries as they walked the tree-lined avenue illuminated in rainbows from Turkish lanterns, already lit in preparation for dusk. Scented bouquets of fresh flowers hung from overarching Elm tree limbs. The shadier areas of the gardens darkened with shadows from the setting sun. All along the walk, jesters and mimes danced, chortled, and entertained, but were met with stiff competition, as the guests stared past them, dazzled instead by the duke and his betrothed.

Instinctively, Liz slowed her gait behind her sister, creating distance. The crowd scuttled to each side of the avenue, a parting sea for the duke and his lady, all eyes watching, all hands covering mouths as people gasped, cooed, and remarked on their great luck of seeing a noble in the flesh.

Wishing for a tree to hide behind, Liz took shorter steps, slower steps, allowing the crowd to fill behind the duke and separate the two couples. Sebastian at her side didn't seem phased by her machinations. Not until they were quite alone in the crowd of onlookers did she realize he might mistake her intentions.

So be it.

She would rather him think she craftily sequestered him than be forced into the spotlight with all eyes upon her, never mind that she, in point of fact, was walking with no lesser of a personage. An earl should be bound to catch as much attention as a duke in a crowd full of penny-pinching commoners who saved for a rare treat to escape into exoticism, yet this earl had an uncanny ability to disappear into a crowd, as if he could cloak himself in anonymity.

His clothes may be custom tailored and the finest London had to offer, but he lacked the glitz of his cousin who fairly sparkled in the limelight. Never had she felt safer or more at home than on his arm.

They walked in companionable silence, admiring waterfalls, pavilions, bowling greens, iron bridges, and even a fake castle. Without the other pair, she was vulnerable to gossip, walking unchaperoned with an unmarried gentleman, but she neither cared nor fretted, as the throngs of people acted as a shield. Any concerned person could assume any one of the crowd members as a chaperone. And blast to anyone else who wanted to gossip about Sebastian. He didn't deserve such rumors. She proudly walked at his side, smiling at the lush gardens.

Glancing beneath eyelashes at her companion, she admired his chiseled jaw and aquiline nose. He could have been a Roman emperor, she mused. Her memory flickered back to the veranda when their fingers entwined, him leaning within inches of her face, a hot mess of masculinity.

"Would it be rude of me to ask why you always wear the cameo?" He asked throatily, eyeing her sideways as they continued forward.

Startled, she reached up to touch the engraved amethyst. It hung on a shorter chain this evening, resting in the hollow of her throat.

"It belonged to my mother." She raised it and angled her head so he could see it. "Papa commissioned it for her as a wedding gift. When she died, he gave it to me, not that I would need a gem to remember her." She ran her thumb across the engraving. "It's made in her likeness. I find it comforting, as though she's with me when I wear it. Sentimental drivel to you, I'm sure."

He paused his step to look down at the necklace. "Not at all. I hope you don't think so harshly of my ribbing when we first met. I'm more sentimental than I confess. May I?" He reached hesitantly for the cameo.

The backs of his fingers grazed her throat as he captured the necklace in his palm. A shiver of warmth shuddered down her spine.

When she looked into his eyes, expecting to see her lust reflected in his, she saw instead raw pain, his brows furrowed, and his jaw clenched. His expression wrenched her heart.

What on earth had happened to this man to drown him in eternal heartache? He certainly didn't murder his wife, for those eyes were not the eyes of a killer, rather the eyes of a victim.

"You were close to her, then?" he said, his words gravelly.

Liz nodded but didn't respond.

"When did she pass? If my questions are too probing, forgive me."

Her heart fluttered. The warring emotions raged inside her, as she wanted so much for him to show interest in her, yet she worried he wouldn't share in return, especially about the more personal questions she desperately sought to ask.

Liz replied, "My mother died in childbed with Charlotte when I was seven. She was my dearest friend, my mother."

Releasing the cameo, he took a step to continue their walk, one slow step after another, taking in the sights of the gardens around him as though unperturbed.

She braved a personal question in return, "Are you close to your mother?"

He stiffened but continued to walk. "No."

A heavy silence fell, pregnant with unspoken words. And this was what she had feared. That impenetrable wall at a single personal question. And that hadn't even been the question she wanted to ask.

She was about to change the subject, when, shockingly, he answered.

"Funny, these coincidences in our lives. It will be your turn to think I'm fibbing, but I promise you now that I'm not. My mother, too, died when I was seven."

He paused, but when she didn't interject, he added, "Unlike you, I hardly remember my mother. We weren't close. I recall glimpses, shared moments, scattered images, but few specifics. I remember her tucking me in at night, kissing my forehead. I remember her walking along the coast while I built sandcastles. I remember one day when my father was in a mood, she came to the nursery and read to me and—," he stopped short before continuing, "and her words drowned out his shouts from somewhere in the manor."

"I'm happy you have those memories, even if they're so few." The comment about his father startled her, but she tucked it away for later. One hurdle at a time. "How did she die?"

"A fever, I was told," he said, the words clipped, his lips pursed. "Complete balderdash. The woman died of heartbreak. But a fever is the official tale."

"Oh, no. I'm so sorry. Was there naught a doctor could do to help?"

"A doctor was never called," he answered sharply.

His good mood turned to gloom. She waited to see if he would explain, but he held his silence, avoiding eye contact.

Well, she decided, she had already managed to ruin his mood with a single question about his mother so how much harm could come from another daring question? If she didn't ask now, she may lose her nerve later.

"Sebastian," she steeled herself, gripping her cameo for courage, "are you widowed?"

He looked at her askance, one eyebrow raising quizzically.

"You realize, I would have to have married to be widowed. No, I'm not widowed. Didn't we have this conversation at your aunt's townhouse? The reasons neither of us have ever married? Or was I talking with another wonderful woman named Lizbeth?" A quiet laugh accompanied a bemused expression, his mood altered for the better. "Why the devil—pardon my language—would you ask me that?"

Well, hmm. If not Sebastian, then whose wife had died, and who had children hidden away in a tower or buried in the back garden, or whatever it was she had overheard? If it wouldn't sound so humiliatingly silly, she would share the whole story with him, for surely he would find it humorous, thinking him a dark villain in a tale of spousal homicide when he had no spouse to murder. Not wishing him to think she had gone mad, she decided against telling him the truth.

"Oh, no particular reason. One does wonder how someone like you could remain unmarried." *Dash it!*

Her desire to divert the truth had just inserted her foot in her mouth.

"Someone like me?"

"Well, you know, handsome, intelligent, titled—"

"Good heavens, Lizbeth. You had better stop before you inflate my ego enough to carry both of us up and away. Keep talking like this, and I will be forced to whisk you down a dark path, and that wouldn't do any favors for our friendship or your reputation." He grinned devilishly, his brows angled with mischief. "I suggest we turn this tide, my lovely. Tell me if you've read *Gulliver's Travels*."

He held out his arm for her to take as they walked.

Resting a hand on his forearm, she said, "I'm acquainted with Swift, yes."

She hoped the embarrassment of the previous moment subsided quickly with the new diversion. How mortifying to have asked such a faux pas question, and then to fumble with those bold compliments. If she could disappear into one of those dark paths, she would.

"Splendid!" he said, all smiles. "I knew you'd have read Swift. Now, I want to pick that brain of yours. What do you make of Swift's criticism of science?"

Science seemed a far cry from a murder mystery. She could already breathe easier. *Deuced women and their gossip*, she cursed to herself.

Lizbeth tried to ignore a jester attempting to court her with a few handheld flowers, but Sebastian stepped forward to snatch the proffered arrangement, giving both the jester and Lizbeth a courtly bow as he handed her the small bouquet. With a curtsy to them both, she accepted the flowers and inhaled the musty fragrance of earth.

With the flowers in one hand and his arm under the other, she continued to walk, a fluster of emotion. What in heavens had he asked her?

"Oh, heavens. Let me think." *Science. Something about science. Oh, yes!* "Well, hmm. As I recall, Swift is quite critical of all things new. I believe he was worried that new discoveries and tools would destroy our belief system, especially how we view the world around us."

"Mmm. He does distort the descriptions of human bodies when Gulliver visits Brobdingnag, doesn't he?"

"Indeed. I believe that was his way of showing the absurdity and impracticality of such new tools as the microscope. Instead of relying on our imagination, our faith, and our admiration of the beauty around us, we are interpreting what we see through a magnified lens, distorting reality, reducing nature to the details of a flea's body."

Sebastian grinned, his good spirits fully restored. Perhaps he enjoyed having a woman of intelligence on his arm, she mused. Or maybe that was her vanity talking and she read into his behavior what she wanted him to think of her.

"How did you enjoy the part where Gulliver visits the Academy at Lagado?"

Liz's response rang with laughter. "I laughed for days over that! They were extracting sunbeams from the cucumbers with their newfangled equipment! Such a delightful even if harsh satire."

"Did you catch when Gulliver pokes fun at Richardson's *Pamela*?"

"Wait, no? I don't remember that at all. You've made that up just to rib me!"

"Honestly, I haven't. Re-read it when you have a chance to see if you catch it. He mocks both *Pamela* and *Robinson Crusoe*. Given our previous conversation and especially your harshness of poor Pamela, I thought you would rather enjoy his mocking the ideal woman and ideal man by societal standards." He winked at her as they continued the walk.

The crowd around them began to thin as people made their way back to the supper boxes.

"That does sound delightful. I will hunt for it with conviction." She fleetingly questioned what Annick and Charlotte were up to, likely down one of the dark paths.

"I hope you'll take this as an endearment when I say you are the most enlightened woman I've ever met." He paused their walk and turned to face her, looking at her in reverence. "You're exactly the woman I had assumed could never exist, a woman for whom I could fall." Their eyes met, his filled with yearning.

Lizbeth found herself nearly alone in the avenue with this potent man who was exhaling an elixir of heady passion.

"What was it you were saying earlier about my being handsome and intelligent?" he asked, his voice lowered.

"You're fishing for a compliment, my lord," she rebuked.

"Maybe I am. But if you don't think of a good one fast enough, I'll be forced to recite Burns to counter what I'm tempted to say."

Liz nearly collapsed against him with laughter. "Anything but Burns! You're incorrigible, Sebastian."

"Not quite the compliment I was hoping for, but I'll take it all the same. Incorrigible. Do you think if I added that to my calling card, I would receive more invitations?" The corners of his eyes crinkled.

She caught a glimpse of two figures walking towards them. Before she lost her chance, she asked one final question, hoping she wouldn't ruin the mood.

"Do you have any children, Sebastian?" she blurted, her words tumbling together.

Not quite the reaction she expected, he bellowed in laughter.

"Does a small army of illegitimates count?" he said between peals of laughter.

She swatted at his arm. "That is inappropriate, and you know it! Oh, heavens, do you really have a small army?"

He wiped tears from the crinkled corners of his eyes. "No, I don't have any children, illegitimate or otherwise. Where the devil, pardon my language again, did that question come from? Oh, wait, I see, this is some sort of proposition, is it not, an offer to bear my children?"

Liz huffed indignantly to stifle her own laughter. "It most certainly was not. You are incorrigible and ungenteel, and I am horrified you would say such a thing. You are the basest man, I have—"

A blushing Charlotte and smug Annick approached then, interrupting Liz's scolding. Sebastian laughed all the way back to the supper box, winking at her flirtatiously every time she glanced his direction.

When they settled into the Prince's Pavilion, Liz admired the painting on the wall behind their seats, a Shakespearean scene from the look of it. They had a spectacular view of the orchestra building and the dancing couples in The Grove.

Although Liz didn't want to be the center of attention sitting in Prince George's supper box, she couldn't deny that it was undoubtedly the best box in the gardens. The delight of dinner thrilled them all; cold meats cut transparently thin, custards, cheesecakes, tarts, and other sinful foods littered the table.

After the sun set, thousands of oil lamps ignited in an instant by lamp-lighters at the ready. Gasps from every table filled the air at the sight of such magic and beauty. Just as the gasps were dying down, the sweet notes of a soprano resounded through the night air. The harpsichord and violins joined in accompaniment soon after. Annick said that if he wasn't mistaken, it was one of the arias from Handel's Teseo, although he wasn't familiar enough with the opera to identify which aria or even which character. Liz was a tad surprised the duke knew anything at all about music.

Midway through the meal, the musical entertainment changed pace for dancing. Their group stayed seated to converse.

"If it weren't already official, it is now," declared Annick. "I've written to Mother about the engagement." He puffed out his chest proudly.

"Oh, Drake, what did you tell her about me?" Charlotte touched his arm.

"Absolutely nothing, of course! You're to be a complete surprise for her. I said," he cleared his throat for effect, "'I have the pleasure to announce that by the time this reaches you, you will be mother-in-law to a most amiable new daughter.'"

"That doesn't tell her anything about me!" Charlotte sniveled, her lower lip pouting.

"I told you, silly goose. You're to be my gift to her from London. She'll love you, I swear." He turned an accusing eye to Lizbeth and Sebastian. "And what were the two of you up to in the gardens?"

Liz sat up straighter, refusing to be the center of scandalous talk. "We talked about *Gulliver's Travels*, actually. A thoroughly scholarly discussion, I will have you know."

Annick turned to Charlotte and said *sotto voce*, "How did you ever turn out this lovely with such a bluestocking for a sister." They both snickered.

Joking or not, Liz felt the sting. His words were true and could have been complimentary, for she did consider herself an intelligent and educated woman, but his meaning was derisive. She was neither involved in the bluestocking society nor frumpy, which she believed was exactly his implication. She had half a mind to point out that he didn't seem bothered by her reading habits when he approached her at the masquerade, but that would be tasteless indeed, especially in front of her sister.

Sebastian leaned to Liz and said in retort, "Goes to show your resilience for tolerating a disreputable dandy as a brother-in-law."

The duke slapped his knee with laughter. "*Touché*, cousin! *Touché*!"

As the meal wound to a close, Annick suggested, "Let's stay until sunrise. The gardens remain open until the last guests leave, so let's be the last guests."

As though he could read her mind, Sebastian said, "Aside from your betrothed, I don't believe anyone in this party is remotely interested in traversing the dark paths with you all night. I suggest, instead, we all visit the British Museum in a few days. See the discoveries of worldly voyages, entrench ourselves in other cultures with Greek antiquities, explore the South Seas vicariously through Captain Cook's collection." He wriggled his eyebrows at Lizbeth.

"That sounds wonderful!" Liz nodded eagerly.

Annick groaned. "The most boring suggestion you've ever made, old man. How do you ever expect to woo a woman when recommending we look at coins and vases as a source of entertainment?" He lolled his head back and feigned a snore. "I'm game if that's what you want to do, but I question how we could be related."

The evening passed faster than Lizbeth wanted, concluding with an explosive colored light show of London's finest pyrotechnics. As all eyes looked upwards into the sky, Sebastian slipped his hand into hers.

In spite of the rocky start to her evening, the whole affair turned out to be one of the best nights of her life. He had shared with her the personal anecdote about his mother, and they had spent a good portion of the evening talking about various and sundry ideas and viewpoints. And there had been the none-too-subtle flirting for her to hold lovingly to her breast.

Almost the perfect man may need to be amended to the *most* perfect man if he kept this pace. Her initial fears of his not opening up to her dissolved with each passing moment in his company.

When they returned to their respective homes, all in the Collingwood residence were abed. Lizbeth settled into her own bed after Bettye helped her out of her gown and into her nightdress. She snuggled into the covers with Goethe's *The Sorrows of Young Werther*, a relatively new publication her father had surprised her with earlier in the year. Next time she saw Sebastian, she must ask him if he knew of Goethe.

"I'm glad you're not asleep yet." A voice whispered from the door, startling Lizbeth into nearly dropping her book.

When she saw Charlotte peeking in, a candle in her hand, she heaved a sigh of relief and relaxed. No ghosts of murdered wives haunted her door this evening.

"You know me better than that, Charlotte. Come in. Are you unwell?"

"Oh, nothing so grim." She shuffled over to the bed, setting the candle holder on the nightstand and climbing on the bed with her sister. "I simply wanted to offer my sincerest apologies that you must spend so much time with that boor, all for my benefit. I do appreciate your sacrifice. It means so much to me that you tolerate him so that I may have time alone with Drake," Charlotte squeezed Liz's hand.

"Thank you, but in the boor's defense, he's not the least bit boorish."

"You're too kind for your own good, Lizbeth. He is a boor. And I'd like to add a bore to his list of traits, now, as well. The British Museum? Egad! Who wants to walk around and look at some dead man's rubbish?"

"I thought it a lovely suggestion. Maybe you don't want to see antiquities, but I do. I don't find him the least boring. Like me, he doesn't favor crowds and would rather be somewhere quieter. This may shock you, but Lord Roddam and I share a good deal in common, and I'm beginning to consider him a friend."

Charlotte snickered unbecomingly. "You really are too kind, you know. I don't like anything about him. Drake on the other hand…"

Liz only heard half of Charlotte's crooning, as she lost herself to the memory of the depths of Sebastian's eyes. She was drawn as a moth to those depths. Mmm, she recalled tastily the moment he said he could fall for her. He hadn't been facetious, she didn't think. He spoke with genuine ardor.

But what had he meant by it? A light infatuation, friendship with affection, love? And more to the point, what would he do about it? His words brought such elation with a world of apprehension. Their time together was fleeting, each passing day drawing them closer to returning to their homes on the opposite sides of the country. Assuming he did fall for her, she wondered if he would act on it, and if so, how she would respond.

Chapter 11

Between his mornings at the House of Lords and his evenings with his cousin, Sebastian devoted much of his afternoons at a local coffeehouse. With everyone he knew visiting White's or Brook's, or the less popular Boodle's, he avoided the clubs to enjoy his coffee black and in silence.

Being surrounded by the merchant class felt more natural to him than listening to Tories and Whigs whine about one revolution or another, not to mention he preferred the anonymity the coffeehouse offered. Even in his oldest and most worn attire, he still stood out, but no one paid him heed, just as he liked.

He had ample opportunity in such a setting to overhear industry strife, worker worries, and the flow of money. Talking with cits wasn't beneath him given his interests for new industry in the north, namely coal mining. Above all else, he simply welcomed the quiet of the coffeehouse. As noisy as it could become on a busy afternoon, it still afforded a level of personal quiet, where nothing at all concerned him and no one called his name.

A man could think in a place like this.

With simultaneous business deals on his plate, the correspondences with his stewards to address, the recruitment and hire of several new positions on his lands, including an overdue blacksmith and a long-awaited physician, along with various other concerns, it surprised him to discover Miss Trethow on the fringes of his mind.

Understatement of the year. She wasn't on the fringes. In fact, he could think of nothing else. His correspondences untouched, his business dealings ignored, he filled his every waking thought with Lizbeth.

Over the past week, his feelings had deepened, aided by the time spent with her family. Never again could he think of her as a potential mistress. He respected her father Cuthbert, grew fond of her cousin Walter, and found her aunt Hazel humorous. Being with Liz and her family showed him the future he wanted. He couldn't stop imagining them all in his parlor sharing laughs, playing charades and cards, taking walks along the beach.

He saw the family he wanted, the family he never had.

The highlight of the week had been the card games, of all things. On one evening in particular, after a civilized game of piquet, Lizbeth, with a gleam in her eye, recommended penneech. Sebastian couldn't recall the last time he had played the game, but it would have been at White's during his dissipated youth, his memory tainted by the haze of endless inebriation at the time.

Up for the challenge, he accepted, and never had he witnessed a more competitive woman than Lizbeth with a new trick every turn. At one point, he thought she might come across the table to swat at him after one of his own tricks, but instead she sharpened her play, examining his every move for signs of weakness and clues to his next play. Her eyes were bright and intelligent, flashing with sly craftiness and a refusal to be bested.

Not that he intentionally meant to distract her, but his foot found its way to her ankle during the game. She would deny it under duress, of course, but he knew she enjoyed his attentions.

His affection for her shifted during that game.

No, no, that wasn't entirely true. He knew during the game he could never take her as a mistress. But it had been the evening at Vauxhall that etched her into his heart for eternity.

From beginning to end of the evening, he was exhilarated by her conversation, proud to walk at her side, possessive when other men favored her with a glance. As she chattered on, he had imagined her not as an acquaintance, but as his wife, the two of them sharing an enchanted evening together. Never had he laughed so much as during that outing. Never had he felt so complete as when their hands embraced during the firework display.

He had begged for the night never to end or else for the world to end in that moment so he would know nothing but the moment itself, the feeling of elation, the uncomplicated attraction of two people perfect for each other.

Alas, if life were different.

He wondered if Lizbeth was God's joke on him. Had God created two people meant to be together, but with a sardonic twist of fate, ensured they would live estranged? If only Sebastian had been dealt a better set of cards, if his mother had lived, if he hadn't let down his father so abominably, if *she* hadn't died. He squeezed his eyes shut, blocking the last memory, blocking *her*.

He needed to stop torturing himself. He needed to put an end to this blossoming friendship before he compromised them both, leaving him no choice but to drag Lizbeth into his hellish life.

She tempted him something fierce. Besotted. Smitten. Head over heels. All he wanted to do was sweep her into his arms and make love to her.

He was in so deeply he needed either to get on the first carriage out of town or ride hell for leather to speak with her father. If only he could offer her a man worth loving.

Not for a moment did he deceive himself that a life with him would be happy.

One sleepless night had been spent convincing himself he could make it work. With a bit of pretense, a few lies, some untold truths, he could keep her enough at arm's length to make life livable between them for quite some time. Assuming she didn't ask too many questions. He couldn't see how such a life could be sustainable, though. There were aspects about himself he couldn't hide. How would he explain some without revealing all? He couldn't reveal all.

If he told her everything, she would leave him in a heartbeat. No one, not even the most tender woman on earth, could love a murderer, regardless of the circumstances in which he earned that title. Two deaths weighed on his conscious, even if not by his hand directly. Two people's lives for which he would exchange his own if he had the power.

God, but he wanted her. If circumstances were different. If he were different. If his past were different, he would be courting her now without a second thought, making a grand showing to her and all the world that he wanted no woman but her.

Oh, Lizbeth. Oh, you wonderous woman.

She would be his undoing.

The more he revealed, the more she would see the war mural beneath the gilded wallpaper. The more he revealed to her, the more she would see the scarred man piecing together his life after a history of violence. The more he revealed…

He couldn't survive her rejection if she left him. If he ended their friendship on his terms, all would be well, because he would add her to the list of his many regrets and move forward with life. But if he gave himself to her and she ran from him, as he knew she would, he could never move forward.

He slammed his fist on the table, rattling his coffee cup in its saucer and attracting curious stares from other guests in the coffeehouse. *Stop thinking about her.*

Flattening his palm against the wood, he ground his teeth. This would not do. This simply would not do. He had to stop. Everything was moving too quickly, too unexpectedly. He had to stop before he did something stupid, something rash, dooming her to the misery of living with him, a brooding devil steeped in sorrow and regret.

Chapter 12

Sebastian walked beside Lizbeth through Montagu House, the home of the British Museum. As fascinating as the exhibits, he concentrated on little else aside her.

She was a far rarer treasure than anything the museum offered. How was he supposed to resist her charms, charms she wasn't the least aware of possessing? He watched her mouth when she spoke, observed her dilating pupils, and appreciated the tightness of her bodice when she breathed deeply.

His willpower teetered on the edge.

For the days they'd been apart since Vauxhall, he'd oscillated as to what should be done between them. By that morning, he'd talked himself into leaving her. It was for her sake. He didn't deserve her. She didn't deserve to be entrapped by him. The best decision for them both was his leaving London, or at the very least avoiding her until he could leave. But oh, such wasn't so easy to accomplish.

He was a drowning man.

It didn't help they were alone. Annick and Charlotte had abandoned them for the reading room when the pair stopped to examine the surviving copy of *Beowulf*. As scandalous as it was to be left unchaperoned, he doubted anyone noticed or cared given the few people milling about them were children and nannies.

Lizbeth paused to study a case, Sebastian hanging back to study her. With her back to him, he could openly admire her. Namely, her coiffure. He longed to undo it one hairpin at a time. Several strands of auburn fell loose from the coil, waterfalling over her ears, onto her shoulders, and down the length of her back. He marveled at how unruly she always managed to look, beautifully, naturally unruly, a freshly tumbled appearance even during the most mundane of activities. Mmmm.

"Sebastian?"

He started, unaware he had slipped into a daze. "Pardon. Woolgathering."

"Obviously. Were you imagining pirates stealing coins on the high seas?" She turned to him, gesturing to the display of coins he hadn't noticed until now.

"Not exactly." He racked his brain for something to say that didn't involve lips or bodices or how thoroughly he wanted to kiss her. "Those coins were from Sir William Hamilton's collection, a Scottish diplomat who, among other hobbies, is a volcanologist."

Hell and damnation. Was that really the best he could think to say? He might as well hold a sign above his head that read, *I'd rather kiss you than talk about coins.*

"He isn't really. You jest!" The green flecks in her eyes twinkling with amusement.

"No jest. He sent reports to London from the Mount Vesuvius eruptions in Naples. Quite the daring adventurer, wouldn't you say?"

"He sounds reckless." She tutted.

"All in the name of science. Should I even mention his study of earthquakes? Musician, archeologist, politician—the list goes on. If only we were all so accomplished."

"Don't start." She wagged a scolding finger. "*You* are accomplished and can't deny it."

"I most certainly can and will. Working myself ragged isn't an accomplishment," he protested.

"Why do you do this, Sebastian? Why are you always so harsh on yourself?"

Her tone wiped the half-smile from his face.

Their conversation lapsed into silence.

When she pressed her nose against the glass of the next case, a fog of breath formed. "I think you have much to recommend yourself," she said in half whisper. "When you told me at Annick's dinner the deplorable state your father left the lands when he died, I knew you were a man to be admired. You've worked so hard to rise from poverty. How can you say that isn't an accomplishment? Not every man can rebuild five earldoms and a barony, you know. Most can't turn a profit with one!"

Sebastian lumbered to the nearest wall and leaned against it, arms crossed. "Change topic, Lizbeth. Business isn't the subject for mixed company."

She pivoted to face him. Her eyes narrowed, and her lips pursed. "Do you still understand me so little? Just because I'm a woman doesn't mean I don't know ledgers, accounting, or investment correspondences. Just because I'm a woman doesn't mean I don't want to hear about what is important in your life. Just because—oh." She exhaled, exasperated.

"Oh, forget it." She turned her hands palm out. "Sometimes conversation with you is beyond enriching. Other times it is impossible. You're edgy today, and I don't appreciate it. Why did you bring me here if you were going to be edgy?"

"I'm not edgy. I simply don't want to talk about myself. I'm sorry for snapping. Truly, I wouldn't hurt your feelings for the world."

Unsure what else to say, he remained silent. He didn't want to talk about himself.

The work he'd invested over the past decade to save his lands from poverty, to build trust amongst abused and financially raped laborers, was a source of pride for him, but it was a modest pride, a humble pride, an embarrassed pride. He hardly deserved the accolades he knew she would shower on him. All he had done was fulfill an obligation to the people and give meaning to his otherwise empty life.

He was not a hero.

It had started with his grandfather, and then continued with his father. After his great-grandfather depleted the family coffers on a dream to turn a pile of ruins into a livable castle, the heir was left penniless. In an attempt to replenish funds, Sebastian's father and grandfather grew greedy. They dropped wages below livable percentages and refused any improvements to the villages. Several of the towns didn't have proper water or sewage systems when he inherited, and none of them had resident physicians. He was not surprised by the state of affairs, but he was certainly appalled.

This had been his plight for a decade.

Lizbeth touched his arm, sending tendrils of heat racing through his veins. He hadn't noticed her approach him. Her touch, however brief and light, made him quiver despite the gravity of his thoughts.

Acquiescing, his lips twitched into a smile.

"Let's not quarrel. I brought you here because I knew you'd enjoy it. Don't let me spoil the day," he said, taking her by the elbow to lead her to the next exhibit.

Absently, without forethought, he added, "If you must know, what I want to do is speak with your father."

Not until her eyes widened did he realize what he said.

Hell and damnation.

Before she could respond or misconstrue words further, he clarified, "You wanted to talk business, didn't you? Well, I'm considering coal mining, as either an investor or sole proprietor. Distant future, mind you. Given your father's experience, a conversation with him is warranted, don't you think?"

She stared, digesting what he said, he supposed.

After several minutes, she responded, "It was my grandfather's tin mine, my mother's father, that is. Papa was his apprentice. He's quite proud of the mine."

He raised a quizzical brow.

They continued their exploration of the exhibits as she explained how her father, of landed gentry, came to apprentice at a tin mine.

He said nothing after she finished her story, feeling her eyes on him rather than the cases.

Clearing his throat to dislodge the lump forming, he said, "I'm not accomplished, you know, just strategic. Coal mining is just such a strategy. I've learned how to maximize profits, generate income, and invest wisely. Originally, the key was in finding ways on the outset to minimize costs. Bargaining, repurposing tools, and greasing elbows, namely. Are you bored yet? Are you ready to concede I'm not as accomplished as a volcanologist?"

She laughed heartily and shook her head.

Sebastian struggled between how she made him feel with her reverence and how he felt about himself. In his estimation, he didn't deserve her respect. Yes, he had worked hard, but no more than any man in his position. Lizbeth was only seeing the man he was trying to become, not the man he had always been.

Liz said, "I think everything you've done is admirable. Your heart is with the people and the lands, where it should be. You've complained before of what all you haven't repaired, but look at what you have done instead!"

Chagrined, he glanced away, realizing they had walked through three exhibits without pausing. Vases from the orient sat empty on shelves in whatever exhibit they walked through now. He didn't much care. All he cared about was this woman on his arm.

"But even the castle is in disrepair, Lizbeth. It is far from finished. Well over half the curtain wall remains in rubble, along with the old towers. Thankfully, most of the keep's renovation was completed before my time, but it did sit empty for two generations."

"No more berating yourself! You act modest, but I know this is your passion." She sighed wistfully. "Oh, I wish I could see the castle."

He resisted saying he too wished she could see it, could roam the halls with him, make love under a blanket of stars in the courtyard. He ground his teeth to blot out that vision and held his tongue before he said something they would both regret. If he gave too much credence to how she made him feel, he would take her into his arms and make a clod of himself in the middle of Montague House.

Struggling not to blurt out his thoughts or to look at her lips, luscious and inviting, he walked to a shelf of decorative vases, none of which interested him nearly as much as the thought of unleashing her passion.

Their solitude was momentarily disrupted by a gaggle of screeching toddlers leading their nanny a merry dance. The children whisked by without a second glance to Sebastian or Lizbeth, but the nanny bowed her head in embarrassed apology as she chased after her wards.

When he glanced at Liz, she stared back at him in rapt interest. What had they been discussing? The only image in his mind was of her standing in his gazebo, arms open in welcome embrace.

He was a drowning man.

She laid a hand on his coat sleeve, a sensation incredibly intimate for such a simple touch, not to mention such a public place. Did she want to ruin her reputation? Did she want to compromise them? Did she know how hard he fought his desire for her own benefit?

"I'm no different than a common laborer, Lizbeth. You see that, right? Beneath the titles, I'm just a laborer. It began in my attempt to build trust with the field hands and villagers, people who had only known a wrathful employer. It began that way, but I liked the work. To prove I was as good as my word, I built the new houses myself, repaired cottages myself, all with my own hands. And I enjoyed it."

For effect, he removed his gloves to reveal callused hands, hardly the hands of a gentleman, much less an earl. "I plowed fields alone. I scythed alone. I didn't do these things once, you understand. I did them every day. I still do them, but now I work alongside my men. I enjoy the work."

"And here I've always thought peers hosted fox hunts and played lawn bowls for entertainment." Lizbeth teased, making light of his words. He replaced his gloves, as she continued. "You *are* accomplished. I wish you could hear yourself, really hear yourself, see yourself through my eyes," she said with a beguiling smile.

The smile disarmed him.

Sliding his hand over hers, public place be damned, he led her to the next room with a collection of busts.

Thankfully, not another soul was in sight. Sophocles stared at him from a shelf, judging Sebastian as if the plaster bust knew his reserve slipped with each step, each smile.

"I've done nothing special or unique, only ungenteel," he insisted. "Every landowner, be they peer or gentry, must work to keep their lands profitable. I merely took the task literally."

"But how many gentlemen would do this on their own? They would go into further debt to hire estate managers to do it all, trusting the expertise of the steward the man's moral compass not to swindle the estate or the people. No, Sebastian, whether or not you wish to take my compliments to heart, I mean them, and they are true. You are the smartest man I know and a man to be respected and admired."

Sunrays shown through the window panes, dancing light across her features.

The look she gave him from beneath long, sooty eyelashes, burning with intensity and curiosity, caused him to misstep, his hand reaching instinctively for her arm, pulling her against his chest as he steadied his footing. Not sure if he should kiss her or apologize for being a colossal klutz, he held her to him for a moment too long, searching her expression.

Her eyes laughed up at him as he cleared his throat, regained composure, and pressed forward in their walk.

His body alive from the brief but intimate touch and his heartrate quickening, he cleared his throat twice, then thrice, before carrying on as though nothing happened.

Sebastian slowed their gait among the sculptures, stopping in front of a scowling man in plaster. "I enjoy the freedom physical work offers, even if it does tan my skin and thicken my muscles in ways civilized society finds grossly unattractive."

"I don't find you unattractive, not in the least," Liz replied coquettishly. "Quite the contrary."

He would have expected her to say it with a blush and downcast eyes, but not Lizbeth. Not this woman who melted his resolve. Her eyes met his, communicating boldly her attraction to him. He studied her for longer than was polite, counting the sun-kissed freckles dotting the bridge of her pert nose and both cheekbones just under her long eyelashes.

A drowning man, treading water.

"So, they trust you now?"

"Who?" He searched his memory of their conversation, recalling only her confession of attraction.

"The laborers," she prompted. "You said you did all this in the beginning to build their trust."

"Ah. Yes. Them. Aye, partly. After a lifetime of abuse, trust doesn't come easily. It takes time to earn and maintain trust. Assuming it ever can be earned." Only after he spoke the words did he realize he was talking about himself.

"Oh, I see," she said cryptically. "Yes, I understand now."

Lizbeth trailed her fingertips down his forearm until she reached his hand, then slipped her palm into his, lacing their fingers. "I want to earn your trust, Sebastian, as you earned theirs. I want you to open up to me. I want… I want *you*."

Before he could stop himself, reacting instinctively to the acceleration of his pulse and the earnestness of her words, he reached for her cheek with his free hand and leaned in to kiss her. Only when he felt her breath against his face did he hesitate.

Sebastian searched Lizbeth's eyes for a reason to pull back but saw only longing, her eyes pleading with him to finish what he started. It was his undoing.

He leaned the remaining inches to press his lips firmly against hers.

Warm. Moist. Tender.

Oh, Lizbeth.

He relaxed his mouth, relishing the softness of hers. Never had such a chaste kiss felt this sensual. He breathed in deeply through his nose to inhale her scent, to fill himself with her, her lips hot and wet against his own. A growl vibrated the back of his throat.

When he began to pull away, her eyes fluttered open, and he saw in them passion and wild abandon, an animal released from its cage. Lizbeth leaned against his chest, her eager lips reuniting with his.

Cautiously, he licked her bottom lip, testing her reaction.

Her lips parted in response, and she pulled in his tongue with her own. He explored her mouth, licking, tasting, drinking the pleasure of her. Lips pressed against each other in fierce yearning, tongues simulating what he wished to do with the rest of his body. He would go mad if he couldn't have her.

A moan, hers or his he couldn't say, reverberated until the sound sobered his intoxication. It dawned on his hazed brain that they stood in the middle of a museum, however deserted. At any moment someone could see them.

Devil take it, what was he doing?

He pulled away so quickly, he had to reorient himself to keep from stumbling backwards. Lizbeth's darkened eyes searched his in confusion of the quitted kiss.

Ignoring her labored breathing, her heaving chest, and the swelling in his loins, he took the opportunity to apologize. He stole her kiss and couldn't offer what should naturally follow such a violation of innocence. He couldn't, wouldn't trap her.

"I shouldn't have done that." He waited, watching her breathing calm, realization dawning in her expression of what had happened, of what he was saying. "Please, accept my apology. I've violated your trust and friendship. It will never happen again."

She stared at him in confusion, shaking her head. She tried to speak, but only mouthed silently, words caught in her throat.

Never had he felt such an uncontrollable longing for another person. It frightened him. From this moment forward, he must stay away from her before he destroyed her with selfish desire.

With another mumbled apology and all due haste, he escorted her on wobbly legs to the reading room, ready to put distance between them.

Chapter 13

The carriage jolted, rattling the windows and sending Lizbeth bouncing across the seat. Papa Cuthbert sat across from her, holding onto an overhanging leather strap for balance. As they traversed the rocky terrain, he bellowed laughter at her plight.

Outside, sheep grazed in the surrounding fields, a welcome sight after the hubbub and industry of London. The gatehouse with its elliptical arch rising from imposts yawned before them. They passed through and down the drive, happy to be home again.

Home was a two and a half story, five-bay rectangle with two wings enclosing a courtyard. The elbows of the house had decorative quoins with pedimented gables at both wings. The front door stood under a triglyph frieze, Tuscan columns to either side.

Teghyiy Hall came into view as they crested the hill, all the doors and windows open to greet the returning master and friendly cross breezes. The housekeeper, cook, coachman's wife, and two maids waved as they approached.

If Lizbeth never rode in a carriage again, it would be too soon. Her bum would be sore for weeks, she was sure, after the trek from London to Trevena.

Although the family left London together, Aunt Hazel and Walter ended their journey in Exeter, while Papa and Lizbeth continued to the coast. Lizbeth knew the household would be sad when Charlotte didn't exit the carriage, but the news of her matrimony would more than make up for her absence.

As happy as she felt to see the wildflowers in bloom and hear the roar of the ocean, she felt an emptiness. She hadn't spoken to Sebastian since the British Museum.

He had been at the wedding, but he was curt at his kindest. He had eyes only for the wedding party and gave her nothing more than a cursory nod. Watching her sister marry Annick had made the day even gloomier, but she couldn't say it hadn't been a handsome ceremony.

It surely must have been the wedding of the Season. While only immediate family attended the ceremony, curious onlookers crowded about the church doors, awaiting the bride and groom's exit, for it wasn't every day a duke married. When the doors opened, and the crowd caught sight of the couple, cheers erupted from all sides, along with a fair share of swooning. Those who knew the duke rained flower petals along the walk from the church to the carriage.

The newlyweds matched in picture-perfect serenity, Charlotte in blue satin with ivory lace overlay and Annick in a dark blue cutaway the same shade as Charlotte's dress with a silk cravat mimicking her overlay. Annick made a show of their departure, unbuttoning his tailed jacket to show off a brightly colored and embroidered waistcoat and catching flower petals in his hat. When they reached the carriage, he tossed coins to the crowd before dipping Charlotte into a very public and very decadent kiss.

While all eyes had been on the bride and groom, hers had been riveted on Sebastian who kept his distance. Of course, he would ignore her. She couldn't blame him. After all, he'd made it clear from the beginning he didn't want to be hunted down like a fox by some marriage minded female, and what had she done? She'd thrown herself at him, quite literally. He'd been the best friend she'd ever had, and she'd acted wanton.

Her heart still ached over what happened. She was ashamed and embarrassed. For all her talk of not being interested in romance or marriage, she had proven herself a liar by flirting and lascivious behavior. He must think her a fortune hunting wanton. Her cheeks burned with the humiliation of it.

It didn't matter that, technically, he kissed her first. Her behavior was deplorable: telling him she found him attractive, fawning over him, touching him, and finally pushing herself onto him. *His* kiss had been chaste. *Hers* had been a ghastly display of affection. It was no wonder he avoided her.

Even despite her reservations about a marriage with him, she had hoped against logic he would do something rash, sweep her off her feet, show her that this was, after all, the beginning of love, the start of a fairy tale romance that would be sung about for generations, and by doing so, inspire her to throw all her inhibitions to the wind on the chance that this was true love.

She felt downright thick. The daftest cow in Cornwall. He hadn't swept her off her feet. Instead, he had kissed her in a way that would torment her for the rest of her days, and then he left for the north. She blamed herself, not him.

What she should be is relieved. As deeply as she'd fallen for him, she had reservations. All would be far better to realize before committing herself to him that it would never work. She would not be a caretaker to a brooding man. She would not be an invisible wife to the lord of the manor. She would not live with a man who couldn't trust her enough to speak honestly. And yet…

At least now she was home. The sea would recharge her spirit, the healing ocean, the embodiment of magic. If she wanted true love, she need look no further than the capped waves. And she could enjoy the fields, the cliffs, the beaches, and all things naturally wonderful without society or propriety breathing down her neck.

Within an hour of settling in at Teghyiy Hall, Lizbeth grabbed her bonnet and ran for the door to head straight for the seaside, eager to begin the cleansing process and forget all about *that man.*

Papa shouted out the door after her with his rough and tumble Cornish accent, "No going for a fair stank, Lizzie, my dove, for 'tis some late already. Two hours, na more. Cook is baking summit special tonight, p'rhaps stargazy pie, like."

With a dismissive wave behind her, she ran down the drive. Liz had no intention of going for a long walk as Papa worried she might. More like a long swim. The sea called to her.

She ran across the field and over the hill, skittering down the other side past fieldstones and sheep, the sun hot against her back, the wind pushing her onward. She threw her bonnet into the wind and let loose her hair, the gust of nature's breath blowing it wildly about her face and torso.

She hopped toward the rock wall between her and the cove, peeling off her shoes and flinging them over her shoulder to join the bonnet dancing a minuet with the wind. Reaching the ledge above the cove, she climbed down the rock face, her feet expertly gripping the crag.

Only an hour remained of low tide, just long enough. She reached the bottom, feet sinking into wet, sandy beach. Toes slapped, sloshed, and sucked the sediment with each step, marking her footsteps towards the lapping waves. She walked straight into the waves, water licking her ankles before surging against her knees.

The cold sea chilled her bones, cleansing her. She slipped into the water, pushing out towards the ocean until the waves splashed about her neck, bubbling in her ears. Curious mackerel swam around her, and kelp tickled her toes. She could see clear to the sea floor below. With abandon, she slapped the waves, kicked the currents, splashed and dove into the icy waters, a child at heart.

After her fill of the sea haven, she perched on a flat rock in the cove, her limbs sprawled, the sun warm. The rock face would soon shadow the cove, so she took advantage of the heat while she could to dry her drenched clothes. Wet hair clung to her arms and face, her petticoats soaked and weighty against her skin.

Three small clouds moved above her. She watched them inch across the sky, overlapping to form one large cloud shaped as an angry god who threatened to pound fists against the headland's cliffside. When her mother was alive, the two of them had lain for hours, guessing cloud shapes and concocting stories of the cloud adventures.

Every waking moment had been spent with her mother, the two of them traipsing the land in search of new escapades. If her mother were here now, they would go together to visit the miners. Tomorrow, she decided, she would bring them breakfast. Cook would bake pasties for her to take. She laughed in memory of her mother's old tales of buccas, those mythical fairies that caused mining mischief if not bribed with food. She hoped the miners' luck had held while she was away. No one else would know to leave pasty crumbs for the buccas.

She missed her mother. She hadn't cried over her death in years, but she did now, a nostalgic cry tinged with remorse. She missed sharing these moments, missed the song of her mother's voice, missed stories of the Cornish pixies, mermaids, and pirates. Above all else, she missed her best friend.

During her brief acquaintance with Sebastian, she thought she might have finally found someone with whom she shared an emotional kinship, but alas, she was alone again. She had Papa, of course, but it wasn't the same.

She fought the weighty shadow of despair.

In London, when surrounded by family, she held her chin high and proud, ignoring the bleeding of her heart as Sebastian turned his back on her. Now, alone and a lifetime away from what could have been, she slipped into a hopeless gloom, feeling the sharp cut of betrayal at his behavior, the helplessness of abandonment, and the heartache of never seeing him again. The tears for her mother blended with tears for Sebastian. In her stomach clenched a tight ball of heartbreak, while in her heart, all care drained to emptiness.

After so many years of being alone, she had found someone to relate to, a true kindred spirit, yet he didn't want her. Undoubtedly, he felt the connection, too. Not enough to find her irresistible, not enough to fight for her, to slay whatever demons haunted him.

To him, she wasn't worth the sacrifice.

Allowing herself to cry over the loss at last, she rationalized what happened. He hadn't deceived her. Never had he promised her a future, never had he courted her. He made it clear from their first day that he had no interest in any relationship beyond friendship. And besides, marriage would have never worked, for as much as he began to open to her, he remained distant, secretive, shielding himself from her prying eyes. At no point during their acquaintance had her worries about him subsided, so why grieve for a future that wouldn't have worked?

Before she could give into temptation, the decision had been ripped from her breast, and all for the better, for now she didn't have to live with regret. Now she didn't have to live with a poor decision. Now she could live freely and independently the life she had always planned where only she was master.

Feeling empty, drained from the expenditure of emotion, she released him from her heart. He had been a lark and nothing more. Today, she would be renewed of spirit. Today, she was home.

Her fingertips felt the shadow before she noticed the setting sun. A cold chill from the whipping wind bit her fingers in contrast to the warmth on the rest of her body. The tide would rise dangerously soon to cover the beach with white waves, trapping anyone remaining on the rocks. Making quick work of it, she climbed up the naturally jutting rocks in the cliff-face to reach the plateau above and searched for her discarded bonnet and shoes.

What would Sebastian say at the drenched sight of her? If he had become her husband, would he have allowed her to swim so scandalously? Not that anyone came to this secret place of hers to cause scandal, but what would he say if he saw her now, plodding barefoot across the grass, still dripping wet despite the sun's best efforts, her soaked hair sticking to her bare arms and about her sodden gown?

With delight, she imagined the ton's reaction to a countess diving fully clothed into the ocean then walking a half mile home looking like a used mop.

Bonnet and shoes in hand, she walked into the open door of Teghyiy Hall, hoping she could sneak to her room and arrange for Bettye to prepare her bath and evening dress before Papa spotted her.

Too late. He stood in the doorway of the vestibule, his hands clawing at his sideburns in horror.

"Lizzie, my bird! Tell yer Papa ye didn' go to the cove like. Yer some ummin and stagged now. Dirty and muddy to the bleddy bone."

She laughed at his horrified expression, comically exaggerated, and ran upstairs before he could scold her more.

Following a warm bath and change of clothes, she joined him before dinner, hoping to exchange stories of homecoming and plan the next week's exploits, be they calling on neighbors or reading in the parlor. One look at him told her he wasn't in a playful mood.

He perched next to the fireplace with its carved sea scenes and embedded sea shells. An arm propped against the mantel, the hand running through his salt and pepper hair.

"I've done ye a disservice in yer upbringing, my bird. I never should 'ave indulged ye. I let ye sit with yer cousin an' 'is tutors, learnin' what a boy ought, not a proper lady. I've raised a headstrong daughter."

"Oh, Papa. I'm just like you. And just like Mama, too. That's not so bad, is it?"

"Na. *Ny wonn*, my bird. It were fine when ye were young, but now? *Ny wonn*. I just don't know. 'ow will ye make a dutiful wife jumping in oceans?"

Liz's jaw tightened. "You know I won't be a dutiful wife, Papa. You know that. You've always accepted how I felt about marriage, never once questioning my decision."

Oh, she didn't need this now, not after finding an infinitesimal micron of peace today.

"I love 'aving ye as my companion. But what will ye do when I'm gone? I shouldn't'a let ye run free as a wildcat, shouldn't'a spoiled ye with books and business. I made ye wild and some smart. I ruined yer chances."

"You haven't ruined anything, Papa. You've taught me what being free really means, what being independent feels like, and I wouldn't sacrifice that for anything. If I truly love someone, just as you loved Mama, it wouldn't be such a sacrifice, and I would consider matrimony, but not as a dutiful wife, rather as the equal of my beloved. If I must sacrifice my freedom, I won't do it. Would you have me sell myself to someone like Charlotte's husband, someone like the Duke of Annick?"

"Would it be so bad? 'e's a good'n. I 'ave no qualms with 'im. I think Charlotte did herself well marrying 'im, and I only wish 'e had a brother for ye."

"But he's not a good one," she protested. "He's self-absorbed. I won't begrudge Charlotte her choice, as it was her decision to make, but I can't abide that man. If he had a brother, he'd be just like him, and I wouldn't consider the courtship for a minute. He would strip me of my own self before the honeymoon ended. No, I'll never let someone control me or my decisions. I will never be helpless. I don't need anyone," she wrenched her words defensively.

"Don't speak ill of yer new brother-in-law," Cuthbert rebuked. "Your views are tainted by headstrong ways. Ye can be independent and still love. Real love doesn't control, but ye 'ave to let go and let it happen, not hold so tightly that ye don't let it in. Ye must open yerself to it, admit ye need the other person, admit yer only whole with 'em, helpless without 'em. Independent is a selfish way to live. You sacrifice for the other person because ye want them to be happy and ye want the marriage to work. It is selfishness not to make the sacrifice."

Liz felt salty tears sting her eyes. "*My a'th kar*, Papa. I love you. I don't agree, but *my a'th kar*. You loved Mama so much that I think your love has blinded you to what marriage is like when you *don't* love your spouse. I don't believe Annick loves Charlotte. And I have yet to meet a man who could love me as you loved Mama, to love me enough to make the sacrifice." She wiped her eyes with the heel of her palm, sniffling like a schoolgirl at her father's words, for he knew not how much they pained her.

"What about that cousin of his? That Roddam? You spent a fair time together."

Her heart caught in her throat. She stared at her hands knowing her father could see straight into her wounded soul.

Trying not to sob, especially over a silly man and after her speech about not wanting to marry, she finally managed a choked whisper. "He didn't want me."

"Ah. Now we have it." He ambled to her, his voice soft and his arms wide.

Wrapping his arms around her, he laid her head against his chest. She could hear his heart beating steady and strong under her ear. The thumping strengthened her, comforted her woes, just as it had as a child sitting on his lap during story time.

The only man she could truly be herself with was Papa. Powerless wasn't the right word. She couldn't think of a substitute, but the meaning held the same feeling. With Papa, she could be powerless while he slew the dragons for her. Only with Papa.

"Did you want him, my bird?"

"I don't know, Papa," she whimpered. "Yes. No. I liked the idea of him. It's all too late now. He's forever away. I gave him every reason not to want me, but I thought maybe, just maybe he could be the one."

"There it is, Lizzie. He's a dolt not to fall for you." He rubbed her shoulders and kissed her hair as she nuzzled against his shirt. "There's a good girl. I'm happy we found yer worries so we can feed them to the sea. Let's go tomorrow and toss those worries into the sea like."

Lizbeth nodded against his chest.

Chapter 14

Drake stretched out his legs in his favorite chair, slinking into the cushion in a most ungentlemanly manner. Folding his fingers over his chest, he said complacently, "I had her calling my name for three hours straight. Drake! Drake! You young buck. Ride me!"

Sebastian grimaced at the image of Maggie in the throes of pleasure. "I really don't want to know about your exploits with your mistress."

"Listen and learn. You could pick up a trick or two." Drake sighed with satisfaction, reaching for his snuff box. "There's something to be said about being with an older, experienced woman, and especially one beyond childbearing years. I don't have to worry about accidents or those wholly uncomfortable French letters." He shuddered. "Nothing worse than thrusting and feeling nothing but tight sheep skin."

"Wonderful. Now I'll need to pour alcohol into my eyes to burn out that vision."

"Sebastian, what you need to do is get out more. Live a little. Whatever happened to the man who enjoyed ale and women by the bushel? I remember when you used to favor your nights wild with a penchant for fawning ladies. The more the merrier," he added with a waggle of his eyebrows. "You've grown dull and celibate, my wayward cousin. You know, I could always ask Maggie if she has any friends who prefer young grass for grazing."

"Don't you have a new wife you're supposed to be infatuated with, making love to every night?" Sebastian probed, ignoring Drake's absurdity.

Drake waved a hand. "Mother keeps her busy learning her duties. They've been planning dinner parties and socials enough to make my eyes bleed."

"Too busy in the evenings, as well? I would have thought she would have kept you too busy to even think of the marchioness."

"She's exactly what you would expect her to be." Drake scoffed. "Stiff as a board. I like my women *experienced*. If she's not climbing on top to use me like a stable boy, I'm frankly not interested. My wife? Frigid. I tell you, it took me almost an hour to get her to come out from behind the bathing screen on our wedding night. Just not my thing, Sebby."

After turning the snuff box over in his hand for several minutes, he took a pinch, sneezed, then wrinkled his nose. "I'm not overly fond of this blend."

"Be serious," Sebastian prompted.

"Couldn't be more serious." Drake poked at the snuff. "Winston recommended it. Clearly he has terrible taste."

"Focus. We're talking about your bride. We've been home less than a fortnight, and you're already dallying."

"I hardly call Maggie dallying. Mother says it's my *duty*, but I don't want to poke a board." Drake's voice turned nasally in imitation of his mother. "'You must produce an heir. Don't let my sacrifices be in vain. Do your duty to your lineage, Drake.' If I must hear that one more time, I'll throw myself into your moat."

"I don't have a moat. I have meres, and they're all quite shallow."

Drake grinned. "All the better. More dramatic to drown in a few feet of water, don't you think?"

Sebastian rolled his eyes.

"I think, Sebby, we should talk about your bumble with the bluestocking."

"I'd rather not." Sebastian's voice edged with warning.

He didn't want to be reminded of her. The last few weeks had been spent ardently trying to forget her, not that she would be so kind as to get out of his dreams, waking or sleeping.

"Yes, let's. Botched that, didn't you, old man? She was ripe for the picking and clearly fancied you. I thought you'd thank me for all of those times I distracted Charlotte to leave the two of you alone." Drake smirked.

"You did no such thing. You were off fondling your betrothed in dark corners, leaving us in the lurch." Sebastian glared at his cousin. "And I really don't want to talk about it."

"Nonsense. It was all part of my plan. I had my blushing bride to myself and the two of you alone to become better, er, acquainted. What's wrong with you, man? Don't you have any interest at all? If I hadn't seen you in your heyday, plowing the fields of the brothels, I would think you a molly. You aren't a molly, are you? Not that I would judge if you wanted a romp in the stables with the coachman, mind."

"You're unbelievable." Sebastian stood, striding to the cellaret in Drake's billiards room to pour himself a drink.

"What you should have done is get her into one of those dark corners, pretend you dropped something on the floor, and then wrap your hand around her ankle. You could have followed that leg all the way up her thigh, lifting her dress as you went. Then, with that skirt hiked up, you—"

A shoe hurled across the room at Drake's head, narrowly missing him and thudding against the wall behind him.

Drake roared with laughter before rising from his chair, his head shaking as he stood. "You're an imbecile. I'm only being honest with you. You're an imbecile who let go of the best thing that ever happened to you."

Drake swaggered to the mirror above the mantle, licking his hand and running it through his hair. He brushed his hair forward then tussled it. "Date night, old man. Stick around if you like, but I'm off to see my special lady."

Without awaiting a reply, he left Sebastian alone in the room, the door clicking shut behind him.

"Unbelievable," Sebastian said to an empty room. He took a seat and stared into his glass absently.

He didn't need his cousin to remind him. He knew himself a fool. But what choice did he have? He acted in the best interest of Lizbeth, knowing she deserved someone better, someone whole, someone who wasn't broken and beaten by his past. His leaving her behind was for her benefit, no matter how it ripped his heart to shreds.

Despite knowing he made the right decision to walk away, he kicked himself for being a coward. So vividly Liz's image shown in his mind, laughing with twinkling eyes. It seemed such a great loss that her strong spirit, her independent mind, her soulful eyes would one day blend in with the wallpaper as someone's employee. Could she truly be happy as a lady's companion?

She would certainly be happier than married to him.

His night dreams replayed the kiss with variations on the theme. In one dream, she slapped him and stormed away. In another he lifted her against one of the museum display cases and made love to her. In yet another she told him she loved him. His worst dream, which returned more frequently than the others, ended with her so repulsed by the kiss that he turned into a grotesque goblin, chasing her as she screamed in terror.

His day dreams replayed the kiss as it happened, only with him making different choices—asking if he might court her, telling her how deeply he had fallen for her, begging her not to return to Cornwall but to run away with him. As much as he wished he had made a different choice, he knew he had made the correct decision for them both. He had survived a great many traumas, but only because he encased his heart in a steel trap. Sebastian wasn't sure he could survive if he unhinged the steel and left himself vulnerable.

More to the point, he had no right to live happily, not with blood on his hands.

On the edge of his memory, he saw a girl no older than eight. Black hair and dark brown eyes. Knee deep in the ocean, calling his name. His soul despaired at the memory. Violently, he shook his head of the recollection and scorched his throat with whatever liquid was in the glass.

He did not have the right to happiness.

Chapter 15

Days passed. Days of confusion, depression, relief. Days of longing for her, rejecting her, wishing he had done something to keep her, congratulating himself for letting her go.

She had been the first real person he had met. He could have talked to her for hours and never grown tired.

After another week of torturing himself, an idea struck. It came to him while he sat in his study, eyes trained on the tapestries of Arthur and Guinevere. The idea was not without risk, not without scandal, not even without heartbreak.

But he knew he couldn't carry on like this. He couldn't have her but damned if he would live without her.

They lived on opposite sides of the country, so no real harm could come of his idea. The idea, if it worked, would enable him to sustain himself on the merest contact without risking her future happiness or risking rejection. He could reach out and hold onto her from the safety of his stone walls.

It was perfect. Given what a lurch he had left her in, he wasn't at all confident she would respond, but it was worth trying. For sanity's sake.

That very evening, he sat at the desk to write her a letter.

~~Light of my life,~~
~~Darling Liz,~~
~~Lizbeth,~~
Miss Trethow,

I write to you from lonely stone walls, dreaming of your lips. Run away with me.

~~Yours always~~
~~Yours faithfully~~
~~Yours~~
Your humble servant, Lord Roddam

Crumpling the letter, he pulled a fresh sheet for a sensible letter devoid of strikethroughs.

Dear Miss Trethow,

I hope you returned safely to Trevena. Forgive my rudeness at our last parting. I knew not what I did. If you could find it in your heart, then I am

Your humble servant and friend,
Earl of Roddam

Dear Lord Roddam,

You need not ask for my forgiveness, for I will always consider you a friend. Are you well? Do you know how my sister fairs in her new home?

Always your friend,
Lizbeth

Dear Lizbeth,

I was both surprised and pleased to receive your reply. I trust this letter finds you well. Thank you for inquiring of my wellbeing. I am fair to middling.

I was honored with a dinner invitation at Lyonn Manor with the Duchess of Annick &co. I am pleased to inform you she is adjusting well. She has taken a shine to the dowager duchess (known to me as Aunt Catherine, for she is my father's sister). If I'm not mistaken, and I could be in the way of young women, the duchess and her new sister-in-law Lady Mary appear to be the closest of friends. Are they not just two years apart in age?

I detected the aroma of lavender in your letter. Intentional? I remain faithfully

Your dearest,
Sebastian

Sebastian,

I challenge you to guess the scent of this letter.

Thank you for the information about Charlotte. I have received only one letter from her and longed for news.

I have wondered at the kinship between you and Annick. Were your father and his mother close siblings? Did you and Annick grow up together in a close-knit family? I do wish to know more about your family, if you'll permit me the familiarity.

This may strike you as a non-sequitur, but I know you'll be honest and educate me. I know not who else to ask. I must say, it is disconcerting not to be taken seriously by men who know the answers yet refuse to divulge to a woman, telling me instead not to worry my pretty head over such matters and that all is well. All is not well. There remains severity towards my sex when discussing matters of war and politics, even among friends and family. I find myself blind even in an enlightened age. My concern: There is, of late, a stir of local skirmishes, namely between the young men and older generations. Many of the young men have enlisted in the regiment. Not unorthodox, but for some reason unbeknownst to me, the elders disapprove of the enlistment. I do hope there won't be another war in the Americas. Papa is usually forthright about politics, but he says it is all too loathsome to discuss. Enlighten me if you know the cause to the rising hostility in and around my humble parish.

Your Cornish pixie,
Lizbeth

To a silly Cornish pixie indeed,

I feel absurd sniffing paper. Was this previous letter scented with jasmine, perchance? In keeping with your game, I have crushed a scent to these pages. I challenge you, in return, to guess the aroma. Sniff if you dare.

The answer to your question of rising hostility is not simple. While I'm not versed in the dynamics of your parish, I can attest the rumblings in Parliament. We have decided to strengthen our naval fleets and take advantage of France's weakness. Their country is in chaos with one faction attempting to restore the monarchy and the other attempting a radical revolutionary republicanism. We can't possibly know how the shift will affect sentiments towards us, so it is an opportunity to conquer France while it is in turmoil; thus, recruitment of new soldiers has increased. The decision is contentious at best.

Enough of politics. How is Mr. Trethow? I had grown fond of our talks in London and should pen him a letter. I never had a chance to discuss mining. My own fault, I know.

You are most welcome regarding the news of my nearest neighbors and kin. The dinner I attended with your sister would have been far better with you at the table to laugh at my jokes. No one at the table appreciated my cynicism or my puns.

Your bravest,
Lord of a Haunted Castle

Dearest Sebastian, Lord of a Haunted Castle,

I have sniffed your paper in a most lady-like fashion and deduced the smell of grass. In response, I've included eau de mint for your olfactory pleasure.

Is your castle haunted? Does the ghost rattle chains or merely hide your toiletries in ghostly humor?

By the by, I eagerly await stories of your family. What is your aunt like? Did she help your father after your mother passed as my Aunt Hazel did for Papa? Do you have any siblings or cousins aside from Annick and Lady Mary? Don't think I didn't notice your careful avoidance of my questions.

Today was splendid, and I only wish I could have shared such splendor with a dear friend. I visited the cliff overlooking the inaccessible remains of King Arthur's birthplace, a sight to behold. One can sense the mysticism.

Do you favor the sea at all? I don't know what I would do without the sea at my fingertips. How does anyone live in a landlocked city like London? A rhetorical question, of course.

Your favorite cliff sitter,
Lizbeth

Lizbeth of the grassy cliffs,

You've guessed right. I pressed grass against the paper and hoped it would stump you. Your nose knows no bounds.

I hope my castle isn't haunted. I wanted you to imagine me fighting ghosts while reciting poetry. A romantic image, no? I don't believe such an image could be more gallant, unless perhaps I battled windmills. I hope you'll enjoy the humor of the windmill reference.

I would have enjoyed sharing the view with you, although I may have been too distracted by you to admire ruins. If you didn't blush like a proper miss, then I have failed at flattery.

Should you ever visit, I would love to take you north into the Scottish highlands. The vistas are spectacular, and if you were brave, we could hunt the mighty haggis. You're missing opportunities to explore rugged lands while hiding out in your pirate cove. In the wilds of the north, I am

Your haggis hunter,
Sebastian

Sebastian,

Do you think me so gullible as to believe there's such a creature as a haggis? You're teasing me, and I shan't fall for it.

Your flattery, however, succeeded. Blush achieved. My only consolation is that you cannot see it to enjoy the victory.

I will not reproach you for not answering my more personal questions, as they were presumptuous of me. All the same, I am disappointed not to learn more about your family. Could you at least humor me as to how you and Annick came to be such good friends when the two of you are so very different? I am

Yours,
Lizbeth

To the fairest flower,

I have, admittedly, intentionally omitted information about family. It is not a subject on which I wish to dwell. I will answer your question about Annick, however. He is, after all, your new brother-in-law, and despite your dislike of him, he deserves your favor.

Annick has a heart of gold, and I am forever in his debt. I hesitate to write the origin of our friendship, for it does not shine me in the best light. I do not wish you to think less of me since there is not much to recommend me as it is.

I grew up estranged from my relatives. I met Drake for the first time when he saved my life. He developed a habit of rescuing me over the coming years.

I believe I was around sixteen or thereabouts when I left home with no intentions of returning. My feet took me into the duchy where I found a pub. I did the only sensible thing I knew to do, drink away my sorrows. At sunrise, Drake found me face-first in a ditch, battered and bruised, heavily intoxicated, and drowning in mere feet of water. He saved me from whatever fate awaited me in that dank hole.

These next words are difficult for me to write, as I keep the darkest parts of my past under lock and key. I do him a disservice by saying he only saved me from a ditch, for, you see, before he found me, I had no will to live.

I stayed with him until Aunt Catherine notified my father of my whereabouts. My cousin is a good man, despite his pomp. He is mostly show, you should know. He has hidden depths beneath the vanity and lace.

We have been close since the incident, and I have been reunited with my family since my father's death. One of the initial attractions to restoring Dunstanburgh is its proximity to my family. It is naught but 15 miles from Lyonn Manor.

I recently finished reading The Castle of Otranto *and am starting* The Surprising Adventures of Baron Munchausen. *Have you read either by chance? I would welcome your thoughts. To this day, I remain*

Your greatest admirer,
Sebastian

To my admirer from afar,

I am touched you shared the personal memory. Annick does sound more than fluff from your estimation. I wish I could thank him for saving you, for without him, you would not be in my life. Why were you estranged from your family? You've not mentioned an uncle. Did he pass some time ago?

I have not read either of the books you mentioned in your correspondence. Shall I? I will check the circulating library, although our collection is dismally small. I've been reading Thomas Clarkson's essay on slavery and am currently reading William Blake's Song of Innocence. *I doubt you'll have heard of Blake. Papa met him at an intellectual meeting this Season, and he was kind enough to gift Papa a book.*

Papa says Blake has ideas about women's rights to happiness and marrying without love that moved him to tears and helped him better understand my views. While I found the poems beautiful, they are tragically sad and hit close to home, for a great many of the tin mines in Cornwall still use children as laborers. Speaking of slavery, Papa wants me to inform you he has been working with William Wilberforce MP on a bill to abolish the slave trade. I believe he valued your conversation in London and would wish to know your thoughts. This is where I prompt you to write to Papa.

Yours,
Lizbeth

My dearest Lizbeth,

I don't wish to be a naysayer, but the bill will never pass the House of Lords. I have penned a letter to your father, as requested, with humble insight that may strengthen his cause. In the letter, I warn him that while there are potential advocates of such a bill in the Lords, the current majority will never pass it.

You'll be interested to know, I live not far from the North Sea. You missed a coastal walk today that would rival your cliff of myths. All it lacked was you by my side.

I have enclosed with this letter a gift. You should know that I am

Always yours,
Sebastian

Chapter 16

With a bonnet for a pillow and the grass for a chaise, Lizbeth lounged at the top of a cliff, re-reading Sebastian's letters for the hundredth time. The edges were creased and the ink smudged. He had written faithfully every week.

The autumn winds of mid-August and the song of the seagulls dampened all sounds aside the rustle of letters in her hands. The letters had become her lifeline to a fairy tale. For all her dogged determination to forget him, the possibility of a second chance began to overshadow her deepest fears of unrequited love.

Perhaps he hadn't spurned her after all. Perhaps she had read too much into his actions after the kiss, expected too much from him. His renewed attentions enlivened the fantasy of the perfect mate. These letters made her giddy, fluttering her heart as an eclosed butterfly.

It all seemed ridiculously silly to be infatuated with a man who twice had turned his back after sharing moments of intimacy, but she justified his actions so as not to spoil his renewed attentions. After all, he may feel the same reservations as she, the same fears of commitment, all of which could be overcome in time as they established trust.

She laughed to learn her sister lived in a home named Lyonn Manor when she would have guessed Sebastian would live in a Lyonn Manor and Drake in a Duckling Park. Unlike his many letters, her sister had written only once, informing Liz the new marriage was going splendidly, better than she could have dreamed. Liz doubted her sister's professions, but she did respect her sister's decision to make the best of her choice without hints of regret.

She held Sebastian's letter to her nose, the scent of him lingering to the pages. She imagined him sitting on a stone throne in his castle, his mane loose about his shoulders, lips curved in a sardonic smile, affectionately seducing her with his eyes.

The plan to be a lady's companion was still viable, certainly the most realistic plan, more so than a future with him. But what if Sebastian renewed his attentions with fervor? What if he increased his flirtations? What if he showed up at her doorstep to sweep her off her feet?

She feared hoping too deeply. He could close the door again at any moment. Or even worse, he could continue to write to her forever into their dotage, only ever teasing, only ever a friend.

All her foot stomping that he would only ever be a friend now stirred anxiety that her original wish may be granted. She didn't want to be proven right. She wanted to be proven that love was real, that fairy tales do come true.

As if to declare his affection, three gifts accompanied his most recent letter.

Two custom bound books, *Estoire de Merlin* and *Suite du Merlin*, both written in French and both containing the handwritten inscription "To My Lady of the Lake," had already been read and re-read enough times she could recite from them by heart.

She liked the *Estoire de Merlin* the best, for it contained the early history of Arthur and Merlin. The *Suite du Merlin* introduced Excalibur and the Lady of the Lake. She needed to acquaint herself better with the legend to keep up with Sebastian's passion for the lore, especially if that passion had helped him see the light during a time of darkness, as he had mentioned in London.

The third gift lay against her chest, a miniature painting the size of her thumb of the churning sea with hurling mist and foam mid-splash against a rock.

He had given her the sea.

On the days she wore her cameo, she slipped the miniature into her stays so it would remain close to her heart. On other days, she fastened it to a chain to wear as a necklace. Sebastian understood her kinship to the sea. For a man to recognize her love for the sea surely meant him destined for more than friendship.

Salt permeated the air, tickling her nose. Lizbeth closed her eyes and listened to the wind whipping around the cliff, the water licking the rocks, the sheep bleating in the pasture.

Rising from euphoria, she packed the now empty basket with her letters and the *Estoire de Merlin*, donning her bonnet. The sun played hide and seek in the low-lying clouds above, threatening to overcast the hills and valley below.

Anxious to reach home before the rain, she started on her trek. She wanted to write him a letter before dinner, telling of her exploits with the miners. Three times a week she brought them baskets of food. The week before, she had done more than bring sandwiches, pasties, and well wishes. She spent every morning of her visit that week with a small hammer in hand working alongside the Bal Maidens as they broke apart the ore brought up by the men in the mines.

While Mama and Papa had always taught her respect for the workers, it was Sebastian she thought of when she made the decision to dirty her hands and soil her gown.

His words of building houses and plowing fields sunk deep into her soul, showing her there was more to being a kind employer than bringing treats and smiles. The nights she spent crying over Blake's poetry and listening to Papa talk about the slavery abolition bill strengthened her resolve to do more for the miners so they would know appreciation for their work.

There was still a difference, despite her good intentions. She could work for a few hours, then go home to comfort and a lady's maid. Her livelihood didn't depend on a day's worth of dirty and dangerous work. The crossing of the line between master and servant was a step in the right direction, all the same, and she knew Sebastian would appreciate her efforts, although she didn't want her kindness to be construed as bragging.

No sooner had she walked into Teghyiy Hall than she spotted a letter from Charlotte. The ducal seal emblazoned in red wax distinguished it from the other missives. She set her basket and bonnet on a table and shrugged out of her pelisse, laying it next to the other discarded items.

As she picked up the letter, Papa descended the stairs.

"*Myttin da*, my bird. Good mornin'! 'ave ye been at the mines all mornin' like?" He squeezed his widened girth between the snug arms of his favorite chair.

"I have. Eseld should be having her baby soon. I caught her hammering again and walked her home myself for rest and a fresh cuppa. I told her no working until the baby comes."

"Ah. Old 'abits die hard, and Eseld is some hard worker. Is that another letter from yer man then?" He nodded to the still unopened letter in her hand.

"He's not my man, Papa. And no, it's a letter from Charlotte. Would you like me to read it aloud?"

"Ya! Read it, my dove. Let's see what she says now that she's paused in 'er busy life to send word. Maybe a happy word about a babe herself, eh?" He winked. "Wouldna' be grand? I'd be a grandpapa!"

Liz broke the seal and unfolded the stationary with the engraved house name in gold under the ducal cornet.

My dearest sister, Lizbeth,

I fear I've made a terrible mistake. I loathe it here. Drake ignores me as though I were not here. I see him only at dinner because his mother requires attendance. I am nothing more than her puppet. I despise her. She controls everything I do, watching me, berating me, reminding me of my duties. I hate it. I hate it. I hate it. Please come to me. You'll know what to do. I've taken the liberty to send a missive to Aunt Hazel, along with a banknote to cover costs of transport, inns, et cetera. Please say you'll come, Lizbeth. Awaiting your response, I am

Your grieved sister,
Charlotte Annick

After a tangible silence, Papa spoke first. "We can be assured never to say he's a pinch-penny."

"Oh, Papa. I feared this would happen. I was doubtful about her first letter, but I was so proud of her for taking the situation into her own hands. There's nothing I can do for her now!" Lizbeth waved her hands in exasperation, letter clenched in her fist.

"Go to her. Bring a piece of home to her. Help her turn this into a life she'll love. Only you can do that, my bird, and Charlotte knows that. While yer there, see about sweethearting that fellow of yours."

"Papa! Charlotte is grieving and all you can think of is that?"

He shrugged exaggeratedly, smiling wickedly. "Charlotte made 'er choice and will soon see how 'appy she can be. A babe is what she needs ter set things ter right. You, my bird, 'ave a second chance to snare that man o' yers. I expect the first letter from ye to be a marriage announcement like."

Chapter 17

The coachman rapped against the top of the carriage. In an unintelligible northern accent, he shouted, "Look tae ye left, marm! Ye's'll sae herry coos! Bet ye no' be sae'n'em afore!"

Lizbeth stared wide eyed at Aunt Hazel. "What did that man say?"

The coachman continued bellowing at them. "Fella' breeds 'em, brought dern from Scotland. No' but a wee bit farther north ye's'll sae wild whi' chattel."

Hearing only a series of grunting from the man, Liz raised her brows at her aunt.

"I believe, love, he's talking about cows and cattle, though I've no idea why. Where did the good Lord send our Charlotte, I wonder." Hazel peered outside, on the lookout for peculiar cows.

After a fortnight of traveling rough roads, first by Walter's ambling carriage from Exeter to Birmingham, and then by post to expedite their travel, Lizbeth was desperate to stretch her legs with a walk and sit without being bounced and jostled like a rag doll.

At least she enjoyed seeing so much of the countryside. She did not, however, enjoy seeing the inside of the country inns along the way. Her aunt was right; bringing their own linens and cutlery for the overnight restorations saved them from a dirty fate. They had made good timing, all things considered, but this last leg of the journey had her feeling cramped.

Her legs ached, her back stiff, her priority a hot bath. Never again would she dare complain about the much shorter ride from London to Cornwall. Within the hour, she would have the ducal estate in sight.

She gazed out the window to admire the sea of heather, a blanket of fading purple on the land, the summer blooms shading to dull brown in patches.

They had passed undulating dales, oceans of flowers, small and flat hills, bubbling rivers along valleys, sunken hollows, brown moorlands, and now a vibrantly colored painting of wide meadows with clumps of autumn leaves nestled between high, rolling hills.

Lizbeth didn't know what to expect when she arrived. It had been over two weeks since she received the letter from Charlotte. She could only imagine what state her sister would be in after two more weeks of misery. Much discussion had occurred during the trip, as Aunt Hazel and Lizbeth tried to develop a plan of action to help Charlotte come to terms with her new life.

They couldn't save her from a poor decision. All they could offer was support and guidance on how to accept her decision and move forward with her life despite an inattentive husband and overbearing mother-in-law.

Walter and Hazel wanted to convince her to fall in love and make the duke love her in return, but that had been met with boos from Liz, as no one could *make* someone fall in love. Shushing Liz's naysaying, Hazel said, in time, Charlotte and Annick would come to an understanding, just as all *ton* spouses did, and with a little encouragement from Charlotte, love would blossom.

That morning, over breakfast at the Black Swan Inn, they jotted a brief note to the manor of their pending arrival. Liz hadn't slept a wink thanks to the boisterous voices from downstairs. Her stomach was knotted and her head ached.

The carriage banged and groaned as it descended a steep hill. Through a gap in a cedar grove, Liz glimpsed tall black spires, but before she could nudge Aunt Hazel to look, the view disappeared behind the tree tops.

Along the road, she spotted other hidden gems peeking through trees, a narrow river with a little walking bridge, a few garden follies, and a columned rotunda. The park surrounding the manor was rustic, naturalistic, with hints of luxury, rewarding those who investigated the wilderness walks. As much as she should be thinking of her sister, she already itched to explore.

After another turn, the manor rose in sight of the carriage, a gothic palace. Rounded towers ornamented the otherwise flat-fronted facade; spires reached skyward; a staircase tower wound upwards three stories to the right of the front door. Liz counted fifteen windows across the front, but part of the house was obscured by a handful of trees, so there could have been more. A far cry from their humble five-bay hall.

Hazel tapped Lizbeth's knee with her fan. "Lizbeth, darling, close your mouth before you drool on your dress. You're gawking."

Liz leaned back against the seat, embarrassed. The clop-clop of the horses slowed as they descended the drive. A row of servants standing at the front awaited the coach's approach.

"Oh, Aunt Hazel. I had no idea it would be so grand. I feel silly for not expecting this."

"Imagine living here. No less than 200 servants I would wager." Hazel fidgeted with the plumes on her wide-brimmed hat.

"I wouldn't want to live here. I would feel insignificant." Liz touched her cameo to draw inner strength.

"We'll live in the finest luxury has to offer for the next month, perhaps a touch longer, depending on Charlotte's state, and then it'll be home again before winter."

The carriage lurched to a halt at the queue of servants. A footman rushed to the door to place steps and help down the women.

Charlotte stepped forward, beaming at her guests. Beside her stood Annick, as laced as ever with skin-tight buckskins and Hessian boots with silver tassels. Liz groaned at the sight of him.

On the other side stood two ladies Liz had never met, but it wasn't difficult to surmise who was who. A haughty looking albeit impressively handsome older woman with a gold handled cane stood next to a bashful girl who could barely be sixteen years of age. The family resemblance was startling. Both ladies favored Sebastian with raven black hair, dark eyes, and the aristocratic nose, but their frames favored Annick, all with striking lithe figures.

It took a few moments to recover from the dowager duchess' handsomeness, tall and graceful with high cheekbones and commanding eyes. She defined elegance and demanded admiration. The closer Lizbeth drew to her, the better she could see the signs of age, but such were limited and sparse, a bit of gray lacing the black hair, a few creases between her brows and around her mouth.

Next to her, Charlotte looked simply pretty, which Liz found shocking since Charlotte was considered the beauty of the coast back home.

Charlotte approached them, arms stretched to clasp hands. "I'm so happy you've arrived. Please, come meet my mother- and sister-in-law." Holding their hands, she led Hazel and Liz towards the ladies.

Lady Mary eyed them curiously, Annick smiled gaily, and the dowager duchess scowled.

"My two favorite beauties!" Annick pulled both into an unexpected hug that defied genteel greetings. "Allow me, my wife." He turned towards his mother, an arm wrapped around Lizbeth's shoulders. "Mother, this is Miss Trethow. And this is Hazel, The Lady Collingwood." He turned back to Hazel and Liz, relinquishing his grip at last. "And this is my mother, The Dowager Duchess of Annick, and my sister, Lady Mary."

The widowed duchess condescended to incline her head a nearly imperceptible fraction of an inch.

Lady Mary's welcome tumbled in a waterfall of excitement. "I've heard ever so much about you both. I believe we'll all be the best of friends!"

"You both must be exhausted," Charlotte said. "Your luggage carriage has yet to arrive, but I'll have you shown to your rooms for a hot bath all the same. We'll await you in the Red Drawing Room."

When a footman escorted Liz to the Red Drawing Room, she discovered Aunt Hazel already in conversation with Charlotte, Annick, and Lady Mary. The dowager duchess declined to join them until dinner.

Dark, rich reds filled every corner of the room, from the window curtains, valences, and window seats, all the way to the red Morocco Leather chair covers and the motif wallpaper within recessed panels. If she hazarded a guess, she would say the room used to be a grand ballroom repurposed into a drawing room.

The group sat in the far corner of the room, looking a tad cramped in comparison to the openness of the room. The sitting area encircled a round table in front of a marble fireplace. Tea and treats waited. Without missing a beat in conversation, Charlotte readied Liz's cuppa.

Liz sipped the sweet nectar of the gods, closing her eyes to savor taste and warmth. Divinity.

Annick stood next to Charlotte's chair, one hand on her shoulder. Unabashedly, his gaze swept over Liz, lingering at her mouth.

With a smirk, he said, "You'll find today peaceful because I've decided to delay my message. Brace yourself for tomorrow."

Liz looked at the faces around her, all of which appeared as bewildered as her. "Pardon? What message?"

"To Lord Dunderhead, of course. My imbecile cousin wanted to be here for your arrival. I would give my best horse to see his expression if he knew

I told you that." Annick winked. "I've decided to delay notification until tomorrow so you have an opportunity to rest and visit with Charlotte first. I know you're dying to hear how well she's getting on. Becoming quite the little duchess!" Annick beamed, resting his hand against the back of Charlotte's neck.

"I appreciate your thoughtfulness, Your Grace, but I don't know why Lord Roddam would wish to be present for our arrival. We aren't well acquainted." Liz swallowed against the lump in her throat.

She set the tea cup and saucer on the table before her shaking hands belied her words. While her aunt knew how she felt, she certainly didn't know Lady Mary, hadn't spoken about it to Charlotte, and most assuredly wouldn't dare ever utter such feelings to the duke.

Annick had the audacity to laugh. "Deny it if you'd like, but I know all your dirty little secrets. The two of you have been corresponding since London. I'm scandalized just thinking about it!"

Charlotte gasped. "Drake, enough! Lizbeth isn't accustomed to your humor. She's mortified."

"She knows I mean well." Annick winked. "And why shouldn't she know the truth? He's talked of nothing else for a month. If he plays it shy while you're here, I'll give him a good thrashing for your viewing pleasure."

Liz could do nothing but swallow again and nod self-consciously. She felt great sorrow for Charlotte if this is how her husband behaved in company. Her distaste of and humiliation at the conversation was almost overshadowed by her desperation to know what Sebastian had been saying about her.

Aunt Hazel saved Lizbeth any further embarrassment by drawing everyone's attention to the paintings. "Charlotte, love, tell us about the portraits."

Charlotte shrugged off Annick's hand to walk over to the two largest paintings, one clearly of a young dowager duchess. "All of these paintings are of Drake's father's family, so I'm afraid I don't know much about them, but these two are of Mama Catherine and her husband Marcus Mowbrah the Duke of Annick. She was only sixteen when this portrait was painted, the new bride of His Grace."

Annick joined her, his hand returning to the back of Charlotte's neck. "Tell the story right, love of my life. My mother married at sixteen a man almost thirty years her senior. He was a dirty old man, wasn't he?" He roared with laughter, embarrassing them all. "No one says no to a duke when he wants a bride. But if you know my mother, you must wonder whose decision it really was, for she was the most coveted woman of the region, and no one says no to her, not even a duke. As much as I enjoy a joke at my father's expense, I suspect it was my mother who trapped him, not the other way around."

He touched the gold frame of his mother's portrait.

"I look forward to getting to know your mother." Aunt Hazel said with sincerity.

Drake's response surprised them all. "Right. Now is where I take my leave. No one has to say it, but I know you're all dying to gossip like twittering maids. Come, Mary. I know you want to stay, and they won't be rude enough to eject you, but let's let the family alone. I'll let you ride my horse if you promise not to pout." The duke frilled his lace sleeves and reached for his snuff box as he walked to the double doors.

After an audible sniff, he waved a hand over his head to signal the reluctant Mary to follow him. Mary nodded to them, blushed, and scurried after her brother.

Not until the drawing room doors closed did they turn to Charlotte with quizzical eyes.

"I'm so happy you're both here!" Charlotte's cheeks were rosy. "I haven't been this happy since my wedding!"

"Out with it," commanded Hazel. She lifted her lorgnette to study her niece. "That mother-in-law of yours looked severe enough, and your husband couldn't be crasser if he tried. An abomination to gentility, but I suppose when one's a duke, one can say and do most anything. Now, how are you, love? We came as fast as we could, sacrificing comfort for speed."

"Oh dear. I never meant either of you any discomfort. I spoke out of turn in my letter. I should have been patient. All is well now, can't you see? I couldn't be happier!"

Hazel's eyes narrowed, her lorgnette lowering half an inch. "Don't speak rubbish. Your letter was most expressive."

Charlotte's neck flushed, her eyes looking down at her wringing hands. "I'm so ashamed for writing that. Everything really is better. I've spent the past two weeks soul searching, and I've come to terms with my new life. In a way, it's what you've always wanted, Lizbeth—independence. I have an allowance and privacy. I've even made peace with Mama Catherine in a fashion. She means well. She's still quite bossy, but that's to be expected of someone in our position."

Charlotte paused, looking back and forth between Hazel and Lizbeth as though questioning if they believed her. She continued, "I've had ever so much fun these past weeks. I've designed a meal plan for our kitchen to serve the needy in the villages. I've written invitations for a shooting party this autumn, hosted a bazaar for the tenantry, and I've even arranged the seats for the dinner party we'll be having in honor of your visit. There's ever so much to do, but I'm learning."

They sat in silence, Charlotte still wringing her hands, Hazel still squinting at her niece, and Lizbeth gaping. She was dubious. Had Charlotte come to terms with her new role, or was she struggling to speak her true feelings in person?

Lizbeth probed. "What of Drake? Your letter mentioned he's ignoring you. Is the marriage unhappy?"

Charlotte bit her bottom lip before she looked up from her hands. "All is much the same with him. I'm not overly fraught by it anymore because I realize I can focus on my duties. In a way his behavior is a blessing. I can live my own life."

Hazel lowered her lorgnette. "Is that what you want, my love?"

"I've never wanted love. You both know that. I've only ever sought a good match, and I have that. Now, though, I find myself wanting more. In many ways it is a blessing to have him away more than he is here, but I find myself wanting to *know* my husband. Let me be clear. He has never mistreated me, and even if he did it would be within his right, but he hasn't. He has shown me nothing but patience and kindness. I just wish, somehow, I could be his *wife*, not his object. Is that selfish of me?"

Lizbeth went to her sister. Perching on the arm of Charlotte's chair, she embraced her. "It's not selfish. You deserve happiness."

"I thought I could live without love, but I'm lonely all the time. I shouldn't feel lonely, for I have Mary, but it's not the same." Charlotte didn't cry or show any signs of despair, none of the remorse of the letter, only a soft sadness, a mix of acceptance and longing. She leaned her head against Lizbeth.

"We're here now, and you won't be lonely," Liz said, kissing the top of Charlotte's head. "Soon you'll make new friends in the area. I imagine you'll serve on all types of committees and stretch those wings of yours, my little butterfly."

Hazel chimed in. "Make him love you."

"Pardon?" the sisters said in unison.

"Make him love you. He's a young man still wet behind the ears. He doesn't know what he wants only what he thinks he wants, so teach him that you're what he wants. Seduce that man."

"AUNTIE!" Charlotte shrieked. "I, I couldn't!"

"Seduce him well enough, and he will fall in love with you. If you can stomach the embarrassment, I will share my best kept secrets, although not in the presence of Lizbeth."

Charlotte stuttered while Lizbeth flushed.

Liz cleared her throat and turned to Charlotte. "I'm proud of you. I really am. I came here worried you had dissolved into depression over what is out of your control rather than controlling what you can in your new life. Make the best of it, and you'll be as happy as any of us can ever hope to be. I'm so very proud of you, Charlotte."

"Thank you, Lizzie. I'm so happy you're both here. Auntie, if you don't mind terribly, I'd like to invite you to my private parlor this evening after dinner. Maybe you could divulge those secrets."

For the rest of the evening, Liz was silently reminded of why she had never wanted to marry. Being tied to a man like Drake seemed a fate worse than death to her. Maybe it was for the best that Sebastian hadn't done something rash in London.

Chapter 18

A heavy rain pelted the windows of Lyonn Manor. The wind howled, blowing the rain sideways, upwards, and back down.

Sebastian tapped a riding crop against his leg, puddles forming on the marble floor around him.

"This way, Your Lordship," the stern-eyed butler quipped without visibly moving his lips.

Tucking the crop under his arm, he followed the servant from the foyer to the double doors of the Blue Drawing Room, leaving wet footprints in his wake.

"The Earl of Roddam," announced the butler.

Sebastian walked into an obnoxiously blue room to a welcoming sight: Lizbeth rising from her chair.

His pulse spiked.

Devil take it. She was more beautiful than he remembered. Such a pity he couldn't close the gap between them and pull her into an embrace that would inspire poets for centuries. *This time,* he told himself, *I will not bungle this.*

"I say, man, you're dripping on my rug." Drake stood by the hearth holding a forgotten snuff box, clearly diverted. "I sent word but never expected you to brave high water. You're soaked to the bone."

He blanched at Drake's words and bowed to all in the room, which thankfully was a small crowd.

Liz, Drake, Charlotte, and Hazel, no signs of Aunt Catherine or Mary.

The minute he had received notice of their arrival, he had made haste, not thinking of how it must look to take flight on his horse in a torrential downpour. His original plan had been to stand in the receiving line when their post turned down the drive, but the rain had dashed that dream.

"Good heavens, man. I'm sure neither of our guests wants to spend the afternoon with a drowned rat. Have my valet see to drying your clothes." Turning to Charlotte, Drake commanded with a nod, "Ring for additional refreshments."

Sebastian's eyes flitted to Liz. Her eyes brightened, her lips smiled, and her body leaned forward as if she too wanted to embrace him.

She couldn't possibly be as excited to see him as he was to see her, especially after he left her bewildered in London. They may have corresponded since then, but he envisioned a long road ahead in regaining her trust. Hell, he had a long road just to silence his inner voice, that ever-present reminder of his unworthiness.

After running from her once, he wouldn't do it again. Inner voice be damned. He would not bungle this.

Drake interrupted his thoughts, as well as his fixed stare on the enchanting Lizbeth. "If you stand there one minute longer ruining my rug, I will assume you've not come to see these beauties, but rather have come to rescue me from polite conversation. I will be forced to take you into my study for the remainder of the afternoon. Consider that a threat."

"I shall return momentarily." He eyed Lizbeth again, another lingering look he suspected was not lost on present company, and certainly not lost on the baroness who raised her lorgnette, her lips curving into a sly half-smile full of impish suggestion.

With another bow, he left the room, dancing past the glowering butler. He bounded through the west gallery, up the winding stairwell, down the bedroom corridor, and into Drake's private rooms.

Why hadn't he thought to keep an extra set of clothes at the manor for such occasions? Because it was oh-so-frequent that he rode his horse hell for leather over fifteen miles of sideways rain just to see a woman, he thought dryly.

Without another set of clothes, he would have to wait for his to dry, which could take hours. The alternative was less appealing, but his only viable option. He would attempt to fit into something of Drake's. The problem? The duke's clothes were tailored for a slenderer frame. Nigh impossible. What had he expected would happen after riding through a rainstorm? Hell and damnation.

He found Drake's valet in the dressing room cleaning Drake's shaving set. The valet looked up in surprise to see Sebastian barreling towards him, cursing a string of profanities.

After more time than he cared to spend in a dressing room, Sebastian barked at the valet, "Get on with it. How long does it take to knot a cravat?"

"My apologies, Your Lordship, but His Grace prefers the *trone d'Amour*. I assumed you would, as well." The squat man with thatched brows fiddled with the neckerchief.

"Do I look like a man who flaunts flouncy cravats, much less cravats so starched I can't turn my head? I'd prefer you tie an Osbaldeston." Any more time wasted on such ridiculousness and Sebastian would be hard pressed not to return to the room without a cravat.

"Yes, my lord, but you'll pardon my saying, my lord, that at the present time, you do look like a man who would prefer a more elegant style." The valet worked at untying the knot of the foppish cravat.

Sebastian cursed at the mirror. Surely the wet clothes would be superior to this. He didn't fit in Drake's clothing, as he knew he wouldn't. While the two men may be of similar height, they were not of similar build, style considerations be damned.

The clothes, especially the breeches, stretched taut across his physique, straining at the buttons. He tried to adjust himself behind the fall flap, but there wasn't much he could do to disguise his parts.

As long as Lizbeth didn't smile, flirt, or move, he may survive without disgracing himself, but one sensual twist of her lips could be his undoing and cause for an embarrassing afternoon indeed.

"I look like a court jester," he grumbled to the reflection, a frightening sight of silk and lace.

"You'll pardon me again, my lord, when I say you look most elegant and youthful." The valet replaced the starched fabric at Sebastian's neck with a softer, thinner linen.

"I'm neither elegant nor youthful." Sebastian scowled. "Well, perhaps still youthful if you consider one and thirty young, but never elegant, at least not in this dandified sense. I look and feel ridiculous."

"Please, try not to flex your shoulders." The valet stepped back to admire his handiwork. "You are the image of sophistication. Care for His Grace's scented pomade?"

Sebastian snorted.

Turning from the mirror, he tested the length of his stride against the strain of the breeches and coat. So help him, if anyone laughed, he would climb back on his horse and leave.

He jetted across the bedroom corridor, down the winding stairs, through the west gallery, and into the unpalatably blue room, narrowly missing the disgruntled butler carrying a tea tray. Dancing past the disapproving countenance, he stepped towards the group, immediately regretting his decision not to wait for his clothes to dry.

Drake's face lit with amusement. The baroness eyed him with lusty appreciation. Charlotte hid a smile behind her hand. Lizbeth looked nothing less than bemused.

"Well, well, well, cousin." Drake wolf whistled. "Don't you look…dashing. Less sullen bachelor and more man-about-town. But let's ask the audience, shall we? Lizbeth?"

She whipped her head towards Drake, eyes wide.

"What do you think of his new look? The tailoring accentuates his, er, features, don't you think?" Drake drawled.

Sebastian would kill him. Next time he had Drake alone, he would wrap his hands around that laced neck and strangle him.

Lizbeth turned to Sebastian, a tell-tale blush creeping up her neck.

Don't smile. Please, don't smile. He chanted to himself. The humiliation of being stared at was enough. The last element he needed was lust. He tugged at the coat self-consciously.

Liz studied him thoughtfully while Hazel and Charlotte tittered. Then, to his dismay, she declared, "Upon reflection, I must agree he does look rather dashing."

The corners of her mouth curved upwards.

His body responded in kind.

The only safe route was a mad dash to a chair before anyone witnessed the result of her assessment. Silently blaspheming, he made the mad dash. No better than a randy schoolboy. A damned randy schoolboy with his first infatuation.

Oblivious to the entire exchange, Charlotte poured him a cup of tea. "You're just in time for a game of loo. I've decided it the perfect game for a rainy afternoon."

He reached for the offered tea. "I mean no offense, but I'm not much of a loo player."

Crestfallen, she pleaded with Drake in a single glance.

Drake wrapped his arm about her shoulders and said, "I'm anxious to have an audience with Hazel regarding the upcoming dinner party. Why don't you entertain us at the pianoforte, dear wife?" He purred. "You have such extraordinary skill."

Glad for a hot liquid after the sharp rain, Sebastian savored his tea while Charlotte and Drake argued with furtive glances. He hoped Charlotte would take Drake's suggestion, for while he wouldn't find a more intimate setting than a room full of onlookers, at least he could speak with Lizbeth without being overheard.

Lizbeth appeared as anxious as he felt. She fidgeted with the embroidery on her dress, circling the embossed thread with one finger then the next. They exchanged glances.

Time slowed. He could hear the tick of the mantel clock.

Another sip of tea. Then another.

With a huff, Charlotte marched to the pianoforte at the opposite end of the room. Drake missed not a beat, pulling his chair next to the baroness and launching into discussion without acknowledging either Lizbeth or Sebastian. Subtlety was never one of Drake's assets. Matchmaking cad.

Lizbeth cast him a knowing look before retreating to one of the far windows.

He was about to follow when the sway of her hips gave him pause. The dress clung enticingly to her curves, snug around the hips, loose down to the ankles, sending a renewed wave of warmth through his body.

He remained seated, feeling conspicuous, though no one paid him any mind. Through the last dregs of his tea, he willed himself into submission. Did she have to look so damned alluring? So damned kissable? Stunning came to mind as an apt description of her.

The dress color showcased the auburn of her hair, and he knew without having to see that it would enhance the color of her eyes. Green suited her. His stomach knotted; his muscles tensed; his loins burned.

He continued to sit, teacup in hand, as he steadied his nerves and tried to think about politics instead of kissing her. The last time he had spoken to her, she had been in his arms, her lips reddened by his.

Ah! This would not do. An entire summer spent thinking of nothing but her had left him depraved. He refocused his mind, imagining the House of Lords and white wigs. Political thoughts doused him in metaphorical cold water. *Don't think about her lips. Don't think about her hips. White wigs. White wigs. White wigs.*

Confident he had himself under control, he returned his cup and saucer to the tray and approached her.

She stared at the gray backdrop outside. The sky had turned even blacker than when he arrived.

"I hadn't expected to see you again so soon," he said in way of greeting. "I presume you'll stay until November?"

"We're planning to stay for only a month, actually," she admitted.

Her words sank in. One month. Did he have only one month in which to act?

"Only one month? But the journey roundtrip takes as long as that."

One month wouldn't possibly be enough time. It would take three weeks to have the banns read, assuming she said yes, of course, leaving only one week, this week, in which to woo her, and he was already down one day because of Drake's delayed message.

One week wouldn't work at all. He had to make amends for London, build her trust, proceed with an official courtship, and finally propose, all before the three weeks of banns. In a pinch, he could get a special license, but even that would take several days since it would involve riding all the way to London and back.

He didn't even know if she would reconsider her plan to remain a spinster, much less accept him as a suitor. He needed time. At least two months, maybe three.

Devil take it.

"The trip here is long and the visit short, but it's worth it for someone I love," she said, her meaning cryptic.

His breath hitched.

Don't be foolish, he scolded himself. She meant her sister, of course, not him.

"Ah, yes, I understand," he responded, feeling dim-witted.

"Do you?" she asked, raising her eyebrows.

He raised his eyebrows in return. Attempting to sound articulate and focused, he clarified, "I know you share a close relationship with your sister. Why not stay longer?"

God, she was beautiful. Had she been this stunning in London, or had the summer in Cornwall brightened her beauty?

"Charlotte asked me to visit so that I might help her with a project. She is busy with her fetes and socials, so we shan't overstay our welcome. But she needed me, and so here I am. I have to confess I think my aunt has been of more service than I have been." She laughed. "It might seem silly to come all this way for only one month, but loved ones are the most important people in my life. I will always place their happiness before my own, because, in a way, their happiness is my happiness. Don't you agree?"

His chest tightened. Her words, regardless of how poetic, left an acrid taste in his mouth, for their meaning unearthed his loneliness, his bitterness about his life. If only she meant those words for him. No one had ever felt that way about him.

His voice strained, he replied, "I would like to think that I, too, would do anything, but I have no experience on which to base an answer."

A crease formed between her eyebrows. "You've never known love, not even from family?" she inquired, her tone both sorrowful and curious.

He shook his head. This was not the conversation he had anticipated. All his plans to talk of traveling, poetry, and politics, and she wanted to talk about love and family. Part of him wanted to take this opportunity to turn the tide in his favor in preparation for courtship, but her words of a loving family resonated too close to his demons, striking the deepest chords of his soul.

When he spoke, his voice was throaty, guttural. "My life has been tumultuous, my family built on obedience and status. I admire that you would do so much for your sister's happiness. I am envious."

After studying him, she turned back to the window, deep in thought. The rain lessened its beating against the glass to a patter, the sound competing against the sonata on the pianoforte.

He wondered what it would be like to be loved by such a woman, to have her console him when he suffered the nightmares, to stand by him when he slipped into the depressions. Would he even suffer from terror or sorrow with her by his side, filling his world with the pure light of happiness?

With a mischievous grin, she looked back to him, her eyes no longer shadowed, but twinkling with silent laughter. "Come to think of it, aren't we officially family now? What would we be, cousins-in-law?" she said, her cheeks tinted pink.

Relieved by the redirection of the conversation, he returned her grin. "I'd be an extended family member, at best. A distant and extended cousin-in-law of no actual relation."

She laughed. "Oh, Sebastian. You're such a dear friend. I want you to know I would do just as much for you as I would do for my sister. All you need is to ask."

Rain be damned, he was glad he had come. Hope soared, and his heart pounded. Was this his cue? Should he mention courtship now? No, not yet. He wanted to go about it properly by asking her father permission, or in the absence of Mr. Trethow, by asking Hazel.

He stood in spellbound silence, admiring her, memorizing her. Outside, the rain continued to soften, the black clouds moving swiftly west.

"I hope you didn't have long to travel in this storm," he said, clearing his throat. "When I received notice this morning of your arrival, the storm was well underway. No carriage is safe in muddy conditions or with limited visibility."

"Much safer riding through the storm on horseback, then?" She teased.

He flashed her a provocative smile, "I felt it worth the risk."

He ached to kiss her and be done with the pretense. Knowing they would be forced to marry if he kissed her now in front of all, he was sorely tempted, especially considering his shortened timeframe. Trapping her would be the worse way to win his suit, though. He couldn't do that to her. This had to be her choice, her decision to set aside dreams of independence to shackle herself to him.

What if, after all, she didn't want to marry him? What if she only wanted to flirt without commitment, as he had once wanted to do? What if she wanted to initiate a physical relationship without marriage, as he had once wanted? He needed to test the waters before he asked permission to court her.

"I'm not happy you risked your safety, but I am glad to see you." Lizbeth peeked at him askance. "Our letters don't do our conversations justice. Incidentally, though, we arrived yesterday morning, not today."

"That sly rat," Sebastian grumbled.

"Oh, dear. Who?" she asked.

"Drake. He promised to send notice when you were due to arrive." Sebastian bit his tongue for saying that aloud and seeming overly eager.

He leaned, unrefined, against the blue wallpaper next to the window. The coat stretched uncomfortably against his shoulder.

"That man is most vexing." She visibly bristled.

"Agreed, but I assume he had his reasons for waiting."

"It's not only that." Lizbeth's spine straightened, upright and rigid. "I'll have you know, he announced to all the world yesterday of our correspondences. Never mind that it is true. He had no business saying it to a room full of my family, especially given what it implies." Liz pursed her lips and glared in Drake's direction.

"He means well, however vexing. I apologize on his behalf if he embarrassed you."

"He gave everyone the impression we've come to an understanding. You know as well as I do it's inappropriate for people not betrothed to correspond, and then I was called on the rug for doing just that. The very idea," she scoffed. "I suppose no one has heard of the word friends."

"Yes, I can see why you'd be embarrassed. It would be the height of embarrassment for others to think us secretly betrothed." He winked, making light of it.

"That's not at all what I'm saying, and you know it. Don't be a tease. We are friends, nothing more, and that man could have put us in a sticky wicket."

Sebastian frowned. This was not the answer for which he'd been waiting. Friends, nothing more. Her words relayed only one message.

She didn't want him.

In that moment, his world crumbled. How had he misread the signals so abysmally? Her flirtation belied her attraction, but she must not want marriage, not even to him. Friends, nothing more. Why flirt with him, then? All his elation of her arrival drained. He felt empty. A cold shell. She didn't want him.

"I pity Charlotte for being married to such a louse," she continued, oblivious to his turmoil.

Until he had time to think, Sebastian didn't want to continue their conversation, much less talk about his cousin or her sister, but what else could he do? "Charlotte doesn't seem all that poor from my vantage point."

The lady in question ended the sonata she'd been playing.

Liz waited for Charlotte to resume playing before continuing. "He doesn't love her. He makes that clear enough. I've only been here one day, and I can already see there is no love in this house."

"What has love to do with an aristocratic marriage? Marriages of their kind are political, nothing more than a career move. Since when do you place romanticism on a marriage of convenience?"

A marriage between them wouldn't be like that—convenient and loveless. If only she'd give him a chance. If only he could convince her to take the leap. But he couldn't *make* her love him. Nothing he could do or say would make her return his affection or accept his proposal, see him as more than a friend.

"Just because my sister is a duchess doesn't mean she doesn't deserve love," she insisted. "He's trapped her in a miserable marriage."

"Slow down." Sebastian held up his hands. "Where do you see misery? I don't approve of all Drake's decisions, but he's not the enemy. Drake is a better man than you imagine. He has a way of seeing the world and seeing people for who they are and speaking truths no one wants to hear. I value his candor, even if he does tend to put his foot in his mouth."

"None of those characteristics give him the right to abuse my sister."

"I've never known him to be abusive, verbally or otherwise. He puts on airs, but he is a deeply emotional person. If I had to describe him in a word, aside from insufferable, I would say he's a lover. Has your sister given him any indication his love would be welcome?" Sebastian couldn't believe he was defending the cad.

"He is nothing more than a shallow, vain oaf. All at the sake of my sister." She stiffened, her feathers ruffled.

"I believe you mistake his vanity. He acts spoiled, which comes from both his title and his mother, but he is a passionate man who wants love as much as you claim your sister does. He wouldn't assume she'd accept his love, though. His upbringing has not seen marriage synonymous with love, only convenience, so from his perspective, both he and Charlotte got exactly what they wanted. Charlotte wanted a title, and he wanted a wife. Their dreams have come true. Where does love enter into this if neither made that clear during courtship? How would he know he could have the love he wants from his own wife if she hasn't told him?"

"She shouldn't have to tell her own husband the obvious," Liz defended. "A wife shouldn't have to beg for her husband's affection or his attention. I've seen this time and again with friends. They marry and then get tossed in a cupboard, another possession. Drake is no different than every other husband. He is ignoring her and carrying on with his—his affairs. He hasn't given her an opportunity or reason to express her love."

"Not to lessen your sister's pain, but has she given him any indication she wants his love? How would he know she wants more than the title? If he believes she's happy with the title, then offering her unwanted affection could tip the scales, causing an uncomfortable marriage. You forget that aristocratic marriages consist of women who are raised only to be dutiful to their position and their husband, avoiding intimacy of any kind. Your sister might be surprised to discover he too wants love but assumes he would never find it from his wife, and thus will never tip the scales without provocation."

In a fashion, he spoke of his own desire to love Lizbeth and be loved by her, if only she would give him some encouragement that such was possible, but he doubted she would read between his words. She was angry on behalf of her sister, angry at Drake for embarrassing her, and angry at the whole institute of marriage. None of this would help his cause.

He searched her eyes for clues to her thoughts, any indication that she may be receptive to him. Surely, they weren't just speaking of his cad of a cousin and her priss of a sister.

The crease between her eyebrows softened, and she pulled her bottom lip between her teeth.

"I didn't mean to snap at you, Sebastian. I've been so looking forward to seeing you, yet look how dreadfully I behave." She gifted him a half-smile. "I've been so afraid of being trapped in a loveless marriage all I see in Drake is my worst fears realized."

Sebastian scratched his chin. "But you would never marry someone like Drake."

"It's not so much the choice of man that's the problem, but that any man could reduce me to a possession and tuck me away for his convenience. I look at the life my sister is living and see my fear realized through her. I could only ever be with a man who includes me in all aspects of his life, who talks to me and never shuts me out, someone who trusts me enough to share himself even if he worries it would tip the scales, as you say. And thus, I'm prejudiced regarding my sister's situation."

He stood in stunned silence. He couldn't be sure if she still spoke only of her sister or if she knowingly spoke of a potential union with him, but her words struck his heart like a sharpened dart.

In some small way, her words should fill him with renewed hope. She wasn't opposed to marriage, then, not entirely, just a marriage wherein there was distance and inequality. Her words should renew all hope he'd lost moments ago. Alas, they deepened his sorrow.

How could he ever offer her happiness? He could claim as the day was long that what he offered was uninterrupted, unconditional love, but how many times had he already shut her out, and how many times would he do so again? Not even he could promise it wouldn't happen again. It would take far more than a week to earn her trust, and it would take a lifetime to strategize a way to keep her happy while maintaining a lengthy distance between her and his past.

He was waging a losing war to win her love.

"Don't look so forlorn, Sebastian. You look as though you've been thrown under the carriage wheels. I didn't mean to insult your cousin, merely his lack of communication with my sister." She brushed a fallen strand of hair behind her ear.

"You haven't offended me," he reassured, feigning a smile. "I've simply been reminded of something I had pushed to the back of my mind."

He folded his arms across his chest.

Dawning gradually lit her eyes before she cast him a devilish smile. "Oh. Oh, I see. Now, don't be coy. You were recalling the masquerade dinner, weren't you? The 'misunderstanding' we had about coincidences and legends, yes?"

He furrowed his brows. "Something like that."

"Don't be terribly upset about that. We sorted the confusion, and look at us now, friends to the end. And it's not as though you're considering me as anything more than a friend, so don't take my words to heart."

After some minutes, he turned the conversation to mutual reading interests.

Throughout their conversation, he remained conflicted. He had been so sure of his intentions that morning but hearing anew her distaste for marriage reminded him of the reasons he hadn't pursued her from the beginning.

Trepidation almost blighted his best intentions. He wouldn't consign them to an unhappy marriage or an awkward friendship shadowed by unrequited love, but how would he live with himself if he walked away without at least trying, without bluntly, boldly expressing his desires? If she rejected him, so be it. He would know without the shadow of doubt she didn't want him, and it would be over. He could walk away without a backward glance. But at least he would have tried.

God, he wanted her. He wanted everything about her. He wasn't worthy of her and doubted he could make her happy, but selfishly he wanted her more than anything else in life. The light she shone into his life, the physical and mental stimulation she stirred, the hope, all spurred him to continue with his original plan. His fears couldn't hold a candle to his desire for her. If he needed longer than a week, so be it, but he would try his damndest to turn friendship into love, to make his intentions known.

Chapter 19

"At least I have more mobility with the shorter sleeves." Lizbeth raised and lowered her arms as Bettye braided her hair into an up-do.

The past two mornings involved posing in the Red Drawing Room while Charlotte entertained callers. Her nicest dresses constricted her movements as well as her spirit as she sat silently, affecting poise for one visitor after another. She wanted nothing more than to wear her favorite cotton and walk the landscape. Alas, silks and drawing rooms had been her plight.

Charlotte lived by a strict time schedule. Liz had lost count of the number of times she changed her attire per day to follow proper decorum. Morning dresses, walking dresses, tea dresses, riding habits, dinner gowns, and what felt like a few dozen more in between. Liz missed the freedom to dress comfortably and run barefoot on the beach.

The dressing room door opened. Charlotte peeked around the corner.

"Ooh, you have a coffee tray. I finished mine ages ago. May I have yours?" She plopped on a pink couch next to the bureau, cozying herself against the cushion as though she hadn't spent the previous couple of days personifying sophistication.

"Help yourself." Liz fiddled with the fichu tucked into her bodice, modestly covering her chest.

Bettye added the finishing touches to Liz's hair.

"I'm delighted for our shopping and picnic plans today," Charlotte exclaimed. "What fun we shall have! It's a pity we must spend the day with that boor. It's bad enough he and Drake spend so much time together, but I'm at least spared from socializing with him except the occasional dinner. I could hardly believe my eyes when he walked in on your second day. I thought to myself, 'Oh, no, he'll ruin Liz's visit!'" Charlotte sipped Liz's coffee, eyeing critically the watercolor painting on the wall above Liz's head.

Lizbeth sighed. She had never spoken with Charlotte of her attraction to Sebastian. Aunt Hazel knew and even liked Sebastian, but Charlotte was less inclined to empathize, especially when she identified Liz as being irrevocably on the shelf.

Charlotte continued her bubbling spring of dialogue. "I'm distressed Drake teases you about him. He teases everyone, so don't take it personally, but I'm horrorstruck every time he says something about you and his cousin." She tutted. "As if either of you would ever be interested in each other."

Liz remained silent, ignoring her sister's prodding. Not that she'd admit aloud, but her sister might have a point. Was he as interested in her as she in him? During their first conversation after her arrival, she had emphasized their *friendship*, angling to see if he'd take the bait and express wanting more. He never did.

After their failed attempts at delving deeper than friendship, she hesitated to press her attentions where they might not be welcome. Over the course of the month, she would proceed under the pretense of friendship, but not without more baiting. Short of throwing herself at him as she had done at the museum in London, she wasn't altogether positive how to show her desire for more without scaring him off or humiliating herself. Today, subtlety was key.

The lady's maid clasped a chain around Liz's neck, the miniature Sebastian had given her resting sublimely against the white fabric of the fichu.

"Is that your walking dress?" Charlotte nodded over her coffee mug to a gown lying over a rack, slightly soiled with mud at the hem. "When did you go walking? We've only just risen."

"On the contrary. I woke early for a walk around the gardens. You've only just risen." Liz wondered at her reflection, worried she looked too modest, too schoolmarmish. Maybe she should forego the fichu. "I stumbled on your mother-in-law in the park. Frosty around the edges, but a skilled conversationalist. We shared a lovely chat about the wilderness walk and whinged about the weather."

"Hmm. All she does is complain about me when we talk. She hated all of my seating charts for the dinner party. 'No, no, no, no, no, no. You can't put Lord Fiddlesticks next to Lady Sheepbrain, and you can't put Lord Horsehead next to Lady Bigbosom.' As if I know any of these people other than from the list of titles she gives me. She says it's my duty to learn all local gentry before I make a disaster of a dinner party."

"I doubt you'll make a disaster of anything, Charlotte. You've always had a gift for entertaining. I'm pleased, honestly, to hear you're doing what you enjoy." Bettye slipped the pelisse over Liz's gown and tied the bonnet. "Well? Are you ready for a grand adventure into the wilds of Northumberland?"

"Drake hasn't taken me for a ride anywhere." Charlotte pouted. "I'm only sorry we're going to Roddam Village instead of one that belongs to me."

"I'm sure we can manage a way to visit some of your own property during my stay. It'll be an excuse for you to do more shopping." Liz clasped her sister's hand after the empty coffee cup had been returned to the tray. "Shall we check on Mary and Aunt Hazel?"

Sebastian had invited them on a picnic, including a visit to his principal seat, only a few miles from the border of Scotland. Drake and the dowager duchess both declined to join. Liz wasn't the least disappointed.

Before long, the merry group was tucked inside Charlotte's state coach, the ducal arms emblazoned on the doors. Sebastian had recommended they ride in the sociable with its folding hood to better see the countryside, but Charlotte had insisted on taking the duke's carriage in all its finery to avoid the sun during long stretches and, true to Charlotte's disposition, to be seen.

The farther north they traveled, the hillier and more forested became the terrain to the west with expanses of rocky patches between wide open meadows and farmlands to the east. Lizbeth admired the views, as well as Sebastian's visage. There was a mischievous glinting in his eyes and a reserved smile on his lips. He was up to something.

He watched her unabashedly for most of the drive north, only looking out the window long enough to point out the border between the Annick duchy and the Roddam earldom and to explain the cultivation of the farmlands. More than once, his foot stretched across the coach to bump hers.

When they reached Roddam Village, Mary and Charlotte set out together, arms linked. Hazel accepted Sebastian's arm and walked beside him as the group toured the village. Liz trailed behind everyone.

To his credit, Sebastian behaved a good sport throughout Mary and Charlotte's prattling and Hazel's whinging. The stolid demeanor he usually donned in social settings transformed into an engaged and interested affect. For an accused boor, he epitomized gentility.

He doted attention on Hazel, all the while casting Lizbeth those mischievous grins. He showed to the ladies a side of himself only Liz had seen, the relaxed and witty flirt.

The few people they encountered greeted Sebastian as a friend rather than an employer. No one cowed in his presence, averted their eyes, or tugged at their forelock. No one ogled him or waited to be acknowledged before speaking. The men in the village shook his hand, while the women regaled him with tales about their little ones.

She felt proud of him, proud to walk with him, and more than a bit smitten. Liz loved seeing this side of him, seeing him in his element away from the London snots. Not once did he act elitist. The same couldn't be said about her sister, who bore the ennui of nobility.

All about them, people took note of him and those with him, especially her, although she couldn't say why unless they witnessed the attention he danced upon her from time to time, but he was just as attentive, if not more so, to Aunt Hazel.

The group finally made their way to the millinery. Draped caps, mob caps, lace caps, headdresses of straw, crape, velvet, and a veritable cornucopia of other materials, ribbons, veils, feathers, and beads, filled the room, an overwhelming assortment of womanly delights. Charlotte and Mary flitted about the shop, trying on one pre-made hat after another. While Hazel spoke with the shopkeeper and milliner, Sebastian snuck behind Lizbeth.

His hand on the small of her back was her first awareness of his presence. His lips whispering in her ear was the second.

"I've instructed Mrs. Mabry to charge anything your heart desires to me. I recommend anything green."

And with those words, he dashed off to recommend a new hat that flattered Hazel's eyes before the pair, thick as thieves, snuck out of the hat shop together, leaving Charlotte, Mary, and Lizbeth to finish their exploration of bonnets and turbans. The warmth of his hand lingered, and the tickle of his breath on her cheek sent shivers down her spine. That had not been an action between friends.

Her pulse racing, her stare fixed on the door where it had followed his retreating back only moments before, she jumped to find the shopkeeper standing silently beside her.

"Ye ken His Lordship, miss?" the woman asked, assessing Lizbeth.

Liz replied cordially, "Yes, I know him. My sister married his cousin, the Duke of Annick."

"Oh, aye, we heard His Grace brough' home a new lass." The woman glanced at Charlotte and Mary who were speaking with the milliner.

Waving Liz to a corner of the shop, she offered to show a design that would complement the dress and be customized to Lizbeth's liking with matching lace and ribbons.

While dressing Liz's hair with a becoming bonnet, the shopkeeper chattered.

"Yer fortunate tae ken the master. He's as guid a mon as ever ye'll find. Ah were only able tae open me shop after he inherited. Built new shops, he did. This shop be me pride 'n joy, i'tis."

"Your shop is lovely. May I see this with a bow?" Liz asked politely, admiring the woman's handiwork in a mirror.

"Ah have ribbons o' shades that be mos' fetchin' tae ye coloring, they would." The shopkeeper, a stout woman with a mop of gray hair under a lace cap, waddled over to the collection of ribbons.

After they warbled about colors, Liz selected three she favored, as well as an ivory brooch her aunt might wear to match the ivory handled fan she favored.

"Ye have a fine day with His Lordship. He's a guid mon, unlike his sire."

Lizbeth paused while collecting her goods. She hesitated to ask for clarification, as it wouldn't be polite, but the woman obviously baited her.

"May I inquire of the previous earl?" she asked tentatively.

"Le's look at a special bonnet tae add tae yer purchases? Comes from Milan, it dae." She bustled to the other side of the shop to retrieve the bonnet, assuming Liz would follow her.

The woman whispered conspiratorially, bonnet in hand, "He beat me Robert in the street fur all tae see, Lord Roddam did. Gave my wee bairn a skelping with a horsewhip."

"His Lordship, the current Lord Roddam?" Liz gasped, her hand covering her mouth in shock.

"Nay, don' be daft. His sire. He bea' me boy. I'm a Christian woman, so I shouldna say, but I thanked the Lord when tha mon died. He bea' me Robert fur pickpocketing. Me bairn werena pickpocket. He were only six years auld 'n a guid boy."

"That's terrible! The current Earl of Roddam hasn't done anything like that, has he?"

"Nay, he's a guid mon, ye ken." Realizing she had an attentive audience, the woman rattled on about several other incidences of violence, including the public whipping of laborers rumored to have complained about wages.

Lizbeth was too stunned to hear all of what was said or to pay attention to the woman's sly request that Liz compliment the shop to His Lordship and recommend it might need a larger space for wares.

She was shocked at the shopkeeper's verbosity, but more so about the stories shared and those left untold. He must have felt such shame that his father would behave that way, even if such treatment was considered acceptable by lords to their tenants. She wondered if Sebastian's running away had anything to do with his father's treatment of the villagers.

After purchasing the bonnet, along with more ribbons than she wanted, she joined Charlotte and

Mary. They found Aunt Hazel and Sebastian two shops down at a confectionery. Sebastian treated them to Turkish Delight, a sweet recently brought over from Istanbul, if the confectioner were to be believed.

Once Aunt Hazel ordered a side table from the furniture maker, which she murmured to the girls would look rustically charming next to her Chippendale, and Mary purchased silk for her needlework, the quintet piled into the state coach, bound for the location Sebastian had chosen for the picnic.

The coachman followed the border of Scotland west before turning south into a valley, stopping next to a narrow river nestled under a clump of trees. The groomsmen secured a sheet beneath the trees and prepared the food and cutlery, Sebastian lending a hand throughout the process.

Mary exclaimed over the red squirrels, while Charlotte wrinkled her nose at the scene. "Why didn't we order the servants to meet us here? They could have brought a table and chairs."

Liz rolled her eyes. "Sit down, Charlotte. Only a few months ago you were picnicking in Hyde Park without a table and chairs. Don't tell me your new title has gone to your head already."

"Well, no, but I don't want to rumple my dress." Charlotte pouted.

"Then stand," Liz said, crawling onto the sheet.

Once the food had been laid out, they ate contentedly, even the duchess.

The sounds of bubbling water, the rustling of leaves against the breeze, and the songs of the birds filled the air. Their canopy hued a vibrant shade of autumn, colors ranging from radiant reds to drab yellows.

"I've decided," proclaimed Charlotte, "to turn part of the conservatory into an aviary for Captain Henry. He'll live in the Gray Parlor, of course, where he is now, except when I'm in the conservatory. Just imagine his surprise when he'll really be able to fly. Isn't it a grand idea, Lizbeth?"

"Yes, lovely," Liz replied absently, running her hands through the greenery so it tickled her palm. "This grass is as soft as silk. I've never felt anything like it." She wasn't thinking of the grass. She was thinking of Sebastian's hand on the small of her back.

"Honestly, Lizzie, I don't go around feeling grass." Charlotte scoffed. "The very idea."

Sebastian stretched out on his side, propping himself on one arm, ankles crossed. "I've been thinking, Charlotte. You should ask Drake to take you to see the Drake Stone. The Cheviot Valley and lake would make a fine outing for two lovebirds. Tell him I told you he was named after the rock."

Charlotte eyed him curiously. "And why would I want to see a stone?"

"The point isn't to see the stone. Tell Drake you want a lover's tryst. He'll go, and you'll both enjoy every minute of the outing. I promise." Sebastian's smile was downright wicked.

"What a vulgar thing to say." Charlotte huffed. "You're so uncouth. I'll pretend I didn't hear you."

Sebastian shrugged, tugging at the grass until he pulled out a few blades. "As you wish. But I've known my cousin long enough to understand how he thinks. You'd thank me if you took my suggestion."

Ignoring him, Charlotte grabbed Mary's and Hazel's hands and tugged them to stand for a game of blind man's bluff, which couldn't be much of a challenge with only three people. Before long, Charlotte and Mary were screeching and squealing like children.

Alone at last, Lizbeth boldly moved closer to Sebastian. Kneeling a few inches from him, she tucked her legs beneath her and fiddled with her dress, unexpectedly nervous.

Sebastian watched her.

"I've written to your father," he said, interrupting the stretch of silence.

Startled, Liz echoed, "Written to my father." Her heart skipped a beat. There could only be one reason he would write to her father.

Was she ready for this? Was this what she wanted? Should she leap feet first and say yes or play coy and tell him she'd think about it? Was this really what she wanted? No doubts or second thoughts? Oh, she had so many doubts, but...

"About the slavery abolition bill," he added.

Oh.

"The one you mentioned he's working on with Wilberforce." He twisted a blade of grass around his thumb. "I offered insight into the Lords' perspective, for what it's worth. I stand by my belief that it won't pass the House of Lords, but I support your father's efforts and hope my suggestions helped."

Her heart sank. That hadn't been at all what she expected him to say.

Hoping not to sound too dejected, she replied, "Yes, I remember, but I didn't think you really would."

"You don't find me a man of my word?" His eyes widened, and he placed a hand over his heart. "I'm hurt you don't trust me." The twitch of a smile revealed he wasn't truly offended.

"Don't be silly. I didn't think you would feel obligated to help an MP with what might be perceived as a pet project."

"I don't consider it a pet project. Ambitious, rather. After seeing the conditions of the workers under my father's iron fist, I have an invested interest. I recognize tenants and laborers working for their livelihood aren't comparable to slaves stolen and transported, but the treatment is none too different from my viewpoint."

"In that case, I want to tell you of my work with the tin miners this summer."

He visibly stiffened. "Tell me you didn't go into the mines, Lizbeth. You don't belong there, and it's entirely unsafe."

"Oh, no, I didn't go into the mine," she reassured, "but I did help the workers in my own small way. I've always brought them treats and visited with them, just as my mother did, but after hearing your stories of working alongside the laborers, I wanted to do more. I don't think it was enough to thin the line between employer and employee, but I tried to join their ranks for a time. If that makes any sense."

The breeze was light but persistent, freeing some of her hair from the braid. She tucked the disobedient strands behind her ears.

"Doing too much, I think, patronizes their labor," he replied. "They have their jobs, and we have ours. I'm sure they appreciated your efforts all the same. If more of the gentry were like you, what a different world we would live in."

He reached into the picnic basket, rummaged, and pulled out a small box. Eyes averted, he slid the box to her.

"What's this?" she asked.

He shrugged, turning to watch the others play their game.

The wooden box was only a few inches long, not much larger than a snuff box. When she opened it, she was rewarded with a palm-sized flower, hand-whittled from wood and painted purple with a green stem.

"Oh, Sebastian," she breathed, cradling the flower. "But you've already given me so much." She rolled the flower in her hands, studying the craftsmanship, rubbing her fingers along the grains. "How beautiful. What kind of flower is this?"

If a masculine man could look sheepish, Sebastian did. "It's cranesbill, the flower of Northumberland. It's plentiful near the castle." He cleared his throat and fidgeted, inspecting the grass.

"Did you get this in the village? My compliments to the woodworker. It really is beautiful."

He shook his head. "No, I whittled it myself. You'll find plenty of blemishes. My first attempt at decorative woodworking, you see. I think some of the stem is purple, so don't look too closely."

Her cheeks warmed. She hardly knew what to make of him, this moody man who one day kissed her and the next spurned her. He broke the rules of courting. First with his familiarity at the British Museum, then with the correspondence, and now with gifts, all actions socially accepted only between betrothed couples, of which they certainly were not.

He wasn't even courting her as far as she knew. Did he want to court her, or were these all gestures of one friend to another? Friends didn't find opportunities to bump legs in carriages or touch the smalls of backs. Friends certainly didn't kiss each other. Did he still regret their kiss?

She was sorely tempted to wrap her arms around him and kiss him again, as wantonly as she had in London, to show him exactly what she thought of his so-called friendship. Instead, she tucked the flower back into its box, set it next to her, and reached into her reticule for a bundle of her own.

"It's a good thing you gave me this first so I don't appear coy." She handed him a round object wrapped in a handkerchief.

He unfolded the kerchief to reveal a black rock, his brows furrowing in confusion. "Hmm. Thank you? I've always wanted a, uh, rock."

Lizbeth laughed. "It's so much more than a rock."

"Is it?" He held it up to the sunlight, squinting.

"Yes. It's volcanic rock from a sea cave in Trevena. I wanted you to have something from King Arthur's birthplace. You could use it as a paperweight, I suppose."

She watched his confusion metamorphose to surprise and wonderment.

"That beach is special to me," she explained, "so I wanted to bring a piece of it to you as a thank you for the books you sent. And, you'll think this part silly, but in the *Suite du Merlin*, Nineve, or the Lady of the Lake, uses her wiles to trap Merlin in a cave. She tricked him into falling in love with her so she could steal his magic, and then she used it against him. Well, I suppose you already know that. When I read it, I thought of the cave I oft visit at low tide, and I also thought about the inscription you wrote in the book, to the Lady of the Lake. This rock is me giving you my magic, so you trust me never to be false."

She had never given a man a gift before, and certainly not something so personal. Her hands trembled so much she gripped the edge of her pelisse, wringing the fabric with sweaty palms.

He fixed his eyes on her for what felt like an eternity before he wrapped the rock back in the handkerchief. As he folded the edges, he paused, spotting the initial on the linen. The kerchief was hand-stitched with silk embroidery, an R for Roddam sewn in blue, surrounded by a wreath of meadow flowers that serpentined along the hem.

She chewed her bottom lip as he studied the embroidery. He would think it all silly. Vulnerability sent a bead of sweat down the back of her neck.

Girlish squealing infiltrated the silence. To distract herself from the embarrassment of the gifts, she watched the three ladies chasing each other along the river. When she looked back to Sebastian, she caught him wiping the corner of his eye.

"What's it like?" he murmured, his words catching in his throat.

"What's *what* like?"

"Love." Sebastian's eyes glistened when he looked up. "What does it feel like? To love and to be loved by family." His composure began to crumble, his shoulders rounding, his features lined. "What is it like to love so much you would suffer four hundred miles of bumpy and dangerous roads?"

Lizbeth mulled over his question. Hesitantly, she said, "I'm not sure I can describe love. For me, it feels warm, tickling inside right down to your toes. Not always, though. Sometimes it's a sensation of longing, as if someone's tugging at an invisible rope around your midriff, a pull at your belly button. It can even be a cold fear for another's wellbeing. Mostly, it feels like home, that comfort you have when you're sitting by the fireplace in winter. I believe it feels differently to everyone and is something you must experience to recognize. That doesn't help, does it?"

"It does," he said, his voice husky. "Lizbeth, I—. That is, when I'm with you, I—. Damnation. What I'm trying to say is that you make me feel—."

Charlotte and Mary ran between them, screeching and flushed with excitement. Aunt Hazel huffed and puffed behind them. Liz held her box protectively from getting trampled, her heart beating frantically at whatever Sebastian was about to say.

"Lizzie! Come dance!" Charlotte squealed, grabbing Liz's wrist.

"What are you talking about, Charlotte?" Not that Lizbeth begrudged her sister the fun, but she wanted to know what Sebastian might have said.

"Come dance! Auntie can be your partner."

Aunt Hazel heaved her way to the picnic blanket and sat, leaning against a tree. Breathlessly, Hazel said, "I most certainly will not. You are the silliest girl, duchess or not."

Sebastian tucked his gifts discreetly into the picnic basket and stood, offering his hand to Lizbeth. She slipped her own gift into her reticule. Taking his hand, they joined Charlotte and Mary.

Chapter 20

In the growing darkness of night, Sebastian could see the child silhouetted against the rising moonlight. A full moon hung low in the sky, filling his world with a bright glow. She waded into the ocean, splashing her hands in the knee-deep water.

"Come swim, 'Bastian! The water is so cold I have gooseflesh!"

"We need to go home, or he'll find out," he called back.

"Come play, 'Bastian!"

Long, black hair flowed around her, trailing in the water that now lapped at her waist. She slipped in deeper, her hair fanning about her body.

As he turned his back, the night air shattered with the sound of a blood-curdling scream. He looked back to see the child dangling from the mouth of a tentacled beast with flaming eyes.

He ran to fight the beast, but his legs wouldn't move. Sand sunk around him, pulling him under. He screamed to the child as the sand swallowed him whole.

Sebastian woke to find himself wading in a pool of sweat. His bed sheets were soaked, his body drenched.

Devoid of the transitional confusion between sleep and wakefulness, he knew instantly where he was and that he had been dreaming. This was the first time he had dreamt of a giant squid, he thought wryly, but not the first time of the child he couldn't save.

He wouldn't stay in a soggy bed and doubted he could fall back to sleep, so he fumbled for the bedside candle, lit it, and reached for his pocket clock on the nightstand to check if it were a decent hour to wake his butler to arrange for fresh sheets and a bath. He paid his staff well enough to wake them any damn time he pleased, but on principle, he refused to be a grouchy lord of the manor in the wee hours.

The dials read four in the morning. The sheets could wait. The bath could wait. He untangled his legs from the wet mop of bedcovers and escaped his newly sweated in-home swimming pool. It only took his purposeful stride a handful of minutes to bring him downstairs, outside the curtain wall, and down the slope to the beach.

The night air, autumn cool, whirled around him, trying to push him left, then right, back, then forward. It tickled the beads of sweat still clinging to his skin.

He pulled off his nightshirt, letting the wind breeze through his legs and across his stomach. The last thing he needed was his shirt escaping for an airborne adventure through all of Northumberland, so he tucked it under a rock. The grassy dunes met black, basalt rock before the ground transformed into sweeping honeyed sand.

Despite the wind, the sea remained calm, gently lapping at his feet as he stepped, bare as the day he was born, into the frigid waters. His body shivered at the icy touch until he dived into the depths, letting the undertow pull him into the waves before rocking him back to shore.

No sea monsters. He wouldn't mind pitting his wits against one. He fantastically imagined Scylla the Greek sea monster with her twelve tentacles and six heads surfacing from the water, begging him, posing as Poseidon the god of the sea, to release her from her monstrous curse, to defeat the monster she had become and release her back into a fair sea nymph.

The water cleansed his nightmarish visions. Somewhat ironic, he mused, given his nightmares were of the sea, yet it was the sea that healed him, mind, body, and soul. He swam well past where his feet could touch seabed, clearing his mind of the visions of the young girl who haunted his dreams.

He returned to the castle only after the pre-dawn on the horizon lightened the night sky. It had been a full moon, he noticed. A fool's moon.

He pulled the bell-cord, waited, then requested fresh sheets and a hot bath. He had estate business to complete today before the dinner party. The doctor he recently hired for the parish of Balan never arrived, and Sebastian discovered the physician had chosen a position in Italy instead without bothering to send notice. Fickle leech. He needed to sort through possible replacements so the parish wasn't without medical care.

Concentration, he realized, was difficult with the looming evening. With so much work to be done, it amazed him he could be distracted by something as mundane as a dinner, but alas, distracted he was.

He felt in over his head and unsure how to proceed. Courting was not a natural behavior for him.

There were strict rules on courting, and he knew he had already broken half of them. He offered her his given name and used hers as though they were family. He had walked arm-in-arm with her in London, a physical touch only socially acceptable between engaged couples. He had corresponded with her. They had exchanged gifts. He had even kissed her. None of these were acceptable unless affianced. It was amazing he hadn't unintentionally compromised her.

Then, perhaps he had. He was so removed from gossip circles, he wouldn't know the latest on dit even if his name were at the center. Presumably, her aunt would approach him if there were any gossip. He assumed no one paid much attention to a recluse and a spinster.

But, he humored himself, who cared? So what if tongues wagged and scandal raged? They were both wallflowers in the social scene anyway, he being mostly ostracized socially except by those willing to look past his foul temper for his wealth and titles. What's the worst they could say—that surly man has scandalized that spinster's reputation? Not much to scandalize if he planned to marry her, or hoped to marry her at any rate, if she would have him, if he didn't lose, if he could dredge bravery from the depths of his soul.

Never had he thought it possible to think those words: planned to marry. He spent his life despising the institution of marriage and hiding himself from the world, afraid of rejection and scorn. Yet here he sat, rolling the words over his tongue, tasting them: planned to marry.

He wasn't foolish enough to believe marriage begot happiness. Non-sequitur, as they say in Latin. It did not follow that infatuation blossomed to love or love to marriage or marriage to happiness. However, at this point, with Lizbeth, he wanted to try to make it work. He feared losing her more than any reason he had not to marry. Knowing what it felt like to lose her after leaving London, that tug at his belly button she described at the picnic, he would be damned if he felt that again. It may destroy them both to marry, but he would not bungle it this time.

He likened his attraction more to an obsession than love because he couldn't stop thinking about her, couldn't stop making love to her in his waking dreams, even found himself asking into empty rooms for her opinion as though she sat across from him. If his butler didn't already think him half mad, he certainly would after witnessing the conversations to empty chairs.

The rest of his day flittered by with little accomplished despite his best efforts to concentrate. He arrived at Lyonn Manor when all in the house were still dressing, all except his aunt. The butler escorted him into the lesser parlor. Aunt Catherine sat in her favorite chair staring up at the new paintings of Drake and Charlotte.

"You're making a fool of yourself," were her opening words to him.

"And a lovely evening to you, as well, Aunt Catherine."

She thumped her gold-handled cane against the floor. "You'll be sitting with Lady Argot at dinner."

"No, I will be sitting next to Miss Trethow." He straddled the floor, feet apart, hands folded behind him, shoulders pulled back.

"Do not defy me in my own house. You will sit with Lady Argot and stop making a fool of yourself." Although she remained seated while he stood, she managed to look down her nose at him.

"In what way do you perceive I've made a fool of myself?"

"Over that girl. Don't think I haven't noticed. It's bad enough Drake married below him to some lowly gentry gel, but to have you gallivanting after that vulgar sister of hers is beyond reproach." Seeing the conversation as over, she turned back to the paintings.

Sebastian prodded. "Don't tell me what to do. Because you never knew love doesn't mean I can't love, or at least try. Need I remind you you are only in my life because I make it so? If I want to 'make a fool of myself,' as you say, then I will. I don't need or seek your approval."

She stared at the paintings with deaf ears.

As he turned to leave, she harrumphed. "Do what you will, but while I reside here, you will sit where I tell you or not dine with us a'tall." She punctuated the sentence with a thump of the cane.

He gave a curt nod, pivoted, and left her to her thoughts.

Stationing himself in the far corner of the Red Drawing Room and hoping to remain unobserved until Lizbeth graced the room with her presence, he waited. Momentarily, he considered going to Drake's study for a book and solitude, but then he would be too conspicuous when returning.

The last thing he wanted was for the butler to formally announce his arrival and have all eyes turn his way. He already knew everyone on the guest list, his aunt's usual guests with the addition of a few ladies meant to tempt him, no doubt, but that wouldn't dissuade any of them from scrutinizing him.

Much to his great pleasure, Hazel was the first to join him in the drawing room, clearly wanting also to station herself, but unlike him, angling to be part of the receiving line for guests.

She was a tad too much like Charlotte for him to keep in company for long, but she proved herself wise in the social arts, a good judge of character, and amiable in all ways. He certainly enjoyed her sense of humor. How different might life have been if his first arrival to Lyonn Manor had been met with Hazel as his aunt instead of Catherine.

He braved removing from his sanctuary to speak to her. Already, several days had passed, nearly a week in total. He was running out of time. Even as he watched the calendar days tick by, he struggled to work up the courage to act on his desire. This was no easy task. The entirety of his future hung in the balance of his actions.

Given this may be his only opportunity to have Hazel to himself, he approached her, his hand reaching for his pocket clock, the feel of the cold metal soothing his nerves.

"Lady Collingwood."

"Oh, good heavens! You startled the life out of me. Where were you hiding, you sneaky man?" She fanned herself for a moment then gave a robust laugh. "Hazel, please. I thought we were well past formalities. We're family now."

His chuckle joined hers. "Your niece says the same thing. And speaking of your niece, I'd like a private word with you about her."

She raised her eyebrows, continuing to fan herself. He had expected more dialogue first. It seemed rude to blurt out such a request without preamble. Where was the instruction book explaining how such things were done? A step-by-step guide on how to ask for permission to court a young woman, and then a follow up manual on how to do the courting.

He gripped the watch until he was sure an impression of the engraving imprinted in his palm. *Give me strength.*

Hazel bored of the silence. "Out with it. The room couldn't be more private if we were on our own island."

"I request permission to court your niece, Lizbeth," he stammered, hoping some of what he said sounded confident. He didn't feel confident.

"Took you long enough. You've done it backwards, you know. You've wooed her before asking permission. And, technically, you should be asking permission of her father, although I will gladly serve in his stead."

She patted his arm affectionately and continued, "Lizbeth is a silly girl with romanticized notions of independence in spinsterhood. I've tried for years to talk her into marrying my boy, but she'll have nothing to do with the institution. Perhaps you're the man to talk sense into her. If she'll agree to your proposal of courtship, then I have no qualms about the matter. Do be quick about it, dear boy, for we leave at the end of the month, and I do hate long engagements."

Resuming his post in the far corner of the room, he watched as the family came in one-by-one and formed their receiving line to welcome guests, some of whom had yet to meet the new duchess.

Lizbeth had joined the party shortly after her sister, but she hadn't seen him in his hiding spot. No one had. He preferred it this way, observing from safety, watching her when she didn't know she was being watched. Several times she touched her cameo, the jewelry of choice this evening.

He remembered with a tightening in his chest that at the picnic she had worn the miniature he gifted her. The sight had made his heart pound and his stomach flutter. However subtle, it had fueled him with the hope he needed.

Tonight, she must be calling on her mother's strength to survive an evening amongst the nobility of north England. Lizbeth moved swiftly through the room to stand against the wall near a set of double doors leading to the garden. She looked anxiously around her, speaking to no one. Did she look for him in the crowd? For a moment, he imagined what it would be like to walk in with her, the butler announcing them as the Earl and Countess of Roddam. He could only hope she truly returned his affection and didn't think of him as only a friend.

The butler, Mr. Thin-Lips, as Sebastian thought of him, announced the arrival of a young lady who pranced into the room as though she were the new duchess. Kid gloves, pink fan, pink bow, blonde straw-colored hair that would have confused a hungry horse. He groaned. She must be Lady Argot, his dinner companion. She looked like someone his aunt would want him to fancy.

Shortly behind her another young lady was introduced, peach hair, purple bow, lace gloves. Maybe that was Lady Argot. He really should have been listening to the butler, but he didn't care enough to pay attention. He already found his appetite waning at these dinner prospects.

Before long, a third girl, identical to the other two, walked in. They always seemed to come in threes, these vapid blonde chits, apples of their mama's eyes, spoiled and entitled. He'd like to ask them what they thought of the slavery abolition bill, if they'd ever hammered ore at a tin mine, or better yet if they liked to swim nude in the ocean.

Chuckling, he decided to save that last question for a terribly awkward social moment, as it would be sure to get a rise from polite society. Somehow, he suspected Lizbeth would approve of his little joke.

Three sets of double doors along the back wall opened by way of invisible footmen, and Aunt Catherine invited everyone to walk the gardens and take cocktails before dinner.

Enough. He pushed himself out of the chair and with long strides closed the gap between the far end of the room and Lizbeth.

Probably his imagination, but he would swear on the bible her eyes brightened and her posture relaxed when she saw him. She released her cameo and held out her hands to him. Short of embracing her, he stopped a few feet from her and clasped her hands, bringing the buttoned gloves to his lips one after another.

"Escape with me," he dared.

"I'm yours," she whispered.

They followed the other guests who walked onto the grotto to collect their cocktails and explore the park. While he couldn't quite abscond with her into the wilderness, at least they were in the open air.

Hazel stepped over to them, then, and said much louder than necessary, "I wish to see the rose garden. Would you care to show me, Your Lordship? Come, Lizbeth."

He offered his arms to them both and escorted the two away from the crowd around to a hidden vista where a clump of trees concealed the walled garden.

"Oh, I see a lovely bush in the far corner there," Hazel remarked. "I must go sniff the flowers because I'm sure those smell differently from all the others." Without waiting for a response, she strolled to the far side.

No matter that he had visited Lyonn Manor every other day since their arrival, and no matter that this private moment may be his only chance to settle things regarding courtship, he found himself dumbstruck as to what to say. Now was his opportunity to ask her permission to court her officially and publicly. Not a task to be taken lightly since all would know his intentions of courting would inevitably lead to a proposal of marriage. How does someone who swore against marriage and even spurned the woman in question now present himself as a serious suitor?

His voice caught in his throat.

He had her alone and may not get the chance again this evening, or even the next time he visited. Now was his chance. He stared at her, knees locked, back stiff, tongue tied.

She spoke first to break the silence. "Charlotte informed me that I will be sitting with a Lord Cavanaugh at dinner. Am I pleased or disappointed?"

He grimaced in repugnance. "Lord Cavanaugh is nearly fifty with ear hair and nose hair that could reach out and devour his food for him."

"Oh dear. That does sound dreadful. Shall we send smoke signals to each other from our seats?"

"Better yet, let's disguise our bites into secret messages. If we nibble, conversation is tedious. If we take large bites, the present company is loquacious. Or better yet, the choice of food sends the message. Vegetables could signify boredom while meats indicate wits' end. Bread rolls could be the cue for drastic measures, perhaps the need for one of us to break into song and dance midmeal."

"And if we should stop eating altogether?" she inquired, full of laughter over his absurd scheme.

"That would mean the nose hairs have waved hello, so you've lost your appetite." He grinned impishly. "If it makes you feel any better, I'll be sitting next to Lady Argot."

"Is that the one with the purple, pink, or green bow?"

"No idea. They all look the same to me." He confessed.

"I did get to peek at the seating chart earlier today, and we are seated diagonally, one seat removed, so not too far. I found that reassuring even if it would be impolite to talk across a table."

"Then let's be the most impolite dinner guests ever to eat at Lyonn Manor. We'll never be invited to a dinner again. Wouldn't that be wonderful?" He joked, partly in earnest.

"For shame, Sebastian! I don't want to embarrass my sister *too* much, so I shall try to be polite, but you know how we country girls lack decorum. I may forget a rule or two when it comes to fine dining. In fact, you might not be at all surprised if I start a food fight." She winked at him, smiling deliciously, her lips ripe for nibbling.

He slipped the glove off his right hand and touched her cheek with his thumb. In response, she tilted her head to rest her cheek in his palm. Caressing her silken skin, he sighed audibly. A vision of loveliness.

He lowered his head, his lips meeting her left cheek. Tracing her jaw line, he kissed a trail to her mouth, brushing her lips teasingly. She smelled like home and tasted like heaven. He purred.

Opening his mouth against hers, his tongue pushed inside, hungrily licking and suckling. He felt her arms snake around his waist and up his back, pulling him against her body, her bosom pressed against his chest. A rush of heat assaulted his body, arousing him, hardening him.

Wrapping his arms around her, he lifted her against him, sliding her body along his hardness, feeling against his breeches the apex between her legs. Instinctively, she tightened her own grip and deepened the kiss. He moaned against her gasping mouth, lost in time and place.

"Ahem!" Hazel loudly cleared her throat, breaking their embrace.

As they untwined limbs, blushing with embarrassment, Hazel began rattling louder than necessary, "Thank you for sharing such horticultural genius, Your Lordship. Yes, I would like to visit the conservatory during my stay. Thank you for the offer."

He realized, then, that although Hazel stood with her back to them for a modicum of privacy, she was pretending to talk to them because someone or several someones were approaching the garden. He made quick work of distancing himself from Lizbeth.

Slipping on his glove, he turned his back to Lizbeth to adjust his nether region so his dalliance wouldn't be quite so obvious to everyone. He could hear them now, voices of three maybe four people coming closer. When he turned, he saw with chagrin that Liz's lips were red and swollen from his embrace.

With a hurried hush, he commanded, "Sniff the roses. My attentions have left a mark."

He snuck a hasty cheek kiss before he retreated to Hazel's side, picking up where she left off. "Aye, the conservatory has clippings and seeds of several genus of roses that you may wish to take with you for your own garden."

He would buy Hazel a rose arbor after being, to his advantage, the most improprietous chaperone he'd ever met. She had the power to force them to marry on the morrow after witnessing such a display of affection, but she knew his intentions were genuine. He suspected she wanted him to romance Liz before the proposal in case her niece held any residual prejudices to marriage. At least that was the impression he received from her earlier.

Three guests entered the garden, then, and eyed Sebastian and his duo with disinterest. Liz's face was buried in the roses, but he noticed with a touch of pride and a chuckle that her neck matched the color of the rose petals. The intruders incuriously passed through the walled garden and out the iron gate at the opposite end.

As naturalistic as the landscape tried to be, Sebastian had always found the garden pretentious, especially the hidden temples and walled sections. Until today. Today he gave a silent thanks to Mr. Brown for designing secret areas in which to hide. Their privacy had, however, been trespassed upon, with more guests entering the rose garden.

As they traipsed back to the house, he cursed at himself for not asking the question he had sought privacy to ask.

An hour later, they found themselves at the dinner table. Everyone removed their gloves to begin the course. Aunt Catherine bragged at her end of the table about taking snuff with Queen Charlotte in the snuff room. Lizbeth sat not far away from him, eyeing Lord Nosehair in alarm. She probably thought Sebastian had exaggerated the man's hair. Now she would realize he had understated the length.

Lady Argot, with the pink bow, sat to his left and demurely blushed, batted eyelashes, and giggled in his direction. He cast her his most forbidding scowl, hoping to discourage her flirtation, for clearly someone had apprised her of both his eligibility and his wealth. Unperturbed, she increased the speed of her eyelash flutter.

By the third course, Lady Argot had nearly driven him to distraction with her incessant chatter about her new wardrobe for next Season. In terms of lady's wiles, he tried to surmise how her wardrobe was supposed to impress him or make for engaging conversation in which to snare a titled bachelor.

He had not said a single word yet, not that the blonde twit noticed or cared. In desperation, he turned his most menacing frown her way, which usually sent little ladies like her running for the hills, but this one was persistent, not the least abashed by his poor mannerisms or rude behavior. Aunt Catherine must have numbered his titles for the vixen. He admired her determination at the very least.

He cast a silent, desperate plea to Lizbeth. She looked back, taking enormously unladylike bites of a bread roll. It took all his fortitude not to howl with laughter as he racked his brain to remember what they had agreed large bites and bread rolls would signal.

A diabolical smile spread across his face.

Turning to Lady Talksalot, he said just loud enough for Lizbeth to hear, "Have you ever eaten haggis?"

Lady Pinkbow stopped talking to gape at his first words of the evening. "Hagwhat?"

"Haggis. There's a most endearing ode to the delectable dish by the illustrious poet Robert Burns that you simply must hear. After which recitation, if you're duly impressed, I will invite you to swim with me in the Annick lake at midnight tonight, in the buff if you're daring. What do you say, Lady Argot?"

Without his needing to say more, the young lady gasped and glowered, her face red with humiliation. As appalled as she was by his uncouth reply to her new wardrobe, he was honestly surprised she didn't slap him in front of all and sundry. The lady turned away from him to initiate conversation to the gentleman on her other side.

Disappointing. He had hoped to recite Burns for her listening pleasure.

A quick look towards Liz rewarded him with a face equally tinged red, but only from holding back what likely would have been raucous laughter. Her eyes sparkling, she shook her head at him, then said across the table that he was the silliest man in England.

Without a shadow of doubt, he wanted to marry this woman.

Chapter 21

The second week passed uneventfully, at least by her estimation. She helped her sister organize an autumn fete, sat rigidly in drawing room chairs while Charlotte entertained, and was treated to steady visitations of Sebastian, who insisted several times on talking with her privately but never offered more than polite conversation, fidgeting with his chronometer instead of speaking his mind.

Lizbeth's third week in Northumberland arrived to find her bereft. Nothing had been settled with Sebastian.

For all his sultry glances, he appeared only to desire friendship. She couldn't fathom why he had kissed her in the garden if he weren't interested in courting her. Was she so terrible at kissing?

To her relief, he had not made overtures of wanting her as a ladybird, which she feared was an impending offer. She began to suspect he saw her as a friend with whom he could safely pursue a physical relationship without worrying she would trap him into marriage. As unorthodox as it would be to proposition a spinster as a mistress, it wasn't outside the realm of possibility, not after they had both expressed such disinterest in marriage. What other explanation could there be for his refusal to court her properly?

The thought made her sick. No, she didn't want an unhappy marriage wherein she would be a piece of property. But she didn't want to be someone's mistress either. To think that might be his only interest in her made her ill for nearly the entire second week of her visit. Her hope for more waned with each passing day.

While they still had time, all the days in the world couldn't motivate a disinterested man to make a move. Had she sent the wrong signals? Had she made too much of a deal of not wanting to marry? Did he truly not feel the same way about her?

Her heart ached that he hadn't made any declarations or given her a reason to extend her stay. The winter months were far enough that if prompted, she could extend her stay another month. Alas, no such prompting came from either her sister or Sebastian.

She sat in the parlor with Captain Henry, reading a book from Annick's study, a surprise from the duke himself who had been making a concentrated effort to befriend her. Not an entirely losing battle, as much as she disliked him, since her sister did appear happier. Whatever their marriage woes, the encouragement from herself and the private words from Aunt Hazel seemed to do the trick.

The cockatoo serenaded her while she read the same line in succession, her mind otherwise engaged. During Sebastian's most recent visit, he had extended an invitation to the entire family to lunch at his home, Dunstanburgh Castle. Charlotte and Annick declined, and thus did the dowager duchess and Lady Mary. Hazel and Lizbeth were the only two to accept his offer. She suspected Hazel accepted to prompt Lizbeth to do so. Hazel's matchmaking, however much in vain, was obvious.

The clock couldn't possibly tick slower. The words in the book blurred as Liz stared unseeingly at the page, too busy counting the minutes to his arrival.

Even if she did have a somewhat disparaging vision of a ruined lean-to for his home and Sebastian welcoming them to the pile of rubble with claims it needed light restoration, she nevertheless looked forward to seeing his castle. He was, after all, the first Lancaster to live there for several centuries.

She wondered if seeing his home would bring them closer together, if somehow the intimacy of being in his private dwelling would break the barriers, initiating a proposal. Bah! She needed to release the dream. He would never propose. He would never open to her.

She had begun to heal after London, but then this trip dredged up all the buried feelings for him. Marriage was out of the question. He was nothing more than a dream, an ideal she'd created that didn't exist. The sooner she accepted the truth, the less she would be hurt by his rejection. Again.

The parlor door opened. Liz straightened imperceptibly to find the dowager duchess in the doorway. Cane thumping, Catherine walked to her favorite chair, sat, and said not a word. Liz resumed reading, and Captain Henry resumed serenading.

"He was my fourth child," announced Catherine.

Liz looked up at her sister's mother-in-law, the woman's eyes fixed on Annick's portrait.

"I thought you had two children," Liz declared.

"You thought erroneously. He was my fourth, the first to survive beyond a year of age."

"I'm so sorry, Your Grace."

"No, you are not. You did nothing for which to be sorry."

The woman turned her eyes on Lizbeth, eyes the same dark shade as Sebastian's, only devoid of emotion, cold orbs of coal.

"Marrying the duke was the best day of my life," Catherine continued, "but marriage was not without trials. I've fought for my son to have everything I never had."

Liz wriggled uncomfortably in her chair, unsure about the intimate conversation. The dowager had spoken to her several times during the visit, but never anything personal aside from gardening and her fondness of Lyonn Manor.

"Arguably, I have overindulged my son." Catherine admitted. "And he thanks me by marrying beneath him."

"I beg your pardon?" She closed her book.

"Don't get haughty. It is a fact, not a judgment. Even you cannot deny it, for you know as well as I do that he married beneath him. I am fond of my daughter-in-law. She may be of embarrassingly low birth, but she is his gift to me, and I accept. I am devoted to completing her training. Once she overcomes the silliness of youth, she'll make an exquisite duchess."

"I'm not sure how you expect me to respond. You've insulted my sister, and me in the process, but in the same breath complimented her. What are you hoping I will say, Your Grace?" Lizbeth questioned, clutching the book in anger.

"Nothing. I do not insult or compliment. I state facts. It is my prerogative to do so. You and your sister are landed gentry, but not of noble lineage. Fact. She will make as great a duchess as I, if not greater. Fact. Both my son and my nephew are enamored of the Trethows. Fact. And now is your turn to state a fact. I will know if you lie." Her face was austere stone. "Are you trifling with my nephew, or do you love him?"

Lizbeth choked on air.

Locking eye contact, Liz answered honestly, consequences be damned, "Yes, Your Grace, I love him."

Catherine scrutinized her in silence, the black eyes searching Lizbeth for evidence of lies.

"I suspected as much." The dowager tapped her gold-handled cane on the floor then stood. "As you were." She about-faced and left the room, leaving Liz in a daze.

Without inflection, her words could mean anything. Did Catherine disapprove? Was she angry? The tap of her cane felt like a stamp of approval, oddly, but that couldn't be right, not after she had insulted both Lizbeth's and Charlotte's social station.

Lizbeth had little time to reflect on the duchess' behavior before Aunt Hazel bustled in to announce the carriage's arrival, open topped, vis-à-vis seating, Sebastian at the reins.

"He looks positively wild, my dear," Hazel exclaimed. "You'll enjoy the view, I declare, if you sit facing him."

Liz tied her bonnet and donned her gloves before leaving the parlor, then followed her aunt to the horseshoe drive. Sebastian stood waiting, looking dashingly untamed. While his hair was pulled back with a ribbon, loose wisps whipped freely about his face. He looked splendid. Make that breathtaking. Positively ideal.

Hat in hand, he bowed to them, his lips curving into a wide smile. He returned the tricorn to his unruly locks and held out both hands to take Hazel's, kissing her on each cheek with exuberance. Turning to Liz, he snuck a peck on each of Lizbeth's cheeks, as well, before showing them to the sociable carriage.

For the entirety of the drive, he entertained them with the bawdiest folk songs she, and Hazel, had ever heard. Hazel laughed beneath her parasol and insisted on learning the words so the two of them could sing a duet of mismatched notes and vulgar lyrics.

The sun beat down on her bonnet, the wind fought to unhand Hazel's parasol, and the meadow flowers weaved a merry dance. She couldn't remember when she had been happier or more amused.

As they closed in on the last few miles of the drive, the landscape changed, becoming less developed, more windswept and dramatic. Sebastian pointed out a herd of deer grazing in the moor, not far from a mob of sheep. Meadows with habitats of birds dipping in and out of the flowers stretched as far as the eye could see. Hills speckled the horizon, inviting observers to roll down their slopes.

Sebastian glanced back at them and grinned. "We're almost there!"

The farther they traveled, the windier it became. Hazel finally closed her parasol and held tight to her bonnet. Liz sniffed the air. Salty. She would know the smell of the sea anywhere. How close were they to the coast? Charlotte hadn't made any mention of the sea, so Liz had assumed they were at least a day inland, but her nose did not lie.

The carriage bumped along a narrow path until Hazel nudged her to look left. Past a large mere, the sun glinting off the surface of the lake water, the land soared upwards into a low-lying fog. She couldn't see beyond the gray cloud, but she knew she had arrived at the Isle of Avalon.

A patch of forest stood not far to the right, the remainder of the area an uncultivated park. Tall, grassy dunes blocked views beyond. She hoped, wistfully, there might be a beach tucked behind those dunes, perhaps even a cliff or headland. The roar of the ocean was unmistakable. Although she still couldn't see it, she could hear it, the sound of the crashing waves competing only with the howl of the wind.

Sebastian drove circuitously around two of the three meres that surrounded the steep hill, slowing the horses to cross a drawbridge leading to a stone outer gatehouse. Liz peered over the edge of the carriage into the watery depth of the lake.

If her reading of the terrain proved correct, the castle would be quite impervious to assault. Between the meres, the sand dunes, the steepness of the hill, and what she believed would be the ocean to its back, there would be only one way into the castle.

Sebastian stopped the carriage just beyond the outer gatehouse. A path before them led straight into the gray shroud.

Hazel and Liz waited, staring curiously at the fog. Sebastian turned to his guests, smiling broadly, also waiting.

"Well," said Hazel, impatiently. "I'm not staying here in the wind and sun. Lead on!"

"Patience," Sebastian cajoled. "The wind has only enhanced the beauty of my two guests, and the sun will hide behind the clouds for another few minutes yet."

And so, they waited. The lighter fingers of fog around the dunes began to lift, revealing narrow glimpses of beach beyond. Liz spied black rock and sand swallowed by a high tide to the left of the curtain wall and a small marshland on the south shoreline where seagulls trumpeted a welcome.

A hearty laugh brought her attention back to Sebastian as he stretched his arms towards the fog. As though by magic from his fingertips, the wind whirled the mist northwest, leaving in its wake a stone majesty, its backdrop a glittering sea. Liz gasped.

"May I present my humble home."

The land sloped upwards. A twenty-foot tall stone curtain stretched to each side of the outer gatehouse. Beyond, the castle rose from the earth, monumental. Two round towers that must be at least twenty or thirty feet wide each and four or more stories tall stood to either side of an imposing door.

Sebastian, apparently satisfied with their awed reaction, turned back to the horses and continued forward to the second gatehouse.

Despite the formidable stone, this was the most enchanting visage she had ever seen. Just like the castle's lord. Rays of sun broke through the clouds to illuminate the towers.

He drew the carriage to a two-story entry and helped them both down. Double, black oak doors studded with iron nails greeted them. While it would have been quite a sight to see those great doors opened by half a dozen footmen, a butler opened a smaller wicket door instead.

She stepped forward then realized Sebastian hadn't followed. He stood by the carriage, talking with a stable boy who soon led the horses around the wall to an unseen stable. Hazel saw herself through the wicket door, leaving Sebastian and Lizbeth standing outside alone.

Sebastian came to her. He took her hand, lacing his fingers with hers. Her pulse raced.

"Well, my darling, are you ready to step into my world?" he asked, squeezing her hand.

With an anxious nod, she walked at his side through the portal, transported to utopia.

They entered a wide foyer with doors to either side and an open room ahead. The butler took their bonnets and accessories before they proceeded into a two-story gallery that ran the length of the two towers. A sweeping stairwell to the left led to the next floor. The arched ceiling was painted to mimic the sky, and a railing on the floor above looked down to them, teasing them to explore further.

Never would Lizbeth have assumed the inside would be this grand.

Directly in front, along the long wall of the gallery, lined glass double-doors open to a massive inner courtyard. From this vantage point, she could see the other wings of the home surrounded the courtyard, all with open glass doors.

Inside the gallery, the walls were decorated with tapestries hanging from iron rods. Every inch of the gallery breathed warmth, meticulous planning, and personal touches. She had never felt so at home.

Sebastian walked into the center of the room, arms outstretched. "I am your servant today. What would you like to do first? Lunch? Cliff diving?"

"Oh heavens, young man. I'm too old and too sensible for cliff diving. I would like a tour before lunch. We've come to see the castle, have we not?" Hazel turned to her niece, brows arched.

"A tour sounds divine. Show us what all you've done. Start with these tapestries. Shouldn't a gallery feature family portraits?" Liz admired the decor.

Sebastian waved her to join him. The nearest set of tapestries, hanging between the open doors, wafted in the breeze. "Roddam Hall houses the family portraits. The last thing I want are the eyes of my predecessors judging me. I'd much prefer to surround myself with beauty, not to mention these are in keeping with the castle motif, don't you think?"

Liz nodded. Hazel walked to Liz's other side and studied the tapestries.

"The collection in this gallery is exclusively the art of François Boucher and Francesco Zuccarelli," Sebastian explained, intimately touching his hand to Lizbeth's lower back, sending tremors down her spine. "I prefer tapestries over paintings because of the craftsmanship and artistry of the jacquard weave. I'm thankful this collection is complete because both factories I order from have halted production given the turmoil in France. I have a list of future orders that I would like for the dining room, if they ever re-open, that is." He shook his head, dejected.

With a nudge of his hand, Sebastian led her through the gallery. Not a single tapestry stood as a solo piece. All belonged to a thematic set, many steeped in mythology. They circled the room, pausing at a tapestry with cherubs and women lounging in the clouds looking below to a man holding a sword.

"I very much like it. The man resembles you." Liz spoke before noticing the man in the scene was nude except a strategically placed red sheet. The sight of the muscular bare chest flushed her cheeks.

"You think I look like the god of fire?" he said huskily, his lips inches from her ear.

She opened her mouth to respond but found she could do no more than imitate a fish.

Sebastian chuckled throatily, his breath tickling her cheek. Stepping away from her, he said, "This is *Vulcan Presenting Venus with Arms for Aeneas*, the final piece in the set from when Venus seduced Vulcan to forge weapons for her son. The set, if you'll walk further down, includes Venus seducing him, asking for the weapon, and then Vulcan forging the weapon. There's another piece, not in the set but matching the theme, where Vulcan catches Venus in a compromising position with Mars. A naughty work, but I'm desperate to add it to the collection."

Liz studied the other works in the set and blushed again, her face likely a blotchy red, for it certainly felt feverish. In each piece, Vulcan draped the red cloth only between his legs, and in one of the tapestries, the cloth slipped suggestively low.

The man in the tapestry looked so much like Sebastian she felt pure, carnal desire. Vulcan's muscular physique recalled the feel of Sebastian's back when she held him to her in the rose garden, and Vulcan's strong thighs reminded her of how the buckskin had stretched across Sebastian's own muscled legs that day after her arrival.

"You'll pardon my saying, but the people in these pieces are scantily clad, to put it mildly." Hazel's voice startled Lizbeth from her reverie. "Not that I object. On the contrary, it's refreshing to see. The world has gone prudish."

She had forgotten about her aunt. Mortified to be thinking such dirty thoughts in the presence of her aunt, she pressed her hands against her cheeks and stared at the floor.

Hazel paid no heed to her niece, having wandered to the far side by the stairwell.

Sebastian, brave soul, walked to Hazel and joked, "You're a woman of good taste. I'm not surprised to find you appreciative of the honest bareness of the flesh."

"Oh ho, young man. You're a rogue in disguise!" Hazel opened her fan and waved it furiously about her face.

They spoke about one of the pieces, allowing Liz time to recover. Despite the flowing breeze, the gallery felt overly warm. Liz was still recuperating when

Sebastian returned, taking her by the hand, and leading her up the broad staircase.

"Come upstairs with me," he said, seductively.

Lizbeth hesitated, her heels digging into the runner. Was her imagination overreacting, or had his intentions turned as disgraceful as her thoughts?

"Come, Hazel!" Sebastian called. "I want to show you the armory before we tour the other wings."

As if realizing her uncertainty, he cast her a reassuring smile and waited for Hazel to catch up to them. When they reached the next floor, positioned directly above the entrance, they found themselves in an armory. An open railing looked over the gallery. A set of narrow, spiral staircases positioned at both corners of the room.

Swords, pikes, horns, and axes decorated the walls. A series of tapestries hung at intervals between the weapons, all depicting Neptune's triumph. Liz recognized a few of the artists: Poussin, Giordano, Gherardini, Spranger, Francken.

The most striking element of the room, however, was the larger-than-life statue of Neptune holding his trident.

"How in the world did you get that into the castle?" Liz inquired, wide-eyed.

"The artist designed and sculpted it here in the armory. Did you expect to see King Arthur? It might surprise you to learn I have other passions." He winked. "My si—that is to say, someone in my past, used to call me Poseidon as a joke."

"It's beautiful," Lizbeth drawled. Then it dawned on her that Neptune stood in glorious nakedness. How had she not noticed right away?

Shamefaced, she turned away. As if the tapestries weren't erotic enough, now she faced a floor-to-ceiling statue of a naked god. She trained her eyes upwards until Sebastian began explaining one of the maces to Hazel. Unobserved, she curiously flitted her eyes back to the statue and gaped. When she averted her eyes, resting them on the Neptune's upper region, she discovered staring at the bare chest wasn't a vast improvement from staring at the lower region since it showcased strength, masculinity, and virility.

She wondered what Sebastian's bare chest looked like. She pressed her hands to her cheeks again. What a hypocrite she was. She didn't want him to be interested in her as a possible mistress, yet all she could think about was what he might look like unclothed.

How could art be so sexually charged? Everything about this home so far, from the landscape to the art communicated feral, uninhibited sexuality, carnality. Even more interesting, it all seemed perfectly natural, not improper, only a celebration of physical beauty. And it all fit him so well.

Despite his reservations and his solitary demeanor, Sebastian was a man of raw passion. She had felt it before, suspected he bottled a volcano of emotion, but to see that inner passion infused into his home as though the home itself was his outlet, convinced her he was far more impassioned than she would have ever dreamed. What would it be like to unleash the beast?

The realization excited her as well as frightened her. Who was this man, and what else about himself did he keep hidden from the world's prying eyes?

"The point of the guardroom is to admire the arms rather than the statue, you know."

She whipped her head towards him, eyes wide, only then registering she had been standing perfectly still, staring at the naked Neptune the entire time.

Her saving grace from humiliation was Hazel ascending one of the spiral staircases.

Sebastian darted in front of the woman, baring the stairs with his arms. "No, actually, that's off limits."

Hazel huffed. "You're a terrible guide to close rooms. What's up there that's such a secret, hmm?"

"Well, you're welcome to proceed if you'd like." He stepped to one side to let her pass. "But you'll only find my bedchamber."

He laughed as Hazel's cheeks turned pink.

"Oh, I see. Yes, well, that's better left not toured, then," she professed.

"I believe my bedchamber is tidy enough for your quizzing eyes, but I won't accompany you if it's all the same."

"No, a description will suffice," Hazel said.

"Well, let me paint a larger picture first. The gatehouse, where we are now, is five stories tall. The ground floor is the gallery, which you've already seen. The first floor is this armory." Sebastian pointed upwards to the ceiling. "The next floor is only accessible from the spiral staircases. One side, the one you just mounted, Hazel, leads to my bedchamber. The other side, which I would like to save for the finale of our tour, is the library. There is a stairwell within each of the rooms leading to smaller towers with windowed-walls. They were once watchtowers for archers, but now they're nothing more than rooms for meditation. The bedchamber and library are connected in the middle by a sitting room."

"Why can't we see the library now?" Liz was more curious at this point about his bedroom but scolded herself on such impure thoughts.

He smiled slyly. "I expect it to be your favorite room, so I've saved it for last. Interestingly, this room we're in now used to be the great hall, while the gallery on the ground floor used to be the guardroom. I took some liberties with the renovations because I wanted a more modern layout, as well as one more suited to my life preferences."

"I'm envious the lord's chamber is next to the library. If I could design my perfect home, that's exactly what I would do. But where is the lady's chamber?" Liz asked, biting her lip sheepishly.

He coughed a laugh, rubbing the back of his neck. "As I said, I renovated to suit my life's circumstances. Since I never intended to marry, I turned the original lady's chamber into the library. Should I change my mind…" He paused to look knowingly at Lizbeth, making her stomach flip-flop. "…my poor wife would have to sleep in the library."

Liz and Hazel both laughed until he added, "I would assume she would prefer to share my bedchamber, however."

The three stood awkwardly, Hazel's laughter the last to die.

They followed him back to the gallery and into the north wing. The drawing room opened on the left with sets of windowed doors looking out to the beach, and opened on the right into the corridor, which had its own set of windowed doors leading to the inner courtyard. Beyond the drawing room was the dining room.

"Past this door is the kitchen, bakehouse, and servants' quarters, which leads out to a small gatehouse for a private entrance into the curtain wall from the north slope. The stables are there, as well. This is where we continue our tour to the south wing."

They walked outside and across the inner courtyard into the south wing, which housed upstairs the guest accommodations, and on the ground floor a ballroom and a parlor, doors from the parlor leading back to the gallery. Such rooms seemed out of character, and when pressed, Sebastian explained that many of the rooms had already been renovated and designated by his great grandfather, so he left them to focus on the areas more meaningful to him. In time, he may repurpose the entertainment areas since he never entertained.

"All rooms in the castle," he explained, "are two-stories high, have a view to both the courtyard and to the ocean, and feature a fireplace large enough to walk into. In the dead of winter, the chill creeps its way through the stone, so fireplaces are essential. During the summer, the castle becomes quite warm, hence all of the doors to the outside to promote crosswinds."

Liz wondered if Hazel was bored silly. If this had been any other home, she might have been, as well, but she couldn't help throughout the tour imagining herself living here with him, envisioning what his life must be like within these walls, and certainly she couldn't deny him the pride of showing them around when he had made it clear that no one other than his cousin had ever visited his castle after the renovations. Given their first quarrel had been over the legend of his castle, she knew without doubt this was one of his most valued lifeworks.

Linking hands again, Sebastian walked them through the guest accommodations, and then showed them the morning room and conservatory of the east wing, followed by the upper floors of both wings, many of the rooms still a blank slate ready to be designated into a music room, a billiards room, studios for woodworking and craftsmanship, additional guest quarters, or whatever his imagination could fathom.

Following the completion of the indoor tour, he ushered them out to a sheer cliffside. With each passing minute she fell more in love with Dunstanburgh.

"I don't know how much either of you know about castles, but since I'm giving this tour, you'll have to suffer through some of my renovation processes." He winked at Liz, his hand still holding hers. "What you've just seen is the don-jon, often known as the keep. The term is misleading, in a way, because this castle has a concentric design with an outer quadrangular curtain and an inner quadrangular wherein the inner walls of the castle serve as the keep itself rather than a central and separate building as the keep. It's the same design as Windsor Castle.

"This is all I've been able to renovate. My great-grandfather who first began to rebuild it in its original splendor, made massive structural changes. I followed his plan with alterations of my own. His purse was much larger than mine at the outset of restoration, so I am pleased he renovated as much as he did or else I would be deep in debt already and living under a leaky roof."

Walking along the perimeter of the cliffside, Liz could see where the curtain wall ended, leaving much of the property open to the sea.

Sebastian continued, "It may be a castle, but I wanted it to feel more like a Tudor manor, a comfortable home with those one-hundred-and-eighty-degree views so valued by the Tudors. I've added glass doors, where at one point there were only arrow slits or walls. I took liberties to make it feel more like a home and less like a fortress."

The wind whipped around them so fiercely, she had to strain to hear him. A strong gust sent her side-stepping towards him. She grabbed onto his arm and used him as a shield against the wind as they walked. He laughed and wrapped an arm around her shoulders, pulling her to his side.

She felt at home here, much like she felt on her cliff in Trevena. Rather than walking half a mile to visit her cliff, this castle lived on a cliff. The cliff and beach were different, the terrain more so, but she felt at home nonetheless. She never wanted to leave. She wanted to send her aunt on her way and remain in this myth-steeped castle forever.

"I'm not accustomed to you being so quiet. You aren't disappointed by the views, are you?" He eyed her, his thumb caressing her shoulder.

"Far from it," she reassured. "I could look at these views every day for the rest of my life, Sebastian." Liz said before she could stop herself.

"Could you?" he questioned quietly, studying her from between the flying wisps of his hair.

She smiled self-consciously, looking back to the ocean. The sun still shone, bouncing off white-capped waves, but dark clouds loomed to the south, bringing in a fierce wind that pushed the waves against the one-hundred-foot cliff below.

Liz had once imagined kissing Sebastian on a cliff. At the time she had dreamt of her favorite headland in Trevena, but now it all made more sense that she would kiss him on this cliff, on his cliff. She closed her eyes to listen to the ocean, feel the wind against her skin, and imagine his lips against hers.

Oh, to live here with him, to kiss him on this promontory every day. She didn't just feel at home with the castle, but at home with Sebastian. She was seeing a piece of his soul, this castle a reflection of him. Never had she imagined he lived in such a place, that he was so naturally at ease here without any of the reserve or unhappiness she often saw in his eyes.

Hazel interrupted her fantasy by saying, "Carry on, young man. What's next?" Hazel shielded her eyes from the sun, clearly wishing she had grabbed her parasol.

"Well, there's naught else that has been renovated, sadly. I hope to one day turn the two ruined towers into astronomy conservatories, but for now they do at least have climbable stairs that afford a marvelous view of the cove on one side and Embleton beach on the other. If the two of you are daring, we could walk down to explore the beach." Sebastian, too, held his hand to his forehead in mock salute to block the sun.

The darker clouds from the south were briskly heading their direction, promising to blot out the sun.

She wondered what might happen if they were forced by foul weather to stay at the castle for the night.

"I will leave such exploring for younger legs, thank you very much," Hazel said. "But if you wouldn't mind, I am ready for that lunch you promised."

Lizbeth doubted Aunt Hazel would be derelict in her duties long enough for a private beach stroll with Sebastian, but she would much rather that than lunch, especially when this may be her only chance to see the castle and one of her last chances to have Sebastian alone. She silently prayed for a torrential downpour to trap them at the castle.

"One last part of the tour before we return," Sebastian insisted.

Hazel huffed but followed him as he led them down the slope to a peninsula where a large gazebo with stone benches looked out to the sea.

Sebastian waved his hands for them to sit and promptly took the spot next to Liz. Hazel sat on the far side to admire the unobstructed view of the sea, her back to them. Liz wondered if the curtain wall had once extended this far, as well, or if the cliff had been protection enough against assailants.

"This is one of my favorite seats, especially in the early mornings," he said to Lizbeth, knowing Hazel couldn't hear him over the wind and waves.

The clouds rolled in, pulling behind them another fog. *Please rain. Please rain. Please rain.* Lizbeth chanted as the fog worked its way around the south side of the hill, the view to the north, humorously, still brightly sunny.

Sebastian seemed unmoved by the looming darkness. "As you know, I have five earldoms and one barony. This is the barony. It is small, only one thousand acres before it becomes the Annick duchy, but it is my oasis. Along the outskirts, I've developed a bit of the land to generate money, namely with a timber farm and sawmill, a bee farm, a deer park which we passed through, and sheep and cattle farm. All are tended by tenants. I've kept all the land leading to the castle undeveloped for my private residence. I plan to keep it that way. I want the landscape to remain natural, void of formal gardens or Scottish golf courses, not on my moors," he said with a soft laugh.

Liz admired the twinkle of his eyes. He was so alive. No brooding, no sullen moodiness, just full of life and happiness.

"I love it here, Sebastian," Liz said adamantly.

"Do you?" He implored, as though he had hoped to impress her, hoped she would love it here.

Or maybe that's what she wanted him to hope.

"Everything here is full of magic. Can't you feel the tingle?" She shouted to Hazel.

Hazel tittered and shouted back, "I think that's the sea air, love, and possibly a spot of rain."

Sebastian cut in. "No chance of rain today. The fog here is a haar, or a sea fret as we call it in Northumberland, and it haunts the coast. It is most common in the early mornings when the warm air meets the cold sea temperatures. Depending on the wind, the fog can stick around for hours, making travel nigh impossible, and sometimes, as with today, it will move on in minutes."

Even as he spoke, the clouds descended on their gazebo, shrouding them in the same gray fog that had shielded the castle from view earlier. The mist was so thick, she couldn't see Hazel across the gazebo.

Before she could remark on the weather, Sebastian leaned towards her and pressed his lips against hers, taking advantage of the limited visibility and her vulnerability. As soon as his lips touched hers, a wet warmth throbbed between her legs.

She reached for his shoulders and gripped them with hungry desperation, greeting his lips with hers parted. His tongue flicked against hers, and then he was gone, hidden by the fog and out of reach.

Oh, heavens, what if that was their final embrace, she thought despairingly.

She stopped herself from crying out for him. Closing her eyes, she cooled from his touch and tried not to swoon from the onslaught of loss at his departure.

"If we wait," he said against the roar of the wind, "the clouds and mist will pass."

They waited until the clouds passed, taking with them the fog and the promise of rain.

He looked between Hazel and Liz, the corners of his eyes crinkling. "Thank you both for coming. It means more than I can say to share this. Although Drake has been here a handful of times, he's only made it as far as my study and reminds me often the whole renovation is a preposterous waste of time and money."

"But it's not a waste. Not when you've produced such splendor, not when you live in this paradise,"

Liz defended, still tingling from the magic, or the sea air, or maybe from his kiss.

Hazel cleared her throat. "The tour is much appreciated. That said, you two may enjoy these noisy winds, but I've had as much as I can handle. I can barely hear myself think. May we retreat inside for lunch?" Hazel stood before either could argue.

After lunch, Sebastian offered the tour finale of the library. Lizbeth was ever aware of the ticking of time, their visit nearly at an end. While she knew she needn't be too disappointed yet since they weren't to return to Cornwall until the end of the following week, she suspected if he wasn't going to take advantage of her visit to his home, the prospects were hopeless. Hazel might say she was giving up too early, but she felt she had waited long enough. Stolen kisses were wonderful, but if that was all she could ever expect, it wasn't enough. It bordered on insulting.

Now, as much as she had looked forward to seeing the library, she hardly saw the point anymore. Why torment herself with yet another room she'd want to live in but never be given the opportunity to do so?

Hazel seemed just as unenthusiastic with his suggestion. She retorted, "I don't mean to disappoint either of you, but I do believe I cannot climb another set of stairs. You have no small home nor shortage of inclines, sirrah. Lizbeth, you can see it if you wish, but I'm staying in the parlor. Think of me what you will."

"We won't think any less of you, Hazel," Sebastian reassured. "I fear I will lose Lizbeth to a fantastical world of literature as soon as we ascend the stairs, so consider yourself momentarily fortunate to retire to the parlor. Lizbeth, would you still care to see the library?"

With a nod, she followed him.

Chapter 22

Sebastian's library, a dark-stained oak sanctuary, greeted the pair with an impressive two-story domed ceiling, wall-lined shelves with tens of thousands of books, and floor to ceiling windows punctuating the lengths of the shelves. To Sebastian, ascending the stone stairwell into this room was an ascension into heaven itself.

His desk, a slab of polished wood, stood guard in front of a floor to ceiling stained glass window of Excalibur held in the hand of the Lady of the Lake. Rolled parchment littered the desk next to neat stacks of paperwork. An almost hidden stone staircase next to the stained glass led to the smaller tower, and a doorway on the opposite side of the room led to the private sitting room.

Jacquard woven tapestries with wooden and gold placards framed the hearth on the far wall, a sitting area in front of the walk-in fireplace. Half of the room rounded with the tower, custom shelves crafted to fit the concave shape. Two railed ladders leaned against the shelves to aid in reaching books.

A catwalk stretched around the room to allow access to the second-floor books, a rounded oak staircase leading from the main floor to the catwalk tucked in a far corner. A rococo style mural encircled the ceiling with the Arthurian knights parading around a center medallion that instead of being decorative plaster as with most ceilings, was an open glass sky light, flooding the room with bright indirect sunlight.

Sebastian searched Liz's expressions for hints to her perceptions. She seemed to like his home, and that meant more to him than words could say. He let nerves get the best of him over the week, causing him to worry about her reaction to the castle. Even if she favored him, she may not care for his way of life.

What if she thought it was too far from civilized society? What if she hated the temperamental weather? What if she turned in disgust from his choices in decor? What if the glimpses of his passions, nay, his obsessions, frightened her?

So many what ifs. He felt exposed showing her his home, part of his soul laid bare for her. If she didn't love his home, she could never love him.

As far as he could tell, so far, she appeared enchanted, or perhaps that should be enchanting. He couldn't keep from touching her, from looking at her, a school boy infatuated by his first crush.

He stepped back, inviting her to explore the room at her leisure, to touch and inspect. She stood in front of his tapestry collection, all Arthurian themed. The largest one in the room told the entire tale from left to right in pictorial form, the first scene showing Arthur pulling the sword from the stone, and the last scene showing him in armor with his knights.

Her slender fingers touched the tapestry as she read its story.

Drake had always told him how foolish he was to obsess over myths. His passion would not be quelled, but that didn't lessen the hurt he felt when everyone, even his cousin, dampened his interests. Studying legends is foolish. Restoring a castle is a waste of money. Reading of other religions is sacrilege. He finally learned not to share his personal interests.

While some might find his collecting a fascinating hobby, it was much deeper. The studying of legends gave him a reason to live during his darkest hours. He found in King Arthur a role model, the kind of man he wanted to be. Few would understand that. Would she?

Lizbeth stood in front of a tapestry inspired by *The Faerie Queen*. "What is this one? It doesn't have a placard."

"It's 'The Red Cross Knight Slaying a Dragon' from that very book you were reading when we first met." He walked over to her, placing his hand on the small of her back and looking up at the tapestry with her.

"But why would you have—oh! Spenser mentions Arthur and Merlin, doesn't he? How funny I've never made that connection before."

He smiled down at her, more in love with her than she could imagine. Only she would understand without him having to explain. She leaned her head against his shoulder for a moment before walking to the centerpiece of his entire collection—the tapestries of Arthur and Guinevere, each serving as the lady's and lord's portrait. She bent to read the wood carvings beneath.

"'Gwenhwyfar / Guanhumara.' I'm afraid I don't know what either of those words means," she confessed.

"Guinevere. The first is in Welsh because the legend of Arthur originated in Wales. The second is in Latin from Monmouth's manuscript accounting for the history of King Arthur and the other kings of Britain."

He joined her, returning his hand to her back, his new favorite spot to touch, his hand nestling comfortably against the arch of her waist. He traced her spine with a finger until he touched the nape of her neck. Goosebumps rose to meet his fingertips as he brushed his hand against her bare skin, trailing up to her ears and around her jaw.

She was perfection itself. She could bring happiness to his life, help him keep his demons at bay. A panic deep in the pit of his stomach surged. She would leave in a countable number of days. All should have been settled well before now. He couldn't lose her, yet he was deathly afraid of what it would take to keep her. He wasn't sure he was strong enough.

"Wasn't Guinevere adulterous?"

He shook the direction of his thoughts as he tried to focus on what she had just said. She stared at him, awaiting an answer.

He stammered, "I don't follow."

"You have a tapestry of Guinevere. I realize she was his queen, but didn't she have an affair with Lancelot?"

Sebastian laughed. "I see your confusion. Yes, but no. Monmouth made no allusions to infidelity. Guinevere was all that was good in this world, Arthur's perfect match. The French, as only they can do, gave her a lover when they rewrote the original tale. I can hardly forgive them for besmirching her name. Chretien de Troyes is the poet who invented Lancelot and the affair with the queen. Other writers followed suit. I will never believe the real Guinevere would have done such a thing, and neither did our Arthurian historian Geoffrey of Monmouth. Therein lies the difference between the writing of histories and fiction. I think of the queen in much the same way as Odysseus' wife Penelope, faithful to her love despite years of absence and rumor of death. They were perfect queens, perfect mates, counterparts to their husband's soul. Loyal, faithful, loving, supportive, leaders, equals. Some might argue they were stronger than their husbands, ruling in the king's absence. I could go on, but I don't want you to think I'm swooning over other women."

Lizbeth chortled, then turned back to study the tapestry. Not being able to resist touching her more, he leaned over and buried his face against her neck, nuzzling her. She still smelled like meadow flowers. The perfect mate. His perfect queen. The only one who could stand by him in the darkness of night, who could love him despite flaws. King Arthur would have never hesitated to pursue Guinevere. He felt every bit the coward for his own hesitancy.

He wrapped his hand around her waist and held her for an eternity, afraid to let go, afraid to speak, standing motionless, irresolutely, breathing her in and wondering what he ought to do. He felt a frustrating absence of initiative, as he did every time he came this close to settling things. If he waited any longer, he would lose his nerve. The silence was expectant, closing oppressively the longer he held his pose against her, ever the coward.

"Sebastian," said the voice of an angel, the word but a whisper, imploring, questioning, tender and loving.

The feel of her hand against his face as she turned her body to face him infused him with the strength he needed.

He spoke laboriously in a hoarse, unsteady voice. "'Yea, said King Arthur, I love Guinevere. And this damsel is the most valiant and fairest lady that I knew living, or yet that ever I could find.'" He stroked her cheek with his fingertips.

In the lingering silence, he blurted, "Marry me?"

Her expression churned with surprise, happiness, indecision, and affection. He held his breath, not sure what he would do if she rejected him. He hadn't gone about this properly, hadn't courted her officially. What if she wouldn't have him without a proper courtship? What if she wouldn't have him at all? He made a fool of himself with his question. He ruined the greatest friendship he had ever known.

Still silent, she rubbed the back of her hand against his face then wove her fingers into his hair. Pulling his head towards her, she kissed him deeply, grasping his upper arm with her free hand to hold him to her.

Without breaking her embrace, her lips still touching his, she said, "I thought you'd never ask. With all my heart, yes."

He tightened his hold, one arm snaking around her back and the other her waist. He rubbed his nose against hers and kissed her lips, her cheeks, her eyelids, her forehead, and her hair before returning to a more passionate kiss, pushing his tongue between her lips in deep exploration, hungry exploration. She leaned against the wall, pulling him against her to feel the curves of her body.

Everything about her body screamed warmth, softness, and invitation. He nestled himself into the curves as much as their clothing would allow. His lips moved from her mouth down to her neck. She gasped against his ear and rubbed a slender leg against the outside of his thigh, opening her stance to receive his hardness as he pressed against her core through layers of clothes. He would go mad if they let this go any further.

He thrust his tongue into her mouth once more, simulating the deed he so desperately wanted to do, even as she trapped his tongue with her lips and made love to it in her own seductive way. With a forceful final kiss, he pulled away, not wanting to leave her embrace.

Her eyes glazed with passion as they looked up at his. He stepped back, clearing his throat and trying to control animal instinct. Strands of her hair had fallen from her chignon, her face flushed. He imagined he didn't look much different.

"I still must write to your father," he said thickly.

She nodded, her chest rising and falling with quickened breaths.

"I could obtain a special license so we could marry before your aunt leaves," he suggested.

She nodded again, reaching up to inspect the state of her hair.

"Wednesday is a new moon. The weather would be perfection itself with the highest and lowest tides of the month around the castle. You would see it at its best."

"We would wed here?" She asked as she regained composure.

"If you like. Wherever would please you. I could return with you to Trevena if you'd prefer to wed there. Your father could be present for the ceremony if we chose that."

"Oh, heavens, that wouldn't be necessary. That would delay things too much. During the new moon, then?" Her smile made his heart sing. He didn't think he could ever be melancholy again.

"As you wish, Lizbeth, my queen, my enchantress." He couldn't help himself, he leaned in and kissed her again, but maintained space between them before he lost himself to her completely.

After he helped tidy the loose strands about her head, and she did the same for him in return, they descended the stairs, hand-in-hand, to announce the news to a patiently waiting Hazel.

Chapter 23

"Oh, Lizzie, you look beautiful!" exclaimed Charlotte.

The lady's maid tied under Lizbeth's chin the yellow bows of a lace-trimmed bonnet. The wedding gown of silver muslin with embroidered blue flowers hugged Lizbeth's bosom, flowing straight to her ankles. Around the high waist wrapped a blue girdle, an early wedding gift from Sebastian.

"But are you sure? Really, truly sure?" Charlotte asked for the millionth time that day.

"Yes, I'm sure, Charlotte. I wouldn't have it any other way, not for the world," answered Liz as Bettye wrapped her in a silk shawl with blue and yellow embroidered flowers.

Charlotte was dismayed when Lizbeth broke the news to her, questioning her sanity for wanting to marry *that man*. Lizbeth tried to explain why she wanted to marry Sebastian and why on such short notice, but how does one explain love to someone who has never felt it and not associated it with marriage?

From Lizbeth's estimation, Hazel was the only person genuinely pleased. Drake smugly said he knew all along it would happen. Lady Mary offered felicitations, but otherwise didn't seem to care. The dowager duchess stood thin-lipped through the entirety of their announcement. Charlotte assumed Liz married to move close to her.

Her father, at least, echoed Hazel's pleasure in his letter, giving his loving approval along with a kind word that he looked forward to seeing them both when Parliament returned to session. He would send Lizbeth's belongings post haste. Cousin Walter had not yet received Aunt Hazel's correspondence as far as they were aware, but she expected he, too, would be pleased for her and send his well wishes.

The days between the proposal and the wedding had dragged. More than a little tension tied Lizbeth's stomach in knots. Although Sebastian had ridden to London without delay to obtain the special license, Liz couldn't stop worrying he would change his mind during the course of the trip. She put her fretting to rest when he returned the day before the wedding, license in hand.

Bettye slipped Lizbeth's shoes over stockinged feet. Earlier that morning, she had written her wedding date inside her shoes, the souvenir of her wedding day she would cherish always and never wear a second time.

Charlotte and Lizbeth walked from one of the guest rooms in Dunstanburgh Castle to meet the family gathered in the conservatory on this most propitious day, a Wednesday, a new moon.

She locked eyes with Sebastian first, instantly igniting a fire within and thumping her heart. Her betrothed, her bridegroom.

This was not a headstrong decision. He was not to be her husband until death did them part because she wanted to delay her departure home. She realized with full awareness that with this decision, she dashed asunder her plans for independence and solitude, her plans to remain her father's companion until he passed. She walked towards her husband, her choice above all others in the living world, because she had fallen in love with him somewhere between his poetical recitations and the first sight of his home.

The decision wasn't without apprehension, as too many unresolved conflicts still lie behind his eyes and trust had not been fully claimed, but she resolved they would do everything together, building trust side-by-side, solving life's mysteries and unveiling secrets one day at a time. Once united, he would open to her, communicate his fears and dreams. She knew it.

Sebastian traded his wildness for elegance today. His long hair tidily swept into a green ribbon, his silk-satin suit embroidered with yellow and blue to match her dress with the addition of green threads. They would wear today's ensemble for many days to come once London's Season resumed, when she would be announced at the first soiree as The Right Honorable The Countess of Roddam.

He held out his hands to her with a glowing smile. Even his eyes smiled, dark brown irises of open admiration, orbs of hope. Clasping his proffered hands, she had eyes only for him, oblivious to all others around them.

"You're stunning," he whispered before kissing her lightly on the cheek.

The walk across the headland was more pleasant than the week prior, the sun hidden behind white clouds, occasionally peeking through to spy on the wedding. Arm-in-arm they walked outside where the clergyman and parish clerk scurried to take their place in the gazebo on the edge of the cliff.

The month's highest tide covered the rocky beaches and brought the waves crashing higher against the cliff, yet the winds were subtler, softer than before, teasing the hems of dresses and cooling the men in their layers of coats and shirts.

The guests included only Hazel, Charlotte and Drake, the dowager duchess, Lady Mary, and a few on-looking servants, including Liz's lady's maid Bettye and Sebastian's valet.

Everyone gathered around the couple as they approached the clergyman. They faced each other, hands clasped, and esteemed each other through the man's speech about the marital duties of each party as dictated by God.

Sebastian, his hands trembling, slipped a gold band on Liz's finger and spoke the vows, "With this ring I thee wed, with my body I thee worship, and with all my worldly goods I thee endow in the Name of the Father, and of the Son, and of the Holy Ghost. Amen."

As she had dreamt so many times since first meeting this strange and wonderful man, he pulled her to him and kissed her on the cliffside, chastely, but full of tender affection. His kiss claimed her for all of time.

The wedding festivities resumed in the dining room with a grand meal, including a sweet mincemeat cake; the first meal, Sebastian told her, that had ever been served for anyone other than himself. While the newlyweds didn't plan to stay with the celebratory group for long, a full evening of dining and socializing was planned for the guests.

The guests, to Lizbeth's delight, acted duly impressed by the castle and grounds, which she knew would please Sebastian. Drake, in all his laced finery and gold-ringed fingers, critiqued the décor and the view, offering more compliments than criticisms.

"But it's so windy here," protested Charlotte. "I wouldn't be able to hear myself think, and I would have to hold my bonnet every time I walked outside." She turned to Liz apologetically. "Then, you always did like walking to the seaside, didn't you?"

Before the meal began, Liz escaped to the drawing room to gather the stowed gifts for each of her guests, including a sewn shirt for Sebastian. As she collected the gifts, all small but personal, the dowager duchess stepped into the room and thumped her way to Lizbeth.

The bride inwardly cringed at her approach. *Please, no insults* today, she begged silently.

"I offer my congratulations on your nuptials," said Catherine, her mouth set in a perpetually dour line, no indication of pleasure in her expression.

"Thank you, Your Grace."

"I do not retract my disapproval of your low station, and I disapprove of my nephew's method of courtship, pursuing you carelessly like a lovelorn swain, but I believe you love him, and I hope you can change him." Catherine glanced at the gifts with a sneer.

"But I don't wish to change him, Your Grace. I love him as he is. And I don't appreciate your insinuation. What would you know of who he is?" She spat, taking the woman's words as a slight to her husband. One day she might learn to curb her tongue. Today was not that day.

"You mistake my meaning and my intention," said the duchess, her lips still sneering.

Lizbeth stood still, narrowing her eyes.

"I approve your marriage, even if you are of low birth. I approve because you bring light to his life. For too long I have watched my nephew lurk in the shadow of his father. You must understand, gel, my brother blamed himself for his wife's death and retreated so far into darkness, he knew not how to raise his son. Do not make my brother the villain, as he faced hardships of his own. Our father was not a doting man, nor our grandfather. In protest of our upbringing, I tried to love my own children, but I had for too long hardened myself to affection; so, I spoiled them to replace the affection I could not give. My brother chose to follow the footsteps of our father to cope with his grief. Love my nephew, Lady Roddam. Love him as no one has, and help him to love himself, or else his soul will be as lost as his father's and yours with it."

Catherine struck the floor with her cane to mark the end of the conversation and turned back to the dining room, disappearing into the sounds of laughter and happiness.

Lizbeth waited to return to the dining room, mulling over the duchess' words. She knew so little about the family, especially Sebastian's side. What did the duchess mean? These were not the thoughts she wanted on her wedding day, not of the man from whom she never wanted to part. The intention of the words seemed of good will, as much as they could be from such a woman, but the timing was poor and the meaning cryptic.

"Anything amiss?" Sebastian asked from the doorway, startling her.

With a nervous laugh, she replied, "I merely underestimated the number of parcels and would be grateful for a helping hand." She collected a few of the gifts into her arms.

Her husband, the Earl of Roddam, chuckled at her stubborn determination to carry the gifts herself before he took them all in his own arms and commented, "You know, you could have had a servant bring them or even had a servant set them on the buffet before we returned from the ceremony. I'm not such a recluse not to have staff on hand, and that staff, may I point out, is now yours to command, my winsome wife."

"Where's the challenge in that? I'd much rather have you come to my rescue so you feel like a heroic and chivalrous knight." She ribbed, following him back to the gathering, his arms full of packages.

"Nothing makes a man feel more heroic than carrying wrapped bundles tied with twine and ribbons."

They returned to the table and dispersed the gifts to the appropriate receiver. Before Liz could see them open their handmade treats, Sebastian tucked his arm around her waist and bowed to the group.

"We must bid you adieu. My home is yours to celebrate my good fortune. Please stay even through tomorrow, as my staff has planned a delectable breakfast in your honor, as well as a few other surprises. I make no promises to see you all before you leave, but I do wish you to enjoy all Dunstanburgh has to offer in our absence." His words were met with cheers, raised glasses, and a few catcalls from Drake.

Even as she smiled to the family, ready to make her own farewells, Sebastian hooked his arm behind her knees and swept her into his arms, carrying her out to the sounds of laughter and whooping.

Not until they reached the spiral staircase from the armory to the lord's chamber did he set her down, the staircase far too narrow for such gallantry. Every other step up the spiral staircase, Sebastian paused, stepped down, and pinned Liz to him for a kiss, each kiss deeper, each kiss longer.

By the time they reached the top steps, she found herself pressed against the stone wall, her husband enveloping her with the deepest and longest kiss they had yet shared. The cold stone against the back of her dress contrasted with the warmth pervading her body, doubling in intensity from the heat radiating from Sebastian.

She wanted this. She wondered if she wanted it more than he did.

She had wanted this since she knew their first kiss of hungry lust, and she had physically ached for him after seeing Dunstanburgh and its risqué art. Even Neptune's nudity teased her, made her question what Sebastian would look like unclothed.

While not entirely ignorant of what happened between a husband and wife, she didn't know quite how it happened, and that blasted statue made her anxious and anticipatory.

Her husband ran one hand down her back, feeling her curves, the other moving towards her buttocks and tugging her firmly against him. Even fully clothed, she could feel his desire for her, spurring her own excitement.

She knew she should be nervous, but nothing about his touches, nothing about the way his lips teased her skin caused apprehension. Quite the opposite. The longer they stayed clothed, the more desperate she was to know him, to unveil the mystery of marital consummation. She ached and throbbed, her skin on fire where he touched.

He led her the last few steps into the lord's chamber, his eyes black with fierce yearning, his skin flushed from where she had explored with her own mouth, tasting his salty skin.

Given this marked the first day of entering this forbidden room, she should want to explore, make note of the decor, the layout, anything, but all she saw was Sebastian, and all she wanted to explore was his body.

They stood in the chamber entrance, admiring each other, touching each other. He ran his fingers up her arms, tickling her until gooseflesh covered her skin, and she, in turn, butterflied her fingertips down his chest, eager to relieve him of his layers.

"My husband," she said possessively, throatily.

"My wife," he replied, his voice more vibration than words.

Light streamed in from large windows. She wanted to see him, all of him, even if it embarrassed her and made her appear vulgarly indecent.

She licked his lips, savoring the taste before he walked her backwards to the four-poster bed. As the back of her legs touched the cold wood of the bedframe, he stopped, holding her to him with one hand around her waist.

"I've wanted to do this since we first met," he confessed as he pulled hairpins from her hair.

A simple act, mundane, the pulling out of hairpins, yet the methodic slowness with which he pulled out each one, the fascination in his eyes as he watched the strands of hair fall down her back, turned the act into sensual eroticism. Once he removed all hairpins and her hair tumbled to her waist, flowing around her, he ran his hands through the tresses, marveling at the length and thickness, the wildness of it. He entwined his fingers in the locks as he brushed his lips against hers.

His lips still on hers, he removed her shawl and reached behind her back to undo the buttons of her gown, feeling his way to each button, his tongue teasing the inside of her lips as he worked. Once undone, she caught the gown from sliding off, holding it protectively against her.

"I desire equality, my lord." She smiled coyly. "Your coat?"

Sebastian shrugged out of the coat, struggling slightly to remove the tailored jacket without the help of his valet. He unknotted his cravat with a dramatized slowness, his fingers pausing between each tug to smile diabolically at her or dash a kiss to her bared neck and shoulders.

Leaving on the waistcoat and shirt, he put hands on hips and waited. She reached up, her gown hanging loosely from her arms, and fingered the bare skin at the hollow of his throat, tufts of black hair peeking out from the v of his shirt. Trailing her hand down his hardened chest, she reached his waistcoat and pushed each button through the buttonhole until it hung loosely open. He tugged off the garment and pulled his shirt over his head, revealing his chest bare for her to explore.

Ravenous, she ran her fingers across the naked flesh, wanting to devour every inch of him. His skin felt velvety smooth and almost feverish to her touch. His chest was well-muscled with a thick pelt of black hair covering the expanse above his erect nipples. A few scars licked over the tops of his shoulders, and one long scar slashed across his chest. Curious, she ran her finger across the puckered white line.

An enticing trail of hair sprinkled down his abdomen and disappeared into his breeches. Her fingertips followed the trail until she heard his sharp intake of breath, his eyes closing. Relishing in this newfound reaction, she palmed the soft flesh of stomach, rubbed the back and front of her hands against the muscles, and leaned forward deviously to press her lips against the naked skin. He held his breath.

Grinning, she ran her fingers through the trail of hair, wandering her hand downwards inquisitively. She eyed with surprise and slight trepidation the shape of his ardor struggling against the fall flap. Averting her eyes, she reached up to cradle his face.

He opened his eyes to meet hers, released his breath, and took a step back from her outstretched hands to slide her gown down her arms until it fell in a heap around her legs. Sebastian smiled so devilishly, so wickedly while loosening the ties on her stays, Liz thought she might swoon. Her body ached and throbbed with desperation as he took his time to remove the stays, then lower her petticoat, baring her breasts to the cool air.

Now was her turn to intake a sharp breath, her nipples hardening at the exposure and her body boiling from his appreciating gaze. Unabashedly his eyes combed her body up, down, and back up. He kneeled to remove her stockings, slipping off her shoes, and rolling the stockings down her legs, lingering at her ankles. Hot hands, rough and callused on the palm, ran the length of her legs. Each stroke sent shivers down her spine.

Before she realized he had risen, his mouth was on hers, probing, wanting, feasting, greedy with desire. Cupping her buttocks, he lifted her onto the bed and laid her against the mattress.

His hands roamed, stroked, and palmed, worshipping her curves, tracing her figure, tantalizing and tormenting her. His palms grazed her nipples until she gasped and arched into his hand. Her body pulsed. She wanted to cry, desperate for release, her body thrumming and throbbing.

"Lizbeth." His voice caressed her name.

Moving off the bed, he stood before her, affording her a full view as he removed his own shoes, stockings, and finally, breeches. His thighs, like the Vulcan god in the tapestry, were thickly muscled. Between those thighs, she flushed to say, his affection for her stood prominently, a hardened muscle curving upwards, surrounded by a bed of dark curls, looking nothing remotely like the statue of Neptune in the armory. Not sure what to do next, she leaned forward and touched his manhood.

"Good God, Lizbeth," he stammered and pushed her against the bed, climbing atop her.

Her husband. Her love. Her Sebastian.

She parted her legs as he lowered his body against hers, nestling into her curves. He exhaled, his muscles clenching as he hovered, loving her only with his eyes. She reached up to feel his arms, his chest, his stomach, encouraging him to satiate her throbbing need. Rubbing her legs against his, her feet sliding along the bed, she tilted towards him, slipped his body further between her legs, pressing the length of him against her womanhood.

Cautiously, he entered her, sheathing his tip. The strange, foreign pressure increased the longing, simultaneously causing an alarming discomfort. She wriggled away from the pain, but her body ached for his in response.

Sebastian shifted to rest on his forearms, reassuring her with his eyes. Lowering himself until his chest grazed her breasts, his lips met hers, hungrily devouring her mouth as he eased himself back into her, driving deeper.

He growled as he pushed forward, slowly, agonizingly slowly, spurring her to precarious boldness. She wrapped her legs behind his buttocks and forced him to her as she arched her hips against him, thrusting him into her, stretching her with a searing tenderness and wave of dizzying intensity. Her muscles involuntarily contracted around him. She cried out with surprise, her nails digging into his shoulders.

He held himself inside her, accustoming her to the feel of him, not moving, just filling her, pulsing within her core. Licking and nipping at her lips, he began to pull out, but her hips followed in frantic desperation, not wanting him to leave, wanting more. That couldn't have been all there was to it. Was it over? Was that all there was?

Chuckling into her ear, he returned to her depths, pausing, then retreating again. Again, he repeated the motion, increasing the pace each time.

As she found his rhythm, she relaxed into the thrusts and contracted against the withdrawals. Her gasps echoed his moans. If they could stay this way forever, she would be the happiest of women, their bodies joined as one, his entering hers, invading her body as a conquering warrior. Nothing could be more intimate. Nothing could bind them together closer than this.

His eyes fixed on hers, drunk with fervor. Their bodies moved in a slow, steady rhythm. He rocked his hips inwards at the apex of the thrust, rubbing his groin against nether lips, causing a shiver of pleasure with each rub, his body stroking her nub, the pace of his thrusts quickening to match her gasps.

Her legs trembled against his thighs. She felt increasingly dizzy. She gripped his shoulders, digging her fingers into his flesh, her lips seeking his as she became lightheaded. *Oh, please don't swoon,* she thought, not wanting to miss a second of him inside of her.

He thrust harder and faster, aggressively kneading and chafing his groin against her nub with each plunge.

"Lizbeth," he groaned hoarsely.

With ragged breath and pounding heart, she experienced a tide sweeping over her, an undertow pulling her down.

His rhythm increased when he parted her lips with his own, his tongue urgently wrestling against hers, the undertow dragging her down, the ocean taking her, and she thrust against him, legs twining around his to force him against her and into her. Her body tensed as she rode him, her muscles squeezing him inside of her, and at last waves of pleasure washed over her as she climaxed.

Crying out, she clung to him, the rhythm turning erratic. He climaxed with her, spilling his seed into her.

"Sebastian," she sobbed in heaving cries as the waves released her ashore.

He held her against him and kissed her face, her jaw, her ears, and her eyelids until she relaxed, their bodies still joined. She laughed against his cheek, exhausted and euphoric.

Her legs trembled, and her body shook.

They held each other, each on the brink of sleep, but neither wanting to lose themselves to this moment. He finally disentangled from her embrace and moved himself to lie next to her, propping his head on one hand, and with his other hand tracing the features of her face.

"Is it always like that?" she inquired.

"I hope so." He kissed her forehead and smiled with obvious satisfaction.

"When can we do it again?" She reached over to run her hand through his chest hair, feeling the silk between her fingers.

He howled in laughter, then shook his head. "It might be awhile, I'm afraid. I need to recover, and you must be sore. I don't want to hurt you. We can wait as long as you need, even if it's days from now."

She shook her head. "No, that would be terrible. Let's not wait that long."

She raised herself on her elbow and leaned in to nibble his ear lobes, then kiss his neck, trailing the tip of her tongue down to his salty chest. She heard his sharp in-take of breath.

Her husband. Her Sebastian.

Brazenly exploring his chest with her mouth, she flicked her tongue against a taut nipple, tickling her fingertips down his sweaty chest to his stomach, following the trail of hair until she felt the damp bed of curls.

She touched his manhood tentatively, the flesh sticky. Wrapping her fingers around it, she massaged it, exploring the texture and shape until it stiffened. Hardening beneath her palm, it pulsed and thickened until her grip spread too wide for her fingers to touch.

The now familiar and burgeoning warmth spread through her body, her stomach fluttering. Pushing her hand away gruffly, he rolled her over and climbed between her legs. Her heartbeat quickened with excitement knowing what would happen next.

Instead of entering her, though, as she had expected, he kneeled between her legs and placed his hand against her mound. He rubbed his hand in the same way he had rubbed his groin against her earlier. She instantly felt the same lightheadedness, the tensing of muscles at this touch. Where he pressed was indeed sore, a tender ache, but not unpleasant, instead intensely sensitive. She watched him, revering him as he massaged her.

The lightheadedness blossomed until she was falling from the side of a cliff, flying, diving towards a warm ocean. Just as she plunged into the water, he entered her, melding his groin against her nub so she could feel every inch of him against her, inside of her, and embracing her as she came. He held himself inside her, still hard, the length of him filling her, the width of him stretching her, as he watched her realize pleasure.

Only when her quivering lessened and she sighed with satisfaction, did he begin a slow, thorough thrust, tilting his pelvis as before to rub himself on her swollen bud. Her second climax hadn't yet finished before she felt another wave, a deeper waver, a stronger undertow.

With every thrust, his pelvis rubbed, and the dizziness augmented until she cried his name with wild abandon, involuntarily thrusting against him, tilting her hips, trapping his thighs and buttocks with her legs, wrapping herself around him in a vice grip. She rode him as he drove her into the sea, the sensation pushing him over the edge with her, their cries in unison.

After lying in a tangle of limbs, panting, sweaty, and sore, they rolled away from each other to lie on their backs, limbs sprawled to welcome the cool air. He reached down for her hand and held it.

The room filled with the musky scent of their lovemaking, intoxicating them until they fell asleep.

When Lizbeth woke, night had fallen. She reached for her husband, but her hand met an empty space beside her. Startled, she sat up and searched the room.

Sebastian stood in front of the hearth, stoking the fire. She could only see his silhouette against the firelight.

She felt a flush of shyness to recall his passionate lovemaking, to remember the feel of him against her and inside of her. However pleasant the memory, she winced at the aching soreness.

Absently she wondered at what point the fireplace had been lit and by whom. Had a servant snuck into the room while they slept or had Sebastian done it himself? What a curious image that made, a naked Sebastian building a fire. She was only sorry she had missed the show.

Stretching her limbs, she realized the soreness wasn't isolated. She ached everywhere below her stomach, including through her hips and legs, the latter still shaky.

"What time is it?" she groggily asked the silhouette.

Sebastian rumbled, "No idea. I'd like to think we're caught in a timeless vortex in which we may make love and laze about for eternity."

He reached for a pitcher of water to fill two glasses, angling his body to pour the refreshing liquid. The firelight illuminated his tall, strong form, revealing the flesh of his back.

Lizbeth's horrified cry startled them both.

Covering the landscape of his back were hideous, uncountable crisscrossing scars, lashing down across his buttocks and the back of his legs. Lizbeth covered her mouth with her hand as Sebastian haltingly turned towards her, fear, pain, and utter betrayal in his eyes.

Chapter 24

Her horror, her disgust echoed in his ears as he looked back at her. So lost in their lovemaking, he had forgotten to cover himself with his shirt afterwards. No one had seen his back before. He had made sure of that. But here on his wedding night he became careless, revealing his disfigured flesh to his new wife.

He could see her revulsion. He could see it in her eyes all the way from the hearth. He resolved never to tell her what he had done to deserve the scars, but some explanation would be expected, unless she decided to run now before he could offer half-truths.

Please, don't run, he thought. *I've only just found you, only just made you mine. Please don't find me hideous.* The steel trap around his heart tightened in anticipation.

She held a hand to her mouth, tears glistening in her eyes, but otherwise she sat perfectly still, wordless. She didn't have to speak for him to know her repulsion.

Carrying the two glasses of water, he set them on the nightstand and picked up his shirt.

"No! What are you doing?" She raised herself to her knees and reached for him.

"Covering myself so you don't have to see this." His hands trembled as he slipped the shirt over his head, hiding his scars.

"No. Please, don't do that. I want to see you." She crawled to the edge of the bed and pulled him to her by his shirt front. "You're beautiful."

He didn't move.

Had she just called him beautiful? He remained still when she tugged the shirt over his head and tossed it back to the floor. Lugging him to the bed, she made room for him to sit on the edge. He refused to sit. If he sat on the edge, his back would be to her.

"Please, Sebastian. Let me admire you. All of you." Tears sparkled on her cheeks, her hands tugging at him to sit.

What else could he do? Leave? What they had just shared made that option impossible, although he was sorely tempted to close the space between him and the door, afraid of her questions and the look in her eyes. Yet, inexplicably, all he saw in her eyes was tenderness.

He could share this one part of his past. One small secret, he decided. Not the *why*, but the *how*. Never the why. He resigned himself to share this but regretted it was being said on their wedding night.

He sat on the edge of the bed, his back to her, nervous that he couldn't see her.

A decade passed, maybe two decades, hell maybe a century. He felt himself aging as he sat on the side of the bed, waiting for her to say something, anything, but then he felt her fingers on his skin, tracing a line across his back. Warm fingers against his cold flesh. He flinched.

Silk fingertips traced back and forth, up and down, following every scar, covering the hundreds of lines on his skin. A few times her fingers reached the back of his arms, as though tracing an especially long scar where the whip had licked his arm.

She whispered, soothingly, observingly, "So many different marks. Some are deep recesses. Some raised ridges. Some are jagged, red lines flat against your skin."

Then he felt her lips against his skin, kissing the length of a scar. He inadvertently arched away from her.

"Don't," he barked more gruffly than he had intended.

They sat in silence for another decade before he felt her lips on his skin again, tentative. This time he closed his eyes and allowed her.

He wanted to weep. Her loving affection swelled his heart against the steel trap, fighting the constraints. He heaved silent, dry sobs against her soft lips.

Kisses caressed his flesh, some he couldn't feel, the skin so damaged where her lips touched, others moist and warm, a healing balm.

"He favored the wet whip." His voice creaked hoarsely.

"Your father?" She asked, wrapping her arms around his shoulders, kissing the back of his neck.

How could she possibly have known that? He must have said something at some point, but he couldn't recall speaking despairingly against his father to her.

He nodded in answer to her question. Her body pressed against his back, shielding him, protecting him. God, he should feel self-conscious, unmanned in this moment, but instead he felt desired, even encouraged through her support.

"When he didn't have the whip, he used whatever was at hand. Cane, stick, horse crop. The first time was the fire poker." He heard her gasp and felt her bury her face against his neck. "You don't have to look, you know. I can keep the shirt on in the future."

She tightened her grip around him, her hair tickling his skin as she moved. "You're beautiful, Sebastian. I want to see you."

He reached for the glass of water and refreshed himself before saying more.

"It started when my mother died. The beatings. After I—." He stopped himself, omitting the catalyst, then continued instead with, "After I disappointed him. Before she died, he ignored me, ignored us, preferring to travel more than be home. I would do things to get his attention. I wanted his attention so badly, naive boy that I was. I became unruly, undisciplined, defying him at every turn. I did things, Lizbeth, things that needed to be punished. I deserved every lash."

"Oh, Sebastian. No, no, no. No one deserves to be beaten, least of all a child. How long after her death did this begin? You were only seven when she died. I remember."

He said nothing, letting the silence fester.

Kissing his shoulder, she insisted, "Whatever you did, you didn't deserve this treatment. The man I know is a good man."

"The man you know hasn't been around for long. I've become this man only since the inheritance. Without Drake, I wouldn't even be alive. I hated my father so much that I tried every means of escape. From liquor to gambling and whores. I had a death wish, welcomed death, really. Drake pulled me out of the muck, literally and figuratively, long enough for my father to die. I swore to turn my life around, to rebuild the family name. While nothing will redeem my wrongs, I have devoted my life to becoming a better person. That doesn't change who I was, who I am at the core."

"You are *this* person, my darling. You are a wonderful person. Please, believe that," she begged, her lips resting against his neck. When he didn't respond, she asked, "What did the doctor say about the wounds? Why didn't he give something to prevent the scarring?"

"My father never sent for a doctor."

She gasped. "But some of these marks are quite deep! It's remarkable you're still alive."

"The sea is the wisest healer I know. After every lashing, I ran as fast as my feet could take me to bathe in the ocean. The salt cleansed the wounds, the water the blood, the waves my soul." His skin prickled as she traced the marks on the tops of his shoulders. "At times, I didn't think I had the energy to make it, but I always mustered it somehow. Pure adrenaline and fear fueling my steps."

She started tugging at his hair. *What the devil?* He swatted at her hand until she laughed, leaning away from him.

"Your hair ribbon is knotted. Let me take it out. I want to see your hair when it's not tied back." She tugged the ribbon right and left until it released his mane around his shoulders.

Hands combed through it, fanning it out, softening the wisps and frizzes caused by their lovemaking and subsequent sleep. He closed his eyes and let himself be petted and pampered.

When her hands slowed, he opened his eyes and moved himself back onto the bed to face her. "You haven't asked what I did to deserve the beatings."

Not that he would tell her, but why hadn't she asked? Everything she did and said was the opposite of his expectation. She hadn't run from the room. She hadn't badgered him with questions. She hadn't done anything but kiss and pet him.

"But you didn't deserve it. Why would I ask such a question? No one deserves to be beaten." She tucked her knees to her chest and placed one hand on his thigh.

"You don't know that with certainty. I deserved the first beating at the very least. If you knew what I did, you would agree. For all you know, I could be as worthless as my father claimed me to be."

"Oh, Sebastian." She scooted closer to him, her feet resting against his shin. "You are not worthless. No child deserves abuse, ever, for any reason. You are all courage and kindness. Just look at what all you've done for your people since inheriting. Doesn't that prove to you that you're not worthless?"

"Not everything I do can redeem a life of poor choices."

"No. No, I will not listen to you abuse yourself as your father did. Do not let him control you from the grave. We can't always control what happens to us or what other people do to us, but we can control how we react, how we internalize it. Don't let him control you. You are brave and good."

She crawled onto his lap and snuggled against him, laying her head against his chest. "I would never have married you if I saw an inkling of darkness. All

I see is kindness. Pain, yes, but that isn't the same as darkness. Let me love you, Sebastian. Open yourself to a future of happiness."

He wished so much he could do just what she said, but it wasn't so easy. How does someone snap fingers and release the past when it has been all consuming, all encompassing? She didn't know the whole story.

He loved her words and the sentiment behind them. He loved that she sat in his lap, still naked, embracing his shame and trying to kiss it away. He loved the idea of being loved and controlling his own future. But it was more complicated than that.

Chapter 25

Two days later, Lizbeth woke to the sound of the chamber door hitting the stone wall. She shoved pillows off her head to investigate the ruckus.

Sebastian pirouetted into the room, a tray balancing in his hands, a bare foot reaching back to close the door.

"That wasn't as graceful or as stealthy as I had planned." He wore nothing but breeches and a smile, his mane free flowing around his shoulders.

He stacked pillows in front of her for a makeshift table and set down the tray. Two plates piled with breakfast treats, two cups of coffee, a pot of tea in a knit tea cozy, and a vase of wildflowers perched on the tray.

"You're spoiling me." She sniffed her plate, filled with more smoked herring, sausage, bacon, eggs, butter, honey, marmalade, jam, and rolls than she could ever eat. "Ooh, where did you get these flowers?"

"I picked them from the grounds, of course. I couldn't bear to wake you, so I snuck away for a stroll and stole nature's bounty." He waved his hand at the buffet. "Breakfast in bed again today. But, I must be the bearer of sad tidings. Cook insists we eat in a more civilized manner from this point forward.

I normally eat in the morning room where Gerald sets up a table for my grazing, so back to usual, I suppose. Ah, and Cook requests your assistance in planning meals. She'll ensure the table is filled with your favorite delights."

He kissed her forehead before crawling into bed beside her.

"Oh, no you don't!" She scolded, trying to push him off.

"What is this abuse? You don't want to break your fast with your husband? Shall I eat on the floor?" He affected a wounded expression as he slid off the bed and onto the floor, peering at her over the side of the bed sheet.

"No clothes! I refuse to be the only one eating naked. Off with them!" She glowered at his breeches.

"You're a vixen of the first degree." He stood, undressed, and climbed into bed, joining her under the covers. "Who am I to argue with the lady of the castle?"

They had spent every hour since the wedding night hiding in the bedchamber. She had not seen the wedding guests since the ceremony, nor had she seen any of the servants. Gerald, the butler, brought food trays when called, but otherwise they had been left in peace to explore each other, converse, and solve the mysteries of the modern world.

"Are you sure you don't want a honeymoon abroad? Maybe a tour of Italy?" he asked as they ate.

"I wouldn't trade breakfast in bed for Italy if you asked a hundred times." She ran the palm of her hand across the thickening stubble on his face. "There is something I do want, though. Desperately."

"If it is the moon, it might take time to craft a rope long enough, but, alas, I will try if it is your wish." He winked and sipped the coffee.

"Tempting, but no. You're off the hook on roping the moon. What I really want is a bath. A hot bath. And you, my lord, need a shave."

"I knew something was amiss. Gerald wrinkled his nose and turned his head when I went down today for the breakfast trays. I must smell like sweat and sex. Mmmm." He moaned, nuzzling his face into her hair. "If I smell anything like you, that is."

She pinched his arm. "That's disgusting! No wonder no one wanted to marry you if you say such vulgar things."

"Oh ho, my lady! There you're wrong. They fawned over me like lost lambs. It was I who would not marry them." He flashed her a toothy grin before shoveling bacon.

"Nonsense. They only wanted you for your money. Why do you suppose I married you? I'm in it for the castle and the piles of gold you have hidden in the dungeon." She tasted the coffee and found it smooth and rich, much more palatable than whatever bitterness they served at Lyonn Manor.

"You think I have an oubliette, do you? Well, I hate to disappoint, but despite popular opinion, few medieval castles had rooms of torture or holes of solitary. There wasn't much point in keeping prisoners alive, you see. Although, if you have an interest in being bound and gagged…"

He reached down to the floor for the cravat in their pile of forgotten wedding clothes. He dangled the neckerchief in front of her before grabbing her wrist.

"How am I ever supposed to have a decent meal when I live with a heathen?" With her free hand, she threw a roll at him.

He laughed and tossed his cravat back to the floor. "I was thinking we could take a walk along the beach today." He eyed her as he noshed a herring.

"Oh, Sebastian, that would be lovely. I've wanted to see the beach since I visited last week. I'll have you know that I only married you for the beach."

"Wait, so not my stack of hidden gold?" He left a greasy and bristly kiss on her cheek.

She wondered if she could ever possibly be happier. There had been that little hiccup the night of the wedding, but nothing of it had been mentioned since, and he had acted confidently since then, making no attempts to cover his back.

This was the marriage of her dreams, the relationship she never thought possible. How absurd to have fretted about marrying him, to have believed for a second that life with him could be distant and convenient. This was the happy-ever-after she had dreamt of when she spurned all former proposals, wanting this or nothing.

Surely, he trusted her now, or was beginning to. After all, he had shared his closest held secret, one she suspected wounded his pride and shadowed his esteem. There couldn't possibly be anything worse than the abuse he suffered at the hand of his own father, but if he held back anything, she felt confident he would share when ready. They had bonded over his secret, and she couldn't be happier with the change in his mood, jovial, self-assured.

They had talked in bed between lovemaking, getting to know each other, sharing wishes, hopes, and dreams, battling wits, exploring viewpoints, exchanging experiences. In two days, she had divulged more to him than any other soul from the mundane to the spiritual. And the physical gratification they shared—oh, God in heaven, she had never known such bliss. If he was to be believed, neither had he, at least not to this level of intimacy, he had explained.

He was hesitant to talk about other women, but with some pressing, he confessed he had never known a gentlewoman's touch, only those paid to love him, and always clothed except the pertinent areas. He swore he had lived the life of a monk for at least a decade, during which time he aimed to repurpose his life. Now he would be remiss to miss a day.

She loved knowing everything about him, having candid conversations as though they were equals. No propriety. No rules. Just the two of them against the world. She also loved his unusual life choices, especially the sleeping arrangements. She couldn't imagine sleeping apart from him, unable to hear his heart beating against her ear, unable to wake in the middle of the night for lazy and exhausted lovemaking.

Deep inside, left unspoken, she was horrified that his father had been so cruel. Nothing on this earth could justify the beating of a child, and from the look of the scars and the tidbits she'd already heard of the father, she suspected the beatings started when he was young and continued until either Sebastian could fight back or be freed by his father's death.

She didn't dare ask for details. If he wanted to talk about it, he could, but she didn't want to press. Something about the way he spoke on the wedding night, something in his tone and body language made her believe she would only gain his trust by letting him reveal the past in his own way at the right time. She couldn't drag out the skeletons in his closet. Their past quarrels taught her the same lesson—he needed time to communicate in his own way. She hoped he was beginning to trust her.

Despite the bliss of the past two days, his self-villainization did worry her. Moving on from abuse was one thing, but accepting he had done nothing wrong, did not deserve that treatment, and would not allow it to control his life, was something different entirely. If he had gone through life letting that identity define him, he wasn't likely to change his self-worth with a handful of compliments from her or even from encouraging pep talks. She didn't know what else to do except show him love and understanding.

They called for a hot bath, and by the time they finished breakfast and loving each other, the tub was ready. They shared the bath, but before the end, they had sloshed most of the water on the stone floor.

Alas, for the first time in days, they readied to step into daylight as man and wife. Her possessions from Lyonn Manor had thankfully already arrived, but she still awaited those from Teghyiy Hall. Bettye freshened Lizbeth in a linen walking dress, and Sebastian's valet shaved away his shadow.

It was decided after Sebastian continuously turned his head during shaving to get a better look of Bettye dressing Lizbeth that a shared dressing room was not the best plan, and Sebastian promised to make the needed arrangements for her private toilette.

They left the castle and half jogged down the steep slope to the north beach. Clouds dusted the sky. A moderate wind whooshed around them, gentle and breezy one minute then bossy and gusty the next.

Given they owned the beach and not another soul other than the household staff lived near them for miles, they violated every clothing etiquette in civilized society. Sebastian wore nothing but his breeches and a shirt, the shirt she had sewn for him as a wedding gift, and she only wore the linen dress. Neither wore stockings or shoes, hair pins or ribbons, hats, or anything else for that matter. Lizbeth felt positively free.

"This," Sebastian explained, his fingers laced with her own as they walked, "is a nice place to dip into the ocean during low tide, but it's a useless place during high tide, as you can see. Nothing but rocks for the shoreline. The beach is a bit farther of a walk but worth every step. A stretch of honeyed sands perfect for running or reflecting."

"I think it's beautifully dramatic." She sighed with contentment, nearly disbelieving this was her new home, and that Sebastian was hers for all times. No more watching for him at a ball or wondering if he'd write. He was hers.

Smooth black rocks bordered land and sea with tall dunes rising to the west and a lengthy stretch of beach to the north. White-capped waves lapped over the basalt. When the sun snuck through the clouds, it tinted the water a dazzling shade of light blue. Lizbeth had never seen nature so beautiful. Her childhood home certainly rivaled this, but the subtle differences made Dunstanburgh mystical.

He snuck a kiss on her neck as they continued to walk north to the beach. She enjoyed his sneaky cheek kisses, a novelty brimming with romance.

"So where are your favorite haunts in the castle?" she asked, wanting to picture his daily life in his natural habitat, a lion in his den. "Implying I haunt the castle?" He arched a brow.

"You know what I mean. Let's suppose I've returned from visiting Charlotte one day, and I want to tell you all about it. Where would I find you? It's a terribly large castle with all those wings and floors. I could do myself a harm running through every room trying to find you. Give me hints of where to look first."

She suspected the library would be where he could find her, although taking a book into the conservatory sounded tempting, as well. But then there were those hidden towers. She would need to try each space to see which she favored.

"Depends on the time of day, I suppose. The library is always a good bet. The south tower, which I've made my temporary astronomy observatory, is a good place after dusk. I favor the morning room over the parlor, I confess, for it affords the best view of the sea. The gazebo and the beach here would be the last places to try after that. If I'm not to be found in any of those places, you should lay yourself naked in the bedchamber and await my arrival like a dutiful wife." He untethered his hand from hers and cupped her buttocks flirtatiously.

She squealed and said, "I'll keep that in mind, you unscrupulous heathen."

"Speaking of the library, would you mind terribly if I slipped off today for a short while? I don't mean to neglect you, but I still haven't found a doctor for Balan. I've narrowed it to two possibilities. I need a few moments to write each an invitation to visit the parish. Before I make an official offer, I want to watch both candidates interact with the people, accompany them through the streets, and show the office I've set up for the parish physician. That'll never happen if I don't write the invitation. You're delectably distracting, you know." He linked hands with her once again, her bottom free from another assault.

"May I help?"

She already missed helping her father with his estate business, and she would love to get to know the people as Sebastian had. She recalled his reception in Roddam Village when the locals approached him as a friend rather than employer. Being a part of that would mean so much to her and set the tone for their marriage. Would he pass this small test? Treat her as an equal rather than as a wife?

"Would you honestly want to?" he questioned curiously. "Business matters aren't normally topics of conversation for the ladies, much less involving wives in estate affairs."

"I understand if you would rather I not know the goings on, but I'd like to be involved as much as you'll allow." She prodded, more than a little nervous that this might prove a moment of quiet contention.

She had made herself clear throughout their acquaintance. Only equality would do. During previous conversations, he had seemed open to her ideas, but hypothetical discussion and actual involvement were two different matters. He might prefer to draw the line between spousal duties and estate business, as would be his right.

After a lengthy pause, he accepted her challenge, offering his own in return. "Come with me to the library, then. I'll tell you about Balan, the two physicians, and ask your guidance on drafting the invitations. It might take some time to acquaint you with everything. If you'd like, we can tour each earldom and see all the estates. Would you like that?"

Relief. He understood her! He wouldn't draw a line or treat her as a woman. Oh, blessed relief.

"Yes, please. You know how important equality is to me. That you're willing to share the burden of responsibility means more than I can say. And thank you for reminding me for the five hundredth time just how wealthy and titled you are. I only married you for your titles, you know." Lizbeth skipped sideways along the shore as she said this, overflowing with happiness that he showed no signs of becoming a dominating husband.

"How fast can you run?" he inquired, jogging to keep up with her skipping.

"I beg your pardon? Ladies do not run, I'll have you—."

Before she finished her sentence, he tickled her sides, sending her screaming down the beach. He chased her across the sand and dunes until they were both breathless and ready to return to the castle for lunch.

Upon their return, they were surprised with a picnic in the gazebo, courtesy of Gerald.

"You really are spoiling me. I wish it could be like this every day for all of eternity," she admitted as she tried the cheese.

"Give credit where it's due, my lovely wife. This was all Gerald's idea, not mine. I suspect he knew we would be sweaty again and didn't want us stinking up the morning room. Now, I've been mulling over a very important matter. What would you say to a husband-wife book club? Each week, we choose a book, both read it, and then we can discuss it. What do you say?" he asked between bites of fruit.

"Oh, that's splendid, Sebastian! We could take turns choosing the book each week. You pick this week, then I pick next week."

"Done. I'll pick one today. We could take turns reading to each other," Sebastian suggested.

"Even better, we should take turns reading to each other in bed." She cast a naughty smile.

"I've always wanted a woman to prefer reading in bed to lovemaking. How did you know?" His eyes twinkled with mischief.

Oh, she loved this man. He seemed equally as infatuated with her, although he hadn't confessed undying love. Love took time in a marriage. He was at least fond of her.

Feeling a spur of boldness, she said, "I've been thinking about my dowry. We could use it to restore the southeast tower into the astronomy tower you want," she offered.

"You remember me saying that? Amazing. I thought I had bored you to tears that day. I had something else in mind for your dowry, actually." He paused while he took another bite of food.

Her eyebrows raised in anticipation.

He continued, "You said once upon a time you wanted financial independence. You worried a husband would block you from ready access to funds. I have it in mind to invite my solicitor next week. Together, we can set aside your dowry money in a separate fund, just for you, accessible only to you. Then, if anything should happen, a disagreement, a separation, anything at all, you would have your own money without needing my consent. You could leave here without worrying about money."

For a moment, she responded with stunned silence. However noble it was to offer her financial security when other wives did not have such, his words upset her, scared her even. He was preparing a nest egg for her in case they wanted to leave, as though he expected the marriage to fail.

Was he expecting her to leave him or for him to ask her to leave? Maybe she was reading too much into what he was saying, but no, he said the words separation and disagreement. It was only day two of their marriage.

"No. I won't accept it," she finally said.

He looked genuinely taken aback. "That doesn't make sense, Lizbeth. Why would you decline financial security? I'm offering you your own money."

"I'm not declining the money, Sebastian. I'm declining your rationale for offering it. If it is offered so that I may separate from you in the chance of a quarrel, then I do not want the money. There is no quarrel we cannot work out with open communication and—and trust." She believed her words but hesitated at the word trust. Were the scars the only secrets he held from her, or was there more?

He turned back to his food and ate silently. The clouds rolling in from the east blackened ominously, the winds picking up speed. They'd have to move inside soon before the storm hit.

She'd need to get used to this temperamental weather, shifting day in and day out, so unlike her own calm sea back home. Then, it wasn't only the weather she needed to get used to. Accustoming herself to this temperamental man would be priority.

"What would you say to turning the second floor of the north wing into a nursery?" He asked the question to his lunch rather than looking up at her, startling her by the change in topic.

"Oh, I've not thought of children. How silly of me. I never expected to have the opportunity. We could already be expecting, couldn't we? Seems frightening. I'd like to spend more time getting to know my husband first. Not that it's an unpleasant prospect, mind you, for I believe I want children, but..." Her words ran together from a fluster of nerves. "Oh, I'm bungling this terribly, aren't I? Yes, your idea is something wonderful." She blushed from her verbal stumbles. "Do you want children, Sebastian?"

She hoped it didn't sound like she didn't want children, but she honestly hadn't given it any thought before. Never had it been a possibility. She wondered what kind of mother she would be, what kind of father he would be.

"I didn't mean to catch you off guard. Like you, I had never thought it a possibility. I've known with certainty I would be the end of my line, and I've felt a sense of pride to end a line of cruelty. Yet, here I sit with my new wife who could already be carrying my heir. I'm just as nervous at the prospect. I don't want to be like my father." He still stared at his food. "That scares me the most. What if I'm like him?"

"Don't say that! You could never be like him. There's nothing about you that's cruel or violent," Lizbeth insisted, touching his arm.

"I don't feel I'm like him. I would throw myself in the ocean before I hit you or a child. It still frightens me, though, the thought of being a father. I don't know how to do that. I have no role model." He avoided her gaze, watching the clouds roll closer instead.

Unsure how to respond, Lizbeth sat in silence, rubbing his arm reassuringly. Then, quite unexpectedly, he turned and smiled. A tender smile after such dreary words.

"Now that I've met you, Lizbeth, I do want to have children, a house full of chaos. Hellions tearing through the halls, dressed as urchins and howling at the moon. What do you think? Let's have a dozen, at least, each one thumbing their nose at Society. We could make up this whole parenting business as we go along, together." He took her hand in his, kissing her fingers. "I envy your family, Lizbeth. I think you could show me how to build a loving household. Would you?"

"With all my heart," she replied.

She hoped her smile reached her eyes, for her mind whirled with his words, his fear, and his worries. As happy as she was, something clearly stood between them. She could feel it. She could almost touch it. And it frightened her more than anything in this world.

Chapter 26

His feet sucked the sand with each step, slowing his movement to the shore. As much as he tried to quicken his pace, the sand tugged at the soles of his feet, pulling him deeper into the earth.

"'Bastian! Come play!" Only feet away swam the black-haired girl.

He called out to her, words dying in the wind. The girl turned her back to him and dove into the waves. He struggled against the sand, breaking free, and racing into the water.

Before him, Lizbeth stood in the same place the girl had disappeared. She reached out to him as the undertow pulled her beneath the water.

"Lizbeth! No!" He shouted, reaching for her hand to haul her to safety. "Lizbeth!"

Even as he reached, she slipped deeper into the waves, being pulled down not by the undertow, but by the little girl. He could see them both under the water, looking up at him, their faces blurred by the waves.

Fighting against the girl, Lizbeth surfaced long enough to scream his name, a gurgled cry as she was pulled under again. "Sebastian!"

He dove into the waves, pushing past kelp, fish, underwater sea castles, and sunken ships, searching for her. He screamed her name against the current. "Lizbeth! Lizbeth! Lilith! Li—"

Then her face hovered above his, wiping the waves from his brow. "I found you," he sighed with relief, pulling her against his chest.

But how had she gotten above him in the ocean? Her cherubic face with brown-green eyes, pert nose, brows knitted in worry—he realized he was in bed.

He sat up, his skin coated in a cold sweat. It took him a moment to shake the nightmare from his head and gain his bearings.

His bed. His castle. His wife. Lizbeth leaned her bare arm against his back, cool skin soothing his feverish flesh. She rested one hand on his arm, the other rubbing his shoulders reassuringly.

"You're shaking," she whispered, kissing the top of one shoulder.

"I'm fine. I'm sorry I woke you. It was just a dream." His voice croaked, unsteady and hoarse. His throat was parched, as though he had been screaming against the wind for hours.

"Don't worry about me," she replied. "Your dream must have been fitful. You kept calling my name. And—another name…What happened?"

"It was just a night terror. It was nothing. I'm fine." Before he could protest, she rose to refill his water glass from the pitcher.

The last dying embers in the hearth flickered as a noisy log shifted, breaking in two with a sooty crackle. Relief filled every pore of his body. She was safe. His wife. His Lizbeth. His love.

She returned to the bed with the glass of water and massaged his shoulders while he wetted his dry throat. He didn't deserve her, and she certainly didn't deserve this. She deserved to sleep the night through, to love a good man who wasn't full of regret and nightly torments, but he loved her, selfishly loved her. He hoped, overtime, she too could love him, could even love his torments and not see him as the monster he knew himself to be.

A slender hand reached around and retrieved his empty glass, then pulled him prone onto the bed. His lovely wife, his angel of a wife, his savior of a wife moved his arm across her stomach and rested his head on her slip of a shoulder, kissing his forehead until he drifted into a dreamless sleep.

Morning light shone through the windows. Squinting, he reached to pull Lizbeth to him, only to find emptiness.

He sat bolt upright, surveying the bed, the sheets drenched in sweat where he slept. Oh, God. Had she been a dream? Had he dreamt the perfect woman and watched her drown in an ocean?

Panicked, he searched the room for evidence of her, trying to orient himself in time and place. A woman's dress hung in the dressing room on the far side of the bedchamber, the door to the private area open. He recognized other familiar items, her shoes, her water glass, her scent lingering on the pillow next to him.

With an almost embarrassed sigh, he accepted she hadn't been a dream, and that he was wide awake in his own castle, his wife likely breaking her fast in the morning room.

He took a moment to wash himself at the washstand, splashing water on his face and freshening his pores from the sweaty dream. Without calling his valet, he dressed in breeches and a shirt, otherwise as undressed as he had been since their wedding night a full week ago.

He found her in the morning room talking with Gerald. Hopefully, he thought in deep chagrin, she had thought to request fresh bed sheets.

When she saw him, her lips stretched in a wide smile, her eyes shining with happiness.

"Good morning, handsome!" She strolled to him, embracing him as though she hadn't seen him in a month. "I hated to wake you. You were sleeping soundly and looked so peaceful."

She touched her cheek to his before leading him to the table. "I finally had that word with Cook, and she assured me the breakfast menu would include the addition of mash and oatmeal. She is also going to surprise you this evening with one of my favorite Cornish dishes, but I won't tell you what it is until you try it. She agreed to it only on the understanding that tomorrow night we have one of your favorite northern dishes."

"I have a favorite dish?" He racked his brain for what Cook thought he liked to eat. Nothing specific came to mind. He generally liked anything if it provided sustenance.

"She seems to think you do," Liz said with a chortle.

Her laugh somersaulted his stomach and fluttered his heart. Bah! When did he become such a sentimental sap?

He heaped bacon and sausage on a plate with a healthy helping of jam, grabbed a coffee, and sat at the table with the most beautiful woman on earth. "Tomorrow will be a surprise to us both, then."

The doors of the morning room were open on both sides, allowing the cool breeze to flutter the curtains and the seagulls to trumpet a morning anthem.

"A letter from Aunt Hazel arrived this morning." Lizbeth picked up a letter stowed under her plate.

"How is my favorite aunt?" Sebastian asked before taking a delectable bite of sausage.

"I haven't opened it yet. I wanted to wait so we could read it together." She broke the wafer, a clear indication Hazel sent the missive from an inn on route home from Northumberland. "Ahem."

My Dearest Countess Roddam and My Newest Nephew.

I have arrived in Birmingham, the return trip home fairing faster with fewer stops along the way. I am to await Walter here and enjoy the remainder of the journey within our own carriage. My devoted son would have arrived ahead of me had a band of highwaymen not been apprehended along his route. His avoidance of that area during the search and seizure of those dreadful ruffians delayed him. The food is terrible. I miss my girls and hope we won't be long apart, for London's Season will be upon us before we know it. If we are invited (this is where you invite us, my dear), I hope to bring Cuthbert and Walter for a summer stay next year. We could spend a month with Charlotte and a month with you, yes? I hope my nephew is making a woman of you. What a virile man he appears to be. I demand to be presented with a great-nephew or niece when I return next summer. Kiss that devilish beau for me, and find me always

Your loving
Auntie Hazel

She folded the letter, blushing from her neck to her hairline, and leaned to him for a kiss flavored of sausage and raspberry jam.

"I'm glad they caught those rapscallions," Sebastian commented. "Will you write to her to extend that sought-after invitation for next summer?"

He waited for her to nod between bites of breakfast before adding, "We have plenty of time before then to plan entertainment. I wish we had an off-season opera house void of the London *ton*. I think both of you would enjoy the opera."

He pushed away his plate, crossing one leg over the other and leaning against his chair-back to admire his wife.

"Fiddlesticks. The opera is only for being seen. No one goes for the music."

"But we would. Wouldn't that be a naughty game? Everyone vying to see the new countess, watching with bated breath our box door for us to promenade around the room during intermission, only for us to disappoint them by hiding in our box the entire time, me fondling you in a dark corner."

"Sebastian, you're a dirty scoundrel! You will do no such thing. And especially not if my aunt is sitting next to us in the box. I do like the idea of the opera, sans fondling, that is. We'll take the ton by storm from inside an opera box."

The twinkle in her eyes was meant for him, her adoration of him. He wanted to know her, inside and out, wanted to know what made her tick, what made her family so tightly twined, wanted to know everything about her.

Loving her hadn't happened all at once, a single moment when he knew he was in love. His feelings deepened with each nuance he learned about her and each time she learned something about him. And now she knew something about him no one else knew. She knew, even if only half the story, what defined him, for good or ill. They shared a secret.

His foot slid under the table to play with her toes.

"Tell me about your cousin," he requested. "I regret I never had a chance to talk with him, but he did seem amiable."

Her foot rubbed against his, their toes gripping each other's, warm skin against warm skin.

"I wish the two of you could become acquainted," she admitted. "He has a heart of gold and a wonderful sense of humor. My uncle and he were thick as thieves, so his world crumbled when his father died in the carriage crash. I think he's still struggling with the responsibility of the barony, as well as the loss. A friend like you could be just what he needs, you know."

"I'll make a point to get to know him in London. Is he married? Any wee ones?"

"Heavens no. Aunt Hazel pushes him too hard, hoping marriage'll settle him and give her grandchildren to spoil. He's too overwhelmed to consider matrimony. I suspect the more Hazel pushes, the more he resists." Lizbeth sipped her coffee, adoring him from over the rim.

Walter would be out of luck if waiting to meet the perfect woman, he mused, as Sebastian had just married her. To express that sentiment, he moved the top of his foot up her calf, marveling at the softness of flesh. He worked his way to the back of her knee, reveling in the feel of her velvety skin.

It wasn't only her delectable figure that excited him. It wasn't just her wit, humor, and tenderness. It was knowing she still wanted him after seeing his disfigurement, after seeing him weak. She hadn't run. She hadn't found him repugnant. He had wept before her, a broken man, a weakling, and she had still wanted him.

She had seen him inside and out and wanted nothing more than to love him. In her own way, she filled him with confidence about himself and confidence their marriage could work. When he looked at her, he saw the most amazing woman, an angel of the highest order, and he, too, wanted nothing but to love her.

"We still haven't chosen a book," he said, tickling the inside of her leg with his toes. "I'm offended you didn't like any of the choices I offered yesterday."

"I hardly consider Frances Burney a serious offer," she scoffed.

"Come now, what could be more enticing than a romantic novel about an illegitimate daughter of an aristocrat searching for love amongst the peerage?" he worked his foot up her thigh, smiling wickedly.

"It's completely unrealistic! And I refuse to believe you've read any of her books," she admonished.

"I have, actually. All of them. I'm determined we'll read her latest release *Evelina*. We can compare the heroine to Pamela of your oh-so-beloved Richardson novel."

"You know very well I despise that book. Ridiculous female." She shoved his foot to the floor, foiling his naughty plans.

"How about Charlotte Lennox? I recommend *The Female Quixote;* or, *The Adventures of Arabella*. It is right up your alley."

"And what alley would that be exactly?" she asked skeptically with a dubious stare.

"The alley of headstrong and stubborn bluestocking nonsense. All of that drivel about independence and strong women." He flashed her a devilish grin. He was rather fond of her stockings after all.

"To the library, then? I think you're tricking me into reading a romance." She stood and walked to the door without a backward glance.

He laughed, admiring the sway of her hips before following her. He felt the all too familiar stirrings in his breeches as her enticing derriere swung side to side.

Over the past week, he had reveled in her lovemaking. Never had he known someone to love with such abandon, such exuberance, and he certainly would never have expected such from virginal inexperience.

If he hadn't witnessed her virtue on the sheets after the wedding night, hadn't felt the barrier between girl and womanhood, he would have sworn on the bible she was experienced in the sensual art of the flesh. She loved his body freely with her own, no inhibition whatsoever. He was enthralled by her, obsessed with giving her pleasure.

With a deep breath to cool his ardor, he followed her through the south wing towards the library, enjoying the view of her backside. At this rate, he doubted he would make it to the library before disrobing her. She wore no petticoat or stays beneath her dress, and the thin, nearly transparent material outlined her figure beneath. Did she purposely tease him?

By the time they reached the armory, his ardor was no longer cooled. He walked with a limp, simultaneously cursing and blessing the transparency of her gown. He jogged ahead of her to lead her up the stairwell, but then halfway up the spiral, he grabbed her by the waist and forced her against the stone wall.

His eyes said it all, he was sure. He licked her lips ravenously, tasting residual honey and coffee. He kissed along her jaw and down to her neck, nibbling until she moaned into his ear, pulling him roughly against her.

Nipping her earlobe, he asked gutturally, "Do you know why they make castle staircases clockwise?"

Her reply was breathy, her eyes closed. "Why do they make them clockwise?"

"Soldiers couldn't swing their swords because of the interior curve. It disarmed them." He licked her neck.

"Oh." She arched her back until the triangle between her legs pressed against his pelvis, rubbing herself against his hardness. "Do you feel disarmed?"

"Let's see if I can swing my sword, shall we?" He drew her gown below her breasts to circle his tongue around the pink skin, suckling each nipple to attention.

She gasped against his mouth, raising her leg to wrap around the posterior of his thigh. Cupping her buttocks, he rubbed himself fiercely against her.

"We shouldn't be here. A servant could catch us." She panted, her eyes still closed. Her fingers dug into his hair, encouraging him to enjoy more of her cleavage.

"Doesn't that add to the excitement?" He muttered against her breasts, his tongue flicking over each nipple.

He tugged her dress down to her waist and wet her gasping lips with his own, grazing on her lower lip. The feel of her hands sliding down his body to unbutton his fall flap hardened him to madness, a nigh painful pulse swelling him. If he couldn't bury himself inside her soon, he would mess on her dress.

Free of the flap, he lifted her off the ground so she could wrap her legs around his waist. In one swift motion, he slid into her slick center. She cried out as he drove deeply, vigorously with fervor, thrusting against her contracting muscles. He surged into her, loving her crinkled brows, her mouth open and panting.

"Open your eyes," he commanded, wanting to watch her pupils dilate when she climaxed, wanting her to watch him love her. "Look at me."

He found nothing more erotic than her watching him, seeing her desire for him. Her eyes made him feel flawless.

Slowly, drunkenly, she opened her eyes, glazed from their lovemaking, darkened from the imminent orgasm. One hand remaining under her for support, he used his other to slip between their bodies and rub her pleasurably, driving her wild.

She gasped his name, her eyes focused on his. Sliding his thumb repeatedly over her swollen button, he thrust aggressively, forcefully, prodded by her fingers digging into his shoulders, desperate to feel her convulse against him.

When her muscles throbbed around him, tightening, gripping, her body shaking with the tremors of ecstasy, he released himself into her with a roar, one hand still on her buttocks, the other hand moving to brace against the wall for support. He reveled in the warm wetness of her womanhood, evidence of her desire for him, and marveled at the intimacy they shared and in her uninhibited passion for him.

Tentatively, she lowered her legs back to the floor, holding him to support herself. A shared laugh filled the stairwell as they tidied themselves, lifting bodice over bosom, buttoning the flap, smoothing frizzed wisps of hair that had been flattened against the stone wall or splayed from roaming hands.

"So, about that book," she said, giggling.

Taking her hand in his, as was his new favorite way to claim her, to hold her possessively and reassure himself she would never leave his side, he led her upstairs into the library.

Upon entering, he released her and bound up the rounded steps to the second-floor catwalk. He browsed the shelves, sated, a perpetual half-smile on his lips.

As he perused, he could hear her pulling books from shelves below, the crisp flip of pages, the thud of a book returned to the shelf.

"What's this collection?" She called up to him.

"I can't very well see to which collection you refer, my less than explicit wife." He pulled two novels from the shelf and started a stack on the catwalk.

"It's hidden behind the stairs, a lonely shelf. Journals perhaps?"

"Ah," he grumbled. "That would be my father's collection. I had all of the books from the estate brought here and the ones of his tucked away."

He could hear pages turning from below. Devil take it. He should have burned the collection years ago.

"They're travel journals," she shouted from below. "This one is from the West Indies, and this one from the Mediterranean. I think he made a travel diary of every trip he took. These must be fascinating to read."

She was having far too good of a time with his father's books.

Leaning over the railing, his ire rising, he demanded through gritted teeth, "Please, put those away, Lizbeth, and don't touch them again. I don't want my father's things touched."

"It's part of the healing process, Sebastian. We should read these together. Listen to this part—."

He took the steps two at a time to close the book before she could read from it. With a tight-lipped warning, he replaced the diary onto the shelf, scooped her into his arms, and carried her up to the catwalk.

"Do not read those again. Leave my father in his grave," he ordered sternly, still holding her in his arms.

Instead of arguing, she trailed her finger across his cheek and said, "I confess. I only married you for your library." With a kiss, she defused his anger.

Chapter 27

"Lizbeth. Lizbeth, where are you?" Sebastian tossed restlessly in the bed next to her.

Perspiration beaded his forehead, a thick crease forming between the brows. He tossed his head side to side, his fists clenching the sheets.

This was the second night in a row he suffered a fitful sleep. Her heart went out to him. What haunted his dreams? Did he dream of his father?

She inched closer to him, rubbing his chest with an open palm.

Whispering in his ear, she said, "I'm here. You're safe. I'm right here."

Sebastian settled, his hand searching for hers. She slipped her hand into his. His head turned in her direction with a soft snore, his eyes remaining closed. Kissing his sweaty forehead, she moved the wet hair from his face before resting her head against his chest. Her fingers ran through the thick bed of chest hair until she drifted back to sleep, the sound of his beating heart against her ear.

She woke to a sliver of moonlight faintly glowing into the room. The bed next to her was empty. Squinting into the darkness, she saw only empty room around her. Somewhere in the back of her mind she recalled a whisper in her ear, a soft growl mentioning a beach walk. Had she dreamt that, or had Sebastian gone for a midnight walk?

Rising from the comforts of the bed, she went to the north facing window to eye the beach below. The negligible sheen of moonlight restricted the distance of her sight. Maybe that was a flash of white by the rocks? Or maybe that was just a wave?

After wrapping herself in a robe and slipping on a pair of boots, she double checked the dressing room, sitting room, and library. Surer now that she had heard his whisper, she strolled out of the castle and towards the beach hoping she wasn't on a fool's errand. Any normal wife would have stayed in the warm bed, especially when the crisp air chilled her to the bone.

Much to her relief and embarrassed surprise, the white she had seen from the window was a nightshirt held down by a rock. She searched the beach for her husband, spying him in the ocean. Sebastian dove into the waves then rode them back to shore before diving again.

She'd married a madman, she concluded.

Before she could hide or return to the castle, he spotted her and waded through the water to shore. When he stood and walked towards her, she was shocked, and admittedly thrilled, to find him nude. Of course, he was nude, she scolded herself. His nightshirt was under a rock, after all. The reality hadn't dawned on her until she witnessed the truth with her own eyes.

He moved towards her, muscles flexing, a cat on the prowl. His body was not of a man who sat idly, leaving the hard work to slaves. No, his body spoke of a man who climbed rocks, swam against currents, ran across landscapes, and labored in fields. The body of a man who wasn't afraid to sweat. She loved his body, this god of the sea. All she saw as he approached was Neptune.

Quickening his pace to close the distance, he swooped her up by her waist, laughing wildly into the night sky and soaking her robe. "Come swim with me, Lizbeth."

"You're naked!" She squealed, the frigid wetness of his body shocking her awake.

"Does that offend your delicate sensibilities? Should I cover my furry parts?" He kept laughing, the corners of his eyes crinkling. "I dare you to join me and feel the healing magic of the ocean."

"What if someone sees us?"

He set her down and ran back to the water, shouting behind him, "We're on our own private island, Lizbeth! Who could ever possibly see us?"

Feeling daring, she disrobed and tucked the garment under a rock next to his nightshirt, the boots next to the rocks, and then waded in, all shivers from the icy water. Before she was knee deep, he splashed towards her, roaring like a charging lion, initiating a game of chase.

They ran, chasing each other into the waves, falling into the water, laughing, and gulping mouthfuls of salt.

He chased her back to the beach until she double backed to take pursuit. She chased him across the shore, over the dune, and up the grassy knoll. Just as she reached him, he turned and caught her in his arms, their bodies falling to the ground. Lizbeth sank into the muddy bank, her hands grasping at the grass, ripping up handfuls as he tortured her mouth with his, searing it with fierce heat.

His mouth and skin tasted like the salty ocean water. She licked the water from his neck, as he plunged hard and thick into her wet and ready entrance. She felt the familiar pressure, the mounting sensation as he thrust, filling her to capacity. Watching him watch her increased the sensation, their eyes locked, his glinting in the darkness, the reflective eyes of a hunter.

Arching to meet his thrusts, she dug her heels into his bottom, forcing him deeper. Sebastian threw back his head and howled, driving into her with long, fiery strokes until they cried out in climax.

Lying on the grass post coitus, they covered themselves with a blanket of stars, warmed only by body heat. The night sky sparkled with diamonds.

"What's that long hazy patch?" she asked him, her head resting on his shoulder.

She nestled against his body, his arms enveloping her protectively, and pointed to an elongated glow in the sky, so different from the billions of twinkling candles overhead.

"That's Andromeda, another galaxy. You're here at the most perfect time, as the autumn nights have the darkest skies, all the better to see with the first quarter moon. In November, I want us to watch the meteor showers."

"I'd like that. Look, there's a river of stars." She pointed. "And then clusters of them over there, and look, over there, too!"

He kissed the top of her head. Feeling brave after such a primal midnight romp, she kissed his chest and said, "Show me your soul, Sebastian. I fall in love every time I see your rawness. Too often, we go through life guarded, fearful. Let's be real; let's be raw, my darling. Show me your soul. Tell me what haunts your dreams."

Tightening his arms around her, he answered her with silence.

Chapter 28

He wasn't hiding from his new wife, not precisely. At least that's what he tried to convince himself of as he used the protective slab of his desk to shield against anyone who entered the library.

Hours before, he had left Lizbeth sleeping in the bedchamber and headed directly to the library without breaking his fast. The full moon had come and gone, marking their third week of matrimony. The first week, oh, that first blissful week, he had slept better than he ever had in his life. He felt safe with her by his side, as though he were embarking on a new life as a new person without his regrets, without blood on his hands.

And then came the second week. The nightmares returned during the second week, leaving him exhausted each morning, embarrassed and guilty for disturbing her slumber and drenching the bed with sweat. As forgiving as she had been thus far, as eternally understanding, she must be growing tired of the constant change of sheets and sleepless nights. No woman was infinitely patient.

The pattern set in that second week. Nightmares haunting his nights, each night fiercer, and Lizbeth questioning him every morning, probing him as to what terrorized him. Every day the same pattern. Sleepless night followed by morning inquisition. For how much longer he could live like this, he was unsure.

Soon she would insist on knowing his dreams, something he couldn't confess to her, not if he wanted to hold their marriage intact, which he desperately wanted to do. For the first time in three weeks, he wished there were a lady's chamber.

But what alternative did he have to the present situation? Now that she had soothed him from the night terrors, he didn't know how he could ever sleep without her by his side, which was unfair to her. But no one had ever caressed him back to sleep, gentle hands stroking him until he dozed dreamlessly, her body a barrier against his warped memories.

The thought of sleeping without her brought a new kind of terror to his waking moments. Such was selfishness. The same selfishness that convinced him to marry her. The same selfishness that destroyed two lives so many years ago. He had to stop being selfish. He had to push Lizbeth away for her own good.

His heart splintered inside its steel trap. Although he knew it wouldn't be possible to sleep soundly without her, he needed to push her away. She never signed up to play nursemaid. From the moment he first saw her, he had feared this would happen. For so long he had resisted marrying her from that fear. But somewhere along the way, he convinced himself she could take the terror away, shield him against the memories, distract him from his past. Instead, he pulled her into his torment.

Marrying her had been the wrong decision. No, that wasn't accurate. He wanted her, still wanted her, would always want her. He felt alive with her, but how cruel to drag her into his world and shackle her to him. She deserved better than him.

It wasn't as if he could talk to her about his demons, and he certainly didn't want to doom her to sleepless nights forever. No, this was his cross to bear. He knew her eyes would turn to judgment, loathing, even disgust if he gave into her unspoken pleas and told her what kind of man he really was.

He couldn't even face the worried and compassionate eyes, eyes that implored him to let her in, eyes that plagued his conscience as much as the dreams agonized his nights. Avoiding eye contact was becoming routine.

There was an alternative, of course. He could tell her. Tell her and be done with it. Could she accept him if she knew the truth? Could she accept the worthlessness he represented? And could he live with her knowing she would side with his father in the end? His greatest fear would never be put to rest if he didn't test her, but that fear being realized by her rejection halted any desire to reveal his past.

Even knowing what he was, he preferred living vicariously in the image she painted of him. Having her see him as the villain and hate him for it would be his undoing. He couldn't live with that pain. He could barely live knowing himself the villain. As long as she kept the heroic image of him, he had hope.

How had they come to this, and after barely a month of marriage? Couldn't his subconscious have given them a year? Two even? Only a few weeks before, he had experienced a new confidence because of her. How had they come to this? As deeply as he loved her, he shouldn't have married her. He should have let her go when he left London.

To distract himself, he pushed himself away from the desk and headed for the stairs to the catwalk. He didn't care what he read, anything to keep from thinking of Lizbeth, of his past, of his world slipping through his fingers.

A hand on the wooden railing, he halted, eyes focused on the shelf with his father's books.

An empty place in the shelf glared at him. Two of the journals were missing. Two of his father's travel journals.

Rage filled him, his hand gripping the handrail. He should set a fire in the hearth and burn them all now, find the two she had taken and throw them on the pyre. How could she disobey his order not to touch the journals? How dare she? She would dig too deeply. She would dig until she discovered the truth.

Why couldn't she leave well enough alone? Her subtle coaxing for him to open to her as part of healing was one thing, but thievery was a new blow, a personal violation, a slap in his face. His past was his to tell, his to hide. How dare she try to force it by digging into his father's things?

Although he'd never opened a single journal himself, that didn't sooth the rage of her taking them after explicitly being told not to read them. His father could have written about what happened. He couldn't be sure. It was bad enough having to live with his mistakes. He couldn't bear to verbalize them. If the journals revealed anything, he would have little choice but to confess all.

Damnation.

To hell with this tiptoeing. He strode across the library to the door, fuming.

The only option was to tell her himself before she read about it. He would bare his soul, show her his darkness, show her the monster beneath the flesh. She wouldn't be so understanding once she learned he had destroyed lives, no better than a murderer, had even destroyed the life of his father in the aftermath of his selfishness.

No, he rationalized, his hand on the door knob. Confessing wouldn't do either of them any favors. To hell with the journals. His only hope was to shield himself from her. If she knew the kind of man she married, she may not be able to live with herself. He needed to strategize. He couldn't salvage their marriage, but if he could protect her from the truth, he could save her the heartache of knowing him a villain.

He had to create distance. Nothing mattered except her. His love for her ran so deeply he couldn't bear for her to turn away from him, for her to reject him, for those loving eyes to harden against him into hate and in doing so hate herself for loving him. Nothing mattered except her.

Chapter 29

Lizbeth watched the castle disappear behind a hill, the carriage swaying to and fro, taking her away from the gloom. She couldn't stay with him a minute longer.

Today marked their one-month anniversary. She had barely seen Sebastian for two weeks. His blatant avoidance of her couldn't be more obvious compared to the obsessive togetherness they shared the first two weeks of marriage.

He had been playful, seductive, passionate, sensual. He had been the Sebastian she fell in love with. And then the past two weeks happened. Just as in London, he changed his tune at a flip of a coin, turning from affection to dismissive without cause or explanation. For two weeks, she had slept in their bed alone, and he had spent increasingly more time in the library working on estate business without including her, wishing not to be disturbed.

His side of the bed remained crisp each morning. Not once had she been awakened by his desire for midnight lovemaking. Not once had she been awakened by his nightmares. Not once had he invited her for an evening of star gazing and ocean swimming.

When they shared meals, rarer with each passing day, he acted reserved, his laugh empty, strained, his eyes stormy. His body showed signs of wear, his face drawn, lined across his brow, dark circles shadowing bloodshot eyes.

She felt him slipping away. If she couldn't find a way to anchor him, she would lose him.

Was this how Guinevere felt when Arthur fought battles? How Penelope suffered when Odysseus left? Did those women feel abandoned while their husband battled demons?

She would never have thought this before, as she loved him above all things in heaven and on earth, but maybe marrying him had been a mistake.

Somewhere along the way, she had failed to tear down his walls, failed to love him enough, failed to earn his trust. This was the kind of marriage she had always feared, the type of marriage she knew she couldn't live with for long. She would not live in a shadow, ignored while the man went about his business, living a separate life.

Sebastian had always needed time to communicate. She was determined to give him that time. She would grant him space and show him support in other ways until he was ready to talk, but if he didn't do so soon, she would have no choice but to confront him or leave. She refused to live like this. She refused to live in a house with a man who wouldn't even look at her, who hid in his library day in and day out.

After the wedding night when he cried in her arms, she thought they had made headway in breaking through his barriers. Now she realized she had merely mounted the curtain wall, still to face the inner wall's defenses. If she could fight her way through the portcullis, she would find his heart, but how? Her love wasn't enough. Her love couldn't conquer all.

Oh, how helpless she felt. Being independent of mind meant never asking for help, never allowing others to control the situation, never being a victim of circumstance. And yet, she felt helpless.

If she couldn't save him, the least she could do was remove herself from the equation, at least temporarily.

And so, she headed to Lyonn Manor, the coachman happy to oblige his new mistress. Charlotte would be the last person to console her over a failing marriage given Charlotte's own troubled marriage, not to mention her dislike of Sebastian, but to whom else was Liz to turn?

Lizbeth felt a rush of relief at the sight of Lyonn Manor. Had this been Charlotte's reaction to see the coach arrive with Liz and Aunt Hazel? Charlotte knew what it was like to be ignored. Although Lizbeth suspected her sister's method for distraction was different from her own. Her sister favored entertaining and socializing. Liz, quite the opposite, slid further into her books as a means of escape.

The travel journals had served for reading material. Five down, ten to go. They weren't exceptionally interesting, she admitted. Lord Roddam accounted for his daily activities but said little about scenery or customs. Bored already, she should stop reading them, but she kept hoping for a glimpse of the man, for some mention of his family, a sliver of a word about his son.

When the carriage pulled into the circle drive, Liz spotted right away the ducal coach awaiting her arrival. A boy greeted the coachman to show him to the stables, and her least favorite thin-lipped butler anticipated her at the door.

He showed her to the parlor and promised to ascertain if her sister was receiving. She rolled her eyes when he left the room, as he knew perfectly well Charlotte expected her and that the carriage waited outside for them.

Her immediate relief waned at the interaction with the butler, so different from Gerald. How depressing to feel homesick so soon. She'd only just left. But so different was her life from Charlotte's.

She tried to imagine Annick and Charlotte sitting at the dining table in undress with bare feet and open collars. Or sharing a joke with the housekeeper who had to order the changing of bedsheets for the third time in the same day from lovemaking. She even imagined the stern butler catching them coupling on the stairs midday.

A laugh caught in her throat, only stopped by the heartbreak. *Oh, Sebastian.*

Squawk.

"Oh, hello, Captain Henry!" She looked up to spy the cockatoo standing expectantly on a branch of his tree. Walking over to him, she scratched his outstretched neck. "I apologize for woolgathering. My husband is a nincompoop, you see."

Captain Henry laughed and bobbed his head.

The parlor door opened with a high-pitched squeal. "Lizbeth!"

Before Liz turned to the door, a flash of muslin and silk rushed her, embracing her in a vise-like hug.

"Lizbeth! You're here!" More hugging. More squeezing. More squealing. "You live nigh fifteen miles, yet I haven't seen you in a month!"

"I've been honeymooning, you might recall."

"Oh. That. Well, yes, I suppose. But today is our day! I'm beyond excited. I haven't been to the village we'll visit today, but the shopping is said to be the best in Northumberland." Charlotte bubbled with glee.

It took over an hour to reach the village in question, but Lizbeth enjoyed her sister's company for the duration, a refreshing change of pace from Sebastian's silence. She never thought she'd find her Charlotte's conversation enjoyable, but at this point, any interaction was better than no interaction.

The village bustled with activity and, as Charlotte promised, an abundance of shops. After two shops, at which Charlotte bought items indiscriminately, they came upon a tearoom with a sizable garden and courtyard.

"I'm parched, Charlotte. Shall we take tea? It'll provide a perfect opportunity to talk," Liz said, one foot already inside the threshold.

Charlotte wrinkled her nose and raised her chin. "It is not fashionable to take tea so early. They'd think us common."

"No one could think you common, and I don't see why we can't take tea any time we want." Lizbeth stepped her other foot across the threshold, staring down her sister.

"You have much to learn of your new station, Lizbeth. You're a countess now. Follow my lead. Tea this early is not done. Now, in one of these shops, there is a reputable modiste with whom I'm eager to talk. Come." Charlotte snapped her fingers.

Liz crossed her arms, readying for battle. "Charlotte, if you don't walk into this tearoom and have a cuppa with me right now, I'm going to steal a horse and ride all the way to Dunstanburgh. And I won't ride side-saddle."

Charlotte narrowed her eyes. "You wouldn't dare."

Liz nodded.

"Very well." Charlotte huffed in defeat.

The small crowd inside turned in curious awe as they entered. While her own dress was plain, Charlotte's emulation of haughty nobility was startling. If Charlotte weren't careful, Liz suspected, she would become her mother-in-law.

They took a table in the garden away from the other guests. A young miss full of smiles and curtsies inquired if they'd like high tea or low tea. Charlotte scoffed at both options, saying no establishment should serve either before four in the afternoon. Cream tea, please.

Lizbeth wanted to hide under the table for the scolding the poor girl suffered. When had her sister become such a snot?

Brow-beaten but still curtseying, the young miss returned with a plate of cakes and tea.

Liz nibbled at the delicious cakes. "What are these, Charlotte?"

"Madeleines. They're all the rage in Paris."

She doubted anything was all the rage in Paris other than people and politics, but if Charlotte wanted to pretend to be in-the-know with fashionable foods on the continent, so be it. The cakes were delicious, wherever they were from.

"How is Annick? Are the two of you faring better?" Liz asked cautiously.

"Never better. We've come to an understanding, as it were," Charlotte answered, adding a dab of milk to her cup. "This tea isn't bad, although a touch over steeped."

Come to an understanding? Never better? Either Charlotte purposely evaded the question or the two had resolved their differences. Charlotte's affect was indiscernible.

Charlotte returned the question. "And you? Have you enjoyed your honeymoon with that brute? You know, when you come to your senses, you can move in with me. Wouldn't that be delightful?"

Ignoring her rudeness and her offer, Liz replied, "My honeymoon has been a dream come true, thank you very much." A half-truth, not exactly a lie. It had been a dream come true.

"What's it like living there? I don't know how you can stand it with all those dreadful seagulls and wind. And can you stomach seeing that vulgar art every day? I'd have it all taken down if I were you. Utterly distasteful. He needs to understand he's no longer a bachelor and cannot display that in his home if he expects to entertain."

Leaning in conspiratorially, Charlotte said sotto voce, "Drake tells me his cousin spent an unbelievable fortune on that pile of rocks. Because he doesn't have perfectly livable estates elsewhere? I don't know how you tolerate it." Charlotte took another sip of her tea. "Still, there is a kind of rustic beauty, I suppose. A well-manicured garden could improve it by leaps and bounds."

Always a tad prissy, Charlotte had rarely been prone to open criticism. Liz didn't care for her sister's transformation into this frosty beast. She really was turning into her mother-in-law.

Liz countered, "I love the castle, especially the landscape, seagulls, and art. I wouldn't dream of living anywhere else, and certainly not a stuffy estate."

"You always were eccentric." The corner of Charlotte's mouth twitched as if to smile. "I almost envy you, you know. I always have." She tucked the almost-smile behind pursed lips and hardened her eyes, a steely duchess.

Liz ate silently while Charlotte turned the conversation, babbling about a soiree she hosted. She found herself distracted, not hearing her sister's words. What Sebastian was doing? Did he miss her? Had he noticed she'd left? Would he gather her in his arms when she returned, spin her in a circle, and declare their next steps into the world would be together?

Oh, blast. Such thoughts were depressing because she suspected he hadn't left the library long enough to notice her absence.

As soon as he stepped out of the library again, she would swap out the current travel journals for two new ones. Guilt lingered at the fringes of her conscience for sneaking the journals out of the library, but it's not as though he forbade her from reading them, merely requested she not. And besides, no harm came from reading a travel journal.

"Why aren't you listening? Is something amiss?" Charlotte's words interrupted her thoughts. "What has he done? Has he hurt you?" Charlotte demanded. "Oh, I will never understand why you married that man, Lizzie."

For a moment, she wanted to defend the love of her life. Then she thought of brushing off the questions. In the end, she admitted to herself she needed to share her woes. Isn't that why she came today? If she couldn't confide in her sister, in whom could she? She abhorred adding more fuel to her sister's dislike of Sebastian, but if she swallowed her feelings for too long, she would burst.

"I am content with my decision. No, far more than content. In fact, 'content' doesn't do him justice. I am truly happy, Charlotte. I don't need for you to understand why I married him, but I do want you to understand he is my choice."

She paused to take a deep breath, not sure how to explain her predicament. "Be that as it may, something is amiss, and I don't know how to resolve it, for I don't know what's wrong. There's not so much wrong with us, as there's something wrong with him. No, I'm not explaining this right. I don't want you to think there's something wrong with him. Blast. He's not been himself these past few days, and I'm worried about him."

Charlotte huffed. With a wave of her hand and a laugh she said, "I told you not to marry him. You should have known he would turn into a savage sooner or later."

Tears stung her eyes and wet her cheeks. Here she was humbling herself to confide in her sibling only to have rudeness slapped in her face.

Charlotte's eyes widened, and her condescension dissolved. She reached across the table to touch Liz's hand.

"Oh, Lizzie, I didn't mean anything. I was teasing. Please, don't think me a terrible person. I'm trying so hard to be a good duchess, a dutiful wife, and a loving sister that I muddle my words these days. I can't seem to do anything right. I never meant to be cruel. Please, forgive me." Charlotte's own eyes glistened with tears.

Lizbeth squeezed her sister's hand.

"Will you talk to me, Lizbeth?"

Liz tried to blink away the tears before she made a spectacle of herself. "Oh, Charlotte. I don't know what's wrong. We had a divine honeymoon, but then he started having nightmares, and now he's all but locked himself in the library. The few times we're together, he makes such a concentrated effort to act normal that he's stiff and foreign."

Charlotte nodded encouragingly, patting Liz's hand.

"I don't know what to do, Charlotte. I can't force him to talk to me, nor can I beg him to be himself. I've never felt so helpless. I take that back because I have, only it was different before. He's done this before, you see, but we weren't living together, so it wasn't quite so difficult. Now, it's unbearable. He ignores me, acts like a wounded cub shying from the pride, hoping no one notices."

Having the words said aloud, she felt their weight, realized the reality she faced. If he was hiding a wound, he wouldn't return to euphoric happiness overnight. With dawning clarity, she saw that now, recognized the problem, at least in theory. He was wounded. He was wounded and hiding his weakness, afraid for her to see him vulnerable. If she could somehow discover the wound, she could salve it, or better yet, find out who wounded him and take them to task.

What would a lioness do if a pride male were injured? Would she protect the wounded lion or leave him for a stronger mate? Being the wounded one, he couldn't take the chance, but how could he not understand her better than that, know she was his lioness, come what may, and would defend him until he healed, fight on his behalf if necessary?

"Show your support rather than telling it." After a bite of cake, Charlotte expounded. "Drake never responds to nagging and can be dim-witted when expressing feelings in words. He's also a proud man who has to solve all his own problems without my interference. I've learned to use other means than badgering to show support when we quarrel. If you can't use words, show him you care for him."

"Thank you for the advice, but I don't think you understand the problem."

"Stop it, Lizzie. You're always Miss Independent, Miss I-Don't-Need-Anyone. You always try to solve everyone's problems for them, bandage them when they're wounded, fight for them when they're defenseless. I knew you would come barreling to Northumberland when I wrote, my knight in shining armor, ready to solve all my marital problems. Well, Lizzie, you can't solve everyone's problems for them. Whatever this is, it is his problem. You can be there for him and support him, but the more you try to solve his problems, the more he'll push you away. You're the brightest woman I know, so if you set your mind to it, you can find a way to express your support without words. Don't badger him, and don't steal his fight."

"It's not that simple, Charlotte. I can't idly stand by while he shuts me out. He's wounded and refuses to reach out. If I stand by doing nothing, he'll withdraw so far into himself I'll never see him again. He needs me but won't admit it. For reasons I can't explain, I believe he's fighting against demons he can't best, the very demons who wounded him. If I can work out the problem, I can fight for him."

"You're not listening, Lizbeth. If you interfere, he'll be so busy trying to protect you, he'll forget to save himself. If you won't listen to me because you think me a silly prat, then talk to Drake." Charlotte poured a fresh cuppa for them both.

Liz almost laughed. What a ridiculous suggestion. "And why would I do that?"

"He's Sebastian's confidant. Sebastian called at the manor practically every other day after we returned from London. They are surprisingly close. Even if Drake doesn't know the problem, he may be able to offer insight. He knows Sebastian better than anyone. If nothing else, let Drake be a glimmer of light when all the world is dark. Promise to talk to him, Lizzie?"

Charlotte's words sounded strange to Lizbeth. Annick—a glimmer of light? When had he ever thought of anyone other than himself? No matter how dark the world turned, she couldn't see turning to Drake for help.

"Charlotte," she said tentatively, "I'm not sure if—"

"Promise me. He may be pompous, but he's a dashed good man to those he loves." Charlotte smiled.

"Only for you, Charlotte. If I lose all hope, I promise to turn to him."

There. That discharged her from the promise as far as she was concerned. She would never lose all hope, certainly not in Sebastian.

Chapter 30

She gathered her courage as she mounted the gallery stairs.

Standby and show support. What a lark. He needed to confide in her is what needed to happen. If he would confide in her about whatever problem ailed him, she would stop at nothing to resolve it.

Her shoulders slumped in defeat. And now back to feeling helpless. There was naught she could do if he wouldn't confide in her.

As she entered the armory, Sebastian stepped out of the library stairwell.

Her heart caught in her throat. He stopped abruptly, searching the room as if to find a hiding place. The circles beneath his eyes were darker, as though he hasn't slept in two weeks. Was he not sleeping to avoid the nightmares? *Oh, Sebastian, talk to me.*

She stood her ground and, as conversationally as possible, as though she hadn't noticed his discomfort at the confrontation, said, "I've had a lovely day shopping with Charlotte."

He clasped his hands behind his back, his shoulders rounded with exhaustion and the weight of the world. His eyes danced, shifting and wandering nervously around the room, focusing on everything except her.

"Good. Glad to hear she's well," he murmured to the floor.

"I didn't say she's doing well, only that I had a lovely day with her. Perceptive of you, nonetheless, as I do believe she's well. We visited a tearoom, a new experience for me as there aren't any in Cornwall," she said, aware of how stiff she sounded.

"Yes, that does sound pleasant. If you'll excuse me, I, uh, need to finish a few things." He turned and took two steps at a time back from whence he came.

Arg! All she wanted to do was throw one of the armory daggers at his retreating back. How dare he dismiss her? How dare he not look at her? His duty was to ravish her in every room of the house, not shuffle back to the library and hide from her. If she ever found the thorn he kept stuck in his paw, she'd crush it under her boot.

Once in her dressing room, she stared at the floor dejectedly, tears welling. This was all so confusing. What if this was her fault? What if it had nothing to do with his nightmares and all to do with her? Blast. Now she was talking foolishness.

Mulling over Charlotte's advice, she wondered if she might ought to try it. Desperate times and all that. They certainly weren't going to talk. If she could show him she loved him despite this quarrel, maybe he would know she was on his side, giving him the time he needed to sort through his troubles. No nagging, no badgering, only support.

Another lark. As often as she told herself she would give him time and space, that he would communicate in his own time, she couldn't heed her own advice. Well, it was easier thought than done.

Standing about being ignored while he worked through issues every few months wasn't a pattern she wanted to repeat for a lifetime. They had to get beyond this, permanently.

Liz took a few moments to regain composure, wiping tears from her eyes. What else did she have to lose?

She marched past their bedchamber, into the sitting room that connected the bedchamber and the library, and straight into his sanctuary.

The library door closed more firmly than she had anticipated.

Sebastian, sitting behind his desk and contemplatively studying the adjacent window, jolted at the *thunk*. He looked up at her with surprise, vulnerability and, could that be… longing? Without acknowledging her, his face darkened, and his eyes returned to the window.

Lizbeth closed the space between them, stopping at the edge of his desk. No stir from the lion, no movement, only a deepening brow furrow.

She proceeded to disrobe.

She started with the half-boots, removing them and tossing them to the side with a *thud,* and then she rolled down her stockings and threw them on the desk, right on top of his papers. She struggled to reach the buttons at the back of her dress, but after some stretching and wriggling, she unbuttoned them and dropped the dress to the floor.

As she stripped, his head steadily pivoted towards her. She unlaced her stays and removed her petticoat. She all but yanked the hairpins out of her hair until the locks flowed around her shoulders. He stared at her, eyes wide and confused. Now he looked, she humored, more like a cornered rabbit than a lion.

Making short work of her plan before he could interrupt, remove her, or protest, she pushed him forcefully against the back of his chair and climbed onto his lap, straddling him. She pinned his shoulders to the leather and kissed him ferociously, her lips communicating every emotion she could infuse into them. He responded, his lips meeting hers, his hands gripping her thighs, caressing her, working their way up her back and twinning in her hair.

After kissing him sufficiently into a fervor, she sat back, breathless. His face, Sebastian's face, looked back at her. Not the face of that stranger who had moved into his body. Sebastian's face venerated her. All curtains removed from his eyes, revealing only affection and adoration. *There you are,* she thought. *My Sebastian.*

He freed himself from the buttoned flap, but as he reached to pull her closer, she grabbed his wrists and lifted them over his head. Not that she could ever hope to win an arm wrestle against him, she still wanted to establish dominance, to be a lioness prowling for her lion, to show him how much she loved him, supported him, and understood him.

Still holding his arms above his head, she positioned herself over him until his hardness touched her lower lips. He moaned at the contact. Smiling slyly, she rubbed herself against him as much to tease him as to pleasure herself.

She rubbed against his shaft until his moans were followed by urgent thrusts against her wet lips. Then and only then did she reach down with a free hand to angle him into the folds, into her, sliding herself over him until their groins met.

She held him there, clenching, teasing, driving him wild and selfishly memorizing his face, his eyes trained on her, full of the beauty she had known at their wedding.

He moved then, suddenly, swiftly, with cat-like reflexes, pulling her arms down against her body with one arm, the other arm wrapping around her derriere in a possessive hug, forcing her against him while freeing himself to move beneath her.

He thrust powerfully into her before removing his arm from hers to reach between her legs. He found her sensitive nub and circled it with his thumb, continuing to pull her against him as he thrust upwards.

The waves rushed over her, plummeting her into the sea. As much as she wanted to close her eyes and focus on the sensation, she refused to lose his face, refused to avert her eyes from his.

She held eye contact, climaxing over him, letting him see the pleasure he gave her. He held her legs down for one final thrust, spilling himself into her, his eyes never leaving hers, revealing nothing less than the greatest love she could ever imagine.

She leaned against the chair, her hair falling around him. She nuzzled his mane, and he pulled her tight against him in an embrace.

"Come to bed with me, my darling," she whispered boldly.

He nodded and lifted her with him as he stood from the chair. Light still streamed through the windows, a far cry from evening. She didn't care. He didn't seem to care either. Lowering her until she could stand on her own, he finished undressing, leaving the heap of clothes on the library floor. She took his hand and led him to the bedchamber.

As evening fell, they lay in the bed, limbs tangled, loving each other with trailing fingers and soft caresses. She had missed his smile, missed his eyes, missed his touch. She especially missed his sarcastic wit.

She thought fleetingly, while she had him in her arms, of pleading with him to tell her what was wrong, but she didn't say a word.

He spoke, though. Between kisses and caresses, he called her his angel, called her perfection, called her his everything.

Well after midnight, he drifted into what appeared a peaceful and dreamless sleep. Was this the first time he'd slept in two weeks?

She fought against sleep. She feared tomorrow. She didn't want this moment to end. Squeezing his waist, she fought the intrusion of darkness. With the light of the moon from the window, she watched the rise and fall of his chest, listened to his gentle breathing.

"You're my courageous lion, Sebastian. I'm here by your side, always."

His features softened in slumber, his arms tightening around her. Maybe tomorrow would be different.

Chapter 31

The next morning, she woke to an empty room.

Depressed, she slunk out of bed, not really wanting to leave it but seeing no point in wallowing all day. She freshened herself at the washbasin and dressed in a simple cotton gown, her hair left free to fly about her. Poor Bettye hadn't gotten to help ready her mistress much since arriving at Dunstanburgh, not with days spent in loose gowns and unstyled hair.

Her first stop was the library to gauge his mood. The room was empty. Walking around to the window overlooking the beach, she leaned against the stones hugging the alcove. Stone window seats, one on each side of the arched glass, beckoned. Crawling onto the stone, she nestled against the glass and looked out.

The waves rushed the shore angrily today, a storm brewing in the distance. From this high in the tower, she could see all the way to Embleton beach where the sun still shone, sparkling the sand, regardless of the dark clouds looming over the castle, shrouding the immediate area in a light mist. Below the ravine hugging the northern outer wall, she saw Sebastian.

He sat on the rocky shore, his feet assaulted by rough waves. She wished he could see himself through her eyes, wished he could rise beyond whatever terrorized his dreams and embrace the here and now, embrace their marriage, embrace the wife at his side.

"Where are you, my king?" she asked to the window pane. "Come rest your weary soul in my arms. Don't you remember that I'm the Lady of the Lake? Don't you remember I can heal you if you come to me?"

With a sigh of helplessness, she turned from the window. Shuffling to the desk, she noticed first the absence of their dispersed clothes, removed by an amused maid no doubt.

It wasn't snooping if she merely wanted to admire the view from his desk and happened to glance down, right? She did just that. Not so much to spy on his affairs, rather to feel close to him, to see the progress of his work. She missed being included.

Disorganized papers littered his desk, so different from how he normally kept his ledgers and paperwork, tidy in stacks. The papers mostly looked to be financial records from the earldom of Eskdale, one of his holdings. Shuffled in the mix was a letter from one of the doctors confirming the invited visit to Balan. Another letter thanked him for the pensions to the widows. A lengthy missive from the steward at his estate in Guiseley verified the employment of new laborers at the mill and detailed the monthly profits of said mill. Next to the inkwell sat an unfinished draft with strikethroughs inquiring about the purchase of a studding horse for a farm in Brayton.

She had much to learn of his holdings and loved him all the more for seeing him hard at work and living up to his promises of being a dedicated employer. All the time he was ignoring her, he had been hiding in his study working on estate business, revealing not only his dedication to his livelihood, but also his choice of distraction. He was burying himself in work to forget his troubles.

If she understood him well enough, she suspected that was what he had done since his inheritance. He threw himself into work as a distraction. He oft claimed it gave him renewed purpose. Did it? Or was it a way to forget?

She recalled their more intimate discussions during the first two weeks. When he was still living under his father's roof, he had no means of escape, no means of distraction, so he drowned his sorrows as many young men did, but after inheriting, the building of this small empire had been his sole focus in life, giving him direction and purpose, a saving grace during the darkest of times.

He worked not so much for himself, but for the laborers his father had cheated in his greedy pursuit of profits. He had told her the focus kept him afloat even during the bouts of depression he suffered, during which times he would work the hardest, but he never would tell her why he suffered other than from the abuse, abuse he still swore he deserved.

Desiring to understand his past more, and with no other means in which to delve, she seized the opportunity to exchange the travel journals. Running back to the bedchamber and up into the topmost tower to grab the travel journals she had been reading, she quickly replaced them with two new ones.

Not that she had learned anything from the journals thus far, but she could hope something would be referenced in the journals. Anything. Any clue to his family life. After all, they were her only link to his father, at least the only link at hand, without her prying by speaking to shopkeepers in Roddam, visiting Roddam Hall, or even interrogating his Aunt Catherine, none of which she was ready to do yet.

With the journals tucked under her arm, she traversed back to the topmost tower where she had set up a little reading room for herself. Both towers were small and cozy, stone seats circling the rooms and stunning views with only slender columns of stone separating the windows.

Settling herself onto her makeshift pallet, she wasted no time in starting the dull as dishwater diary. This diary had been written while in Greece. From what she gathered of the dates, the earl had traveled every summer for several years after Sebastian's birth.

This journal opened with commentary about Turkish conflicts. She wished Sebastian's father would have written more detail, reflected on the people and views, what he saw, not just what he did, or better yet, reflected on his home life and the family he left behind while traveling. The journals really did feel more like travel itineraries than anything. Regardless, she sat transfixed, wondering what the old earl would do next on his trip.

After what must have been two hours of turning pages, she started to doze. Shaking the wool from her eyes, she turned the page.

A letter fell into her lap. Curious, she flipped the book upside down and shook it. Two more letters joined the first.

Setting aside the accounts of Greece, she picked up the first envelope, addressed to The Right Honorable The Earl of Roddam.

Unfolding the correspondence, she glanced first at the sender, a Mrs. Brighton. The stationary was from a parish orphanage in Allshire.

My Lord,

Your donation is welcomed and ample. The amount in question will be enough to support the child through her years at the orphanage. As requested, familial identity shall remain sealed and the donation anonymous. It is unusual for our orphanage to accept a child of her age, but with time she should forget her former life. The additional patronage you offer for us to collect the child is enough for the cost of the travel. The clerk will arrive before dawn on the following Monday. With all matters settled, this is my final correspondence. Wishing you

All the best,
Mrs. Brighton, Headmistress

What child, and why was she being sent to an orphanage? Seeing nothing more to the letter, Lizbeth set it aside and reached for the next one.

Tobias, my love,

I received your letter and wept with joy! We are to be united at last! I must wait until Papa is asleep before I can leave. I will meet you at the stable tomorrow night. You are my true love, Tobias, and I want no one except you. We will show them all the meaning of love once we are wed. No one can stop us, not your wicked father or mine. To think, soon the humble daughter of a coachman will be the wife of an earl's son! Your heart is good to love me despite all that stands between us. Tomorrow, I have a secret to share. I hope you will be as delighted as I. Oh, blessed morrow! Will it never come? Your

One true love,
Lily Chambers (after tomorrow, Lily Lancaster)

Startled, Lizbeth reread the letter. Tobias was Sebastian's father's name, but who was Lily? Sebastian's mother was Jane. Tobias and Jane Lancaster, not Tobias and Lily. Had she misremembered? Jane was a far cry from Lily as far as misremembrance went.

The terms of love and devotion didn't seem fitting to the cruel man she knew Sebastian's father to be. Had he once been a loving man turned cruel, or had he always been cruel and used this poor girl, perhaps ravishing her with promises of elopement? There was no way to know.

Setting aside the second letter, she moved onto the last of the collection, a quickly scrawled note with no salutation or closing, but the handwriting was unmistakably that of Lily from the previous letter.

In this basket, you will find our Lilith. Please do not turn her away. I leave her with you and your new wife in hopes one of you will show compassion.

Lizbeth chewed her bottom lip. She hadn't a clue if any of these letters related to each other or why they had been shoved in one of the travel journals. She did question if Sebastian had seen them. Given his aversion to all things related to his father, she thought not. He had likely never opened the journals.

She re-read the letters two more times. Temptation tickled her toes to take the letters to Sebastian, but she knew his response, knew he would be angry that she had snooped through the journals, and angrier still that she brought him correspondences regarding his father.

If she crafted them into a story, she would guess that Tobias had loved or pretended to love a girl named Lily, gotten her into trouble, then married someone else, by force or choice. Had he loved Lily but been forced to marry Jane? Or had he planned to marry Jane all along and seduced Lily? And who was Lilith?

In her wittily crafted story, Tobias got Lily in the family way, leaving Lily with an illegitimate named Lilith, who Lily then left with Tobias and his wife Jane. The problem with her narrative was, as far as she knew, Sebastian had no siblings.

Then, perhaps he wasn't even aware he had a sister. If she tied in the letter from Mrs. Brighton, she might conclude Lilith had been sent to an orphanage, but no, that wouldn't make sense either because the letter from Mrs. Brighton mentioned an advanced age, not a newborn. If she weren't sent until she was older, Sebastian would know he had a sister, unless they didn't keep her for long or hid her from him? Or he was too young to recall?

Bah! All speculation. Ridiculously fabricated speculation. Her lip was raw from gnawing on it.

Liz didn't have enough evidence to draw any inductive conclusions, only suspicions. Why had he kept the letters? Did Tobias harbor affection for Lily, his love child?

Then it hit her. Slapped her in the face with the cold hand of memory. During at least one of his nightmares, while he thrashed against the sheets and she tried to calm him, he had called Lilith's name.

At the time, she thought little of it, for he had been calling her name, and so she supposed she misheard or he spoke in a feverish fit of confusion. Lizbeth and Lilith didn't sound too different from the lips of a deranged dreamer, after all. But there was no mistaking the memory now. He had spoken that name. He knew of Lilith, yet he had said nothing to Lizbeth about her. He knew full well he had a sister. He hid this from her. As good as lied to her by omission.

Was Lilith who haunted his dreams? What had happened to keep her a secret? Her imagination conjured far wilder stories than were likely true, but given the advanced age at which the girl would have been sent to the orphanage and that Sebastian kept her a secret from his own wife although he still dreamed of her, Lizbeth's imagination took her for a merry ride indeed.

A stab in her gut told her she knew nothing at all about the man she married. She felt ill. She'd married a stranger.

She was sick of being left in the dark, sick of being treated with kid gloves. Confronting him was the only option.

Chapter 32

One of the potential doctors had responded to his invitation. He needed to reply soon to set dates for the physician's visit, but he hesitated, curious if Lizbeth would want to join him in the interview and tour of Balan.

He wouldn't doubt her intentions to join him except he'd been a horse's arse for over a week. He knew he had been. He knew she knew he had been. Yet in her extraordinary way, she cleverly crossed the distance he had created to show him what he missed while stewing. With her simple, wordless act, she showed him she stood by him, understood his need for space to think. Such a remarkable woman, his wife.

Locking his fingers behind his head, he leaned against his desk chair, remembering yesterday vividly. Such a remarkable woman. Despite his being an arse, she still came to him with love and support, reminding him what they shared together and how much he loved her.

Last night, he had slept as soundly as during their first week of marriage, no nightmare, just peaceful sleep. He had dreamed, but not of the past. Instead, he dreamt of Lizbeth walking by his side along the coast, her eyes smiling at him with tenderness.

If only she knew how much he loved her. If only he didn't fear losing her so much that he could be honest with her, lay his past at her feet and ask her to help him sort through the mess. If only he knew with absolute certainty she wouldn't run.

She hadn't run when she saw the scars, so maybe she wouldn't run from the truth. Then, what did it say about her if she didn't run? How could someone so easily forgive another person for what his poor decision had cost, the lives of two people and the torment of a third?

He made up his mind. Not without trepidation. Her demonstration yesterday of unconditional support spurred him to action. He would tell her. For better or worse, for good or ill, he would tell her. She could decide then what to make of him, if she still wanted to shackle herself to a worthless man or if she wanted to seek her life elsewhere. His heart was torn as to what she might choose. As much as he wanted her to accept his flaws, he wanted her foremost to be happy.

He needed another week, a month at most, to gather strength, to spend time with her, to practice how he would tell her, and then he would come clean.

He wanted to perfect the wording to minimize the blow while not lightening the truth. The wording certainly required thought. How best to explain what happened, why he was responsible, and how he has paid the price ever since? Just one more week, at least. He knew she wouldn't badger until he was ready, not after her demonstration yesterday. Remarkably understanding woman.

Before he came clean, he would invite his solicitor to set up for her financially in case she left. The solicitor could arrange for her dowry money, as well as all profits generated from a couple of his estates, to be accessible so she could do with it whatever she liked. Sebastian would also request one of the estates be readied for her to move into. Knowing she would want to be close to the ocean and relatively close to her sister, he decided Creighton Hall would be perfect, for it wasn't far from the coast, nestled on the east edge of the Yorkshire moors.

Yes, she'd like that. His solicitor would draw up the contract, giving her ample funds and the estate at her command. He would see to a child's provision in the contract, as well, should, by any chance, she find herself with child from their coupling between now and then. He yearned for children with her, but he doubted she would want him anywhere near a child of theirs after hearing his tale. She wouldn't dare trust him with a child. Not once she knew the truth.

He wanted her to be taken care of if she chose to leave him, as he couldn't blame her if she did, if she saw in him what he saw, what his father taught him to see, beat into him to see. Everything needed to be in order before he faced her. Devil take it; he should have seen to all of this well before they wed.

He certainly couldn't live like this anymore, keeping her at arm's length. Last night proved that. He had tried, and he had failed, leaving only one alternative: the truth. Just a little more time was all he needed.

No, he didn't trust himself enough, coward that he was.

A ha! A foolproof plan. He would write a letter to his solicitor and require the man deliver it to

Lizbeth at the end of November, no matter what. The letter would explain everything. In this way, if cowardice struck him dumb, his plan would still go into effect, thus saving or destroying his marriage.

With determination, he pulled a fresh sheet of parchment and wet his quill, ready to write his solicitor to begin the process.

Nothing about any of this settled well in his stomach. If only there were a way for it to be like last night every night for the rest of their lives without him having to say a word, or better yet, with his entire past erased.

Lizbeth, I can't lose you.

He jotted the salutation to his solicitor, quill scratching against paper.

A *thunk* from the opposite side of the room announced the closing of the library door. Startled, he looked up to find Lizbeth in the doorway. Behold, a divine angel, beautiful perfection inside and out. A smile curved his lips.

"Who is Lilith?" she demanded, her expression pained.

His smile slipped. He dropped the quill to the desk, ink splattering across the page. Sebastian stared, gaping.

How did she…? He searched his memory for who would know that name, who could have told her that name.

The journals. Devils and damnation. His father must have written about the incident in one of the journals. She must know everything. Before his eyes, his world crumbled.

Fear shook his body, his legs wobbling as he stood from his desk chair. Trembling hands braced against the desk to steady him.

No! No, not yet! He wasn't ready. He needed more time. He needed to meet with the solicitor first. He needed to prepare his words. But then, what more could he say if she already knew all?

Opening his mouth to speak, he chocked, the words caught in his throat.

"Who is Lilith, Sebastian? I have a right to know," she commanded, ignorant of how that name ripped at his heart.

His words didn't rise above a whisper, yet still they carried to her on the opposite side of the room, a gulf separating them. "My sister."

"You have a sister, yet you never told me?" Her inflection wounded, insulted, as pained as he felt. "Why would you keep that from me?"

"*Had*. I *had* a sister. Please, Lizbeth, don't ask more questions, not yet. I need time." Jagged words syncopated his plea.

"And I need you to talk to me, Sebastian. You've had all the time in the world to tell me. Now I ask a simple question—why didn't you tell me you had a sister?"

"It's not a simple question." His voice cracked.

"Talk to me. Why the secrecy? Where is she? What happened to her?"

Each question sounded louder, ringing in his ears. A low humming underlay all sounds in the room. His head ached with a faint dizziness.

"I can't. Not yet. I can't tell you." He leaned against his desk, bracing himself in case he fainted.

The room swirled around him, the humming droning louder. He wasn't ready for this. He couldn't lose her.

Stop asking, and leave the room, Lizbeth. Turn around and go read a book, walk the ocean, drink tea. Please, leave the room, Lizbeth. He repeated this mantra, silently begging her to hear it.

Her words softened, barely audible, her eyes brimming with tears. "I hardly know who you are."

"I'm me. The same man you married. Nothing has changed."

"Yes, it has. You are pushing me away so you can hide your sister. But why? I need to understand. I can't help you if I don't understand why you've lied to me."

"Please stop," he begged. "Stop this line of inquiry. I can't lose you."

The humming drowned out his words. He heard only mumbled words, spoken through a funnel, a distant scene he only perceived rather than participated.

He continued to plead with her in his mind, projecting his thoughts to her, wanting her to receive them and accept them. *Don't make me say it aloud, Lizbeth. I can't bear to say it aloud* yet. *Let me write the letters. Let me organize my thoughts.*

"Why would you lose me? The only way you'll lose me is if you continue this charade, hiding in your library and lying to me. I can't believe you kept this from me." Her chin quivered as she spoke, the corners of her lips dipping with each word.

He turned to look at the floor, still holding himself against the desk. "You don't understand."

"Help me to understand."

The pattern on the rug waved, his vision blurring. Even when receiving the beatings from his father, he hadn't felt this level of fear. He had hardened himself against the beatings. He couldn't harden himself from her. All he knew now was bone-deep fear at vocalizing what he had never spoken to another soul, fear of her rejection, fear of not waking up to her by his side tomorrow morning or any morning.

She continued to plead for answers. "I need you to stop being this stranger in my husband's body. I need you to be the person I married. I can't live with this person who is forever licking his wounds and hiding secrets. This isn't you, not the real you. This is some mask of protection, and you need to remove it so I can see my husband again."

His fear turned to frustration, anger building in his gut. "This isn't a mask, Lizbeth. This is me. If you don't like what you see, then you shouldn't have married me."

He thought she understood. He thought she wouldn't push him until he was ready.

"You think this mask is you? Who, then, is the man I swam with in the ocean? Who is the man I laughed with under the stars?" She took two steps towards him. "That man wouldn't keep secrets from me, especially not to hide an entire person. If that man isn't you, then who is he?"

"An illusion." He turned away from her to face the window, crossing his arms protectively across his chest.

The welling anger centered him, reducing the sound of the hum, giving him balance. He didn't want to be pressed or told who she believed him to be.

"Don't turn your back on me. Don't shut me out. You have lived behind a self-made wall so long that you've forgotten what it's like to be yourself. Or maybe you've never known yourself? I've seen you happy and carefree, an earnest truthsayer. I've seen the real you, Sebastian. Why would you ever want to be this untouchable person who shuts out his wife and turns his back on her? I fell in love with the real you, not this cold mask." Her voice sounded closer, but he didn't turn to see if she had moved.

"How can you fall in love with me if you don't know me? You said yourself you hardly know me. You don't know what I'm capable of, what my father reminded me of every day, never letting me forget my sins. You ask the impossible."

"Oh, but Sebastian, I do know you. I know you better than you know yourself, it would seem. You are you, not who your father defined you to be, not this secretive man afraid to look at me." She stood so closely he could smell the soap on her skin mixed with a hint of book leather and last night's lovemaking.

His heart ached to hold her, to turn to her and ask her to tell him more about falling in love. Had she really fallen in love with him? He braced himself for that to change as soon as he spoke the truth about his sister, as soon as he verbalized it.

"You're mistaken. I'm a man defined by my past, by my choices, by my family."

"That's ridiculous! People don't define you," she insisted.

"But actions do. I killed my own sister, Lizbeth. Now what do you think of me?"

He heard a sharp intake of breath behind him. He waited for a response. An eternity passed, the air thick with unspoken words.

Turning to face her, he saw what he expected to see, fear and pain in her eyes, slivers of hate etched into pupils. "Are you not afraid of me now? Do you not hate me now?"

He turned back to the window, refusing to watch her slipping away from him. Why couldn't she leave instead of watching his heart break?

When she didn't respond, he snapped, "Why are you still here? Leave me. I'm a murderer, Lizbeth. I'm responsible for the death of both my sister and mother, and the heartache of my father, an ache so strong it caused his heart attack, all because of me. I'm not worth their lives. Leave me before I destroy your life, too."

He heard her sobbing quietly behind him.

"Am I not convincing enough? Do you want the whole story? Is my confession not enough for you? Want all the sordid details? I made a choice that resulted in my sister's death, and thus my mother's from heartbreak of losing her beloved little girl. I alone am responsible, and I bear the scars to prove it."

Much to his dismay, the first words she spoke after his declaration, words carried on a sigh, asked, "Are you sure she's dead?"

"Of course, she's dead. Why do you think he beat me? He beat me because I made a decision and had to pay the consequence. The scars are proof of her death."

Only a week ago he thought he could swallow the pain, ignore his past, push it down to the depths of his soul, but now that would be impossible, not when he had spoken the words aloud, not when she knew what he had always known—he was a monster. All his potential happiness washed away.

The cotton of her dress brushed against his leg. A wisp of her hair tickled the back of his arm. For a moment, he thought she would reach out to him, but she didn't.

"No one deserves those scars." Lizbeth's words strained, full of pain and confusion. "What happened? How did she die?"

He had never told the story to anyone, not even to Drake. What more damage could it do to tell her? He flinched at the betrayal she must feel, at the hate she must harbor now that she knew the truth.

Gnashing his teeth, he said aloud what he held in his heart for all these years. "Lilith was my sister. My mother doted on her. She was my mother's little princess. I, too, loved my sister more than anything in this world, even if she did have a knack for getting me into trouble. Every few days, she talked me into sneaking past the nanny to escape to the beach so we could play mermaid and monster or Poseidon and shipwreck or whatever her imagination conjured."

He paused, pain welling in his throat, tears stinging his eyes. "I loved going with her but feared getting caught. Even after dusk, she would refuse to leave, daring me to stay longer, risking Father's wrath. She didn't know it was I who was punished every time we were caught."

Losing himself to the memories, he slipped into the past, watching his sister in his mind's eye splashing in the water, never caring if father punished them, openly defying him by ruining her dresses, covering herself in wet sand, and arriving well past dusk.

"One day, she wanted to stay and play. She begged me to stay. My bottom was still sore from the day before, and while she was immune to his anger, I was not. I didn't want another punishment, so I turned my back and told her I was going home. She begged me to stay, but I left her. I made a selfish choice, and I left my sister alone in the ocean past dark. It was my duty as her brother to protect her, and I willingly abandoned her."

He paused, feeling the wetness on his cheek. He could still hear Lilith calling his name.

His throat scratchy and hoarse, he continued, "I snuck back into the house, relieved not to be caught. The next day, I didn't see her, but that wasn't all too strange, as it was a large house, and often Mother spent days alone with her, doing whatever it is mothers and daughters do together. Another day passed, and I still hadn't seen her. I went to ask Mother, but Father forbade me to go near her, saying she had caught a contagious fever.

"A week passed, in which time I saw neither my sister nor my mother. I didn't know if Lilith had caught Mother's fever, if she had been caught sneaking back in and been punished, or if she were still out there, lost. Childishly, I made plans to rescue her from locked closets, to scout the wilderness and save her with my cunning, to sneak porridge to her if she was sick.

"Finally, I went to my father, worried beyond reason. Why did I wait a week, you wonder? Because I'm a selfish bastard. Because I feared his wrath. Because I feared the punishment when I confessed I had violated curfew. Because I feared his anger when I confessed I left her alone at the ocean. Because I'm a coward. When I went to him, told him what I had done, said I was sorry and wanted to see my sister and mother, I learned the consequences of a moment's rash decision."

Lizbeth's fingers brushed his arm during this pause. He winced, flinching away from her.

"Father stood from his chair, walked to the fireplace, and heated the poker. It was then he told me my sister drowned because of my irresponsibility as a brother, because I failed at my duties as a man. He told me to face the consequences of my decision. And then the fatal blow—my mother died that morning of a feverish fit over Lilith's death and the knowledge her son was to blame. My father taught me in that moment the meaning of consequences, the meaning of remorse. He taught me the cost of my selfishness with not only the fire poker, but the stark reality that the two people I loved most in the world were dead because of my selfishness.

"I was never allowed to speak Lilith's name. Every foul mood, every spilt teacup, every loud noise, he reminded me of what I did, of the pain I brought to the household. He recovered from their death and went quite mad. I might as well have killed them all with my bare hands. All dead because of a single choice I made."

Having spoken the truth aloud after all these years, he thought he might find some relief, but instead his heart pounded in his ears. So lost in the memory of it all, the nightmare of it all, he had almost forgotten Lizbeth standing behind him.

She didn't make a sound.

A life filled with fear, and now he was afraid to turn around, afraid to face the woman he loved, afraid she would look at him as his father had done. He wanted to hold her, wanted to love her. Why couldn't he have had more time with her before the truth was told? Now, he just wanted her to leave him alone to self-loath.

A whisper reached through the fog of his pain. "You told me you were only seven when your mother died."

"And so I was."

"But you were only a little boy, Sebastian."

He let silence stretch and watched the waves crest the rocks as the looming storm clouds gave way to a luminescent sun reflected on the waves.

"I'm a monster. Please, leave me. I want to be alone." Even as he said it, he hoped she wouldn't listen, hoped she would wrap her arms around him.

"You can't be responsible for anyone's death. You were a child," Lizbeth insisted. "But are you sure your sister died? She wasn't sent away?"

The fire poker rose before his mind's eye, blurred by the vision of every beating to follow over the next decade. He howled with pain and rage, his back searing from memory alone, his knuckles on fire from fighting off his father.

"Leave me alone!" he shouted, pounding fists against the stone wall. "Don't touch me! Leave me be!"

It took mere moments to reorient himself, to realize he wasn't shouting at his father, wasn't fighting against the man, but rather was punching the library wall, his knuckles sore and bleeding.

He squeezed his eyes closed and waited to feel Lizbeth's protective arms. Instead, he heard the soft *thud* of the library door closing.

Chapter 33

A maelstrom of emotion whirled in Lizbeth as she entered the carriage less than an hour later, a small bag packed at her side.

Rage at his father. Anger that Sebastian blamed himself for something he hadn't done. Sadness that he bottled it all these years, torturing himself. Helplessness that she didn't know the words to help him see he wasn't responsible. And Love for the man she married.

This man had held misplaced guilt in his heart all his life. She wanted to hold him in her arms and kiss away the pain, but this wasn't her battle. She couldn't alleviate his internal conflict any more than she could sit idly by and watch him rack himself, seeing himself as a murderous beast, which she knew perfectly well he was not.

Despite her belief in his innocence, she felt utterly helpless. Even if everything happened exactly as he had described, which she doubted given he would have been too young to exact details, his father had no right to blame him. If Tobias Lancaster weren't already in his grave, Lizbeth would be tempted to put him there herself.

She suspected Sebastian felt as helpless as she did, but unlike him, she could ask for help on his behalf.

She could swallow her pride, humble herself, and seek guidance from those who knew him best. Without their help, she wasn't at all sure what to do, as he certainly wouldn't listen to her, wouldn't believe her when she told him he wasn't responsible. Somehow, she needed proof that he wasn't responsible, solid evidence.

All this time, she had wanted nothing more than him to open to her. Never had she dreamt he hid so much guilt and pain. She only wanted them to be closer, no more secrets. The confession now seemed such an empty victory. She couldn't battle what his father had done to him. She couldn't battle a ghost.

The carriage bumped and weaved along the path to Lyonn Manor. She didn't know how she would do it, but she had to get her husband back before he drove himself insane. Her life disintegrated before her eyes when he unleashed his burdens, but not because of what he said, only that she realized if she couldn't help him fight his father's memory, she would lose him forever.

The cloud-touching spires came into view at last. She couldn't believe she was taking her sister's advice and intentionally seeking out Annick. She didn't even know what Annick could tell her that she didn't already know, but surely, he would have insights to Sebastian, especially given he would have known Sebastian's father. Could she convince Annick to take her to Roddam Hall? Maybe there was evidence at the manor that would exonerate Sebastian of his guilt, more letters to or from his father, something, anything.

The correspondences with the orphanage seemed key to finding out what happened. Had Sebastian's sister been sent away? Had she died before they sent her? Had she died on the way? It was possible Lilith had drowned, but that wouldn't be the fault of Sebastian, only a child at the time. It was also possible Lilith contracted a fever and died from that. Lizbeth had no way of knowing if the mother died of fever or heartbreak or something far more sinister. Sorting truth from a madman's words to a child was impossible.

Jolting to a stop, the carriage parked in front of the gothic estate. The coachman opened Liz's door and helped her down the steps. After running to the door as dignified as she could manage given her panic-stricken heart, she struck the door knocker persistently, forcefully.

If not for the weight of the situation, she could have laughed. Annick had become a glimmer of hope in the darkness of her world.

The butler answered, scowling before admitting her. He helped her out of her coat and bonnet and took her bag.

"I shall ascertain if the duchess is receiving, madam," he said as he walked towards the far end of the gallery.

"Wait. No. I'm not here to see my sister. I'm here to see His Grace."

Two eyebrows rose in surprise.

"Please. It is a matter of some urgency." She hadn't meant to speak so loudly, but her voice echoed in the hall.

"His Grace is from home. I will take your card and tell him you called."

"No. No, no, no. He must be home. It's an urgent and delicate matter. I must speak with him immediately," she pleaded with the stoic man.

A stern voice called from the parlor door. "What is this about? Why do you so urgently need to see my son?"

The dowager duchess stood in the doorway, the cane gripped tightly in her white-knuckled hand.

"It is a matter I wish only to discuss with Annick." The last person she wanted to see was Sebastian's aunt.

She needed Annick to tell her what to do, how to get through to Sebastian. This woman knew nothing of her nephew and was wasting her time.

"Come. Join me," commanded Catherine.

"No, I—"

"That wasn't an invitation, Lady Roddam. That was a command. Come. Now." Without waiting for another protest, Catherine returned to the parlor.

Liz followed reluctantly.

Captain Henry's tree stood empty today, likely with Charlotte exploring the conservatory. Lizbeth perched herself on the edge of a pink chair, her spine straightened by an invisible string. The dowager sat in her favorite chair and faced Lizbeth, hot coals staring from under thin black eyebrows.

"Something has happened?" Catherine surmised.

"Yes. How did you know?" Liz shifted uncomfortably under the duchess' stare.

"It isn't every day madwomen approach my door with battering rams demanding to speak with my son. Did my nephew strike you?" The question accompanied a casual tone as though they were discussing the latest additions to the flower garden.

"Strike me? Heavens no! He would never do such thing!" What an appalling thing to ask, Lizbeth thought. Sebastian wasn't like his father.

"Then tell me why you are here. Do not feign ignorance. Do not stare at the floor. Do not stutter. I have no wish to wheedle information from you; however, since you are here, and I suspect from your urgency this pertains to my nephew, you may tell me, and I will attempt to aid you." Catherine thumped the cane on the floor. "Know you may seek asylum here if he has hit you. He has the right to do so, but I am a powerful woman and will shield you if you should ask."

Liz's words tumbling out before she could stop them, desirous to defend her husband and get to the point of why she came. "Sebastian is tormented by the memory of his sister."

"What sister? He has no sister."

"Lilith? He doesn't have a sister named Lilith?" For a fleeting moment, Liz questioned if her husband really was mad.

"Oh," Catherine harrumphed, waving her hand dismissively. "That bastard girl. Yes, if you consider an illegitimate offspring a sister. But that's not the point. The point is he couldn't possibly remember her. He was far too young."

"He does remember her, and he's torturing himself. It's destroying him and our marriage. I feel so helpless. I can't convince him he isn't responsible, and I don't know how to convince him that I love him regardless. I'm at a loss, Your Grace. He feels responsible but that's preposterous because he was only a child."

"You're rambling. Responsible for what?"

Lizbeth looked incredulously at the duchess. "Her death, of course."

"What death? She didn't die. What are you talking about?" Catherine thumped her cane in agitation.

"Sebastian says she drowned."

"Don't be ridiculous. Where did he get such a notion? She did no such thing. My brother shipped her off to some parish in Durham or Cumberland or wherever it was to live with all the other bastards. And rightly so. She should have been sent away immediately. A bastard living in my father's estate as though she were a lady. It was unseemly. That wife of his paraded her about Society, I'll have you know, claiming the girl as her own. A shameful disgrace to the Roddam name."

Liz sat stunned. "Then why does he think she died?"

"I'm sure I couldn't tell you. My brother paid a handsome sum to be rid of her, and it was generous of him to do that. My father, if he had ever found out that child lived with my brother, would have drowned her himself."

"I hardly consider it generous to send a child away from her family. But that doesn't answer why Sebastian believes she died. Are you sure she's alive, or maybe there's been some confusion?"

After all these years of him feeling responsible for her death, Lilith couldn't still be alive, could she? Had his father lied to him? But why? Liz had more questions than answers.

"There is no confusion. She was sent to the orphanage, I assure you. No one died in that family except my brother's wife, Jane Lancaster, and she of a contagious fever. Her death destroyed my brother."

"I can hardly believe it. Sebastian feels responsible for a death that never happened. I must find her!

I must go to her. He'll never believe me otherwise," Liz muttered more to herself than to the dowager.

She thanked her own foresight for packing the letters with her, for the letter from Mrs. Brighton contained the address of the orphanage. Lilith would have likely left the orphanage years before, well over a decade ago, but if they could at least confirm the child had arrived and lived there, that she hadn't died, that could be enough. Better yet, maybe they could direct her to where Lilith went after staying at the orphanage.

"That's the silliest notion I've ever heard," stated the duchess. "She's better off where she is and hopefully has no memory of her childhood."

"You don't understand. His father is the one who told him she drowned. He blamed Sebastian for her death and the subsequent death of Lady Roddam."

The dowager sighed. She remained silent while she stood to ring the bell-pull. Catherine returned to her seat, waited, and then after the disapproving butler brought a tray and scuttled away, she poured tea and milk into a fresh cup.

This was hardly conversation to have over tea. She grew impatient. This was wasting time while Sebastian suffered.

Liz watched her, declining the tea with a frustrated shake of her head. Catherine nursed her own cup. Only after emptying the contents did she speak again.

"My brother and I suffered at the hand of our father. He was a proud man, full of righteous indignation. He disciplined corporally when we sinned. If my spine were not straight enough, he would whip my feet until they bled, then make me stand from morning to night balancing objects on my head with my spine aligned. I do not tell you this to gain your pity. I tell you this so that you will understand my brother." The dowager poured another cup to nurse, studying Lizbeth over the rim.

"I married the Duke of Annick when I was sixteen. It was the happiest day of my life to leave that house. My husband may have been far older than me, but he was never abusive. I begged him to take Tobias with us, but of course that couldn't be done. Tobias was only twelve. I left him alone, defenseless against our father. When I left, I removed myself completely from the family, never speaking to my father or Tobias again. I did, however, seek out information about my brother through the servants."

Liz continued to listen, silent and absorbing, trying to place it all into perspective of Sebastian's childhood.

"There were rumors when Tobias was about seventeen that he fell in love with a servant on the estate, a groomsman's daughter or maybe a parlor maid." Catherine paused to eye Lizbeth. "When his father learned of their affections, he married Tobias to the only daughter of a wealthy peer. Jane's death was tragic, especially with Sebastian being so young."

Lizbeth probed, "But what of the servant girl?"

"According to my confidants, Tobias' lover ran away, his by-blow in her womb. A year later, she irresponsibly left the child on his doorstep. From what I understand, his wife Jane took to the child and wanted to raise her as her own. It only makes sense the child would be sent to an orphanage once Lady Roddam fell ill. Tobias wouldn't want a bastard in the house."

Lizbeth had deduced most of this herself from the paltry correspondences she found, but other explanations were possible, of course. Regardless of the reasons, none of this helped her to understand Sebastian's plight. The most she learned from this was that Lilith might still be alive.

The dowager hadn't finished her tale, apparently, as she continued to talk, Lizbeth growing antsy that she wasn't out searching for proof of Lilith or Lilith herself.

"Tobias was a pleasant boy, not unlike Sebastian. Tobias always enjoyed reading and had a passion for exploring. He wanted above all things to travel. But, you must understand, there is only so much cruelty a person can take. My father enjoyed humiliating punishments, especially treatments that debased one's self in front of servants."

A third cup of tea later, she expounded, caught in memory. "Tobias was wild, careless, often purposely inciting our father's wrath. I cannot imagine how badly life became for him after I left. Tobias was never a bad person. He was a person to whom bad things happened. I pity my brother and can only assume he told Sebastian the girl died to spare him the sorrow of her being sent away, or he had already gone mad with grief over his wife. Either way, my brother is not to blame for his actions. I am aware he was heavy handed, but I suspect Sebastian provoked him as Tobias had done with his own father. All in all, you do the right thing to help him. He's always been troubled, and I would rather not see him follow in the footsteps of his predecessors."

It took every inch of restraint Liz possessed to keep from throttling the duchess who defended her brother after the abuse Sebastian suffered at Tobias' hands, after the lies and persecution he suffered.

No amount of sympathy could be given to Tobias after knowing he turned out just like his own father. If anything, he was worse than his father, for he knew all too well what it was to be mistreated, yet he repeated the same behavior against his own son. She refused to see Tobias as a victim. She had no pity for him.

Her heart, however, swelled thinking of Sebastian and how he had broken the cycle of cruelty in the family, violence that had continued for generations. Never could a gentler soul be found than Sebastian. A kind person, a devoted employer, a loving husband. It was only himself he abused, internalizing his pain.

Liz wanted nothing more than to go to her husband this minute and hold him, cover his face and body with kisses and tell him how proud she was, how proud his mother would be if she could see him now. She wanted to lay his head in her lap and run her fingers through his hair. Her lion. Her love.

But she still couldn't do these things. Not yet. She needed to find Lilith, or he would never believe her. She needed to find proof beyond the duchess' words that Lilith did not die as Sebastian had been told.

She fretted about the result of finding proof. Would the realization that he had been so viciously lied to, that he had been blamed by his father for a death that never occurred sink him into an even worse depression, or would it lift his burdens of responsibility? If she found Lilith alive and well and took her to Dunstanburgh, would Sebastian even believe it was her, or would he think Lizbeth antagonized him?

She couldn't know how he might react or what she could say to resolve this, but she would decide after she found proof of Lilith's survival.

"Thank you, Your Grace, for everything that you've shared. You've given me insight to my husband. Do you think my sister would be interested in a brief journey with me this afternoon?"

"Ask her, not me. She's in the conservatory. I believe you love my nephew, and for that I am pleased. If he ever strikes you, however, come to me. I will shelter you as I could not do for my brother. I do not have the legal right to keep you from your husband, but I am a powerful woman and can hide you. In a way, that would atone for my inability to help Tobias."

"Thank you, Your Grace." Liz rose to find Charlotte.

While the dowager meant well with her offer, and Liz did appreciate the sentiment, she realized how little Catherine knew her own nephew, a woman still trapped in her own past, fighting her own demons.

Sebastian glowered at his desk. She had left him, never to return. He knew she would leave, had anticipated her departure, but now he struggled to accept he'd lost her.

All his fears came to fruition in a matter of minutes. His last look at her had been those pained eyes, angry and betrayed. He supposed he should feel angry and betrayed, as well, but he had no anger left, only sorrow.

Gerald had visited an hour prior to inform him the countess had packed and taken the carriage for Lyonn Manor. He knew in that moment she had left him forever.

She had seen him for what he was and left, horrified to have married such a man, knowing he didn't deserve happiness with innocent blood on his hands. People were always predictable from his experience, always acting according to his expectations, living up to his estimations. Even his once unpredictable wife had followed the path he set for her, right through the front door.

Determined to do something right, he had already finished the letter to his solicitor to set up a fund for Lizbeth, asking his man of business to visit her at Lyonn Manor to discuss the details of Creighton Hall, the money, and any provisions for a child.

Waxed and sealed, he still needed to send the letter. And he needed to have her possessions packed and delivered to the manor. He couldn't do either of these now. Maybe tomorrow. Maybe next week.

He buried his head in his hands. If only he had time to craft his words before telling her, he might have been able to share his secrets in such a way that wasn't completely villainizing. He deserved this fate, but he would have tried everything in his power to keep her from seeing him as a monster. If only.

Briefly, he entertained what his life might have been like if his sister had lived and he never had to shoulder this responsibility. Would his mother have lived? Would his father not have gone mad or died from heart failure? Would his father still have beaten him? Would his father, the one person who was supposed to love him, still have made him feel worthless, or was that purely the effect of Sebastian's poor choices?

He imagined life with a sister. Lilith had loved him unconditionally. As much as he wanted to be the protective brother, it always seemed to be the other way around, with her bossing him, convincing him to disobey rules, taking the brunt of Father's anger when they were caught, never realizing he would be punished regardless. He imagined her grown, likely as headstrong as Lizbeth, likely an exceptional beauty. Would they have grown together as best friends or fallen to sibling rivalry?

A vision of a grown Lilith and his Lizbeth picnicking at the cliff's edge flashed into his mind, both laughing at a shared joke, turning in unison to wave at him. What an absurd vision. He scoffed. Lilith would never see this castle, just as she would never grow older than eight years of age. And Lizbeth would never again picnic on these grounds. He had lost everyone who ever meant anything to him, everyone who had ever loved him.

What did love even mean? A useless emotion. Love hadn't kept Lilith alive. Love hadn't kept his mother alive. Love hadn't kept Lizbeth with him. He thought when he married Lizbeth that maybe love would be enough, maybe if he gave it a chance, love would cure his troubled heart.

Had she ever loved him? She mentioned falling in love with some part of him, some sliver of him that she had seen, but her love hadn't been strong enough to love all of him, the darkness and the demons. Loving some small part wasn't enough if she couldn't love all of him, not that he would expect her to love a murderer, but he had hoped, somewhere inside he had hoped she would see him and not turn away, just as she had done with the scars, kissing them instead of being repulsed and shunning him.

God, he missed her, and she had only been gone for two hours. Facing a lifetime without her seemed unbearable. He would do what he did before: bury himself in his estate business and work the fields with the laborers. Keeping busy was his only survival strategy for facing a world without his wife. In time, he could bury her memory.

First things first, he would burn his father's journals. He moved from the desk to the hearth to stoke the dying embers. As he did so, a handkerchief slipped from the side of his desk onto the floor.

Looking up at him with colorful embroidery was the handkerchief Liz had sewn for him. Reaching down to retrieve the fabric, his vision blurred. Grown men didn't cry. Hardened men who built castles and tilled fields, titled men who sat in the House of Lords did not cry.

He sat back in his chair, fingering the kerchief. The soft embroidery caressed his fingers, reminding him of the feel of her skin beneath his hands. The scent of the fabric recalled the intoxication of her hair when he buried his face against her neck at night, the sweet aroma of fresh flowers. He cried into the kerchief until his sobs were silent heaves.

Chapter 34

Charlotte talked nonstop for the entire journey to Allshire, a parish in the heart of Cumberland, a fact they gratefully learned before they set off. As desperately as Liz wanted to head straight from Lyonn Manor the day before, both her sister and the coachman agreed it would be best to wait for a new day to arrange for the horse exchanges that would be needed to make the journey in good time.

Reluctantly, she had agreed, not knowing that Drake would take both the carriage and the coachman with him the next morning on some errand, delaying the trip even longer. Liz had fretted and paced in the parlor until the duke returned. She wanted to make haste, knowing the pain Sebastian must be experiencing now and not wanting to be gone from him for long.

The trip exhausted the day and should have realistically taken two days if they hadn't encouraged the coachman to hurry, even rushing the exchange of horses along the way at coach stops in the duchy. The trip covered nearly eighty miles.

Lizbeth worried it was a fool's journey. Who would logically travel such a distance in hopes of finding a girl presumed dead? It would have been easier to write a missive to Mrs. Brighton inquiring if

Lilith had arrived safely those many years previous and if her current whereabouts were known. Logic didn't weigh into Lizbeth's plans.

If Lilith were alive, she wanted to find her in person. She wanted to drag the woman back to the castle as living proof Sebastian wasn't responsible for anyone's death.

She wasn't even sure if Mrs. Brighton would respond to a letter. A personal visit seemed the best option in her fevered determination to resolve the conflicting information surrounding Lilith's disappearance. If the girl were indeed alive, showing him a letter wouldn't suffice. He may even accuse her of forging it. Only the flesh and blood person would do.

She hadn't quite worked out how she would convince Charlotte or the coachman to go on yet another drive to wherever Lilith may currently be living. What if she lived somewhere like London? Lizbeth hadn't thought of that. The closer they got to the parish, the more of a fool's errand this seemed. Not completely disheartened, Liz knew at least some questions would be answered with this trip.

At one time, Sebastian had questioned her rationale to travel four hundred miles to see her sister after a single letter of invitation, and Lizbeth had responded that she would do anything for the people she loved. Well, now he was on the receiving end of that, for she would do anything for Sebastian, anything to help him slay this demon so he could find peace.

When Charlotte and Liz finally arrived at the parish of Allshire, the coachman asked if they wanted to go directly to the orphanage or to the inn.

"The inn of course," replied Charlotte.

"No! The orphanage! We haven't a minute to lose," countered Lizbeth.

"Don't be silly. The girl has waited this long already. She can surely wait one evening more so we may rest and be fresh for the visit. No one expects uninvited visitors this late. The sun is already setting. At the most, let us send our card to the orphanage to announce our intention to visit tomorrow." Charlotte sat back on the bench, satisfied to resolve the deliberation.

"This is not a social call," defended Liz. "And I don't care about following social protocol. We will go now and at least ascertain if she is still alive."

"Very well. But I'm not getting out of the coach." Charlotte directed the coachman to continue to the orphanage.

Being a small parish, the orphanage was not far from the edge of town, a two-story building connected to the church. Lizbeth exited the carriage, leaving her sister behind to watch out of the window.

Above the door of the building, an engraving read: *Let the little children come to me, and do not hinder them, for the kingdom of heaven belongs to such as these. Matthew 19:13*

Closing her eyes to garner strength, she rapped on the door.

After a lengthy wait, a middle-aged woman, short and lean with a lace cap and high-necked dress opened the door, eyeing Lizbeth skeptically. "May I help you?"

"I'm here to see Mrs. Brighton, please." Lizbeth could only imagine how it must look to be paying a call at dusk to a complete stranger. Perhaps Charlotte had been right after all about waiting and sending a card first.

"Mrs. Brighton is not here, I'm afraid." The woman began closing the door.

Lizbeth, not meaning to startle her, placed a hand against the wood to keep it from shutting. "Wait! Please. This is a matter of some urgency. When will she return? Where might I find her?"

"You'll find her in the Allshire cemetery, ma'am. Mrs. Brighton passed nearly fifteen years ago." The woman stared with alarm at Lizbeth's hand against the door.

"Oh, no. Please don't tell me that."

She had come for nothing. She should have inquired first. She should have written. She should have…

"Is Mrs. Brighton's replacement here? May I speak to the matron of the orphanage?"

The woman narrowed her eyes and was about to turn her away when she saw the ducal coach waiting in the street. Her eyes widened with a fresh head-to-foot perusal of Lizbeth, assuming her to be a duchess here to inspect the premise, pay homage, or some other business of crown and country.

With a new willingness to please, she curtsied deeply to Lizbeth and stammered, "I do apologize, Your Grace. Please forgive me. I shall see you to the matron now, Your Grace."

Lizbeth didn't correct the error in identity, but instead followed her through a narrow hall into a back room that served as a small office.

"Please sit, Your Grace. I will bring Mrs. Copeland to you." The woman curtsied backwards out of the room, dipping and stepping all the way through the door as though the guest were royalty.

She didn't wait long before a tall, slender, and rose-cheeked young woman not much older than Lizbeth rushed into the room, curtsied, and seated herself behind the desk. With a moment's amusement, Lizbeth imagined herself sitting behind that desk, a fate she might once have desired before marrying Sebastian.

"Welcome, Your Grace. I am Mrs. Copeland, the headmistress. You wish to see the children and facilities, then? The children are in the dining room taking supper. I could show you first the classrooms, then the sleeping quarters to give Miss Tolkey time to prepare the children for presentation."

"Oh, no, you misunderstand my purpose. Allow me to introduce myself. I am the Countess of Roddam. My sister, waiting in the carriage, is the Duchess of Annick. We are here not to inspect, but rather to find an orphan who may have once stayed here. We hope to learn if she arrived safely, and if so, her current whereabouts, assuming they may be known. Mrs. Brighton handled her admission." Lizbeth watched as Mrs. Copeland deflated, her expression turning from eagerness to confusion.

"I'm afraid I won't be able to help you, Your Ladyship. Few records are kept once children leave. What would have been the timeframe of the child's stay?"

"I would hazard to guess during the span of the late 1760s to early 1780s." Liz tried to calculate dates quickly in her head based on Sebastian's age, his age when his mother died, and thus the relative age his sister would have been sent to the orphanage. She failed miserably at the hasty subtraction but felt confident the dates were within a relatively safe range.

"No, we wouldn't have any records for the children from so long ago. I'm sorry I can't be of more help. Would you still like to see the facilities?" The woman, eager to please, had already stood in preparation for the tour.

"I've come nearly one hundred miles. Please, don't turn me away. Maybe you would remember the child if I told you her name," Liz begged.

"I'm afraid I wouldn't know any of the children from that time. That was when Mrs. Brighton served as matron. I would have been about the same age as the person you seek, I'm sorry to say."

"Her name was Lilith. Lilith Lancaster or maybe Lilith Chambers," Liz blurted out, not wanting to be dismissed before having her say. "Please, tell me you know a child named Lilith. I don't know where else to turn." Glad her sister wasn't present to witness her groveling to an orphanage matron, Liz stood and implored the woman, her hands clasped in front as if in prayer.

"Lilith? You want to see Lilith? Why didn't you say so from the outset?" Mrs. Copeland looked even more confused now, but with obvious recognition.

"You know her?"

"Yes, of course. She's our schoolmistress. Once an orphan here herself, she has stayed on as a teacher."

A hand over her mouth, Lizbeth released a quiet sob. This all seemed heaven sent. Without first warning the startled Mrs. Copeland, Lizbeth reached out and hugged the matron.

"You have no idea how happy this makes me. Where may I find her? I will go to her now," Lizbeth said, releasing the poor woman who had been crushed to Liz's bosom.

"She's at Arbor House this evening, just beyond the west edge of town. I'll draw you a map, if you'd like."

The matron sketched it on the back of discarded parchment. Lizbeth bade the woman farewell and raced to Charlotte so they could proceed to Arbor House before the darkness of night hampered their task.

Sunrays illuminated Sebastian's world, flooding the gazebo with morning light. He had lain awake most of the night, listening to the waves make love to the rocks and feeling the emptiness of the bed. Hours before dawn, he tired of staring at her empty pillow and walked out to the gazebo on the headland to think.

Sitting in the place where they had exchanged vows didn't make him feel much better, but if he closed his eyes and centered himself in the sounds around him, he could swear she sat next to him and whispered to him on the wind. He saw her in the waves and felt her touch in the sea mist.

Nothing could dissuade him from his next course of action, for he knew what he must do. He must find peace within himself so he could bring his wife home.

The empty halls of Dunstanburgh begged to be filled with the laughter of their children. The beach called to be covered with their footprints. The guest wing waited to accommodate Hazel, Walter, and

Cuthbert. The lord of the manor yearned for his soul's mate.

Finding peace was the only way to bring her home, the only way he could convince her he wasn't a monster. If he could just convince himself first. After a lifetime spent blocking the memories and wallowing in blame, he struggled to focus. Never before had he tried to focus on it, tried to pinpoint exactly what haunted him, what the nightmares meant. Before he could wash the blood from his hands, he needed to know from whence it came.

The nightmares were always the same with variations on the theme. They always started with a clear vision of Lilith playing in the water, calling for him to stay and play. That in itself was a happy memory, one he wanted to hold onto if it weren't associated with guilt. Only the rest of the nightmare twisted the memory, filling in the blankness of when he turned his back. He had turned from her and never saw what happened next, so the dreams filled the void with monsters, epically sized squid, pirates, sky-high waves, and various other absurd ways she could have been taken by the sea.

Was it that he didn't have the rest of the story that bothered him? That he couldn't see what happened to her? Or maybe it was that he had been unable to save her? If he could dig deep enough inside himself, face the pain, he could pinpoint the anguish and free himself. Theoretically.

He had never been able to do this before, never had the courage to face his self-made enemy, but for Lizbeth, he could do this. He had to do this. For Lizbeth, he had to look at himself and understand the truth.

His scars were no exception to this self-exploration. He spent a good portion of the previous evening staring at his own scars, something he had never done before. He had no idea what his back looked like until now.

Gerald and his valet had gathered several mirrors and arranged them to face each other so he could see his back in full view from all sides. The scars had always been a reminder of his decision and the consequence, but the only way he could heal was to see himself how Lizbeth saw him, to accept himself for what he was and what he had done.

The scars had been difficult to look at. At first, they made him physically ill to see. Only through remembering Lizbeth's reaction on their wedding night did he find the courage to return to the mirrors. It took hours for him to work up to an unwavering stare, to study the lines and crisscrosses without casting up his accounts.

Remembering her lips on his back helped him accept what he saw. He touched those he could reach, accepted them as being part of him rather than a reminder of death. Lizbeth saw them as a mark of courage and survival. She had traced every scar with her fingers, kissed every mark and complimented his bravery. These were the marks of a survivor, not a beast.

Sitting by the sea until dawn helped him remember every conversation he had with Lizbeth, even their first one, when they discussed Locke's theories of the *tabula rasa*, the blank slate. Lizbeth, his clever and witty wife, had believed it to be hogwash, that people were not defined by what happened to them, were not molded by nurture alone.

Her belief, so different from what his had always been, held that people were born with predispositions, characteristics and personalities, and while nurture would certainly influence their value systems and their decisions, the inborn traits as well as free will had more to do with anything nurture affected. If a man were beaten, he could blame nurture for turning him into an abuser, or he could look inside himself and realize violence is wrong and thus choose not to beat.

A lifetime he had spent being what his father made him, a worthless, unlovable wretch. Seeing himself through Lizbeth's eyes changed everything. Thinking of what all he had done for his people changed everything. He was not who his father made him. He was a man of worth, both loving and courageous.

Searching his soul, remembering Lilith and his childhood, diving into the memories and facing his fears finally resulted in two conclusions. While he could certainly be mistaken and need to explore his feelings further, he thus far concluded that two aspects afflicted him.

The first pain was that he hadn't been there to help her. The second misery was that he had never been able to say goodbye. Unpacking these two traumas, he discovered a few more things about himself.

As young as he had been and as small as he had been, even smaller in stature than his sister at the time, he wouldn't have been able to rescue her if she had been caught in the undertow, which is most likely what happened.

She excelled at swimming and swore she had hidden gills and a mermaid fin. It made no sense that she would have drowned unless the undertow had pulled her in. Even then, she should have known not to struggle and allow the tide to release her back to shore. Often, they had ridden the undertow together, letting it suck them under the water and release them. She should have known what to do.

If the undertow had taken her, there would have been nothing he could have done, and in all likelihood, he may have been pulled under with her. Part of his agony, he discovered, was guilt that his absence had allowed her to drown. As a rational man fully aware of the motions of the sea, he now realized his presence wouldn't have helped any more than his absence.

What hurt about this now, looking back, was that even if he couldn't have helped her, he wasn't there to try. She had died alone. He hadn't been there for her. He didn't know if she cried out for him or if it had happened all at once. Had she been scared or unaware?

This. This was demon number one that he faced down for the first time in his life, understanding what about the memory tortured his dreams.

The second aspect that tormented him was not being able to say goodbye. He felt his father had taken away that right. No funeral had been held. No acknowledgment whatsoever of her death had taken place other than his father's words telling Sebastian she had died and her name would never again be spoken, as though she never existed. His mother had been buried at Roddam Hall, only a small cross marking her grave, but no such burial had been made for Lilith, not even a cross to mark her existence and passing.

Without an opportunity to mourn the loss of the two people he had loved most in the world, his guilt had been branded onto his body with a fire poker. He realized now he had spent so many years feeling guilty, he had never truly mourned. The more his mind wrapped around this line of thinking, the more he devised ways he could lay them both to rest, especially Lilith, and thus lay this bane of his past to rest.

He could never absolve himself of the blame for not being there, but he saw no reason he couldn't lay everything else to rest. It had been Lizbeth who helped him discover this, in her own way, helping him verbalize it even when he wasn't ready and reminding him throughout their acquaintance that there were no victims, that no one could control or define another person.

Lilith never would have blamed him, and despite what his father had said at the time, his mother certainly wouldn't have blamed him. As Lizbeth pointed out, he had only been a child. He wanted to beg for forgiveness all the same, but they never would have blamed him.

He decided at once to hold a funeral for her, to place a marker for her to memorialize her short time on earth. He could carve her name on the largest rock on the cliff as the marker or sculpt one of the large boulders into the shape of a mermaid in honor of her. Rock sculpture wasn't exactly something he had tried before, but neither had woodcarving, and the flower he carved for Lizbeth had turned out fairly well.

Lizbeth needed to be by his side, even if he had to fight to win her back. He had never fought for anything in his life, not really, only ever emulating the passive victim, letting things happen to him rather than taking control.

This time, he would fight, for he had something worth fighting for. This time, he would fight for what mattered, fight against his father's oppressive ghost and fight to prove to Liz he was not a monster after all, only a remorseful boy trapped inside a man's body.

If he could convince her that nothing else mattered except his love for her, maybe he had a chance to win her back. All her suggestions of talking to begin the healing process now made sense, and he embraced this, wanted to talk about his plan for a funeral, wanted to share memories of his sister, wanted to talk about it all, to heal after all these years.

Even if she wanted to read the travel journals, they could read them together, or better yet, they could travel to each place and compare the entries to their experiences, putting his father to rest in the process. He would do anything she wanted, anything she asked, if only she would give him the chance to be the man she fell in love with.

Funny how she knew him better than he knew himself. She had seen the real him, the man behind the mask. He always assumed the mask was him, but no, it was the face of the remorseful boy, not him. He thought about the things in life he loved, his hobbies and interests, sardonic jokes, bawdy poetry, all of which comprised the real him, not the blame he placed on himself.

He felt awakened. He felt alive after a century of slumber. A future with the woman he loved beckoned.

Much to the surprise of the seagulls, Sebastian laughed out loud, the sound reverberating in the coved ceiling of the gazebo. He laughed from happiness, from release, and he also laughed at himself for not realizing all of this sooner, coming to grips with it all sooner. He spent so much time locking it away, afraid to face his demons, that he never even knew what haunted him. He wanted to take Lizbeth in his arms and kiss her, twirl her in the air, and laugh about how alive he felt.

Only one snag in that plan. She had left. That fact be damned, he was going after her. She could slap him across the face and call him a devil if she liked, but he didn't care because he knew now he wasn't to blame.

As fast as his feet could carry him across the dew-covered grass, he returned to the castle, mounting the stairs two at a time to the bedchamber. He didn't bother calling his valet for he dressed for no one but his love. Stubble grew on his cheeks, and he didn't care. He would use it to tickle her face when he finally kissed her again. He held no illusions he could bring her back to him, but courage welled inside of him, passion fueled him, and a confident self-perception led him.

Dressed to ride, hair sloppily pulled back, and boots on his feet, he jogged to the stables and was riding to Lyonn Manor within minutes.

Chapter 35

When Lizbeth and Charlotte arrived at Arbor House, they questioned if Mrs. Copeland sent them to the right address. A sizable home stood on acreage just outside of town. This was hardly the home of an orphan.

Charlotte suggested, more than a tad impressed, "It would seem she married well."

Lizbeth exited the carriage with Charlotte still declining to join her. Charlotte agreed to accompany her as moral support but didn't want to get involved if she could avoid it. To Charlotte, the whole situation sounded too dreadfully depressing, as if from one of those barbarous novels, *The Old English Baron* or *The Castle of Otranto*. Liz ventured to the white columned estate alone, armed with purpose and courage.

Naught but twenty feet from the door, she stopped in her tracks at an ear-splitting scream from inside the home. Panicked, she burst through the door, following the sounds of the screams down unfamiliar hallways. Not a soul was in sight to stop her as she barreled down the corridors and up a flight of stairs, holding her skirts high and her wits higher.

As she turned down a hallway on the second floor, the screaming stopped. Which door had it come from? She surveyed the doors for signs of life, a flicker of light from beneath the frames, sounds of movement from within the rooms, anything.

A door at the end of the hallway opened. A woman stepped out wearing an apron covered in blood.

Horrified, Liz stared at the blood stains, unable to run in any direction, not even to retreat to the stairwell. The reddened apron moved closer.

"Pardon me, but are you here to see Sir Graham? He's in his study."

Liz shook her head, her eyes working up the bloody apron until they met the face behind the voice. Shock rippled through her body.

The woman before her could be Sebastian's doppelgänger. Although her hair was tied back in a knot, ebony strands flew freely around her face as if she had survived a struggle. Her eyes looked black from this distance, her facial structure the same lean face with the prominent Roddam nose. The look metamorphosed the woman into an exotic beauty.

"If you're not here to see Sir Graham, then why are you here? Who are you?"

Liz stammered, eyes flitting back and forth between the woman's face and the blood-smeared apron. "I'm here to speak with Lilith Chambers."

The woman didn't blink, only stared. "Yes, I am Lilith Chambers. You've caught me red-handed, in a manner of speaking." She chuckled, a deep rumble that reminded Lizbeth of Sebastian's own laugh.

"I, uh… are you well? Are you harmed?" Liz hadn't yet moved, frozen in place from the sounds and sights that had barraged her since arriving.

"Quite well. Tired, but well otherwise. Lady Graham has given birth to twins, I'm pleased to announce. A long day of labor resulting in a blessed event. But why have you come here to see me? Are my services needed elsewhere?"

Recovering herself, Liz said, "It's a delicate matter, perhaps better discussed in private and sitting. My congratulations to Lady Graham. Why are you covered in blood, if I may ask?" The apron made Lizbeth uncomfortable, even though it appeared all was well, and no one had been harmed in the making of the bloody apron.

"You found me here, asked for me, yet you don't even know what I'm doing here? You're a curiosity." Lilith examined Lizbeth from the opposite end of the hallway. "I'm Allshire's midwife. I assume you're not inquiring regarding my midwifery skills, then?" Lilith smiled, despite the unusualness of the situation and the strangeness of a person unknown to her standing in the home of her patient.

Lilith continued after Lizbeth could only nod in response to her question. "Not to be rude, as you appear an affable woman, not to mention of fine attire, but it has been an exhausting day. I need to tidy up here and settle the twins and Lady Graham for the evening, not to mention bring the glad tidings to her husband. Is your request urgent? If not, I will be more than pleased to meet you on the morrow at the church. We could meet in the vestry next to the gardens."

"It's not exactly urgent, no, although time is not entirely our ally." Liz hated to wait until morning, but this moment alone confirmed the dowager duchess' words.

A weight lifted from her shoulders, and with this newfound knowledge, she could accomplish much to help Sebastian find peace.

"Then it's settled. Would ten be too early?" Lilith queried.

"Ten is perfect. Thank you for agreeing to meet with me. I hope not to keep you from your duties, as you appear a busy woman," Liz said.

"I consider myself productive and useful, thank you. I haven't caught your name. You are...?"

"Lizbeth Lancaster the Countess of Roddam." She braced herself for an intake of breath, a start, a flinch, some glimmer of recognition at the surname and title.

Lilith showed no flicker of recall. Instead, she politely replied, "A pleasure to make your acquaintance, Lady Roddam. I will see you at ten. I'm sure you can see yourself out." She turned from Lizbeth and re-entered the room, leaving Liz alone in the hallway.

A few mistaken hallways later, Lizbeth found her way to the front door and back to the carriage.

"Well?" Charlotte held her hands open in inquisition.

"She's alive. She's in there. His sister is in there. Oh, Charlotte, she looks just like him. She's agreed to meet us tomorrow at ten." Lizbeth grabbed one of her sister's hands and held it.

"What did she say when you told her? Does she remember him?"

"I didn't tell her. I will tomorrow. She wasn't exactly in a position for chit-chat. How will I tell her? All my haste and I haven't planned what to say. Do I blurt it out—I'm your sister-in-law? Do I ask if she knows she's the daughter of an earl? Do I open by asking if she knows her brother thinks she's dead? This is impossible!" She closed her eyes and squeezed her sister's hand.

What a glorious dilemma she now faced. Reuniting lost siblings was far more pleasant than battling ghosts.

They proceeded to the inn where Lizbeth expected she would toss and turn all night. Surprisingly, she slept soundly, knowing she would soon be back in Sebastian's arms with a bright future ahead of them.

Chapter 36

"Are we there yet?" Drake pestered his cousin for the twentieth time in the past hour.

"Let's hope so, then I won't have to hear you complain anymore."

Sebastian rode along in good spirits, despite the arduousness of his task ahead. He didn't know if he could win her back, but he held a cheeriness and high spirit new to his disposition.

When he had arrived at Lyonn Manor, Drake hadn't been able to help much more than to agree to join him on his escapade. Neither Charlotte nor Lizbeth had divulged to Drake the purpose of their trip, only that they were bound for Allshire. Sebastian knew the truth, though. She was getting as far away from him as possible. His only hope was to find her before he lost the trail.

Sebastian and Drake followed on horseback, hoping they wouldn't be too far behind, making faster time than would the two ladies in the ducal coach. While he wanted to gallop until he arrived, he couldn't push his horse so cruelly.

Despite their speedy progress, their trip was punctuated with stops along the way to rest and water the horses. Sebastian wanted to travel through the night in hopes of intercepting them, but Drake insisted they stop for the evening in consideration of road visibility and the sake of horses and sore bums.

Drake found the whole trip a grand adventure, likening themselves to Don Quixote and Sancho Panza, Drake playing the role of Sancho, of course, with his witticisms and ability to rope in Don Quixote's fantastical day dreams of knighthood and chivalry.

All Sebastian had told him about their journey was that he had botched things with Lizbeth and meant to make amends before she did something as rash as return home to Cornwall. Drake found the whole plan a lark.

"Here we are, you and I," said the duke as they rounded a bend in the landscape, "gallant knight and squire off to woo our ladies fair!"

For once, Drake was refreshing company, as jolly as a dandy could be, despite tongue-in-cheek comments of his sore bottom needing to be massaged.

"You know what I think you should do when we arrive, Don Quixote?" Drake asked.

"No idea. What should I do, Sancho?" Sebastian was already chuckling at his cousin before he answered the question, knowing Drake would undoubtedly offer jewels of wisdom on chivalrous courtship the likes of which civilized society had never heard.

"Ride into town at top speed, hoist her up by her pannier, throw her over your horse, and ride into the sunset!"

"She doesn't wear a pannier, and we'll be arriving after sunrise." Sebastian smiled nonetheless at the conjured image.

"You are such a critic. Well, how about this. You stop in the middle of the town square and prostrate yourself until she comes crying with words of forgiveness. Some over dramatized, penitent self-flagellation might not be a bad idea to prove to her you're repentant," Drake offered with a wide and goofily lopsided grin.

"Mmm. That sounds tempting. I've always wanted to flog myself in a town square. You say the sweetest things, cousin."

"I have it. Imagine this. She's inside a building, say the second or third floor, her hair flowing out of the window as she sees you approaching—"

"Don't you dare say I should climb up by her hair to rescue her." Sebastian was still chuckling.

"No, no, not at all. You read too much, old man!"

"*Persinette* is a well-known fairy tale, hardly considered 'reading too much,'" Sebastian refuted his companion.

"Ah, then you have not read the latest version where she's renamed Rapunzel instead of Parsley, and it is far more wicked than a fairy tale in his version." Drake winked from his horse.

"Oh ho! My cousin cracked a book! I'm impressed. All these years I suspected you didn't know how to read." Sebastian steered his horse around a rut in the road.

"Not such an unheard of feat. Now, I was saying something of great importance before someone rudely interrupted me. You know you shouldn't interrupt a duke when he's talking, for I have more power behind my name than you have in both of your fists combined. I am second only to royalty! In fact, I could smite you for interrupting."

"I'm quaking in my boots," Sebastian antagonized. "Continue."

"So, imagine her in the window on the second or third floor. You see a tree nearby the window. Climb it! Climb that tree and abduct her. Bind her and gag her, then don't release her until she's agreed to let you have your way with her. No, no, don't even wait for permission. Bind her, gag her, and have your way with her until she agrees to forgive you. Brilliant, yes?" Drake smiled smugly.

"How am I supposed to know she's forgiven me if she's gagged?" Sebastian questioned innocently.

"Right. No gag."

"And if there is no tree?" He raised a quizzical eyebrow.

"Scale the damn building! How should I know? I'm offering sage advice, here, so no need to be pessimistic."

"Your advice is invaluable, to say the least. I think rather than slipping on a tree limb and breaking my neck, I should sing outside her window," Sebastian joked.

If he squinted, he swore he could see a town on the horizon. With any luck, that would be Allshire. They had no way of knowing where the pair of ladies would head after the stop at Allshire, so with any luck, they would still be there or have mentioned to someone their final destination. Or at the very least, the coachman will have mentioned over a pint whereto next.

"Just what every woman wants to hear—you singing. While you find a likely window to entice with your dulcet tones, I will head for the nearest inn. I'm parched, sore, and fatigued." Drake reached beneath him to rub his bottom and wince. He was definitely used to a carriage and not the back of a horse for lengthy rides.

"I'll resist the urge to woo an empty window, and instead go to the inn with you. Hopefully, someone has seen them. I doubt they would be difficult to miss, especially gallivanting around in your obnoxious carriage."

"It's regal, not obnoxious." Drake affected a wounded tone.

As they approached the outskirts, Drake continued his monologue, offering ways Sebastian and Lizbeth could make up for their evenings apart once he got her back to the castle.

Adrenaline coursed through his veins knowing at any minute he could spot her. Just one sight of her and he may leap with joy or sob unattractively or freeze from fear. All eyes following them when they entered the parish. Sebastian scanned every side street and building for signs of the carriage, the coachman, or the sisters.

"Please be here, Lizbeth," he chanted under his breath as they approached the inn.

A young boy took their horses. When Drake tossed him a coin and a wink requesting he feed, water, and cool the horses, the boy gaped, tugged at his forelock, then bowed so fervently, Sebastian's horse became skittishly nervous, snorting at the boy's erratic movements.

They entered the Black Bull Inn, a dark and small watering hole well populated by townspeople eating and socializing. Drake wasted no time in ordering a drink and a table, nonchalantly ignoring the eyeballs trained on him and his ringed fingers.

The people of the parish had likely never seen a dandy in person.

Surveying the room, Sebastian saw a chipper maid bringing drinks and food to the tables. Feeling lost and uncertain, his cheerfulness waning now that the moment of truth was upon him, he joined his cousin at the table and reached for his chronometer, only to realize he had left it at home. Unsure what to fiddle with for comfort, he tapped his fingers on the table.

"Relax, old man. As much attention as we're garnering, imagine how memorable our wives if riding in my coach. Someone in here will tell us where to find them." Drake leaned back in his chair, exuding an air of superiority.

The peppy maid approached their table just as Sebastian saw a flash of blue muslin from the staircase. Ignoring the maid, with a hand gripping the chairback, he rose, taking a tentative step towards the staircase. The dress could belong to anyone, he told himself, anyone at all.

The hem descended the staircase, revealing hips next, then a bosom, and then a face as the woman made her way to the first floor.

And there she stood. Not more than ten feet from him. A vision in blue. His love. Lizbeth.

He dropped to his knees on the stone floor, his hat in one hand, his heart in the other. Around him, a hush fell on the room, prompting Lizbeth to look for the source of the disturbance.

Their eyes met.

The low hum buzzed in his ears as it had in the library. Swallowing his fears, he focused on his newfound courage. He could do this.

Her eyes brightened with surprise and, could it be, happiness? "Sebastian!" She exclaimed, walking towards him. "What are you doing here?"

"Don't say a word. Please, let me speak before I lose my courage." The stone floor bit into his knees, but he didn't care.

"But I— " She tried to interrupt.

He dropped his hat on the floor and held up his hands. "No, please. I must say this. Lizbeth, search your heart and find a way to forgive me for my behavior. You're the only person in this world I want to love and be loved by in return. I should have listened to you sooner. I should have faced my past, but I was a coward. You gave me strength, Lizbeth. You gave me strength to look into my soul. I do not deny I'm still pained by my mistake, but I see now I wasn't responsible." He paused to catch his breath. "Give me a chance to explain myself."

"Sebastian, I— " She tried to interrupt again.

"No, please, let me explain. Let me defend myself. Give me a chance to redeem myself. Give me a chance to beg you to come home. You see, after all these years, I can lay the past to rest, but I need you by my side to do it. Could you ever love me again? Would you consider being loved by me? I want us to be a family. I want to spend the rest of my life proving I love you more than all the stars in the sky. I will prostrate myself before you, climb a tree to reach you, sing beneath a window, anything for you. I love you, Lizbeth. Give me a chance to prove it to you. Will you come home to me, to your family?"

He held his breath as he watched her, as did all eyes in the inn having turned from him to her.

His angel floated towards him and took his bruised hands into hers, tugging him to stand. Unsure if his nerves would let him stand without quaking, he braved the odds and stood, gripping her hands for support despite the sting of his knuckles.

"Sebastian, I never left." She pecked his bristly cheek with a kiss. "I've never doubted your courage, and I see only the man I love standing before me."

Despite the room full of people, she wrapped a hand behind his neck and pulled his face towards hers for a kiss. However chaste the kiss, he tingled from head to toe, her lips snapping the steel trap around his heart and dissolving it in a warm pool of pure love.

Drake shouted to the two, "Get a room!" stirring a round of applause from the onlookers.

Sebastian laughed against Liz's lips, breathing in her familiar scent. All his worries, all his preparations to win her back, and she had never left him. Remarkable woman. This whole time, she really had loved all of him, even the parts he thought she would fear. Then why the devil had she taken off to Cumberland?

"Before we return home, there's someone I want you to meet," she said against his kiss.

Confused and curious, he followed her outside.

Chapter 37

Lizbeth led her husband towards the church.

Lilith had instructed her to meet in the vestry, so with the few minutes remaining before ten, she could talk to Sebastian in the chapel first. The last thing she wanted was him to find out the truth by seeing his sister without warning or explanation. For all she knew, he would think he had gone mad to see a grown ghost.

Her heart overflowed as they walked to the church. Sebastian had come for her. Never in her wildest dreams had she guessed he would do that, that he would spend their time apart reflecting introspectively so that he could come to her as a whole man without self-condemnation.

He had come for her, riding across the countryside to bring her home, believing, she suspected, that his wife had abandoned him after his confession.

She had assumed all along she would be the one to save him, but in the end, he saved himself and came to rescue her. Never had she been prouder of her husband or felt more loved. If they had more time, she would beg to hear how he'd come to terms with the past, but ten approached, and she refused to be late for her meeting with Lilith.

When they reached the chapel door, she poked her head into the room first to ensure the coast was clear. The pews were empty, and more pointedly, free of a certain woman with ebony hair. Lizbeth ushered him into the chapel, closing the door behind him, and found herself immediately pressed to Sebastian's chest by powerful arms.

She looked at him smiling down at her, his eyes untroubled and full of life.

"You're mine." He growled, holding her possessively against his body.

"I am. And you, my lion, are mine forever and always." She lifted her arms around his shoulders, embracing him. He buried his face against her neck and lifted her off her feet.

When her feet touched the ground again, she tried to drag him to the last row of benches. "Sit. I think you should be sitting when I tell you this."

"I'm not letting you go. Tell me whatever it is while I love on you." He nuzzled her hair and ears.

This wasn't going to be easy if he couldn't be serious. The most important moment of his life, and he acted like a schoolboy.

Moving her hands to his cheeks, she said, "Sebastian. I need you to focus. I don't know how you're going to take this."

He stood straighter and studied her.

She held a palm to his chest hoping to infuse him with courage and strength for what she was about to say.

"This may be painful to hear, but you must hear it. You must understand what I'm about to tell you. Know that I'm here for you through all of this. Are you with me?"

His expression pained, he asked, "Are you about to tell me you're going to leave me? Regardless of love, you're going to leave, aren't you? Is it because I became angry? God, Lizbeth, I'd never hurt you. Tell me you know that."

"No, no, no. I'm not leaving, and I know. Now, listen to me. We are about to meet a most important person, and I need you to be ready. Can you prepare yourself for what I'm about to tell you?"

He nodded, brows furrowed.

"Your father lied to you. Either mad as a March hare or a viciously cruel man, he lied to you." She paused, eyeing him. "You are not responsible for your sister's death because—." Her breath caught before she said softly, "Lilith didn't die."

Lizbeth paused again, wondering if she should let the words sink in or continue.

Sebastian stared blankly.

Speaking hurriedly and hushed, she said, "Your father sent her to an orphanage, the orphanage here in Allshire. She's alive, and she's waiting for us in the vestry. I understand if you aren't ready to face her, as this is so sudden. We can leave without meeting her, if you wish, or I can go alone on your behalf."

She watched his complexion pale, his eyes lose focus. His hands slipped from her waist and fell loose at his sides before he collapsed on a bench.

"Do you understand what I'm saying, Sebastian?"

After staring into the ether, he doubled over to rest his elbows on his knees, his head falling into his hands.

Not sure what else to do, she ran her fingers through his hair. She wondered if she had chosen her words poorly. She hadn't exactly planned on telling him like this, but he had shown up less than a half hour before she was to meet Lilith. What else could she do, ask him to stay behind while she met with a mysterious stranger?

He leaned his head against her bosom and hugged her to him. His shoulders began to shake, and her heart went out to him. If he needed to cry on her dress, he could cry all he wanted, soak the dress with tears if he wanted.

But, wait, that wasn't right. The sounds coming out of his mouth weren't sobs at all. His shoulders heaved and shook with laughter, a laugh that grew louder until soon it filled the chapel. Had he just gone mad before her eyes?

"I wonder if she would still want a mermaid sculpture," he laughed.

"What are you talking about?" She continued to brush his hair as he looked up at her through wet eyelashes.

"Everything I've ever known has been a lie. Everything except you. Who am I, Lizbeth?"

"You're the man I've fallen in with, the father of our future children," she replied without hesitation.

His laugh dulled to a soft chuckle. "You really love me?"

"Yes. I do. I have for a long time." She stroked his forehead with her thumb.

"I'm not a killer." His voice husky, he held her gaze in an eternity of silence, a free man's smile on his lips. "All this time I believed you could never love me because you would see only the killer my father told me I was."

She smiled reassuringly.

"My God, Lizbeth, is she really alive? After all these years, she's still alive? Does she remember me?"

"I don't know. I haven't spoken to her yet, only arranged to meet. Would you like to find out for yourself, or shall I? You don't have to meet her if you're not ready, if you need more time," she said, running the backs of her fingers down his unshaven cheek.

Still embracing her, he stood and looked around, as if seeing the world around him clearly for the first time.

"I would like to meet her. I believe I can do it if you're with me. Promise you will stay by my side." He squeezed her.

"I will never leave you, Sebastian, no matter what." She turned them towards the vestry, hoping they wouldn't be late.

She wasn't sure how long Lilith would wait for some strange woman who had hunted her down in the evening hours at another person's home. When she tried to move, he tightened his grip with one arm and reached to cup her face with his free hand.

"You did this for me. But why?"

"I told you months ago. Family is the most important thing in the world. I will do anything for those I love, and I knew how important this was to you." She rubbed her cheek against the palm of his hand, and then attempted to wriggle out of his grip again. "She's waiting in the vestry if you'd like to meet her."

"How did you find her?" His grip of steel held her steady.

"A mixture of the journals and your aunt, but I didn't dare say anything until I knew the truth. Now, if you don't release me and head towards the vestry, she may leave, and then you'll have to hunt her down all over again." She warned, her tone teasing.

He nodded curtly, his lips a grim line.

They walked together into the vestry. The cozy room held a worn couch with equally as worn chairs circling a round table in the center of the room, a mismatched long table against one wall and an empty stone fireplace in the corner.

In one of the chairs, a book in her hands, sat Lilith.

Sebastian gasped. She knew he recognized her, for how could he not when staring at her was like looking at his own reflection.

Lilith looked up at the sound of their entry. Closing the book and setting it aside, she stood, eyes roving back and forth between Sebastian and Lizbeth.

Sebastian stepped forward, hoarsely whispering his sister's name. "Lilith?"

The young woman stood her ground and stared at him curiously. "Yes, I'm Lilith. My meeting was with Lady Roddam. Who are you?"

He took another step forward. "You don't remember me?"

Her eyes narrowed. "Should I?"

Taking a step back towards Lizbeth, he reached his hand behind him to find hers. She took it, and walked them both to a seat, hoping to initiate a cordial conversation.

Liz smiled at Lilith and motioned for her to return to her seat. "Thank you for agreeing to meet with me, Miss Chambers. I have great respect for the work you're doing in Allshire, and I wish to know more about you, as does my husband, Lord Roddam. We are here to inquire if you know anything of your birth family from your time before the orphanage."

Lilith sat hesitantly, her eyes still flicking nervously between the two of them. "No, I do not know anything of my birth family. They keep our records sealed. I do know my stay was fully funded by a generous benefactor, but I could not say who." Turning fully to Sebastian, she asked, "Excuse me for asking, my lord, but should I know you?" She examined his features, no sign of recognition yet lighting her eyes.

Lizbeth spoke again before Sebastian could answer. "If given the opportunity, Miss Chambers, would you like to know your birth family?"

Lilith's knuckles turned white as she clutched her dress, but her voice was strong and sure. "All orphans wonder about their birth family, but few like what they learn when given the opportunity. I will not deny I've thought of what it might be like for my parents to come for me. I'm too level headed now to believe any good could come from that. I take it you know of my birth family? Do you think, from your position of knowledge, that I would want to know of my family, or should I remain ignorant?"

Sebastian's hand squeezed Lizbeth's, his eyes never leaving the face of his sister. When he spoke, his voice trembled. "What if it were not your parents who came for you, but a brother? Would you want to meet him?"

Lilith stared at him, searching his face.

Sebastian broke the silence with a nearly inaudible, "Your brother spent years hoping you had become a mermaid."

Lizbeth watched as Lilith's face contorted, confusion to anger, shock to recognition. Her hands crept to her mouth, her eyes widening.

"'Bastian?" she whispered behind her hands. Liz turned to see Sebastian nodding, errant tears streaming down his cheeks. "I have a recurring dream that two men take me from my brother and won't let me say goodbye. Are you the little boy from my dream?"

"I'm your brother, Lilith. I would have come sooner, but I— I thought you were dead." He made a motion to stand, as if to go to her, but then sat back down, unsure.

Lilith stood instead. With a quivering hand, she reached out to her brother. Lizbeth urged him by unraveling her fingers from his. He took Lilith's hand in both of his and held it to his lips.

Lilith spoke first, her hand still cradled to her brother's lips. "I'm not sure I'm ready to know details, but if you told me a little, I might be able to separate my dreams from memories."

Nodding, Sebastian said, "We lived together in the north, not far from the coast. Most days were spent at the beach. The nursery held a dollhouse you liked, and you found great pleasure in pushing me off of the rocking horse so your dolls could ride. I'm afraid my memory is blurry. Our nanny—."

"Always wore brown, and I thought she looked like an ugly rug," interrupted Lilith, her eyes glistening with memory fragments.

"Aye, you threw your paint at her one day, if memory serves." His words were met with an eager nod from Lilith. "You're the daughter of an earl, Lilith. Our parents have passed, and I am now the Earl of

Roddam. I know you don't know us," Sebastian said, "but we're your family, my wife Lizbeth and I. Would you consider coming home with us?"

Lilith returned to her chair and thought carefully before speaking. "I need time. Thank you, but no. Not now anyway. This is my home, here in Allshire. I've made a life for myself here. I would like to get to know the two of you, though, and learn about my family, learn why I was sent here and what I've missed by being away. I need time for this to make sense before I ask those questions. If you could leave your address, I will come to you when I'm ready. I hope that doesn't sound ungrateful."

Sebastian shook his head and replied, "I will leave you with a complete map to our home so you can find your way to us. You are welcome anytime."

"If it isn't too cumbersome, I may write to you first, gain an acquaintance from a distance. Would that be bothersome?" Lilith asked.

"Not at all. Please, write. This is as startling for me as it is for you, I assure you."

Lizbeth suspected Lilith doubted that very much, but she wouldn't know what her brother had suffered over her disappearance.

Lilith stood again and apologized, "I don't mean to leave you so soon. You must both have come far to see me, but I have much to do this day and need time to think. This is all too much, and I wish to be alone. I have many questions, but I would like to write them instead after I've meditated on what you've told me."

Following words of farewell, his sister departed, leaving Sebastian and Lizbeth standing alone in the vestry. Lizbeth waited silently for everything to settle, for her husband to digest what had just happened.

Sooner than she expected, he turned to her, smiling so widely the corners of his eyes crinkled.

"Thank you, Lizbeth. Thank you for being here, for finding her, for standing by me, for loving me."

Lizbeth leaned against him, resting her head on his chest. "How do you feel about all of this, about her, about your father?"

He sat on the arm of the chair.

"I feel light, as though a weight has been lifted. I suppose…." His words trailed off as he slipped into thought. "I suppose I should be angry at my father, worried my sister won't write, some variation of anxiety, but I feel at peace. I realize now what kind of man he was, and in that way, he has no power over my past or my future. I hope she writes, but if not, I know she's safe. And I have you, the greatest gift in this world. I feel happy, Lizbeth. And you?"

She traced his eyebrows and the length of his nose with her thumb. "I'm happy that you're happy. I've also learned a valuable lesson from my sister, if you'll believe it. I can't fight everyone's battles for them, but by Jove I can wield a shield." She kissed his forehead when he looked inquisitively at her.

"I have a sister," he said proudly.

"Yes, you do. And she seems just as stubborn as you."

He laughed and replied, "Maybe you were onto something with your critique of the blank slate."

"My what? Now what are you talking about?" She racked her brain trying to remember when they talked about blank slates.

"When we first met. Don't you remember? Your opening words to me were a rather harsh criticism about John Locke's theory of the blank slate. You insisted we have natural born tendencies. If my sister and I share any traits, that would validate your belief. I'm insulted you forgot our first date."

"Oh yes, that does sound familiar. I would hardly call that our first date, however. A Mr. Roddam interrupted my solace, called me a romantic, and insulted all my beliefs. You were positively antagonistic!" She admonished playfully.

"Mmm. I think you're misremembering that experience, but you should tell me more about it on our way home so I can antagonize you further. Think they'll let us take the carriage home? I want to antagonize you for the entire journey." He drew her into his arms and kissed her.

Epilogue

Three months later

Outside of the castle, the landscape disappeared under several feet of snow. Inside of the castle, heat from the hearth warmed the sitting area in the library, Sebastian's laughter reverberating through the room. They lay together on the floor in front of the fireplace, atop pillows and under blankets.

Lizbeth reached over Sebastian to grab at the book in his hand. He held it up and away, out of her reach.

In his most nasally and high-pitched voice, he imitated the speaker in the book as he read while swatting away Lizbeth's searching hand. "'For heaven's sake, Cousin, resumed Arabella,' —"

"Stop reading like that! Arabella doesn't sound like that! She has the deep and commanding voice of a strong and independent woman. Give me the book! It's my turn to read aloud before you ruin this heroine now and forever." She leaned over his bare chest in another failed attempt to grab the book. "It's bad enough you wouldn't let me have a turn reading from Lilith's most recent letter about the newest orphan, but now you're hogging my turn at reading Lennox. Give me that book!" She pushed against his shoulder then lunged for the book.

Her nipple grazed his skin. He closed the book and tossed it out of both their reach. "How do you expect me to concentrate if you keep teasing me?" He rolled on top of her, nibbling at her nose.

She tried to push him away. "Get off of me! I did not intentionally tease you. It's not my fault you insist on holding our book club meetings naked. You're a crude and classless man." The rest of whatever she had planned to say muffled beneath his lips.

After pleasuring her mouth until she moaned against him, he rolled away from her and reached for the book to resume reading.

"You can't be serious. That's it? That's all I get? Now who's teasing whom, hmm?"

Tucking the book under the edge of their makeshift bed, he propped himself on his forearm to admire her.

"I've been thinking about your offer to use the dowry money to build an astronomy tower," he announced, as he peeled back the blanket she had just used to cover herself.

He circled her nipple with his fingertip until it hardened. "The astronomy tower really is the most logical choice, don't you think? The November meteor showers weren't nearly as impressive as they could have been if we had a proper space for a larger telescope. Shall we do that next?"

He maintained eye contact as he leaned to tease her nipple with his tongue.

Arching against his mouth, she murmured between gasps, "Terrible idea. No tower." She writhed beneath him, clenching his hair in her hands.

"No? You don't want to see the stars?" He took her breast into his mouth, flicking the peak with his tongue.

"Yes, yes, yes, I want, wait, no. Don't stop. Yes, there. No tower. Nursery first. We need to do a nursery first." She panted against him.

His mouth came to an abrupt stop. She tried to pull him back, but he held steady. "Say that again?"

She grinned at him mischievously. "You should learn to listen more closely. I said we need to renovate the nursery first, unless you want our baby sleeping in the tower reading room."

"We're having a baby? We... Why didn't you tell me? I'm going to be a father? We're… Good God, Lizbeth, why didn't you tell me?" He sat up and tugged her to him for a celebratory hug.

"I believe, Your Lordship, I just did." She encircled his neck with her arms and held him to her.

Gerald, the butler, walked by the library just then and smiled to himself when he heard his master roar from the other side of the door, a bestial sound followed by a laughter-filled moan from the master's lioness.

A Note from the Author

Dear Reader,

Thank you for purchasing and reading this book. Supporting indie writers who brave self-publishing is important and appreciated. I hope you'll continue reading my novels, as I have many more titles to come, including the continuation of this series.

I humbly request you review this book on Amazon with an honest opinion.

Connect with me online at www.paullettgolden.com, www.facebook.com/paullettgolden, www.instagram.com/paullettgolden, and www.twitter.com/paullettgolden. You'll also find me on at such places as Goodreads, Bookbub, Amazon's Author Central, and LibraryThing.

All the best,
Paullett Golden

If you enjoyed *The Earl and The Enchantress,* read on for a sneak peek of the next book in The Enchantresses.

The Duke and The Enchantress
Available 2019

The Duke and The Enchantress

This tale begins at the happy ever after, for Miss Charlotte Trethow has married the Duke of Annick, and all her dreams have come true. Charlotte would laugh with delight if she weren't barreling towards an unknown future in a land far, far away.

The duchess bounced and swayed in the ducal state coach, heading in the opposite direction of civilization and wondering what happens after the happy ever after. She eyed her new husband warily, the nuptials having been conferred hours prior. How could he sleep so soundly through the bumps and grinds of the ride?

A lengthy week's journey lay ahead of them, after which point she would meet her mother-in-law, her sister-in-law, and her new home. Could she do this? Could she be the perfect duchess, the perfect wife? The idea of being a duchess had seemed so dreamy, but as the reality set in, she feared failure. How does one be a duchess?

The mere thought of the pressure caused anxiety to constrict her breathing, an oppression against her chest. Although the finery of wealth and status surrounded her in the plush velvet padding of the carriage, and the handsomest man she had ever met sat across from her, she feared what would happen next with London at her back and Northumberland ahead of her.

To ease her mind, she focused on her new husband, Drake Mowbrah, Duke of Annick. His lean frame wedged in the corner of the carriage, long limbs stretched across the carpeted floor, his breathing punctuated by soft snores. Despite her worries, she did find him irresistibly attractive. He had the slender physique of a fencer, a sabreur to be precise.

She admired his lithe body with the porcelain complexion of a nobleman, his ebony hair fashionably brushed forward, heavy on top and cropped short on the sides and back, his Roman nose well-proportioned to his slim face. And his lips. She loved his lips. Soft and red, almost pouty. Blue eyes, a deep sapphire. All so unlike his cousin.

Her gaze shifted to the man sitting next to Drake, his cousin. He glowered at the window, making no effort to engage Charlotte in polite conversation. His brooding perturbed her and made her first few hours of marriage uncomfortable. She didn't want him in the carriage, but he certainly couldn't ride with the servants in the four-carriage caravan heading north.

The cousin made her nervous. No, on second thought, his entire countenance frankly unsettled her. The two men would look more like brothers than cousins with their matching profiles and black hair, except the cousin looked more like a common laborer than a gentleman. His skin was tanned, eyes black as coals, hair unfashionably long, and broad shoulders with the sinewy body of a worker. He spoke only when spoken to, and even then did little more than grunt.

This wild animal trapped in their honeymoon carriage gave her chills. She had this week's journey to get to know her husband better before entering their new life at Lyonn Manor, but she couldn't see how that would happen with the beast sharing their space.

The carriage slumped heavily to one side, hitting a rut in the road, and jolted forwards, jerking Drake's head against his chest. His eyes flew open as he braced himself.

"Is it highwaymen? Are we under attack?" He surged forward to the window only to see placid countryside.

The beast spoke for the first time since they began the trip. "Just a hole in the road, you dolt. Or, more aptly, your snoring probably startled one of the horses." The brute's eyes never left the window, his face etched in stone.

Drake roared with laughter and slapped his cousin's arm. "Too right, old man. Too right." Turning his eyes on his bride, he smiled wickedly. "How is my wife enjoying the view?"

Charlotte replied, "The meadow flowers are lovely this time of year."

Drake leaned forward and touched her knee with long, slender fingers. "I didn't mean the view outside of the window. I meant of me." He winked, his mischievous expression unmarred by her innocent reply.

She swatted at his hand, eyeing his cousin uneasily. This was hardly proper behavior or conversation in front of company. "I assure you that I know not what you mean." She hoped her tone sounded appropriately scolding.

"Like hell you don't. I could feel your eyes on me as I slept, working their way over my svelteness. Do you like what you see?" He swept his hands over his torso in invitation. "I hope so, because you'll be seeing a lot more of it tonight." His blue eyes lit with an inner fire before he turned to his cousin and ribbed him jovially. "You'll have to stuff the linens under the inn's door, cousin! I'm going to make her scream my name tonight."

While his cousin only snorted, Charlotte gaped incredulously. Husband or not, how dare he speak to her in this manner? How dare he say such things? How dare he speak like a commoner and to *her* of all people?

She felt her cheeks burning with the humiliation of it all. That he said it, that he thought it, and that he said it in front of his cousin. Flicking her eyes to the door handle, she felt a sudden impulse to leap out and run back to London.

Her husband clearly didn't require a response, as he lazily leaned back in his seat, placing his hands behind his head with a smirk of satisfaction before closing his eyes again.

With the heat of her cheeks singeing her skin, Charlotte pressed herself against the cushions, wishing she could disappear into the velvet. Her happily ever after might have been the mistake of the century.

About the Author

Celebrated for her complex characters, realistic conflicts, and sensual love scenes, Paullett Golden has put a spin on historical romance. Her novels, set primarily in Georgian and Regency England with some dabbling in Ireland, Scotland, and France, challenge the norm by involving characters who are loved for their flaws, imperfections, and idiosyncrasies. Her stories show love overcoming adversity. Whatever our self-doubts, *love will out*.

Connect online
paullettgolden.com
Facebook.com/paullettgolden
Twitter.com/paullettgolden
Instagram.com/paullettgolden

Made in the USA
San Bernardino, CA
19 March 2020